Dear Readers,

Many years ago, when I was a kid, my father said to me, "Bill, it doesn't really matter what you do in life. What's important is to be the *best* William Johnstone you can be."

I've never forgotten those words. And now, many years and almost 200 books later, I like to think that I am still trying to be the best William Johnstone I can be. Whether it's Ben Raines in the Ashes series, or Frank Morgan, the last gunfighter, or Smoke Jensen, our intrepid mountain man, or John Barrone and his hard-working crew keeping America safe from terrorist lowlifes in the Code Name series, I want to make each new book better than the last and deliver powerful storytelling.

Equally important, I try to create the kinds of believable characters that we can all identify with, real people who face tough challenges. When one of my creations blasts an enemy into the middle of next week, you can be damn sure he had a good reason.

As a storyteller, my job is to entertain you, my readers, and to make sure that you get plenty of enjoyment from my books for your hard-earned money. This is not a job I take lightly. And I greatly appreciate your feedback—you are my gold, and your opinions *do* count. So please keep the letters and e-mails coming.

Respectfully yours,

William W. Johnstone

WILLIAM W. JOHNSTONE

THE FIRST MOUNTAIN MAN: PREACHER'S JUSTICE

FURY OF THE MOUNTAIN MAN

PINNACLE BOOKS
Kensington Publishing Corp.
http://www.kensingtonbooks.com

PINNACLE BOOKS are published by

Kensington Publishing Corp.
850 Third Avenue
New York, NY 10022

All Kensington Titles, Imprints, and Distributed Lines are available at
special quantity discounts for bulk purchases for sales promotions,
premiums, fund-raising, and educational or institutional use. Special
book excerpts or customized printings can also be created to fit specific needs. For details, write or phone the office of the Kensington
special sales manager: Kensington Publishing Corp., 850 Third Avenue, New York, NY 10022, attn: Special Sales Department, Phone:
1-800-221-2647.

Pinnacle and the P logo Reg. U.S. Pat. & TM Off.

ISBN-13: 978-0-7860-1906-9
ISBN-10: 0-7860-1906-9

First Pinnacle Books Printing: December 2007

10 9 8 7 6 5 4 3 2 1

Printed in the United States of America

THE FIRST
MOUNTAIN MAN:
PREACHER'S
JUSTICE

1

The sky over the Rocky Mountains was a brilliant, crystalline blue. Though it was cloudless now, it had snowed steadily for the previous twenty-four hours and a deep pack on the ground was painfully bright under the relentless sun. It also made traveling difficult, so the man everyone called Preacher had not even attempted to ride his horse this morning. Instead, the mountain man and fur trapper had taken a pack mule with him, and he led the animal, laboriously breaking a path through the nearly waist-deep snow. The mule was carrying a string of beaver traps that, over the previous several days, had been carefully inspected. Repairs had been made as necessary.

Preacher, who was twenty-seven years old, had been trapping in these mountains since he was fourteen. He had a dark shock of hair that he kept trimmed with a sharp knife. Though it was sometimes difficult to do so, he also managed to shave at least two or three times a week so that, while he often had stubble, he never had a beard. His eyes were dark. From a distance one might think they were brown, but upon closer examination they proved to be a deep, cobalt blue. He was a little taller than average, and slender of build, but with broad shoulders and muscular arms and powerful legs strengthened by his years of trapping in the mountains.

Preacher looked toward a distinctive peak and saw feathery tendrils of snow streaming out from it in the cold, piercing wind of the higher climes. The snow crystals glistened in the sun and formed a prism of color to crown the beauty of the rugged mountains and dark green trees. From that peak, which Preacher called Eagle's Beak, the young mountain man got his bearings. Thus oriented, he started up a narrow draw until he found the creek he was looking for.

Preacher ground-hobbled his mule, took some of the traps, then stepped out into the stream, breaking through the thin ice that had formed at the stream's edge. The nearly paralyzing cold shot up his legs as he waded in the water, looking for the best place to put his traps. It would have been easier and less painful to move along the shoreline, but he'd learned long ago to use the water as a means of masking his scent from the beaver.

Finally, he came to the place he had discovered five years earlier, a place rich with beaver that had so far been undiscovered by the other trappers. Since his discovery, he had worked this area as if it were his own private reserve. While there was no such thing as privately owned land here, the trappers recognized and followed a code of the right of territory according to who came first.

Dropping all his traps in the water, Preacher began setting them by depressing the springs by standing on them, putting one foot on each trap arm to open it up. When the trap was opened, he engaged the pan notch, holding it in the set position.

As each trap was set, he would extend the trap chain to its fullest length out toward the deeper water, where a trap stake was passed through the ring at the end of the chain and driven into the streambed.

Finally, he placed the bait. The bait was a wand of willow, cut to a length that would permit its small end to extend from the stream bank directly over the pan of the trap. Bark was scraped from the stick and castoreum was smeared on the end of the switch, so that it hung about six inches or more above the trap. Castoreum was an oil taken from the glands of a beaver. Once his traps were set, Preacher returned to the tiny cabin he would call home while wintering in the mountains.

It was no secret that Preacher had hit upon a mother lode of beaver. Every year his catch was consistently the highest, or very near the highest, taken. While others might have envied him his good luck, they were bound by the code they all followed not to horn in on him.

But there was one trapper who wasn't bound by this, or any other code, and he was determined to find Preacher's secret location. He didn't know where Preacher trapped, but he did know where he lived. He had made camp near Preacher's cabin, surviving the storm just passed, in order to follow him to his secret place.

The recent snow made it very easy to follow, because he didn't even have to stay in contact with Preacher. All he had to do was follow the path left by Preacher and his mule through the snow.

"It'll be like taking a sugar-tit from a baby," he said with a gruff laugh.

His traps set, Preacher returned to his little cabin. This was his seventh year in this same location, and over the years he had made several modifications to improve the living conditions. The thick log walls were well chinked with mud and insulated with moss so that even the coldest arctic blasts were kept at bay.

Initially, the cabin had been heated with a fireplace, but a few years ago he'd bought an iron stove at Rendezvous and hauled it back on one of his pack mules. The stove was a marvel of efficiency, heating the cabin much better and with considerably less wood than was consumed by the fireplace. It also made it easier to cook his meals because he could set a pot right on top of the stove, rather than moving it from place to place within the fireplace.

Preacher had become a pretty good cook over the years of living alone. When he returned home after setting the traps, he was greeted with the enticing aroma of a simmering beaver-tail stew. He rolled out some biscuits and put them on to bake.

Automatically, he made an extra biscuit for Dog, then remembered that Dog wasn't with him. Dog was back in St. Louis, looking after Jennie.

Preacher missed the animal that had been his sole companion out here. He recalled the way he had come by Dog. A few years ago, the traders at Rendezvous had formed an alliance designed to keep the price of pelts down. Preacher had decided to take his pelts back to St. Louis and sell them himself.

He was about three weeks on the trail when shortly after nightfall, as he was laying out his bedroll, he became aware of eyes staring at him from the dark. With the hair standing up on the back of his neck, he slipped his pistol from his belt and stared into the black maw that surrounded his camp.

"Who's there?" he called.

There was no response.

"Who's there?" he called again, and this time he augmented his call with the deadly clicking sound of his pistol being cocked.

A low, frightening growl came from the darkness.

"Are you a wolf?" Preacher called.

Thinking to lure the animal from the darkness, he took a piece of rabbit and held it up. "Come on in, boy. Come get this meat."

Tossing the meat about ten feet in front of him, he raised his pistol, ready to shoot the moment the wolf showed itself.

It wasn't a wolf, at least not a full-blooded wolf, though it clearly had many of the markings and features of a wolf. It was a dog. The animal walked into pistol range, growling, its eyes locked on the mountain man as it moved toward the proffered morsel.

Preacher lowered his pistol and watched as the big dog used its powerful jaws to pull the meat away from the bone. The dog fascinated him, not only by its size and power, but also by the way it carried itself, clearly showing no fear.

When the dog finished the first piece of meat, Preacher threw another piece out, this one closer to him than the first. The dog came for it. By the time he threw the last piece of meat, the dog was quite close. In fact, it was close enough for Preacher to touch. He did so, rubbing the dog behind its ears.

"How'd you get way out here in the middle of nowhere?" Preacher asked.

Though the dog didn't snuggle against his hand, it was friendly enough to be non-threatening. The growling had ceased.

The dog slept near Preacher that night, and when Preacher got ready to leave the next day, the dog jumped onto the boat with him. Preacher named the dog "Dog," and they became companions. Preacher always thought of him as his companion, not as his possession. Dog clearly belonged to no one but Dog.

Last year, concerned for the safety of Jennie, he left Dog with her, charging the animal with the responsibility of looking out for the woman that came closer to being Preacher's woman than any other. Thus it was that when Preacher returned to the mountains, Dog went with Jennie to St. Louis.

Clearly, Dog would have preferred to come back with Preacher. It showed in his eyes as Preacher took his leave. But Preacher had made it personal, asking Dog, as a favor to him, to stay and watch after Jennie. Dog accepted the responsibility without complaint.

"I miss you, Dog," Preacher said aloud. "I can get along

without people just fine. Truth to tell, I prefer it without people. But I do wish I had you around to keep me company."

It wasn't all that unusual for Preacher to talk aloud, even though there was no one there. Although he enjoyed solitude, there were times when he wanted to hear a human voice, even if it was his own.

When the biscuits were done, Preacher took a couple of them, spooned up a generous serving of the stew, and sat at the crude table he had made to enjoy his dinner.

As Preacher ate his meal, he went through the figures in his little ledger book. If he had as good a year this year as he did last, and he had no reason to suspect that he wouldn't, he would be able to add substantially to his bank account.

By the standards of the day, Preacher could almost count himself a rich man. He was worth just under fifteen thousand dollars, and would go over that amount by the end of the season. The funny thing was, money meant nothing to him except as a means of keeping score. With what he had now, he could buy the finest house in St. Louis and live in luxury for many years.

Sometimes he felt guilty for not doing that. He could marry Jennie and make a good life for her and for himself. But even the thought of such a thing was difficult to consider. He looked up from his ledger and peeked through the window—made of real glass that he'd packed in three years ago—at the ruggedly beautiful terrain surrounding his cabin.

"I'm sorry, Jennie, ole girl," Preacher said quietly. "To the degree that I can understand love between a man and a woman, I probably love you. But if I gave all this up, I would have such a hunger for it in my heart that there would be nothing left for you. I hope you understand."

When Preacher returned to check out his traps a few days later, he was surprised to see that they had all been removed, set aside, and replaced by another man's traps. Angrily, he removed the new traps and put his own back in place. The process took most of the day.

It was one thing to crowd in on another man's territory. That was done from time to time, and it nearly always brought about harsh feelings. But to actually remove another man's traps was an affront of the worst kind.

Preacher considered breaking the offending traps, but finally decided against it. Instead, he left one of them on the bank of the stream and placed rocks on the ground in the form of an arrow, pointing toward his cabin, indicating that if the man wanted to retrieve his traps, he would have to come see Preacher to get them. When Preacher returned to his cabin, he hung the poacher's traps up on the outside wall, in plain view of anyone who might happen by.

Exactly one week later, Preacher was tending to his mules when he saw a lone figure trekking across the snow-covered meadow that separated Preacher's cabin from the woods. The man was wearing a buffalo robe and a fur cap, and as he crossed the meadow he left a long, dark smear in the pristine white snow behind him.

No doubt, this was the one who had attempted to poach on Preacher's territory. Preacher had left his weapons inside. However, there was a hatchet nearby. Preacher felt a sense of security in believing that if need be, he could arm himself.

Before the man was halfway across the meadow, Preacher recognized him as Henri Mouchette. He wasn't surprised that this was the man who had so blatantly violated the trappers' code. Mouchette had the reputation of being someone who was very hard to get along with. He was even suspected of stealing from other traps, though as no one had ever actually caught him doing it, the accusation had never been brought before the trappers' court.

"Hello, Mouchette," Preacher greeted him. "What brings

you by?" Preacher knew full well why Mouchette was there, but he decided to play the game.

Mouchette stopped a few feet away from Preacher. He was breathing rather hard from the effort of both climbing and having to cut a trail through the snow. Clouds of vapor surrounded his head.

"You son of a bitch, you stole my traps," Mouchette said.

"I haven't stolen them, Mouchette," Preacher replied. He pointed to the traps hanging from his front wall. "As you can see, they are hanging right here, in clear sight."

"They're here now, but you took them from the stream," Mouchette said.

"Oh, yes, siree, I did that, all right," Preacher said easily. "As a matter of fact, I took them right after you took mine."

"That is my place," Mouchette insisted, pointing to himself with his thumb.

"And what makes you think that is your place, seein' as I was there first?" Preacher asked.

"I been trappin' that stream for years. Hell, I was trappin' it when you was a pup," Mouchette said.

"You know as well as I do that the first person to arrive at a stream has the right to put out his own traps. I didn't see any traps here when I arrived."

"I laid off a couple of years because I didn't want the stream to be over-trapped," Mouchette said. "I quit trapping so it could recover. Then, when I went back to it, I seen your traps there. I didn't figure that to be right, so I took 'em out."

"Are you saying you were trapping there two years ago?" Preacher asked.

"Yeah, that's what I'm saying. Two years ago, I trapped the stream. Then I let it be for two years."

"Well, now, that's where the mistake is," Preacher said. "You must have your streams mixed up. I have been trapping this same stream for five years now, so you couldn't have been here two years ago."

"I ain't the one that made the mistake. It was you," Mouchette insisted. "By all that's right, that stream belongs to me."

"Not now, it doesn't. Put your traps somewhere else."

"I aim to put my traps right back where I had them," Mouchette insisted. "And I plan to get your traps out of there."

Preacher's eyes narrowed. "Well now, Mr. Mouchette, I would strongly advise you against doing that," he said.

Mouchette glared at Preacher for a long moment. Then, without another word, he took his traps and trekked back into the woods, once more leaving his footprints in the snow behind him. Preacher noted, with some satisfaction, that he wasn't heading toward the stream in question.

Preacher waited four days before he returned to the stream. Evidently, Mouchette had paid heed to Preacher's warning, because Preacher's traps were still in place.

It was nearly three weeks after his encounter with Mouchette when the shot came. Preacher was gathering his first crop of beaver pelt. The traps were full, and the beaver were prime with rich coats. He had bent over to check something when a ball whizzed by, right where his head had been. Had the shot been fired half a second earlier, Preacher's blood and brains would have decorated the tree beside him. Instead, there was just a streak of green wood in the tree where the bullet had chewed off a limb and stripped away some of the bark.

Preacher dove to the ground, burrowed into the snow, and turned to look in the direction from which the shot had come. Just below a snow-bearing pine bough, he saw a puff of smoke hanging in the cold, still air. This was where the shot had come from.

Wriggling through the snow on his belly, Preacher returned to his kit. Grabbing his rifle, he rolled onto his back and began loading it. He poured powder into the barrel, then used his ramrod to tamp the wad down. All the while he was loading his rifle, he kept his eyes toward the tree line from which the shot had come. He knew that whoever shot at him would also be reloading, and his assailant had a head start.

Just as Preacher was dropping in the ball, he saw a rifle barrel protrude from the trees, not where the smoke of the first shot was, but from some distance away. His assailant had cleverly changed positions after the first shot.

Preacher rolled hard to the right, just as a flash of fire erupted from the end of the protruding rifle barrel. The ball crashed into the snow where Preacher had been.

"Now, you son of a bitch! You're empty and I'm loaded," Preacher said. Standing, he moved quickly toward the puff of smoke.

But Preacher had miscalculated, because another barrel suddenly appeared, not a rifle, but a pistol. Preacher realized, too late, that his assailant had loaded his pistol as well and was holding it in reserve.

Once again, Preacher had to throw himself to the ground in order to avoid being shot, and once again, the ball came so close to him that he could hear it whizzing by his ear. When Preacher hit the ground this time, he felt himself tumbling, slipping, and sliding down the side of a long hill. When he finally stopped, he was more than one hundred feet below where he started.

Scrambling back to his feet, Preacher searched through the snow until he found his rifle. Cleaning the flint and pan of snow, he worked his way back up the hill. When he got to the top, he started toward the tree line where he had last seen his assailant. He found marks in the snow where the man had waited in ambush for him, but whoever it was had gone.

Following the trail the assailant left, Preacher saw someone hurrying across an open field, trying to reach the safety of the woods on the other side. He was too far away for Preacher to be certain, but there was something about the way the man was moving that made Preacher believe it was

Mouchette. And of course, as he thought about it, Mouchette was the only one who would have a motive to attack him now.

Preacher raised the rifle to his shoulder and aimed. Mouchette, if that was who it was, was just on the extreme outer range of his rifle. Despite the great range, Preacher was an exceptionally good shot. He knew that if he pulled the trigger, there was a good chance he would hit him.

Preacher took a breath, let half of it out, then gradually began to increase the pressure on the trigger. Then, taking his finger off the trigger, he sighed and lowered the rifle. Whoever it was had tried to kill him, and he had every right to shoot. But Preacher's life wasn't in immediate danger right now. To shoot a man in the back, while he was fleeing, didn't set well with Preacher—even though that man had tried to kill him.

Raising the rifle to his shoulder again, he aimed—not to kill, but to frighten. He squeezed the trigger. The rifle boomed and rocked him back, a cloud of smoke puffing up around him. He saw the strike of the ball in the snow, just a few feet in front of the fleeing man, and he saw the fleeing man throw himself to the ground in terror.

Preacher laughed. "Let that be a lesson to you, Mouchette," he said, positive now that Mouchette was the one who had attacked him. "If you come back, don't think you are going to get another shot at me."

Returning to work his trap line, Preacher leaned the rifle against a tree, then loaded his pistol and put it on the ground close by. Keeping both firearms loaded and ready, he went back to work.

"Damn, Dog, this is one time I could've really used you," he said, speaking aloud. "You would never have let anyone sneak up on me like that."

2

St. Louis

Dog lay on the front porch of the little store into which Jennie had gone. There were some buildings he could go into, and some that he could not. Dog never understood exactly why it was like that, but he was aware of the difference, and he knew that this was one of those buildings where he was not welcome.

Being denied entry into a building didn't present a problem to Dog. Whenever he encountered a building in which he wasn't welcome, he would simply wait outside until Jennie came out again. He didn't care that much about being around many humans anyway.

Dog missed the life he had led before coming to this place. Part wolf, he was completely at home in the woods and the mountains. But he was part dog as well, and the part of him that was dog felt some primordial instinct to bond with man. The man Dog chose was well worthy of his bonding. For Dog had seen the man fight a bear and kill him. Others called that man Preacher, but Dog thought of him as Bear Killer.

Dog not only bonded with Bear Killer, but traveled with him as well. In their travels, they wound up here, in this place of many men and few animals. Dog had waited patiently for

Bear Killer to leave this place of many men and few animals so he could return to the woods and the mountains.

Before it was time to leave, however, Bear Killer gave Dog a job to do. That job was to look after Bear Killer's woman. Dog wanted to leave with Bear Killer, but the part of him that was dog would not let him do so. Loyalty was the strongest trait of a dog, and Dog's loyalty was particularly well developed.

Others came and left the little store, but Bear Killer's woman, Jennie, was still inside. Dog slept on the porch, with his nose between his paws. As he slept, he dreamed of the woods and the mountains, of clear, sweet streams of water, and of rabbits he would chase down and eat. Yet, even as he was dreaming, a part of him was still alert. He assessed all who entered or left the store to determine whether or not they represented any danger to the woman he had been ordered to protect. Some would speak to him, others would go out of their way to avoid him, frightened by his powerful, wolf-like appearance. Dog actually preferred those who went out of their way to avoid him.

"There you are, Dog, right where I left you," Jennie said, coming out of the store. She squatted down beside him and smiled at him. Jennie was an exceptionally pretty woman with a smooth, olive-complexioned skin, high cheekbones, flashing brown eyes, and dark hair that hung in easy curls about her shoulders. She held a piece of ribbon beside her face. "Do you think this is pretty?" she asked.

Dog raised his head, then twisted it slightly, as if trying to respond to her question.

Jennie laughed. "Of course you think it's pretty. You're a good dog and you like anything I like. Come, let's go."

Jennie stepped down from the porch and Dog stood up, shook himself, then started after her.

* * *

Philadelphia

Theodore Epson sat across the desk from Joel Fontaine, the president of the Trust Bank of Philadelphia. They were in Fontaine's office, and as a measure of the size of the Trust Bank, Fontaine's office alone was as large the entire River Bank of St. Louis, the bank where Epson had worked before coming to Philadelphia.

"Mr. Epson, I have recently come in receipt of a very disturbing letter," Fontaine said, holding the letter up for Epson to see.

"A disturbing letter, sir? What type of letter?" Epson asked.

"It is a letter from one William Ashley of St. Louis. I'm sure you are familiar with William Ashley, are you not?"

Epson began to get a little nervous, and a small line of sweat beaded on his upper lip. He took a handkerchief from his pocket and dabbed at it.

"Uh, yes, sir, indeed I do know Mr. Ashley," Epson said. He knew that whatever Ashley had to say in the letter about him couldn't be good. "Mr. Ashley is a furrier," Epson continued. "And as such, he is a man who must deal with the most common class of people. Unfortunately, I'm afraid he is sometimes unduly swayed by them."

"Unduly swayed by them?"

"Prone to believe them over the more substantial and trustworthy citizens of the community," Epson said.

"An interesting observation," Fontaine said, stroking his chin. "I would be interested in hearing what Mr. Ashley has to say. What is the subject of the letter, if you don't mind sharing?"

"I don't mind sharing at all, as it concerns you."

"The letter concerns me? How so?"

"According to William Ashley, there was an incident in St. Louis where mortgage money duly paid to the River Bank of St. Louis was not credited."

"Well, now, I don't understand that," Epson said, nervously

patting his mouth with his handkerchief. "Why would Mr. Ashley be writing to you about some business that supposedly took place in St. Louis? It would seem to me that he would take that up with the River Bank. And as I am no longer with the River Bank, why would that information, if it is true, concern me?"

Joel Fontaine cleared his throat. "Well, it has to do with you, Mr. Epson, because I'm afraid Mr. Ashley is accusing you of fraud."

"Me?" Epson said. "This is preposterous. I have no idea what you are even talking about. My record at the River Bank of St. Louis is spotless. Why, you checked my credentials yourself. You were satisfied that they were impeccable. The directors of the River Bank in St. Louis gave me a sterling report. I know that they did."

"That is true," Fontaine agreed.

"Well, then, there you go," Epson said. "If the bank has found no fault with me, then this . . . this preposterous story that Mr. Ashley is spreading about me taking money from some whore, and not crediting her account, has absolutely no basis in fact."

"Whore?" Fontaine asked, screwing his face up in confusion. He looked at the letter he was holding. "And just what whore would that be, Mr. Epson?"

"The woman you said is claiming that I stole money from her. Why, she is nothing but a common whore. As a matter of fact, the house on which we held her mortgage was a house of prostitution."

"Well, now, that is interesting," Fontaine said. "For as it turns out, the money in question was supposed to be paid on a woman's house. But I made no mention of that fact. If, as you say, you have no idea what I'm talking about, how is it that you know that I was talking about a woman?"

"I . . . I just know because both she and Mr. Ashley have tried to make trouble for me in the past," Epson stammered.

"And I'm sure, should you deem it necessary to look into this most preposterous story any further, you will see that I am telling the truth."

"Yes, I'm sure that the investigation will prove you innocent," Fontaine said. "Although I must say, the amount of money Mr. Ashley claims was not credited to the woman, nine hundred fifty dollars, is remarkably close to the amount of money you deposited in your personal account when you arrived at our bank." Fontaine looked at a piece of paper. "The amount you deposited was nine hundred dollars, I believe."

"Yes," Epson said. "But of course, that was a mere coincidence. I assure you, there is nothing to this story. You will recall that when I came to work here, I told you that I had been instrumental in putting some brothel houses out of business?"

"Oh, yes, I do recall."

"I'm sure this all has to do with that. It is spite directed against me because I did my civic duty. As I say, the woman in question is a whore. You ask how I know who was behind this, even though you had not mentioned a name. I can only report that the woman in question has tried shenanigans of this sort before. It is bitterness, pure and simple."

"Well, that may be the case for the woman," Fontaine said. "But what about Mr. Ashley? I have checked on him, and I find that he is one of the most successful businessmen in St. Louis, highly respected by all in the fur-trading industry."

"Yes, but you must understand that William Ashley cavorts, on a daily basis, with whores, trappers, hunters, wilderness guides, boatmen. And one cannot come into such constant contact with such people without being affected by them. Why, I have no doubt but that Mr. William Ashley was himself a habitué of the establishment in question."

"That is quite an accusation," Fontaine said.

"Perhaps so, but it is less damning than the false accusation he has lodged against me," Epson said.

"Why do you think someone like Ashley would make such a charge?" Fontaine asked.

"Oh, that's easy to understand. The whore, Jennie, no doubt talked him into making the accusation against me and bringing it to your attention. I'm sure that she understands that a respectable bank such as the Trust Bank of Philidelphia will have nothing to do with such a spurious accusation being lodged against a bank officer by a common whore."

"No doubt the matter will soon be cleared up," Fontaine said.

"Yes, I'm sure it will be."

"Go on back to work, Mr. Epson. I will investigate thoroughly, but quietly."

"Yes, sir, thank you," Epson said. "I shall return to work confident in my total and complete exculpation."

Shortly after he left Fontaine's office, Epson wrote a letter to a St. Louis citizen whom he knew to be of disreputable character. Such a low-class citizen, however, was exactly what he needed for the task at hand.

The letter went by stage from Philadelphia to Steubenville, Ohio, making the transit in six days. At Steubenville, the letter was put aboard a riverboat for transit to St. Louis. Traversing the Ohio and Mississippi Rivers required another fourteen days so that, twenty days after Epson mailed the letter, the St. Louis postal clerk stepped into LaBarge's Saloon, carrying the letter with him.

LaBarge, who was wiping off the bar, looked up as Toomey came inside. He smiled.

"Well, well, if it isn't our illustrious mail official Mr. Toomey," LaBarge said. "This is indeed an occasion. I don't believe I've ever seen you in here before. What can I get for you, Mr. Toomey?"

"I'm not here to partake of any spirits, thank you," Toomey answered officiously. "I am here on U.S. Government business. I have come to deliver a letter."

"I've got a letter? Who from?" LaBarge asked, reaching for it.

"It isn't for you," Toomey said, pulling the letter from him.

"Well, if the letter ain't for me, what the hell are you doin' in my tavern?"

"Because I am told that the person for whom I am looking can nearly always be found here," Toomey said as he continued to look around the room. "And indeed, there he is."

When LaBarge looked in the same direction as Toomey, he blinked in surprise.

"What the hell?" he said. "Surely, you ain't talkin' about ole Ben Caviness?"

"I am," Toomey replied.

"Well, hell, that son of a bitch can't even read, can he?"

"My dear Mr. LaBarge, whether or not any of the recipients of our mail can read is of no concern of the U.S. Post Office," Toomey replied. "Our job is merely to see that the recipient receives the letter that is sent to him. Getting it read is his responsibility."

At one time, Ben Caviness considered himself a fur trapper, and he had actually spent a few winters in the mountains. But he had never been very productive in what was actually a very difficult job. Then, when his friend Percy McDill got himself killed by the one they called Preacher, Caviness gave up the trade altogether.

Now Caviness made his living by pulling odd jobs when they were available, and by resorting to petty thievery when necessary. It worked well that way because Caviness's personal needs were few. He never wasted money on clothes or personal hygiene. He lived in an empty stall at the livery, paying for it by mucking out stables. And there were a handful of houses in town where the woman of the house felt disposed toward feeding the hungry and clothing the naked, so he could show up at the back door of such a place, hat in hand, and be able to count on a meal.

With those basic needs met, any money Caviness managed to earn through the various odd jobs he performed was spent in LaBarge's Tavern. As a result, Caviness spent every available hour there, often the first to arrive when LaBarge opened his doors in the morning and the last one to leave in the evening.

Caviness was there now, at a table in the back of the room, drinking raw whiskey and talking to a few others whose own station in life was no higher. He had no idea an official of the U.S. Post Office was looking for him to deliver a letter. In fact, if questioned, Ben Caviness would have to answer truthfully that he had never received a letter in his life.

"You would be Ben Caviness?" Toomey asked, approaching the table.

"Who's askin'?" Caviness replied.

"I am an official of the U.S. Post Office," Toomey said. "And I have a letter for Mr. Ben Caviness."

Caviness looked shocked. "You have a letter for me?"

"I do indeed," Toomey replied, handing the envelope to him.

"Ha!" one of the other men at the table said. This was a man named Slater who, like Caviness, lived a hand-to-mouth existence, working as much for liquor as for food. "Who do you know that can actually write? Let alone send you a letter?"

"You'd be surprised at the high-tone people I know," Caviness replied.

Caviness opened the envelope and took out two pieces of paper. One piece of paper was obviously a letter to him, but the other looked official. He had never seen anything quite like this.

"What is this here thing?" he asked, showing it to Toomey.

Toomey looked at the paper.

"That's a bank draft for fifteen dollars."

"What does that mean? What is a bank draft?"

"That means you can take it to the bank and they will give you fifteen dollars," Toomey explained.

"The hell you say. They'll just give it to me for nothin'?"

"No, not for nothing. You will have to present them with this draft." Toomey pointed to a line on the draft. "Do you see, it is made out to you."

"I'll be damned," Caviness said, a big smile spreading across his face. "Who would give me fifteen dollars?"

"Suppose you read the letter," Toomey suggested. "I'm certain you will find the answer to your question there."

"Yeah," Caviness said. "Yeah, I'll read the letter." He began to read and, even though he was reading silently, his lips formed every word.

"What does the letter say, Caviness?" Slater asked.

Caviness looked up from the letter, then put his hand over the words.

"This here is my letter, and it ain't none of your business what it says."

3

St. Louis

It was dark. Jennie and Dog were walking home. For many years, Jennie had made her living as a prostitute, but it wasn't a profession she chose. Born to a half-black mother in a whorehouse in New Orleans, Jennie had been sold into slavery as a very young girl.

The man who bought her, Lucas Younger, had intended to make her into a housemaid; however, as she was a very beautiful young girl, he realized early that if he played his cards right, she could be worth a lot of money to him. When she was but thirteen, he paraded her in front of a collection of the finest and wealthiest gentlemen of New Orleans. The price one man paid for the privilege of being first more than compensated Younger for her purchase in the first place.

He managed to get away with selling her for the "first" time for almost six months, until word got out as to what he was doing and he was forced to flee New Orleans, taking Jennie with him. Going by wagon from New Orleans to St. Louis, he made Jennie available for all who would pay. In those early days, Jennie would sometimes service as many as twenty or twenty-five men in one night, all arranged by Lucas Younger.

It was during that trip north that she met Preacher for the first time. As a twelve-year-old boy, experimenting with beer for the first time, he was easy pickings for Younger, who knocked him out, put him on his wagon, and took him with him. Preacher was called Art then, and Jennie was a full year older than he was. Younger attempted to make the boy his slave, but Art got away, killing him in the escape.

A few years later, their paths crossed a second time. Jennie, now the slave of another, was still being forced to earn her keep by prostitution. At this meeting, Art managed to win Jennie in a shooting contest.

By then, Jennie knew that she was in love with him, and the thought of being his slave actually pleased her. But Art would have none of it. He gave Jennie her papers of manumission, freeing her forever. In turn, Jennie provided the boy, who was not yet known as Preacher, with his passage into manhood.

Even though Jennie was now free, she was a person with a checkered past, unable to earn a living in any way except the only way she knew. Once more she became a prostitute, but this time, working for herself, she was at least able to profit from it. Because she was frugal, she soon earned enough money to start her own brothel, which she staffed with a full complement of girls, carefully chosen for their looks and demeanor.

The House of Flowers, as she called her brothel, quickly became the most successful operation of its kind in St. Louis, and its parlors hosted some of the most influential men in the city and state. It also became a lightning rod for civic action groups, especially the Women's Auxiliary of the St. Louis Betterment League, whose president was Sybil Abernathy, wife of the president of the board of directors of the River Bank of St. Louis.

Once Jennie had her business going, she left "the line," as it was called when one was an active prostitute, doing noth-

ing but administer her house. From that time on, the only time
she was ever with a man was on those rare times when
Preacher would come to St. Louis.

Jennie was in love with Preacher. She never spoke about this
to him, because she knew that it could not work out. Preacher
would never be happy in a city, and she could not live in the
isolation of the mountains. As a result, Preacher's visits to St.
Louis were all the sweeter because they provided little windows
on a life that she could only glimpse, but would never have.

When Jennie learned that Sybil Abernathy intended to
force her husband to call in the loan, she took 475 dollars
from her savings and presented it to the chief teller at the
bank. It was enough money to pay off the mortgage on her
house, thus making it fully hers, safe from the machinations
of Sybil Abernathy.

What Jennie did not realize was that Preacher had also
paid off her mortgage, doing so quietly because he was
afraid Jennie wouldn't take the money from him. In neither
case, however, was the money credited. Jennie wound up
losing her house.

Now, Jennie shared a small house with her best friend,
Clara. Clara, who was a few years younger than Jennie, had
lived in the House of Flowers with Jennie and the other girls.
Although Clara lived there, she was not, and had never been,
one of the prostitutes.

By living together, the two women were not only company
for each other, they also shared living expenses. Clara earned
her money by working in a café, whereas Jennie earned her
income by working as a seamstress. Jennie was a very good
seamstress, but she had to struggle for a living. Many of the
women in town, aware of her past, would have nothing to do
with her.

One of the most vocal woman against her was the one
most opposed to her while she was running the whorehouse,
Sybil Abernathy.

Ironically, it was Mrs. Abernathy's house Jennie was coming from tonight. Though it killed Mrs. Abernathy's soul to have to work with Jennie, the bank president's wife was in a bind. She had been invited to a party at the governor's mansion in Jefferson City, and she had nothing to wear. The only way she could get ready in time was to use Jennie's services.

She decided to do so, but insisted that Jennie make her visits for fittings only at night. In so doing, Sybil thought it would lessen the chances that Jenny would be seen coming to or from her house.

"After all, unlike you, my dear, I do have a reputation to uphold," Mrs. Abernathy had said.

Mrs. Abernathy was a very exacting client, and if Jennie hadn't needed the money, she would have told her to get someone else to make her gown. But she did need the money, so she put up with Sybil's demands, redoing the seams, making adjustments here and changes there. It was nearly midnight by the time she left for home.

Although Mrs. Abernathy had thought she was hiring Jennie in secret, such a piece of gossip was just too juicy to keep. The news didn't come from Jennie, because she had told no one—her sense of integrity extended even to someone like Mrs. Abernathy. But others were aware of the arrangement, and soon the entire town knew that Jennie was making a special gown for Sybil Abernathy to wear to the Governor's Ball.

One of those who knew was Ben Caviness. He also knew that Mrs. Abernathy had demanded that Jennie work for her only at night. Armed with that information, Caviness waited in an alley along the route between Mrs. Abernathy's mansion and the small house that Jennie shared with Clara. As he waited, he reached down to grab hold of himself. The letter had been very specific as to what he had to do to earn the fifteen dollars the bank draft represented. It was going to be fun.

* * *

Unlike some of the larger cities back East, St. Louis had only a few street lamps, and they were in the middle of town. In the part of the city that was closest to Jennie's house, the streets were narrow and shadowed. It was particularly dark tonight, for there was no moon out. Had Dog not been with her, Jennie would have been too frightened to be out.

Dog sensed the man before he smelled him, and he smelled him before he heard anything suspicious. As they approached the alley, Dog stopped. The hackles stood up on the back of his neck. He let out a low warning growl.

"What is it, Dog?" Jennie asked. She reached down to pet him.

There was someone in the alley ahead . . . someone waiting for them. Dog didn't know who it was, but he knew that whoever it was, he was up to no good. Dog lowered his head slightly and moved ahead slowly, deliberately.

Suddenly, a man jumped out of the alley in front of them.

Jennie let out a gasp of alarm.

"Good evenin', missy," Caviness said with an evil smile.

"I know who you are," Jennie said. "You're Ben Caviness. How dare you jump out at me! What do you mean frightening me like this?"

"Missy, you're causing a lot of trouble for a very important man, and he don't like it none," the man said.

"What are you talking about?"

"Mr. Epson don't want no more letters bein' wrote about him," Caviness said.

"I don't care what he wants. I will continue writing letters about him until I get my money back."

"Then I reckon I'm going to have to change your mind," Caviness said, taking a step toward her.

Until now, Dog had merely been watching Caviness. The moment Caviness started forward, Dog leaped toward him, snapping, and nipping him on the leg.

Startled, Caviness jumped back.

"What the hell! Call that dog off! Call him off!"

"I expect you'd better get on out of here," Jennie said.

Dog continued to growl. He wouldn't attack again unless the man attacked Jennie. But if need be, he was in position to do so. He growled and made another lunge toward the man, though he held back at the last minute.

"No! No! Call him off! Call him off!"

"Get out of here, and I'll keep him back," Jennie promised.

Caviness turned and ran, chased down the alley by Dog's barking and Jennie's laughter.

Clara was asleep when Jennie and Dog returned, but Jennie woke her up to tell what happened.

"Oh, Jennie, that is so frightening," Clara said. "You should go see Constable Billings."

"Ha," Jennie said. "A fat lot of good that will do. I have complained about that toad Epson stealing money from me, and the only thing it accomplished was to have him send Caviness after me."

"Well, to be honest about it, what can Billings do about Epson? Epson is with some bank in Philadelphia now. I'm sure that Mr. Billings has no jurisdiction over him. But he could certainly put Caviness in jail."

"For what? For wetting his pants?" Jennie asked. "Because I'm sure that's what he did when Dog got after him. Besides, if Caviness is the best Epson can come up with, then I don't think I have anything to worry about. You know what they say. Better the devil you can see than the one you can't see."

"I suppose that's true."

Jennie laughed. "And you should have seen him run! I laughed so hard that my sides hurt."

Clara laughed as well. "Oh, I wish I could've seen that," she said.

Jennie rubbed Dog behind the ears. "I'm not worried. Not as long as I have Dog to look out for me."

Philadelphia

Once more, Theodore Epson was summoned to Joel Fontaine's office. This time, it wasn't just Fontaine, but the entire membership of the board of directors was present for the meeting. They had been talking among themselves, but they fell silent when Epson entered.

Epson looked around nervously. "You sent for me, Mr. Fontaine?"

"I did."

"To what purpose?"

"Have a seat, please," Fontaine said without directly answering Epson's concerned query.

Whereas the others were sitting in comfortable chairs around a table, the seat Fontaine offered Epson was a small, straight-backed, wooden chair, placed at some distance from the others.

"Mr. Fontaine, may I ask what is this about?" Epson asked.

"Mr. Epson, we have received another letter from Mr. Ashley of St. Louis," Fontaine said. "And this time, he included a report that Miss Jennie . . ." He looked through the letter. "There doesn't appear to be a last name."

"She has no last name," Epson said.

"No last name? Of course she has a last name. Everyone has a last name," one of the board members said.

"Many colored do not have a last name," Epson said. "She is a colored woman."

"Really? I wasn't aware of that," the board member said.

"Yes, well, let us return to business, shall we?" said Fontaine. "According to Mr. Ashley, this is a report filed by Miss Jennie, No Last Name, with a Constable Billings. Are you familiar with Constable Billings?"

"Yes, he is the chief law enforcement officer in St. Louis," Epson replied.

Fontaine cleared his throat. "Mr. Epson, this report which Miss Jennie filed with the constable alleges that you hired someone to threaten her. According to the report, he accosted her late one night. Had it not been for the fact that the lady was accompanied by a dog, he would have done her bodily harm."

"That's preposterous."

"You don't believe the lady was attacked?" Fontaine asked.

"She may well have been attacked, for St. Louis is a wild and mostly undisciplined town," Epson replied. "But I assure you, if that is the case, I had nothing to do with it. Why would I?"

"According to the report, the man who attacked her said that"—Fontaine adjusted his glasses and read directly from the letter—"'Mr. Epson don't want no more letters wrote about him.'" Fontaine looked up. "What do you say to that?"

Epson shook his head. "I don't know what to say," he said. "Other than to say it isn't true. I have hired no one to harm her."

"Do you have any idea why she would make such a claim?"

"Yes, I have a very good idea. She is trying to extort money from me by making the claim that I took mortgage money from her without posting it to the books."

"So, it is your contention that this is part of an extortion scheme on her part?"

"Yes, her part, and William Ashley's as well. Is there any paperwork to substantiate the claim that either of them gave me any money?" Epson asked.

"Apparently not," Fontaine said. "For no such paperwork was included in the letter."

"Then I ask you gentlemen to consider this," Epson said.

"We are all bankers. We deal with money every day. Our only protection against such spurious claims as these is the signed documents by which we do business. Can you imagine passing over an amount of money as large as all that without getting a signed receipt?"

There was a murmuring of agreement from the members of the board.

"Mr. Fontaine, as this is obviously an attempt at extortion, I am the aggrieved party here. I am the one who is being falsely accused. Fortunately for me, the very basis by which we do business, the signed receipt, is, by its absence in this case, proof of my innocence."

"You know, Joel, Mr. Epson has a point," one of the other board members said. "In this business we live or die by supporting documents. It seems to me contrary to everything we stand for to be accusing one of our own of a violation, when there is no evidence, such as a signed receipt to substantiate this woman's claim."

Fontaine looked at the others. "Yes, I agree. Gentlemen, I am inclined to take Mr. Epson at his word," he said. "How say you?"

Most of the board agreed, but one of the members held up his hand.

"Yes, Miller, what is it?"

"In principle, I agree. However, it just so happens that I will be making a trip to St. Louis in a few weeks. Suppose, while I am there, I visit with Mr. Ashley and this woman and talk to them in person."

"Good idea," Fontaine said. He looked up at Epson and smiled. "For now, Mr. Epson, we will take no action. I'm sure that you will be exonerated. But if Mr. Miller is going to St. Louis anyway, we may as well put this whole thing to rest once and for all. I'm sure you agree that would be the best approach."

"Yes," Epson said. Taking out his handkerchief, he dabbed at the beads of sweat along his upper lip. "Yes, I agree, that is best. And I assure you, I welcome a full inquiry into the matter."

"I was certain you would," Fontaine said. "Now, gentlemen, let us all get back to work, shall we? After all, we do have a bank to run."

That night, in his apartment, Epson walked over to the window and looked out onto the street below. What a mess he was in. He had not set out to steal anyone's money. But when the opportunity presented itself, the temptation had been just too strong to resist.

He recalled the sequence of events that had brought him to this point.

The River Bank of St. Louis had just opened for the day's business, and Epson had been at his desk for no more than five minutes when William Ashley arrived. Stepping inside the bank, Ashley looked around for a moment, then came straight over to see Epson.

"Mr. Epson, I wonder if I might have a word with you?" Ashley asked.

"Certainly, Mr. Ashley," Epson replied, standing to greet him. "It is always a pleasure to greet one of our fair city's most powerful businessmen. How are you doing, sir?"

"I'm doing fine, Epson," Ashley said.

Epson's eyes squinted, and he continued the conversation in a somewhat more guarded tone. "I must say I'm a little surprised to see you, though. I've been given to understand that you have started your own bank for the fur trappers."

Ashley shook his head in the negative. "Not at all," he said. "All I'm doing is keeping some of my trappers' earned income on the books for them."

"Isn't that what a bank does?"

"I suppose. But I'm only doing it as a favor for my trappers. Most of them don't like to carry any more money than they need."

"Nobody does," Epson said. "That's what banks are for. You could steer some of your accounts our way, you know."

"Yes, I know," Ashley replied. "And I fully intend to, over a period of time."

"Really?" Epson asked, brightening. "So, have you brought me a deposit today?"

"Not a deposit, but a payment."

"A payment? I don't understand. A payment for what? You don't have a loan here."

"It isn't for me. It is for one of your customers. It's more than a payment actually. I intend to pay off the entire mortgage."

"Why would you pay off someone else's mortgage?" Epson asked. He frowned. "Wait a minute. Have you made the loan yourself? That's it, isn't it? You're paying off the loan because you have made it yourself. You *are* going into banking."

"No. All I'm doing is paying off the loan on behalf of an interested party."

"I see. And what loan are you paying off?"

"I'm paying off the loan on the House of Flowers."

"You are paying off the whore's loan?"

"Yes."

"I don't understand. Why would you do such a thing?"

"I assure you, sir, I am not paying the loan from my own funds. As I said, I am doing so on behalf of an interested party. He doesn't want this Miss Jennie to know that he is doing it."

Epson stroked his jaw as he studied Ashley. "Are you saying that she doesn't know her loan is being paid off?"

"That's right."

"I am curious. Who is her benefactor? Some businessman in town?"

"I don't believe I'm at liberty to say who it is," Ashley said.

"I wasn't told that I couldn't tell, but I wasn't given permission to tell either. Therefore, I feel ethically bound to keep his identity a secret."

"Ha!" Epson said. "I was right, wasn't I? It is some local businessman. And of course he would make the payment through someone else if he wanted it kept secret. Like as not, it's one of the same men who, in public, call for that house to be closed, while in private, are among her biggest supporters. Who is it? The mayor?"

"I told you . . . I don't believe I'm at liberty to say. It doesn't matter anyway. All I intend to do is pay off the note. Now, are you going to accept the money, or what?"

"Yes, yes, of course I'll accept the money."

Later that same afternoon, Jennie herself called at the bank. Seeing her the moment she stepped through the door, Epson went over to meet her.

"Yes, Miss Jennie," he said. "Is there something I can do for you?"

"I wonder if we could speak in private for a few moments," Jennie said.

"Yes, of course we can. Come over here to my desk. We can talk there without being overheard."

There were no other women in the bank, but there were several male customers. Most of them knew who Jennie was, and many of them had been paying customers at the House of Flowers. It would have been easy to pick out her customers, for while the others stared at Jennie in unabashed curiosity, her customers looked away pointedly, pretending they didn't even see her.

Epson led Jennie through the gate of the small, fenced-in area that surrounded his desk. He offered her a chair, then sat as well.

"Now, Miss Jennie, what is it that we can only discuss in private?"

"Recently, some people have been attempting to close down my business," Jennie said.

Epson scratched his cheek with his forefinger. "Ah, yes," he said. "You would be talking about the Women's Auxiliary of the St. Louis Betterment League."

"You know about it?"

"Yes."

"Then you also know that chief among these women is Mrs. Abernathy."

Epson nodded. "Sybil Abernathy, yes."

"Doesn't her husband have something to do with this bank?"

"Yes indeed, he is the chairman of the board of directors of the bank."

"I thought as much." Jennie opened her portmanteau and fished out a piece of paper. "According to the contract, even if I am not in arrears, the bank can call in the remainder of my loan at any time. Is that right?"

"Yes, but . . ."

"That's what I thought. That's why I want to pay off the entire loan today. That way there will be no chance for the bank to foreclose." Jennie began writing a bank draft. "I believe the amount is four hundred and seventy-five dollars."

Epson was silent for a long moment, and Jennie looked up at him questioningly. "Am I not right?" she asked.

Epson wondered what he should do. Though he had not yet posted the paperwork, he had accepted the money from William Ashley to pay off her debt. He couldn't tell her this, though, because he had been specifically instructed not to.

"Mr. Epson, is four hundred and seventy-five dollars correct?" Jennie asked again.

"Uh, yes," Epson said. He would take the money now and decide later what to do.

Jennie wrote the draft and handed it to him.

"I'll, uh, take care of this for you," Epson said.

Jennie smiled at him. "Thank you," she said. "I may be worried for no reason at all, but Mrs. Abernathy seems to be quite a determined woman. I fear she may convince her husband to exercise the foreclosure clause in the contract. I would rather just own the house free and clear, so that there is no question."

Epson nodded again. "Yes, I'm sure you are doing the right thing," he said. He picked up the draft and put it in his pocket. "I'll have the title delivered to you."

"Thank you again," Jennie said, getting up from her chair. Epson stood quickly, then walked with her to the door. He stood in the door and watched as her driver helped her climb into her carriage. Then he returned to his desk and sat there for a long moment, contemplating what he should do.

It was not until that moment that he realized what an opportunity had been dropped in his lap. He was due to leave on the very next day for his new job in Philadelphia. Neither Jennie nor, amazingly, Ashley before her had asked for a signed receipt. That meant he could leave St. Louis 950 dollars richer, and no one would ever be the wiser.

That is exactly what Epson did. And although he had come through some difficulty, it looked now as if Mr. Fontaine was willing to accept his side of the story. The only fly in the ointment was Mr. Miller's trip to St. Louis.

If Miller talked to Jennie, he might believe her version of the story. She was, after all, a very pretty young woman who could be very persuasive. If there was only some way to keep him from talking to her.

Epson stood at the window for a moment longer, and the solution came to him. It wasn't something he would have wanted to do, and it certainly wasn't anything he could do personally. But the situation had been forced upon him. Jennie herself had forced it upon him.

Turning away from the window, Epson sat at the small writing desk in his room and wrote another letter. This one was short and to the point.

Make my problem go away.

With the letter, he included a draft for one hundred dollars. If the intent of his message wasn't understood, the amount of money he was paying to carry out the operation would certainly make itself understood.

He just hoped that the letter reached St. Louis before Miller did.

4

A lone rider, tall and rawhide lean, sat his saddle easily as the horse picked its way down from the high country. Preacher was riding one horse and leading two more. The pack animals were carrying five hundred plews each, beaver pelts perfectly skinned, dried, and stretched so as to be of the finest quality.

The trail followed alongside a meandering brook where cool, sweet water broke white over rocks as it rushed downhill. At the end of the trail there would be Rendezvous, a gathering of mountain men and traders, trappers and fur dealers, Indians, whiskey drummers, Bible salesmen, whores, friends and strangers.

Many a mountain man spent his entire winter thinking ahead to the next Rendezvous, using it as an incentive to help him through the long period of isolation. Preacher wasn't one of them. He reveled in his isolation, and enjoyed being alone in the vastness of the Rocky Mountains. There were times, during the winter, when he would see another trapper in the distance. Some would go out of their way to close that distance, to visit and palaver.

Preacher would not. In fact, he often changed trails to avoid these occasional meetings. For him, Rendezvous was a necessary part of doing business. It was not two weeks of drinking, gambling, and whoring.

Those who knew Preacher best understood this about him, and accepted it. He wasn't exactly a misanthrope—he was friendly enough when he was with others, and no one could want a better friend than Preacher. He had been known to have more than a few drinks on occasion, would bet on an honest game of cards or a shooting match, and was not without experience with women. But for the most part, he was sober, upright, honest, and hardworking. These attributes were admired by all, but few could emulate them.

Preacher could smell the Rendezvous first, the aroma of coffee and cooking meat, the smell of wood and tobacco smoke, and the more unpleasant odor of scores of bodies, unwashed for months, gathered in one place.

Next, he could hear it. The sounds of people began to intrude upon the sounds of nature until soon, the babbling brook was completely overpowered by loud, boisterous talk, raucous laughter, and the high, skirling sound of a fiddle.

Finally, he rode into a clearing and saw it: men and women clad in buckskin and feathers, homespun and store-bought suits, bits of color, flashes of beads, silver and gold. Dozens of tents and temporary shelters had been erected, many of them little more than canvas flaps protruding from the wagons that had brought the traders, dealers, and goods here from back East.

In front of him, and slightly to the right, Preacher suddenly saw a flash of light and a puff of smoke. At almost the same instant he heard the shot and the sound of a ball whistling past his ear.

Looking over in surprise, he saw Henri Mouchette toss his rifle aside, clawing for the pistol he had stuck down in his trousers. This was Preacher's third encounter with Mouchette this year, and it looked like this one was going to settle the score between them—one way or the other.

Preacher leaped from his horse, not away from Mouchette, as Mouchette, might have suspected, but directly toward him. Mouchette was caught off guard by Preacher's unexpected reaction. Rather than pulling his pistol cleanly, he dropped it as he jerked it from his trousers. Preacher shoved him hard, and Mouchette staggered back, a tree breaking his fall.

Mouchette pulled his knife and held it in front of him, palm up, the knife moving back and forth slowly, like the head of a coiled snake.

"That's all right," Mouchette said. "I'd rather gut you than shoot you anyway. Shootin' kills too fast."

Preacher held a hand out in front of him, as if warding Mouchette off. He pointed at Mouchette.

"That was you that tried to shoot me a couple of months back, wasn't it?" Preacher asked.

"You're damn right it was," Mouchette answered. He nodded toward the pack horses Preacher had brought in. "By rights, them should be my plews. You pulled my traps out of the water and set your own."

"We went through all of that," Preacher said. "My traps were there first. You pulled them out and replaced them with yours. I was only returning the favor."

"Who give you title to that creek anyway?" Mouchette asked.

"Nobody has title to any land up here," Preacher replied. "It's first come, first served, same as it's always been. And I was first there."

"You wouldn't even have know'd about it iffen you hadn't heard me talkin' about it last year."

"That's not true, and you know it. I've trapped that same creek for five winters now," Preacher said. "You can ask anyone here."

"That's right, Mouchette. I know he was there three years ago 'cause he took me in for the winter when I got stoved up," one of the trappers said. He, like several others, had been drawn in to the commotion. From other parts of the camp, people were moving as well, coming quickly to see what was going on.

"Yeah, well, it don't matter none now 'cause he ain't goin' to be trappin' it no more. I aim to split him open from his gullet to his pecker."

Mouchette lunged forward and made a swipe with his knife. The move was unexpectedly quick, and Preacher barely managed to dance back out of the way.

"Mouchette, I don't want to fight you," he said. "If you've got a dispute with me, we can take it up with the trappers' court."

Trappers' court wasn't an official court; it was just a group of trappers who would hear arguments from both sides of a dispute, then suggest a settlement. Their suggestions had no power of law, only the power of public opinion, but for most mountain men, that was binding enough.

"Yeah, Mouchette, take it up with trappers' court," one of the others said, picking up on Preacher's suggestion.

"Nah," Mouchette replied, his evil grin spreading. "I think I'll just kill the son of a bitch, then there won't be nothing to settle." He lunged forward again, but this time Preacher was ready for him, and he easily slipped the knife thrust, then countered with a hard blow to Mouchette's ear.

Mouchette jumped back, then put his hand to his ear.

That gave Preacher the opening he needed, and he reached for his knife, only to discover that it wasn't on his belt. He looked back toward his horse and saw that his knife was in a scabbard on a belt that was hanging around the saddle pommel. His rifle was in the rifle boot, and his pistol was in the saddlebag. He was bare-handed against Mouchette.

"Well, now," Mouchette said when he noticed Preacher's predicament. "Ain't this somethin'? 'Pears to me like you've come to a knife fight without a knife."

Mouchette crouched over and held the knife in front of him, still moving it back and forth. The smile that spread across his face wasn't one of mirth, but rather one of smug satisfaction. Mouchette, who was from New Orleans, had grown up with the knife. Even in a fair fight, he might have had an advantage. But as Preacher was unarmed, there was nothing fair about this fight.

Suddenly, a knife whizzed by in front of Preacher and stuck in the tree beside him.

Preacher had no idea who it came from, and didn't know who to thank. But at this point, he had no time to consider such things. He pulled the knife from the tree, then faced Mouchette. The easy, confident smile left Mouchette's face, but the determination did not.

"Good," Mouchette said. "I like it better this way. Wouldn't be no fun in killin' you 'lessen you fight back some."

Armed, Preacher was no longer at a disadvantage. His posture mirrored that of Mouchette's. He came up on the balls of his feet, crouching slightly, holding the knife firmly—but not too tightly—palm-up in his right hand. The two men began moving around each other warily, now entirely circled by people who had come from all over the Rendezvous, drawn to the spectacle of a fight to the death.

Mouchette moved in, raised his left hand as if to shield what he was going to do, then raised his knife hand to come in behind that shield. Preacher raised his left hand to block. Seeing the smile of triumph on Mouchette's face, Preacher realized, almost too late, that he had been suckered. He had reacted exactly as Mouchette wanted him to react.

Mouchette moved his knife hand back down swiftly, as quickly as a striking snake, and he thrust toward Preacher. Preacher managed to twist away, barely avoiding the killing thrust, but not escaping entirely. He felt the knife burn as it opened a cut on his side.

Even as Preacher was avoiding Mouchette's deadly stab, he responded with a quick counterthrust. Mouchette, thinking he had won, wasn't prepared for the instantaneous response. He was wide-open to Preacher's attack. Preacher's knife went under Mouchette's ribs, slipping in cleanly, easily, all the way to the hilt. Mouchette let out a grunt, as if he'd had the breath knocked out of him. The two men stood together for a second. Then Preacher felt Mouchette falling as his body tore itself off the knife, ripping open an even larger wound.

Mouchette fell onto his side, then rolled over onto his back. He looked up at Preacher.

"I'll be damned," he said. "Boys, I come here to kill this son of a bitch. Instead, he kilt me. Now, ain't that a hell of thing?"

Mouchette wheezed a few times; then the ragged breathing stopped and his eyes, still open, glazed over.

"Whose knife?" Preacher asked, holding up the knife he had used to kill Mouchette.

When nobody spoke up, Preacher looked over toward the tree where he had gotten the knife. Grasping the point of the blade with his thumb and forefinger, he threw the knife at the tree, sticking it in the trunk in almost the same place from which he had pulled it a moment earlier.

"You done what you had to do," one of the trappers said, and several others agreed.

"Mouchette was a pain in the ass," another insisted. "If there was ever any son of a bitch needed killin', it was him."

Nodding, but with no verbal response, Preacher walked over to his horse. Taking off his shirt, he lay it across the saddle while he examined the wound on his side. Fortunately, the cut wasn't very deep, and already it had stopped bleeding. He was putting his shirt back on as someone approached him. Preacher could tell by the way he was dressed that this was one of the traders from back East.

The trader looked over the pack animals. "Looks like you had a good season," he said.

"Tolerable," Preacher replied.

The trader looked at the pelts more closely, folding them back to examine several of them.

"More than tolerable, I'd say. These are some of the best I've seen brought in since I been here."

"Thanks."

"You the one they call Preacher?" the man asked.

"I am," Preacher said.

"I work for Mr. Ashley. William Ashley? I believe you know him."

"Yes, I know him," Preacher said.

Preacher had done business with Ashley many times before. In fact, he had once negotiated a peace with the Indians for Ashley and his traders. In this world of few contacts, and even fewer friends, William Ashley was a man that Preacher would count as a friend.

"Mr. Ashley said to treat you fair."

"He always has. That's his way," Preacher replied.

"Oh, and I almost forgot. He told me to give this to you," the trader added, handing an envelope to Preacher.

"Thanks," Preacher said.

"Hey, Preacher," one of the others called. "We got us a shootin' match comin' up tonight. Ever'one puts in a dollar, winner take all. What do you say?"

"What are you invitin' him for, Drew?" one of the others said. "You know he always wins."

"I know," Drew said. "But they's always them that'll bet he won't win, so what I lose by not winnin' myself, I make up by bettin' on a sure thing."

"Yeah, I never thought of that. What about it, Preacher? You aim to get in on the shootin'?"

"I reckon not," Preacher responded. He put some moss onto the cut, then put on a fresh shirt. "But thanks for the invite."

As the trader continued to look through the pelts, Preacher sat on a fallen log. Setting the envelope down, he took out his pipe, poured in some tobacco, tamped it down, lit it, and took a few puffs before he turned his attention back to the letter.

Finally, he reached for it, opened the envelope, pulled out the letter, and began to read.

Dear Preacher,

   It is with great sadness that I must inform you of the death of our mutual friend, Jennie.

"Oh, shit," Preacher said, pinching the bridge of his nose.

"Somethin' wrong?" the trader asked.

"You don't know what's in this letter?" Preacher asked, holding it up.

The trader shook his head. "Wasn't my letter, wasn't my place to read it," he said.

"How long ago was it written?"

"I'm not sure. Six weeks, two months maybe. I've had it at least six weeks."

Six weeks, Preacher thought. Jennie had been dead for at least six weeks, and he didn't even know it. Several times, something would happen that would remind him of her, and he would hear her laugh, or see her smile—if only in his memory. But the ability to enjoy his thoughts and remembrances of her only worked if she was alive.

"Say, Preacher, do you mind if I take these pelts on over to my wagon so I can count and grade them?"

"What? No, no, go ahead, I don't mind," Preacher replied distractedly. Reluctantly, he returned to the letter.

   I wish I could tell you that Jennie died peacefully, but I cannot. She was murdered, Preacher, in a way so vile as to defy any attempt to describe by written words. There were two of them, but one of them got away. I'm sure you remember Ben Caviness, for you had such a difficult time with him when he was part of your trapping party. Nobody knows for sure who the one is that got away, but I believe it was Ben Caviness.

The problem is, what with Jennie being a whore and all, I'm afraid there will be no justice.

Preacher, I know what store you set by Miss Jennie, and I'm sorry to have to be the one to tell you such sad news, but I knew you would want to know.

Your friend,
William Ashley

Folding the letter, Preacher got up and walked over to stick it down into his saddlebag. He glanced over toward where the fight had taken place, and saw that a couple of men were already digging a grave for Mouchette.

How odd, this sensation. Moments earlier, he had been locked in a life-and-death struggle, a struggle that he barely survived. Yet now, it seemed so remote to him that it could have happened to someone else. His thoughts were only of Jennie.

He wondered where Jennie was buried, and if anyone had shown up to say a few words over her. He hoped that they had, but he knew that it would take a brave preacher to risk the ire of his parishioners in order to pray over one of St. Louis's most notorious women.

Preacher felt an overwhelming sense of sorrow over her loss. Then, as he considered the fact that she'd been murdered, the sorrow gave way to anger.

He walked over to the trader's wagon, where the trader was busy counting out and sorting Preacher's pelts.

"It's amazing," the trader said. "All of your pelts are of the very highest quality."

"How quickly can you pay me for them?" Preacher asked.

"Well, if you will take a marker against Ashley, I can pay you right away."

"I'll take his marker," Preacher said.

"Very well, I'll make one out for you."

"Before you left St. Louis, did you hear about Jennie getting killed?"

"Oh, heavens, yes," the trader replied. "It was all anyone talked about for a while. It's a shame about her. Such a pretty young girl."

"Yeah, a shame," Preacher said.

He thought about what Ashley said in his letter about Jennie not getting justice. William Ashley was wrong. There would be justice, all right. It would be Preacher's Justice.

5

The doctor in Ste. Genevieve daubed more wagon grease onto what was left of Ben Caviness's ear.

"It's a good thing you came to me when you did," the doctor said. "This ear was near to mortifying."

"Yeah, well, it's been hurtin' somethin' awful."

"What did you say caused this again?"

"A bear," Caviness said. "I run up against a bear and he mauled me."

"Looks more like something bit this ear off, rather than clawing it off," the doctor said.

"Yeah, that's what I mean. The bear bit it off."

"You're lucky he didn't bite off your whole head."

"Do you have to talk so much, Doc? Just patch up the ear and stop the talkin'."

"I was just being friendly," the doctor said. "It's always good to be friendly with your patients. Puts them in a good frame of mind."

"Yeah, well, it don't work with me."

"I can see that it doesn't," the doctor said. He straightened up, then looked at Caviness. "That'll be one dollar," he said.

"One dollar!" Caviness exploded. "One dollar for a handful of grease you could get offen any wagon wheel?"

"It's not the grease you're paying for. It's the knowing what to do with the grease," the doctor said.

"Yeah, yeah," Caviness said. Still grumbling, he paid the doctor the dollar, then left the doctor's house and walked down to the river's edge to wait for the next boat to come through.

When Caviness got the second letter from Epson, the one that said, "Make my problem go away," he knew what Epson was asking for. Epson was paying him one hundred dollars to kill Jennie.

One hundred dollars seemed like an enormous amount of money then, because it seemed like a simple job. After all, how hard could it be to kill a woman?

Caviness knew about the dog. He had encountered the dog before. But he figured that he and Slater should be able to handle the dog with little difficulty. After all, the dog hadn't actually attacked him the last time. The dog had merely barked and growled.

That sure wasn't the case this time. The dog had attacked immediately. But even as Caviness was stabbing the dog, slashing away at him, the dog was ripping out Slater's throat. Slater was killed before he could say a word.

What started out to be an easy job turned into a nightmare. Slater was dead, and Caviness had to face the dog alone. The dog turned on Caviness, and Caviness threw up an arm to guard his neck. He felt an intense pain in his left ear; then he managed to shoot the dog. The dog fell to the ground—whether dead or alive, Caviness didn't know. All he knew was that the dog was away from him.

Caviness had planned to have a little fun with Jennie, but it was too late for that now. Dog had seen to that. Caviness was bleeding so badly that he was in danger of passing out from blood loss. When he finally did turn his attention to the whore, the expression on her face reflected the horror of the moment.

Caviness was a terrible sight to behold. He had blood all over his face, arms, and hands. The side of his head was covered with blood too, as well as an ugly little piece of shredded flesh that was the only indication of what had once been an ear.

Caviness made one mighty sweep with his knife, not only cutting her jugular, but nearly decapitating her. Leaving Dog dying, and Jennie and Slater dead, Caviness left the scene of the crime. Stealing a rowboat, Caviness started downriver. He had no immediate plan in mind. At this point, all he wanted to do was get out of St. Louis.

He wasn't sure when he came up with the plan of going to Philadelphia to see Mr. Theodore Epson. But the more he thought of it, the better the idea became. He would get more money from Epson. He figured losing an ear should be worth a lot of money. And if Epson thought otherwise, then all Caviness would have to do is go to the law with the letter Epson had sent him.

Caviness wasn't even sure where Philadelphia was, though he had a vague suspicion that one could get there, or nearly so, merely by taking a riverboat. It was his intention to take the next one that stopped in Ste. Genevieve. When he heard the whistle of the approaching boat, Caviness put his hand over the bandaged ear and walked down to wait for it. There was no one ashore selling tickets, but the moment he stepped on board, the purser arranged his passage for him. He found out from the purser that the boat couldn't take him all the way to Philadelphia as he had hoped, but he would take it as far as he could.

Once they were under way, Caviness walked to the bow of the boat and watched the river roll underneath them. He had never been to Philadelphia. He had never been to any city any larger than St. Louis. He wondered if they had whorehouses in Philadelphia.

Kansas City

Jeb Law had his back to the bar as he was putting bottles of whiskey in their place.

"What do you have that isn't poison?" someone asked from behind him.

Jeb didn't turn around.

"Ain't you ever heard the temperance lectures, mister? It's all poison, some of it is just quicker than the other," Jeb replied.

"Well, if you got anything that won't eat through the glass before I can get it down, I'll have a drink."

This time Jeb recognized the voice, and he turned around, then smiled broadly as he stuck his hand across the bar. "Art!" he said. "Well, if you ain't a sight for tired ole eyes."

"Hello, Jeb," Preacher said, shaking Jeb's hand. "How are things here in Westport?"

"It's Kansas City now," Jeb corrected, reaching under the bar to pull out a special bottle to pour Preacher's drink. "Nobody calls it Westport anymore. Come to think of it, nobody calls you Art anymore either, do they? It's Preacher, isn't it?"

"That's the handle folks seem to have hung on me," Preacher said, reaching for some money.

Jeb held out his hand, palm facing Preacher. "Your money ain't no good with me, Preacher," he said. "This drink is on the house."

"I'll let you buy me the first one," Preacher said. "Then I'll buy us both one."

Jeb smiled. "Sounds good enough to me," he said. "What brings you to Kansas City? You don't come this far east all that often. From what I hear, you're about as fixed in those mountains as one of them aspen trees."

"I'm on my way to St. Louis," Preacher said. "Thought I might find a place to board my string here, then take a boat."

"What have you got?"

"Good riding horse, two good pack animals."

"How long you plannin' on being gone?"

Preacher shook his head. "Well, that's just it. I don't know as I can answer that question."

Jeb smiled. "That ain't like you not to have a clear plan of what you're goin' to do," he said.

"Oh, I've got me a clear plan of what I'm goin' to do, all right," Preacher said. "I just don't know how long it's going to take me to do it."

Preacher killed the rest of his drink, and Jeb set another glass on the table, filled both of them, then put his special bottle back under the bar.

"Sounds a little mysterious," Jeb said. He took the coin Preacher gave him, then picked up his glass and held it out toward Preacher. "Here's to you, my friend," he said.

Preacher nodded and touched his glass to Jeb's. "And to old times," he replied.

Jeb tossed the drink down, then wiped the back of his hand across his mouth.

"Now, what is it you're a-plannin' on doin', if you don't mind my askin'?"

"I reckon you heard about what happened to Jennie," Preacher replied.

"Jennie?" For a second Jeb squinted; then his face registered recognition. "You're talking about that pretty little gal used to run the House of Flowers back in St. Louis?"

"Yes."

"No, don't know as I've heard anything about her lately."

"She's dead, Jeb," Preacher said.

"Dead? Oh, the hell you say," Jeb replied. He shook his head. "That's a damn shame. She was a fine woman, for all that she was a whore. Wait a minute. You set some store by her, didn't you?"

"Yeah, I did. I set quite a store by her," Preacher said.

"I'm real sorry to hear about her dyin'," Jeb said. "She come down with somethin', did she?"

"She was murdered."

"Murdered," Jeb repeated. Without being told, he reached under the bar, pulled out the bottle, and refilled their glasses one more time. "Does anyone know who done it?"

"I got a letter from Mr. Ashley," Preacher said. "He thinks Caviness may have had something to do with it."

"Caviness? Ben Caviness?"

"Yes."

"Well, from what I remember about the son of a bitch, he's mean enough to do something like that. Come to think of it, didn't he trail with you one season?"

"Yes, he and his partner Percy McDill."

"McDill, yeah, I remember him. Hell, he was as ornery as Caviness from what I can recall. Whatever happened to him?"

"I killed him," Preacher said. "I just wish I had killed Caviness the same time."

"What happened?"

Preacher took another drink, then stared off, as if looking into the distance. "The son of a bitch tried to rape Jennie."

"Yeah? Then the son of a bitch needed killin'. I'd like to hear about it, if you don't mind the tellin'."

"No, I don't mind the tellin'," Preacher said as he started the story.

* * *

Two years earlier, at Rendezvous

In the darkness, illuminated only by a single candle, Jennie faced a terrifying apparition. Percy McDill burst into her tent and now moved toward her, his face twisted by lust and anger into a grotesque mask. The candle's reflection in his dark eyes gave Jennie the illusion of staring into the very fires of hell. She stepped backward, but found little room to maneuver in the confines of the tent.

Jennie screamed.

Outside, Preacher heard a woman's scream. It came from a nearby tent. It startled him—not because of the cry itself, but because he thought he recognized the voice of the woman who screamed. But it couldn't be. It couldn't be who he thought it was. Could it?

Running in the direction of the noise, Preacher wondered what Jennie would be doing out here. He was certain she was in St. Louis, and yet, something about the scream touched his very soul. He hurried toward the tent.

McDill lunged, clamping his dirty hand over her mouth. Jennie bit his hand and he ripped it away, howling like a wounded animal. She screamed again. Outside the tent she could hear people moving around, and she hoped someone would come to help her. She fought back, pummeling his chest and face with her hands, but he was so big and strong that it had no effect.

"You bitch!" he sneered, cradling his wounded hand. "I was gonna pay you, whore that you are, but now I'm not— I'm gonna take it for free."

"Stay away," she warned. "For your own good, mister. I don't want to hurt you."

"Ha! You don't want to hurt me?" he said with a lopsided, drunken grin. "Tell me, bitch, how are you plannin' on hurtin' me?"

She couldn't stand the smell of him, and his ugly leer. Yet she realized that she had to be careful, that she couldn't rile him even more—or else he was liable to kill her. She had known men like him for her entire life.

She gathered what composure she could, and brushed a fall of hair back from her face. She forced herself to smile at him.

"Look, you're right, whoring is my business. But I was just getting ready for bed and I must look a mess. Why don't you go away now, give me a chance to get ready, then you can come back later," she said.

"No way, little lady. I'm here and here I stay. You'll get to like me when you know me better. I promise."

Jennie doubted that she would ever be able to bear the sight of this man, let alone like him. He was grotesque, and it didn't matter that he was drunk. She had met this kind before, and he reminded her of her old master, among others.

"But you'll like me better if you give me a chance to get ready for you," Jennie said, making one last attempt to get through to him.

"I like you fine just the way you are," he said, starting toward her again.

Jennie felt the world closing in on her and smelled blood in the air; she could only hope it wasn't her own. Again she screamed for help.

At that moment the tent flaps opened, and it was as if God himself had heard her plea. The one man in the world whom she truly loved stepped inside. It was Preacher, the man she had known as a boy—the man who was a part of her life even when they were not together.

McDill turned to see the man he hated most in the world—the man he had thought was dead—moving at him swiftly and angrily. He ducked to avoid Preacher's first swing, and came up with a hard punch of his own, taking Art off guard, smashing into his chin. He laughed as the younger man staggered backward.

"Well, now, if it ain't my ole pal," McDill said. "Are you goin' to preach to me, Preacher? Are you going to save my soul?" He laughed.

Preacher got to one knee and shook his head, trying to clear away the cobwebs of the hammerlike blow. He stared up at McDill, and at the hideous leering grin on his face.

McDill held his hand out and curled his fingers, tauntingly inviting Preacher toward him.

"Well, come on, Preacher," he said. "Come on, you son of a bitch. I'm going to beat you to a pulp."

His head cleared, Preacher leaped up again and charged at McDill. He buried his head in McDill's midsection and both men went crashing to the ground.

Preacher scrambled to his feet and grabbed McDill by the collar, then dragged him outside. He wanted to take this confrontation away from Jennie. By now a crowd, drawn by the screams and the commotion, had gathered just outside. They surrounded the two men, who were locked in a deadly confrontation.

The crowd cheered for Preacher and jeered McDill. McDill managed to get to his feet, and the big man charged like a bull. Preacher stepped out of the way, and McDill went hurtling into the crowd.

Laughing at his awkwardness, the men in the crowd caught McDill and pushed him back into the circle of combat. The two men faced each other again, and Preacher punched him as hard as he could. McDill doubled over. Preacher landed a strong right to McDill's jaw, straightening him out and sending him back on his heels, massaging the hand that had struck the blow.

Ben Caviness was watching with the others in the crowd. He wanted to go to the aid of his friend, but he dared not, for fear of the retribution of others. McDill was on his own now. Caviness melted away into the growing darkness. Even as the fight was going on behind him, he saddled his horse. If Preacher won, he might come after Caviness. If McDill won, he would want to know why Caviness didn't help him. Under the circumstances, Caviness knew that this was no place for him to be.

Jennie came out of her tent then. Preacher turned toward her, then held his hand out, as if telling her to stay away. "Jennie, stay back, keep out of the way!" he cautioned.

Preacher looked away from McDill for just that quick second. McDill pulled his long-bladed hunting knife from its sheath and lunged at Preacher, the knife pointing at his guts. Now, enraged and humiliated by the beating he was taking from this younger and smaller man, McDill was more animal than human.

Jennie saw McDill and called out to Preacher: "Look out! He has a knife!"

Preacher turned just in time to see the blade flash in the flickering light of the nearby fires. He reared back to avoid the killing knife, then circled his enemy bare-handed. Someone from the crowd tossed him a stick. Preacher used it as a defensive weapon, swinging it at McDill to keep him at bay. With one swing, McDill's knife chopped the stick in half.

"What are you goin' to do now, Preacher?" McDill taunted, holding the knife out in front of him. He moved the point back and forth slightly, like the head of a coiled snake. "You think that little stick is going to stop me? I'll whittle it down to a toothpick, then I'll carve you up."

Preacher realized then that he had no choice, he must fight

this madman on his terms—no rules, any weapon at hand, and to the death. He drew his own knife and held it up, showing it to Percy McDill. He said, without words, that he intended to kill the man who had threatened Jennie.

Suddenly, it seemed as if McDill had sobered up. The taunting, leering grin left his face and he became deadly serious and focused. With a steady hand, he held his own knife up, challenging his opponent. His face was now a mask of calm determination.

"You'd better start preachin' your own funeral, Preacher," McDill said. "It's time for you to die."

Now, for the first time, Preacher grinned. It was neither taunting nor leering. Instead, it was confident, and it completely unnerved McDill. "I don't think so, McDill," Preacher said easily. "I think you are the one who is going to die."

"I'm going to kill you, and that damned mutt of yours," McDill said with false bravado, trying now to bolster his own courage.

Out of the corner of his eye, Preacher could see Dog, standing on the edge of the watching crowd. The young mountain man put aside all thoughts other than one: McDill must die. Trying to hurt Jennie was the last evil thing this son of a bitch would ever do.

The two men circled each other like gladiators in a Roman arena. The crowd became silent. Even Jennie, who watched in horror, could neither speak nor cry out. Dog stood at alert. He could have attacked McDill, but somehow seemed to sense that this was something Preacher needed to do by himself.

McDill moved first. He swung his blade at Preacher, missing his face by only a few inches. Preacher felt the wind of the swift knife blade and jerked his head back. In almost the same movement, he swung his own knife low and hard, aiming for McDill's belly. He missed.

The big man then punched Art on the side of his head.

Art was stunned, and for a second he couldn't see anything. He backed away quickly to avoid the oncoming McDill, then stepped to one side. As McDill shot past him, he stabbed with his knife blade and felt it slip into McDill's midsection.

He pushed the knife in as far as it could go, then held it there. The two men stood together, absolutely motionless, for a long moment. Preacher felt McDill's warm blood spilling over his knife and onto his hand.

Howling like a stuck pig, McDill pulled himself off the knife. He stepped back several feet, then came back toward Preacher. But before he could even lift his own knife, he gasped, dropped the knife, and put his hand to his wound. Blood filled his cupped palms, then began oozing from his mouth as well. His eyes turned up in their sockets, showing the bloodshot whites.

From her position by the front of her tent, Jennie looked at McDill's eyes. They had caught the reflection of the campfires, and once more, she had the illusion of staring into the pit of hell. She shuddered, wrapping her arms around herself as she realized that, within minutes, McDill would be in hell.

"Damn . . . you . . ." McDill managed to gurgle through the blood and spit that filled his mouth. "Damn . . ."

Preacher took one step toward the dying man, then stopped. McDill's big body shuddered, then collapsed in a heap on the ground. Beneath him, the blood pooled darkly from his leaking wound.

Jennie ran up and threw her arms around Preacher, kissing him. He stood still, unable to take his eyes off the crumpled heap that had once been a man.

Finally, he spoke. "Where did Caviness go?"

"I think we will never see him again," said one of the men in the crowd. "I saw him sneak away like a dog."

* * *

"That's one hell of a story," Jeb said when Preacher finished with the telling. "You're plannin' on goin' after Caviness, you say?"

"Yes," Preacher said.

"What are you going to do with your string?"

"I don't know, sell them, board them. I was hoping you would have an idea."

"I'll keep your animals for you," Jeb said. "If you don't come back by next season, I'll sell 'em and hold the money for you, after takin' out what it took me to feed 'em."

"I appreciate that," Preacher said.

"Now, what do you say to me'n you goin' down to the Blue Hole Café and havin' us some supper?" Jeb offered.

Preacher smiled. "Sounds good to me."

6

The enticing aroma of pork cooking over a hickory fire drifted down the street to them even before they reached the café known as Blue Hole. Blue Hole was a wood-frame building with a shake roof and a wide-plank floor. The cooking pit was just behind the building, and the aromatic smoke the cooking produced was the best advertisement the café had.

A large woman, known as Aunt Molly, greeted the two men when they came into the cafe. "Howdy, Jeb," she said, smiling at the saloon keeper.

There was only one empty table, and it was covered with leftover bones, but Aunt Molly led them to it, scooped up the bones, then used a soiled cloth to wipe the table.

"Who's your young, good-lookin' friend?" she asked, smiling over at Preacher.

"This here is Preacher," Jeb said.

Aunt Molly looked at Preacher with interest. "Preacher? Are you a man of the cloth?"

"No, ma'am," Preacher replied.

"Oh, heavens!" Aunt Molly said with an expression that was almost awe. "Are you that mountain man folks call Preacher?"

"That's who he is, all right," Jeb said.

"You're gettin' yourself quite a reputation," Aunt Molly said. "They say you're the ridin'st, shootin'st, fightin'st, trappin'st, dancin'st, handsomest man in all the mountains." She switched the handful of gnawed bones from her right hand to her left, then reached out with a greasy palm. "I don't know about all the rest, but I'll vouch for the handsome part," she said. "I'm right pleased to meet you, Preacher."

Preacher hesitated but a moment before he took her hand. Her effusive description of him was a little embarrassing, but he knew that she meant well. He extended his hand to hers. "I'm very pleased to meet you," he said.

At the next table, two men got up to leave.

"You gents come back now, you hear?" Aunt Molly called to them.

One of them grunted in reply.

"What have you got that's good, Aunt Molly?" Jeb asked.

"We got some ribs just ready to come off," Aunt Molly replied. "Perhaps you're a-smellin' 'em now?"

Jeb smiled. "The whole town is smellin' them."

"Well, I certainly hope so," Aunt Molly replied with a little laugh.

"Tell you what. How 'bout you bring us a side of ribs, some beans, bread, and coffee?" Jeb ordered.

"Help yourself to the coffee, and I'll go back to get the ribs," Aunt Molly said.

As Aunt Molly headed out back, Jeb walked over to the coffeepot, where he poured two cups. He returned to the table, a steaming mug in either hand.

Three men were having a conversation at a hitching rail just up the street from the Blue Hole. One was tall, with a very dark, scraggly beard. The other two were somewhat shorter and clean-shaven. They were the two who had just left the Blue Hole.

"You sure it's Preacher?" the tall, scraggly-bearded man asked.

"Oh, yeah, it's him all right," one of the other two said. "I mind seein' him at a Rendezvous a year or so back."

"'Sides which, Jeb's the one pointed him out. They say Jeb's known him for a long time," the other man said.

The tall man stroked his beard and smiled. "Well, now," he said. "Looks like I just got me a streak o' luck, don't it?" He took out his pistol and began loading and charging it.

"Luke, I sure hope you know what you're doin', goin' after Preacher like this. I've heard of him. They say he's one slippery fella to try 'n get a hold of. Lots of men have tried it, and lots of men have died."

"I ain't plannin' on dancin' with the son of a bitch, so I won't be tryin' to get a hold of him. I plan on just puttin' a ball in his brain," Luke said as he continued to prepare his pistol. "Now, are you men with me or not?"

"I ain't got no quarrel with 'im," one of the others said.

"I didn't have no quarrel with Roland Peters either," Luke replied. "But when you went up against him last year, I was with you."

"Luke's right, George. He was right there with us."

"Roland Peters wasn't no Preacher," George replied.

"If they's three of us go after the son of a bitch, they's no way he can handle us all. Hell, he's only got one charge in his pistol."

George sighed. "All right, I'll back you. But you're the one that's goin' to call him out."

"Don't worry, I'll do that, all right," Luke replied.

Back in the Blue Hole Café, Preacher, unaware of the three who were plotting against him, continued his conversation with Jeb.

"You know anything else about Miss Jennie getting murdered?" Jeb asked as they waited for their dinner to be served.

Preacher had chosen the chair that faced the front of the café, which meant that Jeb had his back to the door. "I mean, did the letter tell you how it happened, why it happened? Anything like that?"

"This is all I know," Preacher said, taking Ashley's letter from a pocket and handing it across the table to him.

Jeb took out a pair of spectacles, fitted them carefully over one ear at a time, then read the letter. He concentrated on it for a moment, then clucked sympathetically. "I'm real sorry to hear about that," he said, handing the letter back. "I didn't really know her all that well. Did Miss Jennie have any family as you know about?"

Preacher shook his head. "Nobody that I know about," he said. "I reckon me'n her friend Clara's about the only ones that she was really close to."

"You!" a loud, angry voice suddenly shouted, disturbing the peace of the café.

Looking toward the front door, the patrons of the café saw that a tall man with a black, scraggly beard had just stepped through the front door of the café.

"Are you the one they call Preacher?"

The man was holding his hand down by his side, but Preacher saw at once that there was a pistol in his hand. And even from where he sat, he could see that the pistol was cocked. He could only assume that it was also primed.

"I'm the one they call Preacher," he said.

"My name is Luke Mouchette. That name mean anything to you?"

Jeb, who was sitting with his back to the door, turned to look.

"Jeb, I reckon you better move away," Preacher said quietly.

Instead of moving out of the way, Jeb turned toward the intruder. "Look here, Mr Mouchette, I don't know what this is about but . . ."

"Jeb, get the hell out of the way! Now!" Preacher insisted, interrupting Jeb in mid-sentence.

Jeb got up from the table and walked over to the side of the room. He wasn't the only one to move, as every other table in the café emptied. The patrons, left their food on the tables, as they scrambled to get out of the way.

"You didn't answer me, Preacher," Mouchette said. "Have you ever heard my name before?"

"Yes, I've heard it," Preacher said, easily.

"Where have you heard it?"

"I killed a low-assed, mealy mouthed, piss-complexioned, maggot-infested son of a bitch by the name of Mouchette," Preacher said, his voice clipped and cold. "I take it there is some connection?"

"He was my brother," Mouchette said. "He was my brother, and you kilt him, you son of a bitch!"

"He needed killing," Preacher said.

"Yeah, well, so do you," Mouchette shouted. He raised his pistol and aimed it at Preacher, who had so far made no effort to move.

Suddenly there was a loud bang . . . not from Mouchette's gun, but from under the table. A hole appeared in the table and chips of wood flew as a ball passed through the tabletop. That same ball plunged into Mouchette's chest and he staggered back toward the door, a surprised look on his face, blood pumping from the wound. In a reflexive action, Mouchette fired his pistol as he staggered back, sending the ball into the wide-planked floor.

From just outside the café, George saw Luke stagger back. With his own pistol drawn, he started toward the front door.

There was a large hole in the top of the table where Preacher had been sitting. Preacher stood then, and as he did so, everyone could see that he was holding a smoking pistol in his hand.

"How the hell did you do that?" Jeb asked, pointing to the pistol.

Preacher didn't respond to Jeb's question. Instead, moving quickly, he hurried to the front door and stood to one side of it. A man came running in.

"You son of a bitch!" George shouted, pointing his gun toward the table where Preacher had been sitting. Not seeing him there, George raised his pistol in confusion. He had only a second to be confused, though, because Preacher hit him right between the eyes with the butt of his own pistol.

George fell back upon the body of Luke Mouchette, and as he fell, Preacher dropped his own gun and grabbed George's.

Rearmed, Preacher stepped out the front door, where a third man fired at him. The bullet whizzed past Preacher's head and buried itself in the door frame right beside Preacher's head. Preacher fired back and the man went down.

With no other adversaries on the scene, Preacher stepped back inside, still holding the smoking gun. He tossed it to one side, picked up his own spent weapon, and walked back over to the table, cognizant now of everyone staring at him in shock and awe.

Aunt Molly was standing by the table holding a plate of ribs, her eyes wide, a shocked expression on her face. Smoke from the discharges gathered in a billowing cloud under the ceiling. Quickly and carefully, Preacher reloaded his pistol. From outside, voices could be heard as people started running toward the café. When the first man came in, he stepped back in fear and surprise when he saw that Preacher had leveled his gun toward him.

"Hold on! Hold on!" the man shouted, putting his hands up in the air. "I mean you no harm."

Slowly, Preacher lowered his pistol, then nodded for the man to come on inside.

Luke Mouchette was on the front porch, his head hanging down over the step, his feet just inside the door. The right foot was pointing straight up, the left foot cocked to one side. There was a hole worn in the sole of his left boot. The man Preacher had knocked out was just now coming to, and he stood up, shook his head a few times, then walked away, leaving the café behind him. He didn't even look down at the body of the second man Preacher had shot.

Another man hurried over to the café. Stopping on the front porch, he looked down at Luke's body, then came on inside. He was wearing a badge.

"What happened here?" he asked.

"This here fella didn't have no choice, Sheriff," one of the café patrons said quickly. "Them three others all come for him."

"That's the truth of it, Paul," Jeb said. "We was all witnesses."

The sheriff stood there for a moment, then looked at Preacher. "Do you know why he come for you?"

"I killed that one's brother," Preacher replied, pointing to Luke.

"Where'd you do that?"

"At Rendezvous, out in the Rockies."

"At Rendezvous, you say?"

Preacher nodded.

"Trappers is normally pretty straight about things. If you killed him at Rendezvous and they let you go, you was probably in the right," the sheriff said. "Besides which, ain't no concern of mine what happened out there. And if all these folks say you was in the right here, I don't plan to do nothin' about this either."

"Thanks," Preacher said.

"I'd appreciate it, though, if you'd put the gun away."

Preacher stared at his pistol for a moment, then stuck it back in his belt.

The sheriff looked at Aunt Molly. "I'll get the undertaker down here to pull the body off your front porch," he said.

Aunt Molly chuckled. "No hurry," she said. "Long as he's out there, folks will come have a look. And when they do, why, they'll just naturally want to come in and have dinner."

The others laughed.

"Lord, I hope not, Aunt Molly," the sheriff said. "Else you'll be draggin' anyone that gets shot down here."

More laughter as the sheriff left the café.

"I'm sorry about the table," Preacher said to Aunt Molly after the sheriff was gone. "If you tell me how much it is, I'll pay to have another one built for you."

"I reckon a dollar will pay for your food and fix the table," Aunt Polly said.

Preacher pulled out a silver dollar and handed it to her, then reached for the plate of ribs.

"Thanks," he said. "This looks good."

7

On board the riverboat Nathanial Pyron

At first, Caviness thought that the interest people were paying him was because of morbid curiosity over the fact that he was obviously missing an ear. But the second day into the trip, he was standing at the railing when the captain and two deckhands approached him.

"Mister, you want to tell us how you lost that ear?" the boat captain asked.

Caviness put his hand to the wound on the side of his face.

"What business is it of yours how I lost it?" he asked.

"Well, you see, the thing is, some of our passengers are down from St. Louis. And according to them, there was a young woman murdered up there recently. But it turns out, she had a dog who defended her. The dog bit the ear off her attacker."

"Yeah, well, I don't know nothin' about that," Caviness said. "I got this ear bit off by a bear."

"That may be," the captain said. "But I intend to put you in irons now until we get to Cape Girardeau. There, I'll turn you over to the constable, and he can take you back up to St. Louis until you get all this worked out."

As the men started toward him, Caviness hesitated only for

a moment. Then he climbed onto the rail and leaped down into the Mississippi River.

"The son of a bitch is getting away!" one of the deckhands shouted, and he and the other two ran to the railing. Looking down into the river, they could see only the roiling water, but no sign of the man without an ear.

"Where is he? Where did he go?"

"I think we can forget about him, boys," the captain said. "The currents and eddies are so strong right through here that it's damn near impossible to swim. More'n likely he's drowned already."

"Yeah, well, that's good enough for him," the first deckhand said.

"If he's the one that done the killin'," the second said.

"He's the guilty one, all right," the captain said. "Otherwise, he wouldn't've jumped over like that."

On the Missouri River, on board the Missouri Belle

Preacher booked passage from Kansas City to St. Louis on the steamboat *Missouri Belle*. He had enough money to afford first-class passage, and could have easily occupied the most luxurious stateroom. The fact that he chose not to was due less to parsimony than to the fact that he was genuinely more comfortable on the open deck than in one of the fancy staterooms.

While in Kansas City, Preacher got himself some new clothes, though his new duds, like those that he'd gotten rid of, were made of buckskin. He rented a bathtub and got himself cleaned up, even going to the barber for a haircut and a shave. As a result, he cut quite a handsome figure when he stepped aboard the *Missouri Belle*. Two of the passengers, Misses Emma Purdy and Cynthia Cain, took note of him, smiling at him from behind the fans they were carryng.

The two very pretty young ladies were from well-to-do

families in Kansas City. Their families, believing that Kansas City was too provincial a town for them, were sending them to St. Louis for finishing school.

Although the young women had noticed Preacher the moment he came on board, they made no effort to approach him, believing that he, as most other men they had encountered, would make the first move. When, by the evening of the second day, it became obvious to them that he wasn't going to come to them, they approached him.

Preacher was standing by the rail, looking at the shoreline. Preacher had been through this country many times before, and was sorry to see that even here, civilization was beginning to creep in. Now he saw farmhouses and cultivated land where, on previous voyages up and down the river, there had been nothing but wilderness. He wondered how long it would be before civilization, and all its ills, encroached upon the West that he knew.

Though the scene was bucolic, it wasn't silent. The boat was a cacophony of sound as it moved down river. The steam-relief valve was booming, the engine clattering, and the side-mounted paddle wheels were slapping against the water. Because of all the noise, he didn't hear the two women approach. The first time he noticed them was when they suddenly appeared, one on each side of him.

Recovering quickly, Preacher smiled at them. "Good evening, ladies," he said.

"Good evening," they replied.

"Nice view from here," Preacher said, struggling hard to make some small talk. Truth to be told, he was uncomfortable in situations like this.

"Yes, quite lovely," one of the two girls replied.

"The captain said you are called Preacher," the other one said.

"But he also said that you aren't really a preacher," the first added.

"That's true," Preacher said. He turned away from the

shoreline, and leaned back against the rail as he spoke to the two pretty women.

"I'm Emma Purdy," one of the women said.

"And I'm Cynthia Cain."

Preacher nodded his head. "I'm pleased to meet you, ladies."

"If you aren't a preacher, why do they call you Preacher?" Emma asked.

"It's just something that happened to me once," Preacher said.

"Oh, please, do tell."

"It's a long story."

"Well, it's a long time before we get to St. Louis," Cynthia reminded him.

Preacher laughed. "I guess it is at that," he said. "All right, here goes."

Preacher began telling of the time he had been a prisoner of the Blackfeet, with no chance of help or escape. From somewhere an idea formed in his head and he began to sermonize, speaking in the same singsong voice he had once heard used by an itinerant preacher on the waterfront in St. Louis. He preached like a born-again, water-baptized, true believer in the Lord Almighty.

"The Indians didn't understand what I was saying," Preacher said, "but they listened anyway, and I continued to preach all through the night.

"Come the next morning, I was still preaching, amazed that I still had the strength to do it."

"What were you preaching about?" Emma asked.

"To tell the truth, I almost didn't even know what I was saying myself, but I kept on talking, kept on preaching.

"I preached all through the rest of that morning without stopping. The people of the village, men, women, and children, gathered around to listen, although they didn't have the slightest idea what I was saying.

"Finally, the elders of the village held a council where they decided I was crazy. And maybe I was."

"What do you mean, maybe you were? Do you think you were crazy?" Cynthia asked.

Preacher chuckled. "Well, I might have been a little crazy at the time. I don't know," he admitted. "But here's the thing. The Indians think that anyone who is crazy is touched by the Great Spirit. They're afraid to do any harm to him, because they don't want to offend the Great Spirit.

"So, the next thing you know, a couple of the old chiefs came over to me and untied me. And let me tell you, they didn't do it a moment too soon, because by then my mouth was parched and sore, and my vision was so blurred I could barely see. I don't think I could've lasted more than another five or ten minutes."

"And they just let you go?" Emma asked.

Preacher nodded. "Yes," he said.

"Oh, what a wonderful story!" Cynthia said.

The brothers Rance and Leon, scions of Angus Culpepper, owner of Culpepper Stage and Freight Lines, were making the trip to St. Louis on the same boat. Because they, like Emma Purdy and Cynthia Cain, were occupying first-class accommodations, they considered the two young ladies to be their exclusive property by right of social position.

Rance and Leon stood for a while at the rail, smoking their pipes and looking toward the flora and fauna of the riverbank as it slid past the boat. While there, they couldn't help but overhear the story Preacher told the two young women. Now, walking toward the stern of the boat, they were engaged in a private discussion about the man called Preacher.

"What a lout," Leon said. "No doubt, this is the longest conversation that creature has ever had with any woman who wasn't a whore."

"Probably even including his own mother," Rance replied.

"Do you mean he hasn't had a long conversation with her? Or do you mean that she is a whore?" Leon asked.

"He hasn't had a long conversation with her," Rance replied. Then he added, "And she probably is a whore."

Leon and Rance both laughed, though their laugh was brittle, like the shattering of crystal.

"You have to admit, that was some story he told," Leon said. "Do you believe it was true?"

"No. Mountain men are know to be great storytellers. And liars."

"He had the ladies hanging on every word."

"Yes, unfortunately, he did," Rance said. "But it is obviously a story of self-aggrandizement, designed to make himself a hero in their eyes."

"What I don't understand is why Miss Purdy and Miss Cain would allow him to talk to them in the first place," Leon added. "He is traveling steerage, and one wonders where he even got the money for that."

"He is taking advantage of their innocence," Rance answered. "And I am personally offended by that."

"Mountain men are barely civilized; they spend months at a time with no company other than bears," Leon said.

"And no doubt, the bears find the presence of such men to be an affront to their dignity," Rance added. Again, the two young men laughed brittlely.

"He obviously has no sense of his proper place," Leon said.

Rance smiled. "Perhaps, before we reach St. Louis, we should teach him some manners."

"Yes," Leon said enthusiastically. "But let's not hurry. If we are patient and observant, I am positive that the opportunity will present itself."

The *Missouri Belle* carried two very long poles, called spars, at the bow of the boat. Whenever the boat got stuck on a sandbar, which was fairly often in the transit of a shallow river like the Missouri, those two poles would be put down to the river bottom at about a forty-five-degree angle. Then they were driven back by cables attached to a steam capstan. The result was a very powerful poling of the boat. That action was technically known as sparring, though as the poles looked like grasshopper legs when in the water, it was often referred to as "grasshoppering."

When they were four days out of Kansas City, they got stuck on a sandbar. It wasn't a bar they had blundered onto as a result of poor piloting, but a bar that covered the entire channel—and thus could not be avoided. Now their only hope lay in attempting to traverse the sandbar at its most advantageous part.

The poles dug into the river bottom, then strained and bent slightly. The boat crept forward, creaking and groaning under the exertion. Finally, the poles became extended and the boat could go no further. The poles would have to be retracted and the operation repeated.

Though Preacher had offered his help, the captain had explained that the best thing any of the passengers could do was stay out of the way, and now Preacher was accommodating him on that request.

The poles were reset, and the operation started a second time. Again, the poles strained backward, and again the boat started sliding forward. The poles bent as before, but suddenly one of the cables snapped, and it whipped back around with a loud whoosh.

"Look out!" Preacher shouted and he dove toward Emma and Cynthia, taking them both down. The cable whizzed by over them and smashed through the flagpole, breaking it as cleanly as if it were no more than a matchstick.

The operator of the capstan also dove to the deck just in time to avoid it, but because the capstan was still running, the cable continued to whip around, flaying and smashing everything in its path. The operator could not stand up because the cable was whipping over his head, which also meant he couldn't get to the throttle lever to shut down the capstan. As long as the capstan turned, the cable would continue to whirl about madly.

"We've got to get that engine shut down!" the captain shouted. "If that cable flies loose and hits the boiler, we are going to have one hell of an explosion!"

The cable continued to whirl about, but as some of the steam pressure was vented off, it wasn't whirling quite as fast as it had at the beginning. That was little consolation, though, because it was still moving with enough force to make a shambles out of the bow deck. It took down the flagpole with its first revolution; then it smashed through the railing, and now the operator was still trapped beneath the slashing line.

Preacher watched it spin for two more revolutions. When he had it timed just right, he leaped up, ran to the bow deck, ducked at just the right moment, and reached the engine lever. He pushed it shut. The cable, without the whirling momentum of the capstan, fell whistling into the river.

"Great job, lad!" the captain said, congratulating him, and the rest of the passengers and crew applauded him.

"You saved our lives," Emma said.

"That would have killed us if you hadn't gotten us out of the way," Cynthia added.

"Don't forget, I was saving my life too," Preacher said modestly.

Preacher's heroism had elevated him, not only in the opinion of the two young women, but in the eyes of the passengers and crew as well. For the Culpepper brothers, though, it just made them more determined to take care of him before they reached St. Louis.

That opportunity came on the last night before they were to reach St. Louis. Leon and Rance came out of the grand salon, where they had been gambling and had had a run of bad luck.

"I lost twenty dollars," Leon said. "How about you?"

"Thirty-five dollars," Rance replied.

"I know that gambler is cheating," Leon said. "But he is too good. I couldn't catch him at it."

"Yeah, I never saw such bad luck," Rance said. They had stepped out to the rail to get a breath of air, when suddenly Rance stuck his hand out to keep his brother from advancing any farther. "Brother, I think perhaps our luck is about to change," he said quietly.

"What do you mean?"

"Look."

Rance pointed to the stern of the boat. There, curled up next to a stanchion, they saw Preacher. It was obvious that he was sound asleep.

"You know what would be funny?" Rance said.

"What's that?"

"I think it would be really funny if we just sort of quietly walked back there and rolled that son of a bitch off the boat. He'd be three feet underwater before he knew what happened to him."

"Brother, you are a genius," Leon said.

Moving quietly, and staying in the shadows, the two men crept to the back of the boat.

One of the side-mounted paddle wheels jerked out of sequence as they often did, and it caused the boat to make a sideways lurch. It splashed a little water onto Preacher, and he opened his eyes. Just before he closed them again, he saw Leon and Rance Culpepper slipping through the shadows toward him.

He wasn't sure what they were up to, but they had already let him know that they considered his friendliness toward the two women to be above his station. He was fairly certain that, whatever the plan, they were up to no good.

* * *

Leon and Rance moved out of the shadows, then covered the open space between the after cabin and the stern of the boat. Leaning forward, they stuck their arms out, intending to roll Preacher over the side of the boat.

Preacher timed it just right, reaching up and grabbing their arms just as they were leaning forward. With their forward momentum already established, it was a simple maneuver for him to pull them past him. Shouting in alarm and surprise, both Leon and Rance tumbled overboard.

Preacher stood up and looked back into the churning wake, where he saw both heads pop up. The two brothers shouted, but the boat was making so much noise that, even to Preacher's ears, their shouts were barely audible. Preacher looked around to see if anyone else had seen them go overboard, but nobody appeared to have done so.

He watched the brothers swim toward the bank. Reaching the shallow part of the river, they stood up. Turning, they shook their fists angrily at him. Preacher saw a couple of farmhouses nearby, so he knew the brothers weren't in any mortal danger from being stranded there, but they would have a long walk into St. Louis. With a little laugh, he rubbed his hands together, then lay down again and went back to sleep.

As they approached St. Louis from the river, Preacher marveled at the changes the city had undergone since he had first laid eyes on it. He had come to St. Louis the first time in 1813, and from there, he had joined a regiment of volunteers to fight against the British at the Battle of New Orleans.

Even though Preacher was only fourteen years old, he had been breveted a lieutenant in that battle, earning the respect of his commanders and the men who had served with him. Since that time, Missouri had become a state, and St. Louis had grown from a frontier town to a bustling, prosperous city of nearly twenty thousand people. That was a lot of people— too many people for someone like Art, who had grown accustomed to life in the wilderness and went for days or weeks without seeing another human soul.

St. Louis was a vibrant city, alive with the pulse of commerce and enterprise: the scream of a steam-powered sawmill, the sound of steamboat whistles from the river, the hiss and boom of boats' engines, and the clatter of wagons rolling across cobblestone streets. To someone used to solitude so complete that he could hear the flutter of a bird's wings, the noise of civilization was almost unbearable.

Preacher had not planned to visit St. Louis during this trip down from the mountains, and had in fact not planned on any visit in the near future. But, upon learning that his dear Jennie had been murdered, he'd felt that he had no choice. He had to come, to find out just what happened, and to find justice for her.

"I say, Preacher," the purser said, coming to him shortly after the boat docked. "I seem to have lost the Culpepper brothers. Have you seen them recently?"

"Yes," Preacher said.

"Where are they?"

"Oh, they got off the boat last night," Preacher said without further explanation.

"They got off last night? My word," the purser said, scratching his head as he started back to his office.

Emma and Cynthia came to the deck of the boat, preparing to leave. They were accompanied by the headmistress of the finishing school they were to attend, and followed by three young black boys who were struggling to carry their luggage.

"Oh, Miss Peabody, this is Preacher," Emma said by way of introduction.

Miss Peabody held her glasses up on a long stem and looked at Preacher. Seeing by his dress that he was a frontiersman, she turned away from him without even acknowledging his presence.

"Come, ladies, we mustn't tarry," she said.

"He saved our lives," Cynthia said.

Miss Peabody hesitated for a moment, then turned to Preacher. "I'm sure the families of these young ladies would be more than willing to provide you with a reward for your service," she said.

Preacher nodded. "Thank you, ma'am, but seeing their pretty smiles is reward enough."

Both women giggled in delight, but Miss Peabody just let out a disapproving "hurrumph" and, again, ordered the girls to come with her.

Preacher watched them get into a beautifully lacquered carriage, then drive away. He picked up the roll he kept his own gear in, tossed it over his shoulder, and walked down the gangplank and up the street.

A neatly painted sign on front of the building read: FURS BOUGHT AND SOLD, WILLIAM ASHLEY, PROP. Squaring his shoulders, Preacher went inside.

A little bell hanging from the door summoned the proprietor from the back. A tall, rather dignified-looking man came up to greet him. Then, recognizing Preacher, he smiled broadly and extended his hand.

"Preacher!" he said. "If you aren't a sight for sore eyes."

"Hello, Mr. Ashley," Preacher said, returning the handshake. "It's good to see you again."

Ashley leaned over to see beyond Preacher. "Did you bring your own plews?"

"No, no, I sold them to your representative out at the Rendezvous."

"Oh? Well, then, what brings you to St. Louis? Not that I'm not pleased to see you," he added quickly.

Preacher pulled the letter from inside his shirt. "I came because of this," he said.

The smile left Ashley's face, and he nodded. "About Miss Jennie," he said.

"Yes."

"To tell the truth, I rather suspected that would bring you to St. Louis."

"I would like to visit Jennie's grave," Preacher said. "Is it marked?"

"Yes, I put up a marker for her."

"Thanks. Where in the cemetery will I find her grave?"

"I don't even need to tell you that. You'll find her easily enough," Ashley said.

Preacher looked puzzled. "What do you mean?"

"The cemetery is just down at the end of the street here. Go on down there and look for yourself. You'll see what I'm talking about," he said mysteriously.

"May I leave this here?" Preacher asked, taking the roll from his shoulder.

"Yes, of course," Ashley said, taking the roll from Preacher and putting it down behind the counter. "Go visit Jennie's grave, then come on back. We'll have dinner at Chardonnay's."

"Thanks."

Leaving the shop, Preacher started down the street toward the cemetery, wondering what Ashley meant when he said he wouldn't have any problem locating Jennie's grave.

As soon as Preacher reached the gate to the cemetery, he saw what Ashley was talking about. There, on the far side of the cemetery under a spreading maple tree, he saw a familiar-looking dog lying on one of the graves.

"Dog?" Preacher called.

Dog raised his head. Then, seeing Preacher, he bounded across the cemetery toward him. Preacher dropped down on one knee. When Dog reached him, Preacher began rubbing him on the head and behind his ears, one of which, he noticed, was only half an ear. In addition, there were half a dozen scars on the dog's head and body.

"Is that Jennie's grave over there?" Preacher asked.

Whether in sorrow or shame for having failed in his duty, Dog lowered his head.

"I'm not accusing you, Dog," Preacher said quietly. "From the looks of you, you did all that you could. Come on, take me to see Jennie."

With Dog leading the way, Preacher followed through the cemetery until he reached Jennie's grave. Dog lay down. Putting his nose between his paws, he looked up at Preacher, sharing his grief.

Preacher read the inscription:

> *Precious Flower,*
> *Divine providence hath seen fit to pluck thee*
> *from this earth*
> *and transplant thee to the garden of Eden*
> *where a more fitting abode awaits thee.*
> *Cherished one,*
> *As long as blood flows through the veins*
> *of the hand that pens these lines,*
> *Thy memory shall be kept ever green.*
> *Gone but not forgotten,*
> *Carla*

8

"You found Dog, I see," Ashley said when Preacher returned with the dog several minutes later.

Preacher sat in a chair, tipped it back against the wall, and began rubbing Dog behind his ears.

"Yes," he said.

"Did you see the inscription on the tombstone?"

"I saw it."

"Carla had me put it there. You remember her, don't you? She was one of Jennie's girls, but not really one of her girls. Carla never was a whore."

"Yes, I remember her. She's what now, sixteen, seventeen?"

Ashley laughed. "She's twenty-two now, and quite a pretty woman. She's waitin' tables down at Little Man's Café."

"Mr. Ashley . . ."

"Lord, Preacher, haven't we known each other long enough for you to call me Bill?"

"Bill," Preacher said, "you said you thought Ben Caviness was one of those who killed Jennie?"

"That's right. Nobody saw who did it, but if I had to make a guess, he's the one I would pick."

"In the letter you said there were two of them, but only one got away."

"Yep."

"What about the one that was caught? Haven't you been able to make him say anything?"

"If he does say something, he'll be saying it to God," Ashley said. "We found him at the same time we found Miss Jennie. He's dead."

"Dead? How? What happened to him?"

Ashley nodded toward Dog, who was now sleeping with his head resting on Preacher's foot. "As near as we can figure it, Dog killed him," he said. "I mean, Dog must've put up one hell of a fight."

"If nobody saw it, and you found one man dead, how do you even know there was another one?"

"Because when we found Dog, he was more dead than alive," Ashley said. "And he had a man's ear clenched in his teeth."

"An ear?"

"Yep. And that ear didn't come off the dead man, 'cause he still had both his ears. That means there was another person involved."

"Speaking of ears, I notice that Dog just barely has both of his," Preacher said. "He also seems to have several scars."

"Like I said, Dog was more dead than alive when we found him. We really didn't think he was going to live," Ashley said. "He had a gunshot wound, and six stab wounds. He was lying in a pool of blood, though most of it was Jennie's blood. He was lying on her body when we found him."

"What was his name? The fella who was killed, I mean. Do you know?"

"They called him Slater, but nobody knows if that was his first name or his last. He drifted in here about a year ago. Some say he had been a river pirate; others say he was just a petty thief. He was almost always in some kind of trouble, I know that. Folks all agree that Dog did the city a favor by killing him."

"I suppose," Preacher replied. "But it would've been good to talk to him, to find out for sure if Caviness was the other man."

"Well, whether it was Caviness or not, whoever did it is not in St. Louis," Ashley said. "We know that much at least."

"How do we know that?"

"Because everyone in this town is wearin' both their ears," Ashley replied with a little laugh.

The men were quiet for a moment. Then Ashley nodded toward the dog. "I have to tell you, I'm surprised to see him here," he said.

"Why is that?"

"Because this is the first time since the day Miss Jennie was buried that Dog has left the cemetery. Folks have taken notice of him, and someone is always bringing him something to eat, just because they want to. There are a lot of rabbits and squirrels out there, and Dog is pretty resourceful. There is also a stream that runs through the place."

"I wonder why he won't leave the cemetery," Preacher said.

"Oh, I don't think that's all that much of a mystery," Ashley replied. "You did leave him to look out for Miss Jennie, didn't you?"

"Yes."

"I think he's feeling guilty for not being able to do what you asked."

"I'll be damned," Preacher said. "You might be right." He looked down at Dog. "Dog?"

Dog opened his eyes and looked up at him.

"Dog, you don't have anything to feel guilty about," Preacher said. "You did the best you could do. You killed one of them, and you fixed it so that when I find the other one, I will recognize him." He reached down and rubbed Dog on the head again. "You did a good job, Dog, and I am very proud of you."

Dog stretched, stood up, then shook himself so that the loose skin slipped around noisily. He licked Preacher's hand.

Ashley laughed. "You know what? I think you just took a

big load off his mind. I really do think he was worried about what you would think of him failing his responsibility."

"He didn't fail anything," Preacher said.

"Nevertheless, I bet he won't spend all of his time down at the cemetery anymore."

"Listen, didn't you say something about buying my dinner?"

"I did. Chardonnay's is just down the street. That's the best restaurant in St. Louis."

"Yes, I've eaten there," Preacher said. "But if it's all the same to you, I believe I'd just as soon eat at—where is it you said Carla works?"

"Little Man's."

"Yes. Let's eat at Little Man's," Preacher said.

"Preacher!" Carla squealed in joy when Preacher and Ashley stepped into Little Man's Café. She was carrying a pitcher of water and she put it down, hurrying over to give Preacher a big hug.

Preacher returned her hug, and she hung on to him for a long time. After a moment, he felt a wetness on his cheek and realized that she was crying. He didn't force her away from him, but let her hold him for as long as she wished. Finally, she drew away and, raising the end of her apron, dabbed at her tear-filled eyes.

"You know about Jennie?" she asked.

Preacher nodded. "Mr. Ashley sent me a letter. I just visited her grave. That was really nice, Carla, what you had put on her tombstone."

"Jennie was like a big sister to me," Carla said. "I've never loved any person like I loved her. She loved me too." She smiled through her tears. "But of course, she didn't love me the way she loved you. She was really in love with you, Preacher, did you know that?"

Preacher nodded. "Yes," he said. "I knew it."

"It wasn't all one-sided, was it? You did love her too, didn't you? I mean, I know you did."

"It wasn't one-sided," Preacher said. "I did love her, perhaps even more than I thought I did. But nothing would have ever worked out between us."

"I guess not. Oh, if you visited her grave, then you saw Dog there. He won't leave it, you know."

"He won't?" Ashley asked with a broad smile. He nodded toward the front door. "Who do you think that is?"

Looking in the direction Ashley indicated, Carla saw Dog curled up on the front porch. She gasped and put her hand to her mouth. "Oh, my," she said. "There he is, on the front porch."

"Yes."

"But I don't understand. Ever since Jennie died, day or night, rain or shine, cold weather or hot, Dog has been right down there, lying on Jennie's grave. He never leaves the cemetery, never. Yet there he is, right outside on the front porch."

"I released him," Preacher said.

"You released him? What do you mean?"

"I had charged Dog with looking out for Jennie. He thought he had failed."

"Preacher told him he did all he could do to protect Miss Jennie," Ashley said.

"But I told him that," Carla said. "We've all told him that."

"Yes, but you weren't the one who charged him with that responsibility," Preacher said. "Only I did that, and in Dog's mind, only I could release him from that charge."

"Bless his heart," Carla said. "Maybe he can find peace now."

Lying out on the porch, Dog looked through the door at Bear Killer and the friend of Bear Killer's woman. Dog had believed that Bear Killer would be angry with him because he had not done his job.

He had tried as hard as he could, and even now, he could recall the warm rush of blood as he ripped open the neck of one of the two men who had attacked Jennie. Even as he was engaged with that one, the one Bear Killer's woman called Caviness was attacking him with a knife, stabbing him repeatedly.

When Dog felt the life drain from the one he had attacked, he turned on Caviness, despite the pain and the weakness he was feeling. He went for Caviness's neck, but Caviness covered it with his arm, and turned his head to one side. Dog ripped off his ear, and heard Caviness scream in pain.

Then Dog saw a flash of light and heard a loud noise. He felt a blow to his side, followed by a darkness. When he came to, he saw that Bear Killer's woman was dead, lying in a pool of blood from a wound in her neck.

Dog felt an intense shame for having failed in his duty. Bear Killer had asked him to protect his woman, and he hadn't done so. He could not bring himself to leave her, even when she was buried. He stayed at the place where they buried her, determined to carry out the responsibility Bear Killer had given him, determined to continue to protect her, even though she was now dead.

But now, Bear Killer had returned. Dog could see that Bear Killer wasn't angry. Bear Killer understood that Dog had done all he could. Dog was at peace.

Ordinarily, the hotel would not allow dogs in the patrons' rooms. But like nearly everyone else in town, the proprietor of the Dunn Hotel knew the story of Dog, how he had killed one of the men who attacked his mistress and had chewed the ear off the other. He also knew that Dog had stayed at Jennie's grave all this time, out of a sense of loyalty, or love, or responsibility that was almost humanlike. Because of that, when Preacher took a room that night, and walked up the stairs with Dog following right behind, the proprietor said nothing.

In fact, he thought, both Preacher and the dog were fast becoming legends. It might well be that being able to say they stayed in his hotel would mean an increase in business.

Preacher and Dog stepped into the magistrate's office the next morning to find Constable Billings sitting in a chair with his feet propped up on his desk. He was paring an apple, and one long peel hung from it all the way to the floor. He looked up as Preacher came in.

"I remember you," the constable said. "You're the one they call Preacher."

"Yes."

"I expect you're here to ask about Miss Jennie. William Ashley said she was your woman."

"She was."

Billings finished, then tossed the peeled apple to Preacher. "Want this?" he asked. "I don't particularly like apples."

Preacher looked at Billings with a confused expression on his face.

"If you don't like apples, why did you peel it?"

"For the peel," Billings replied. He stretched the long, unbroken peel out on the floor. "How long you reckon that is?"

"I don't know. Three, four feet maybe?"

Billings stroked his chin. "Yeah, that's pretty much what it looks like to me as well." He sighed, picked up the peel, then opened the door to the little potbellied stove and tossed it in. "That's not long enough."

"I beg your pardon?"

"That's not long enough," Billings repeated. "You see, I've got me a two-dollar bet with the mayor of the town on who can make the longest unbroken apple peel. He claims he can do five feet. We're all set to do it come Saturday."

"About Jennie," Preacher said.

"We found her down by the riverside. Her throat was cut, but before that, it looked like she had been beat up pretty bad.

"Found Slater there too. His throat was ripped out. Figure Miss Jennie's dog did that. The dog was still guarding her. We had the devil's own time getting to her. I reckon the dog finally decided that we didn't mean her any harm."

"Mr. Ashley said there was a second man. A fella by the name of Ben Caviness."

"Well, now, we don't know for sure that that's who it was," Billings said. "I reckon Ashley told you the dog had a man's ear clenched in his teeth. Funny that he didn't eat it. It was almost like he wanted us to know there was someone else."

"Mr. Ashley seems pretty sure it was Caviness."

"Well, some folks did see Caviness and Slater together on the night it happened," Constable Billings said.

"All right. If you know that, how come you won't say for sure that the one who got away was Caviness?"

"'Cause we don't have no actual witnesses to the killin', 'cept for that dog there," Billings said, pointing to Dog. He chuckled. "And it's kind of hard to identify someone by his ear."

"Do you still have it?"

"Have what? The ear?"

"Yes. Do you still have it?"

"Now, just what in the Sam Hill makes you think I'd hang on to somethin' like that?"

"Do you still have it?" Preacher asked again.

Billings sighed, then walked over to a chest and pulled out a drawer. "As a matter of fact, I do," he said. "I dried it out in the sun, so it wouldn't rot away."

"I'd like it, please."

"What are you aimin' to do with it?"

"As soon as I find Caviness, I aim to sew this ear back on his head," Preacher said. "Then I aim to kill him."

"Sounds reasonable enough," Billings said, handing the sun-blackened piece of leather to Preacher. "Oh, you might want this as well." He took an envelope from the drawer.

"What is that?"

"It's everything I've got on Miss Jennie: complaints she made, and complaints made against her. I don't know that it'll do you any good, but I got no need to be keepin' it now, so it's yours if you want it."

"Thanks." Preacher said, taking the envelope, then starting toward the door.

"Preacher?"

Preacher was nearly to the door when the constable called him. Stopping, he turned toward Billings.

"Yes?"

"The man you're lookin' for, whether it's Caviness or someone else, ain't in St. Louis. I'm pretty sure about that. If he is here and you find him and kill him, well, I just want you to know you won't be havin' no trouble with me or the law, seein' as any son of a bitch who would do somethin' like that needs killin' pure and simple. But if you find him in some other town, and you kill him there, then you might have some explainin' to do."

"I know," Preacher said.

"What I'm sayin' is, once you leave St. Louis, there won't be nothin' I can do to help you."

"I know," Preacher said again.

"Just so's you understand."

Preacher nodded, then stepped outside. Dog followed Preacher as he headed toward LaBarge's Tavern.

In the shadowed interior of the tavern, Preacher ordered a beer, then sat at a table in the back. Dog curled himself onto the floor beside Preacher's chair.

"Folks don't normally bring dogs into the saloon," the barkeep said.

"You want him out, you run him out," Preacher replied.

"You," the bartender said to Dog. He pointed to the door. "Out! No dogs allowed in here."

Dog made no effort to respond.

The bartender came around from behind the bar. "I said get out of here," he said menacingly. He took a couple of steps toward Dog, but stopped when the hackles went up on Dog's neck. Dog bared his teeth and growled a low, quiet, but menacing growl.

The bartender stopped. "I, uh, guess you can stay," he said, retreating back to the bar. Dog closed his eyes in dismissal.

Preacher had paid no attention to what was going on between Dog and the bartender. Instead, he busied himself with dumping the contents of the envelope.

Examining the little pile on his table, Preacher found a document written in Jennie's neat hand.

> *I, Jennie (no middle name, no last name), do hereby file this complaint against Mr. Ben Caviness.*
>
> *Last night, while returning home from a job I was doing for Mrs. Sybil Abernathy, Mr. Ben Caviness jumped out of an alley in front of me. I believe it was his intention to attack me, but my dog ran him off.*

There was also a complaint filed against the River Bank of St. Louis, and Theodore Epson, for failing to credit her mortgage payment.

In addition, there were several documents that had been filed against Jennie. These were much older, the oldest being six years old, the newest one almost two years old. All of these had been filed by Mrs. Sybil Abernathy. The gist of Mrs. Abernathy's complaints was that Jennie was a prostitute and the practice of her profession prevented St. Louis from realizing its potential as a city of culture and influence.

There was also a letter in the file from Theodore Epson, responding to an inquiry made by Constable Billings.

Mr. Theodore Epson
Chief Teller
Trust Bank of Philadelphia

Dear Constable Billings:

I assure you, sir, that any suspicion you may have that I absconded with cash due the bank is totally without merit. The woman in question, known only as Jennie, was indeed in debt to the River Bank of St. Louis for the mortgage held on her home.

In point of fact her home was not a private residence as she claimed in her loan application. It was, instead, used as a house of ill repute. Thus, you can see that if a case of fraud is to be made, it should rightfully be made against her, for misrepresenting herself in securing the loan.

I cannot believe that anyone would take seriously the accusations of a whore against a respectable banker.

Sincerely,
Theodore Epson

"Preacher?"

It was a woman's voice and, looking up, Preacher saw Carla coming toward him. Generally, only bar girls and women of the street, plying their profession, would enter a saloon. But Carla was very much at ease in LaBarge's Tavern. She was not, and had never been a prostitute, but in her younger days she had worked as a bar girl in this very establishment.

"Carla," Preacher replied. Preacher was a man of the

mountains, but he retained enough manners to stand as she approached his table. "What are you doing here?"

"I thought I would . . . well . . . I mean, if you don't have other plans, I thought I might cook supper for you," Carla said.

"Cook supper for me where?" Preacher asked.

"Jennie and I shared a small house over on Olive," she said. "Well, actually, in the alley behind Olive. I'd be happy to cook dinner for you tonight."

"You don't have to cook for me, Carla. We could have dinner at Little Man's."

Carla smiled. "I work at Little Man's," she said. "Sometimes I just want to get out of there."

"Oh, yes, well, I guess I can understand that. All right, how about if we have dinner at Chardonnay's?"

"Why, Preacher, one would think you don't want my home cooking," Carla said with a teasing pout.

"No, no, nothing like that," Preacher replied. "I'm just trying to keep you from going to any trouble for me, that's all."

"You don't know anything about women, do you, Preacher?"

Preacher smiled, and shook his head. "Not much," he admitted.

"Sometimes, women want to go to the trouble of fixing dinner."

"All right, if you put it that way. I'll be glad to come."

"About seven?"

"Seven will be fine," Preacher agreed.

9

Perryville, Missouri

After leaping off the boat, Caviness managed to swim ashore, though he nearly drowned in the process. He lay on the riverbank for several minutes, trying to get his breath back. Caviness had not considered the fact that someone might be looking for him. No one saw him kill Jennie, so how would they know it was him?

Finally, Caviness stood and hitched up his pants. When he did, he suddenly realized that he had lost his knife. Then he discovered he had lost all of his money as well. He looked back toward the river. Evidently, it had fallen from his pocket when he jumped into the water.

The money was in bills, issued by the Bank of the United States. It was paper money, not coin, which meant that the money was probably scattered all down the river by now.

"Son of a bitch!" Caviness screamed at the top of his voice. "Son of a bitch, son of a bitch, son of a bitch!"

Caviness crawled up to the top of the bank. From there he could see the boat moving majestically downriver, its chimneys belching smoke, the paddles slapping into the water, churning a wake that followed behind.

He had no real idea where he was, and he was wet, cold, hungry, and broke. Now he had to get to Philadelphia. He began following the river south.

That night, he saw a flatboat that had put in for the night. There were two men operating the boat, and he watched as they made it fast, then built a fire for their supper. The smell of the food made his stomach growl, but he stayed hidden until both were asleep. Then, sneaking down to the boat, he slipped the rope from the tree and pushed out into the stream. The current caught him and started him downriver at a fairly good clip.

All that night and the next day he rode the boat downriver. He passed Cape Girardeau, because he knew the steamboat was going to stop there and he was afraid they might know about him. The next town south was the small town of Commerce, so he put in there.

Commerce consisted of no more than a dozen buildings, all parallel with the river's edge. When he landed, a man came down to take the rope and make the boat fast for him.

"Howdy. The name is Ferrell. I own a store here. What is it you are carrying?"

"Axes, shovels, iron stoves," Caviness replied. He had examined the cargo during the trip down.

"Are you looking to sell it here? Or do you plan on going down to New Madrid?" Ferrell asked.

"I'll sell it here."

"Because you know I can't pay as much as they do down at New Madrid."

"What can you pay me?"

"Well, let me take a look here," Ferrell said.

All the while Ferrell was poking through the cargo, he kept glancing up at Caviness. Caviness knew that he was looking at the wound left by the missing ear. Had the boat stopped here as well? Did this man know who he was? Finally, he could take it no longer.

"What the hell are you looking at, mister?" he demanded, angrily.

"I'm sorry," Ferrell said, looking away quickly. "I know it ain't good manners to stare at somethin' like that. I was just wonderin' how you come by a wound like that."

"I was bit by a bear," Caviness replied, sticking to his original story.

"I'm sorry I was starin' at you," Ferrell said, apologizing again. "I know it's rude, I just . . ." He let the sentence die.

"How much will you give me for all this?" Caviness asked.

"I figure I can pay you one hundred dollars," the man said. "Like I said, you'd probably get more for it down in New Madrid, but I'll give you a hundred for it."

"I'll take it," Caviness said, smiling broadly. What a stroke of luck! This would replace the money he lost when he jumped into the river.

"All right, just bring your bill of lading on up to my store and I'll pay you," Ferrell said, stepping off the boat and heading toward the scattering of buildings.

"Bill of lading? I don't have no bill of lading."

Ferrell looked back in surprise. "You don't have a bill of lading?"

"No," Caviness replied. In truth, he didn't know if he had one or not, because he wasn't even sure of what it was.

"Mister, how'd you come by those goods if you don't have a bill of lading?"

"I won the boat and everything on it in a card game," Caviness answered.

Ferrell looked at him suspiciously. "Where?"

"Up in Ste. Genevieve," Caviness said. "If you'll just give me the one hundred dollars, I'll be on my way."

"Can't do that," Ferrell replied.

"What do you mean you can't? Why not?"

"Mister, you may not know this, but time was when we had river pirates somethin' awful. They're most cleaned out now, but ever' now and then there's outlaws will prey on the boats comin' downriver. So now it's a law. Anything we buy off a boat has to have a bill of lading. If you don't have one, I can't buy your goods."

"I'll sell it all to you for fifty dollars," Caviness said, watching the money he thought he had slipping away from him.

"Mister, I wouldn't give you twenty-five dollars for it. Like as not, the man you won it from stole it off somebody."

Ferrell walked away from the boat.

"Ten dollars!" Caviness shouted. "You can have the whole load for ten dollars!"

Ferrell stopped, then looked back toward Caviness. "Mister, I'm going to get the constable. He might want to talk to you about that man you won that from."

Caviness had no desire to talk to the constable, so as Ferrell walked away, he slipped the rope free and pushed back into the stream. He reached the confluence of the Mississippi and Ohio the next afternoon, and there he abandoned the boat on the Illinois side.

From there he started following the Ohio River. About every other day or so, he would see boats going upriver, but he was afraid to take passage on one of them, for fear they might be looking for him.

If it hadn't been for that damn dog chewing off his ear, he could've boarded any of the boats and no one would have been any the wiser. But if they were looking for someone with a chewed-off ear, that would make it pretty hard for him to blend in.

He wasn't sure if the news had spread to the small towns along the river, but there was a good chance that it had. After all, the boats were making better time than he was, and news like that was generally the first thing folks would talk about.

When he abandoned the boat, he took the rest of the food with him, but it ran out after a few days. He had one day of absolute hunger, then happened onto a field of potatoes and dug up several of them. Those sustained him for the next several days. Then he was drawn to a travel camp by the smell of smoke from the fire.

Advancing just to the edge of the golden bubble of light, Caviness stayed in the darkness. That way, he could see but not be seen.

There was only one man in the camp, an older man from the looks of his white hair and beard. The man had no idea that he was being examined, but the horse sensed the presence of a stranger and began whickering. Alerted, the man looked up.

"Hello?" he said. "Anyone out there?"

"Hello the camp," Caviness called. "Can I come in?"

"Sure," the man replied. "Come on in. I've got enough stew for two. I'd enjoy the company."

"Thanks," Caviness said, walking into the bubble of light.

"You got your own pan?" the man asked.

"No."

"No matter, we can get a piece of bark to use as a plate. Have a . . . God's name, man! What happened to your ear?"

"I had a run-in with a bear."

"Bear? In Ohio?"

"Back in Missouri," Caviness said.

"Oh, my, you were lucky to survive," the man said. Finding a flat piece of birch bark, he spooned up some of the stew, then handed it over to Caviness. "I don't reckon you have a fork or a spoon either," he said.

"No," Caviness replied. "But this'll do." He held up a smaller piece of bark and began using it as a spoon.

"If you don't mind my asking, how is it that you are traveling with none of the things you need?"

"I was traveling by boat," Caviness said. "The boat sank and I lost everything."

"Oh. I'm sorry to hear that. Where are you headed?"

"Philadelphia."

"Big town, Philadelphia," the man replied. "My name is Seagraves. Milton Seagraves. I'm on my way to Cincinnati to take a job with a newspaper. What's your line of work?"

"Whatever I can get," Caviness said. "I'm sort of a handyman."

"Well, if you are willing to work, I'm sure there'll be plenty of jobs for you in a city as big as Philadelphia."

"You aren't carrying a gun?"

"A gun?" Seagraves replied. He shook his head. "Heavens, no, why should I carry a gun? Ohio is civilized country."

"I just thought you might have one," Caviness said.

"No, siree, I don't own one and I don't intend to ever own one. I don't hold much with guns. I do have a knife, though," he said, pulling the knife from his belt. It was a good-sized knife, much like the one Caviness had used to kill Jennie, and the one he had lost in the river.

"Good stew," Caviness said. "I appreciate the invite."

"You're mighty welcome. Like I said, I enjoy the company."

"Fire's gettin' low," Caviness said.

"That's all right. 'Bout time to turn in anyway."

"I see a good-sized piece of wood over there," Caviness said. "I'll get it and throw just one more piece on the fire."

Seagraves chuckled. "Go ahead. If we're going to talk a while longer, we may as well be lookin' at each other while we're doin' it."

Caviness walked over to pick up the piece of wood. It was about three feet long and three or four inches in diameter. In truth, it wasn't a very good piece for burning at all, but it was an excellent piece for Caviness's use.

"So tell me about that bear," Seagraves said without turning toward Caviness, who was now coming up behind Seagraves's back. "How did he happen to chaw off an ear without taking off your head?" He chuckled. "That's a story I'd like to—"

That was as far as Seagraves got. At that moment, Caviness brought the club around, holding it in both hands and swinging hard. The blow crushed the side of Seagraves's head, and he fell forward into the fire.

The next morning Seagraves was still belly-down, with his head in the ashes of what had been the previous night's fire. His head was turned to one side and the bottom of his face was burned away so that what flesh was left was blackened and disfigured. Amazingly, the top half of his face was undamaged.

Caviness found a change of clothes that were somewhat less conspicuous than the clothes he was wearing, so he changed. Then, saddling Seagrave's horse, he rode off.

Near Alexandria, Ohio

Two days later, when he smelled pork chops frying, he determined to find their source. Riding through a cornfield, he came upon a small farmhouse, the origin of the enticing aroma. Dismounting, he tied the horse off, then using trees and bushes to mask his approach, eased up to the house.

Looking through the window, he saw a man sitting in a chair, smoking a pipe and reading a book. In addition to the man, there were two women standing at the stove. As he examined them more closely, he saw that one of the women was very young, perhaps no more than fifteen or sixteen years old.

"Papa, supper's about ready," the younger woman said.

"All right, missy, I'll sit at the table soon as I finish reading this page."

"Go get Billy, Suzie," the older woman said.

Nodding, Suzie opened the back door. From his position of observation through the window, Caviness saw that the man was sitting with his back to the door Suzie had just used. That was good. That meant that the door would be unlocked because Suzie had just gone through it. And as Suzie's father's back was to the door, Caviness would be able to sneak in without being seen.

Moving quietly, and with the knife he had taken from Seagraves in his hand, Caviness opened the door and slipped inside.

"Well, that didn't take long," the man said without looking around.

Caviness stepped up behind the chair, then drew the knife across the man's throat, cutting jugular and windpipe. Unable to make a sound, the man grabbed the wound on his neck, then tumbled forward from the chair.

The woman had stepped out of the kitchen for a moment, but hearing the fall, called out.

"Hiram, what was that? What just fell?"

Caviness stepped quickly to one side of the door and waited for the woman to come back into the room.

"Hiram?" the woman called again.

Once again, Caviness made use of his knife, slicing the woman's throat. She died as silently as her husband.

With the bloody knife still in his hand, Caviness walked over to the table, where he picked up a pork chop and began eating.

As soon as the girl came back, Caviness would take care of her . . . though not before he had a little fun with her. Then he would search the house for a gun, any money they might have, and some extra food. Maybe a blanket or a quilt would be nice too.

Outside the house, seventeen-year-old Billy Potter was using a pitchfork to toss hay in the feeding trough when Suzie came to get him.

"Mama says get washed up for supper."

"What are we having?"

"Pork chops," Suzie answered. "And I cooked them."

"Ha! If you cooked them, they are probably poison," Billy teased.

"Well, if you don't like them, you don't have to eat them."

"Oh, I'll eat them, all right," Billy said. "I won't like them, but I'll eat them."

Finishing with the hay, Billy walked over to the well, where he drew out some water and poured it into a basin.

"Billy, are you going to the county fair this Saturday?"

"Yes."

"Will you take me?" Suzie asked hopefully.

"No, I won't take you. Who wants to go to a county fair with a little sister hanging around him all the time?"

"Little sister?" Suzie replied. "I'm near as old as you are," Suzie said. "And I'm almost a woman, full grow'd now."

"Yeah, that's what I'm afraid of. You'll go sparking with all the boys, and I'm the one that will get in trouble for letting you do it."

"I won't."

"You will too. You're the biggest tease in the whole county."

"Ohh, you make me so mad!" Suzie said. She grabbed the pan of water and started to toss it on him.

"No, no, wait! You can go! I was just teasing!" Billy said, laughing.

"Promise?"

"I promise."

Suzie put the water pan down and Billy grabbed it. "I'll show you to threaten me," he said, starting after her.

Laughing and screaming, Suzie ran back up to the house with Billy chasing her.

"Mama! Billy is going to . . ." Suzie started, but as soon as she stepped into the house she gasped, then screamed.

There, on the floor of the kitchen, lay her mother and dad, both with their throats cut. The most terrifying-looking human being Suzie had ever seen was standing there over them, holding a bloody knife in one hand and a pork chop in the other.

Billy, coming in right behind her, saw the scene as well.

"Suzie, run!" Billy shouted, pulling her back outside and giving her a shove. Billy turned and ran with her.

Reaching the barn, Billy grabbed the pitchfork he had been working with, then turned back.

Caviness had come as far as the kitchen door to chase them, but when he saw the boy with a pitchfork, he had second thoughts. He didn't have a gun. All he had was a knife. Even though this was just a boy, the kid was nearly full grown. In a fight between a knife and a pitchfork, the pitchfork would always win.

Turning to go back through the kitchen, Caviness grabbed a couple more pork chops, then ran out the front door and headed for his horse. He managed to get mounted just as the boy came out the front door of the house.

"You son of a bitch!" the boy called. "You bastard! You killed my ma and pa!" The boy chased after him, but couldn't catch up with the horse, which easily opened the distance between them.

Caviness hadn't noticed the boy when he first came upon the house. If he had, he might have been able to surprise the boy and take care of him first. Instead, the boy had almost managed to kill him. Caviness knew that if he was going to survive this, he was going to have to be much more careful in the future.

10

Carla's house was very small, consisting of only one room, which served as a bedroom, living room, kitchen, and dining room. But using curtains and flowers and a handmade quilt, she and Jennie had done what they could to make it attractive.

The pleasant aroma of fried chicken and freshly baked biscuits greeted Preacher when he arrived.

"Please, come in. Sit down and make yourself at home," Carla said. "And excuse me for a moment while I check my biscuits."

"Everything smells good," Preacher said.

"Thank you," Carla said, returning to her work.

As Preacher watched the young woman work in the kitchen, he recalled the first time he had ever seen her. She was Jennie's friend, and had been, even then. But their chance meeting had had nothing to do with Jennie.

Preacher had just arrived in St. Louis when he heard a woman's voice call out. The cry had come from LaBarge's Saloon.

"No, please, don't! It was an accident!" the woman was saying in a frightened voice.

"You bitch! I'll teach you to be clumsy around me!" a

harsh voice said. The expletive was followed by a smacking sound, and as Preacher looked toward the commotion, he saw a young woman who he now knew to be Carla being propelled backward through the open front door. She fell on the porch and a large, gross-looking man stomped out of the saloon toward her.

"Please," Carla had begged. "I didn't mean to spill the beer on you." She tried to get up, but as she did so, the big man hit her again, knocking her back down onto the porch. She rolled over onto her hands and knees and tried to escape him that way, but he followed after her and kicked her. She cried out in pain.

Preacher stepped up onto the porch behind the man.

"I'll learn you to spill beer on me, you worthless whore. I'll kick your ass clear into Illinois," the man growled at Carla, who was still cowering on the wooden planks of the porch.

"Sir?" Preacher said in a calm voice from just behind the man.

"What the hell do you . . . ?" the man started to ask, but he was unable to finish his question because as soon as he turned toward Preacher, the young mountain man brought the butt of his rifle up in a smashing blow to the man's face. The blow knocked out two of the man's teeth, broke his nose, and sent a stream of blood gushing down across his mouth and into his beard. If he had been ugly before, he was grotesque now. His eyes rolled up into his head and he dropped, heavily, to the porch.

Preacher chuckled.

"What is it?" Clara asked.

"I was just thinking about the first time I ever saw you," Preacher said. "You were one miserable-looking soul."

Clara laughed as well. "I reckon I was," she said. "I don't know if I ever thanked you for coming to my rescue then."

"Oh, no more'n a dozen times," Preacher said flippantly.

Clara laughed again. "Well, here is one more time," she said. "Thank you for saving me from the clutches of a horrible man like Shardeen."

"You're welcome," Preacher said.

"Oh, I think the biscuits are done."

Using her apron as a hot pad, she pulled out a pan of golden-brown biscuits and set them on the table, beside a platter of fried chicken. She had also prepared boiled potatoes and green beans for their meal.

"Oh, this looks and smells great," Preacher said.

"Back when I lived in the House of Flowers with Jennie and the girls, I would often cook for them," Carla said. "They all said I was the best cook."

"Well, if this is any indication, I'm sure you were."

"That's why I'm working at Little Man's Café now. One of these days, I'd like to own a café of my own. Oh, I know that's probably just a foolish dream, but like Jennie used to say, a person should always hang on to their dreams."

"Jennie was a wise person," Preacher said.

"She was the wisest person I ever knew, and I miss her terribly. Actually, I miss all of the girls," Carla said. "Oh, I know, they were all whores, and the town didn't think much of them. But that's because they didn't know them the way I knew them. Why, there wasn't a one of them who wouldn't do everything they could for all the others. Especially Jennie. She was like a big sister to us all."

"She started out like a big sister to me as well," Preacher said.

Carla laughed. "I don't think Jennie thought of herself as a 'big sister' to you."

Preacher laughed as well, then coughed in embarrassment.

"No, it didn't wind up that way," he said.

"Why, Preacher. I do believe you are blushing," Carla said with a laugh. "Imagine that. Me, making you be embarrassed."

"These biscuits are really quite good," Preacher said, changing the subject and taking a bite from one.

Carla chuckled again, but she didn't tease him any further. Then, after a moment of silence, she changed the mood.

"You're going after Caviness, aren't you?" she asked.

"Yes."

"I prayed that you would," she said. "Jennie deserved better than to be killed, only to have her killer just walk away without so much as a fare-thee-well."

"Oh, Caviness isn't going to get away with it," Preacher said. "I promise you that."

"Caviness isn't the only one, you know."

"Yes, I know, but if you're talking about the man named Slater, he didn't get away with it," Preacher said. "Dog saw to that."

Carla shook her head. "I'm not talking about him. I'm talking about the man that's the cause of all of this. Theodore Epson."

"Epson? Do you mean the banker?"

"Yes."

"Well, I know Epson cheated Jennie out of her house, but what do you mean that he is the cause of all of this?"

"I've got something to show you," Carla said. Going to her dresser, she took out a letter, then brought it to Preacher.

"One night after coming home, we found this letter stuck in our door," she continued. "I think you should read it."

A single candle sat on the table, its perfectly still cone of flame lighting the distance between them. Preacher held the letter in the golden bubble of light and began to read.

To the Harlot known as Jennie

   I have been informed that you are attempting to make trouble for me by accusing me of stealing. I cannot, and will not, allow my good name to be besmirched by a common whore.

   For your own safety, I advise you to say nothing more of what went on between us.
T. Epson

"You say you found this stuck in the door?" Preacher asked, holding it up.

"Yes," Carla answered.

"Huh. Constable Billings gave me a file he had on Jennie, everything about her. I looked it over pretty thoroughly this afternoon, didn't see any mention of this," he said.

"I know. Jennie didn't mention this to him."

"Why not?"

Carla sighed and shrugged her shoulders. "I think by the time she got this letter, she had given up on ever getting anything done. It was like everything she took to Billings just died there."

"Well, he must've at least contacted Epson, because there was a letter from him in the file," Preacher said. "I believe it was from Philadelphia."

"Yes, that's where he is."

"Well, if he's in Philadelphia, then that means he had to have someone in town leave the letter for him."

"Caviness," Clara said.

"You're sure it was Caviness?"

Clara nodded. "I'm positive. On the night Caviness jumped out of the alley after her, he told her that she had upset a very important man, and he warned her not to do it anymore. That could only be Epson."

Preacher drummed his fingers on the table for a moment. "Then Caviness killing her didn't have anything to do with me and with what happened back in Rendezvous."

"No," Carla said.

Preacher was silent for a moment. "I'm glad," he said. "That doesn't sound right," he added. "I'm not glad Epson had her killed, you understand. I'm just glad that I wasn't the reason Caviness killed her."

"Oh, Preacher, how could you ever think such a thing?" Carla asked, getting up from the table and walking over to lay her hand on his shoulder. "Why, that's as foolish as Dog thinking he was responsible."

Preacher nodded. "I know," he said. "But it was a feeling I couldn't shake until now."

"Well, I know how you feel. I've been thinking that, if I had gone with her the night she went to Mrs. Abernathy's, she wouldn't have had to come home by herself."

"She didn't have to come home by herself," Preacher replied. "She had Dog with her. And if you had been with her, you both would have been killed."

"I know, I think about that as well. Still, I just wonder if my being with her might not have made a difference."

"Do you have any idea where Caviness might be?" Preacher asked.

Carla shook her head, then returned to her chair on the opposite side of the table. "Nobody seems to know," she said. "He hasn't been seen around in quite a while. In fact, he hasn't been seen since the night of the murder. That's one of the reasons everyone is so sure he is the one who did it."

They had been eating all during their conversation, and finally Preacher pushed his plate away.

"Carla, I have to tell you, that was the best meal I've eaten in years," he said.

"Well, I certainly hope you saved room for some of my apple pie," Carla said, smiling sweetly. "I baked it just for you," she added.

"Oh, apple pie? I wish you had told me earlier you were going to have apple pie. I would have for sure saved room for it," he said, rubbing his stomach.

"That's all right," Carla replied with a sweet smile. "We can always eat it after."

"After?" Preacher replied, a puzzled expression on his face.

Carla looked at Preacher with an expression of wonder and barely suppressed excitement. The pupils of her eyes grew large, and she licked her lips. Preacher had always thought she was a pretty girl, but now, at this moment, she was beautiful to him.

"After," she said again rather cryptically.

The momentary confusion rolled away. Preacher knew exactly what Carla meant. Preacher pointed toward the bed, the presence of which now seemed to dominate the single room of the little house.

"Are you talking about you and me, uh, about us being together?" he asked.

"Preacher, in all this time that I have known you, I've never said anything to you about how I felt about you. I never even made the slightest suggestion as to how I felt because . . . well, I know that you belonged to Jennie, so . . ."

"Carla, do you know what you are saying? What you are doing?" Preacher asked.

"Yes, I know exactly what I'm saying and what I'm doing," Carla said. "I'm a virgin, Preacher. All the time I was working in the house with Jennie and the other girls, Jennie insisted that I keep myself a virgin. She said that someday someone special would come along. She wanted me to wait until that someday."

Preacher sighed. "Carla, you understand that the reason nothing ever came of my relationship with Jennie is because nothing could come of it? I don't live the kind of life that would allow for a family."

"Yes, I know," Carla said.

"The same would go with us. I can't offer you anything, or promise you anything."

"I know that as well," Carla said.

"What I'm saying is that, under the circumstances, I may not be that someone special Jennie wanted you to save yourself for."

"Oh, you are the someone special, all right," Carla said.

"You are sure about this?" Preacher asked.

"I've never been more sure about anything in my life," Carla replied.

She began unbuttoning the top of her dress, but just before she opened it, she leaned forward and blew out the candle. A moment later, Preacher felt her arms around his neck, her breath on his cheek, and her soft, naked flesh against his chest.

11

The smell of bacon frying in the pan, and freshly brewed coffee, awakened Preacher the next morning. For just a moment, he wondered where he was. Then he remembered that he had spent the night with Carla.

He smiled as he recalled that it had been an active night.

Dog shook himself, making his loose skin flutter as he did so.

"What are you trying to tell me, Dog? That Preacher is awake?" Carla asked.

Dog walked over to the bed and lifted his paw.

"You didn't have to fix breakfast," Preacher said.

"I know I didn't have to. I wanted to," Carla said.

Preacher looked around the room.

"The necessary is out back," Carla said. "And there's a pump and washbasin just outside the back door."

"Thanks."

Preacher took care of his morning business, washed his face and hands, decided against a shave for now, and came back into the small house. Carla had breakfast laid out on the table.

"Carla, really . . ." he began, but Carla held up her hand to stop him in mid-sentence.

"Preacher, this may be the closest thing to a normal family that I'll ever have," she said. "Please, don't deny me this pleasure."

"Deny it?" Preacher smiled broadly. "On the contrary. I intend to enjoy every bite of it."

"Slater? Yeah, I knew him," LaBarge said, replying to Preacher's question. "Worthless as tits on a boar hog, that one was."

"Were he and Caviness pards?" Preacher asked.

"You goin' to buy more beer, or just ask questions?" LaBarge asked.

"I'll take another beer."

LaBarge drew a mug of beer from the barrel, then set it in front of Preacher. Preacher blew the head off, then took a drink.

"I wouldn't go so far as to say they was pards," LaBarge said. "But I did see them together from time to time. Sometimes they'd sit at that far table over there and talk real quiet about things."

"Things? What sort of things?"

"I don't have any idea. Like I told you, they would talk just real quiet."

"I heard 'em palaverin' about Philadelphia one night not too long ago," one of the other bar patrons said. He had been standing at the bar, about ten feet away from Preacher and LaBarge. Supposedly, he was minding his own business, but the fact that he could respond indicated that he was paying attention to what was going on.

"What were they saying about Philadelphia?" Preacher asked.

The patron shook his head, then raised his glass for a drink. "Well, now, I can't answer that," he said. "I just heard 'em mention Philadelphia."

"Do you know some of the other folks who were at that table?"

The patron stroked his chin for a long moment, supposedly in thought, but obviously waiting for Preacher to make an offer to pay him for information. Preacher slid a nickel down the bar.

"Finch was one of them," the patron said. "They was two more. But it'll cost you a nickel a name."

"No, it won't," Preacher said.

"What do you mean it won't? I'm the one knows who was at that table."

Preacher shook his head. "Finch knows."

Finch was working at the wagon freight yard when Preacher found him. Sitting on an overturned barrel, he was packing grease into the wheel of one of the wagons.

"Your name Finch?"

Finch grabbed a handful of grease and started shoving it into the wheel hub.

"Who wants to know?"

"I do," Preacher said without identifying himself.

"I owe you money, mister?"

"No."

"Have I got your sister, wife, or daughter in a family way?"

"No."

"Did I challenge you to a duel when I was so drunk I wasn't makin' any sense?"

"No," Preacher said. He laughed.

Smiling, the wagon mechanic stood up, then extended his grease-filled hand toward Preacher's.

"Well, then, if you ain't a-wantin' me for none of them things, I reckon I'm the man you're lookin' for."

Preacher started to take Finch's hand, but seeing it all filled with grease, he jerked his hand back.

"I'm sorry," Finch said, reacting to Preacher's aversion. "When you work in grease all the time, sometimes you just forget." He wiped his hand on his own trousers, then stuck it out for a second time. It was nearly as greasy and dirty as it had been the first time, but Preacher took it anyway.

"Now that you know who I am, what can I do for you?" Finch asked.

"Do you know Ben Caviness?"

"Caviness?" Finch's eyes narrowed. "Yes, I know the son of a bitch. Don't tell me he is a friend of yours."

Preacher shook his head.

"He's no friend of mine," he said. "But I am trying to find him. When is the last time you saw him?"

"Oh, mercy, let me see. I'd make it two or three months now, for sure."

"Have you seen him since March?"

Finch thought for a moment, then shook his head. "You mean since he killed that girl? No, and I don't reckon anyone else has either."

Preacher's eyes narrowed. "You think Caviness is the one who killed Jennie?"

"Well, folks is saying he's the one that done it, and knowin' the son of a bitch like I did, there ain't nothin' that would make me disagree with 'em."

"What about this man Slater? I hear he and Caviness were pards?"

Finch shook his head. "Well, if either one of them was goin' to have a pard, it would have to be each other," he said. "Warn't neither one of them worth a pail of warm piss. But no, I wouldn't go so far as to say that they was pards or anything like that."

"But last March, you and some others were seen sitting at the same table as both Caviness and Slater."

"Sittin' at the same table?" Finch shook his head. "No, you

got me wrong, mister. I wouldn't never sit down to dinner with either one of them sorry sons of bitches."

"No, not a dinner table. A table over in LaBarge's Tavern."

"Oh. Yeah, well, I suppose I could have done that from time to time. LaBarge's gets awful crowded sometimes, so's that you can't always be none too particular who it is you wind up sittin' with."

"Do you recall sitting at a table with both Caviness and Slater? According to one person I spoke to, they were discussing Philadelphia."

Finch tried to snap his fingers, but because of the grease, he didn't get a pop.

"I'll be damned," he said. "You know, now that you mention it, I do mind that night. Oh, LaBarge's was crowded somethin' awful that night."

"What did they say about Philadelphia, do you remember?"

"Well, it's not so much what he said, it's just that Toomey brought him a letter, and he's the one that passed the remark."

"What remark?"

"Somethin' 'bout this gettin' to be a habit, him deliverin' letters from Philadelphia."

"What did he mean by that? It being a habit?"

"According to Toomey, that was the second letter that month that come from Philadelphia."

"Thanks, Mr. Finch," Preacher said, extending his hand again.

"Wait a minute, you're the fella they call Preacher, ain't you?" Finch said as he shook Preacher's hand a second time.

"I am."

"This girl that Caviness killed, some says as how she was your woman."

"She was," Preacher said without going into any further explanation.

"I see now why you're so all-fired interested in Caviness. You aim to find 'im and kill 'im, don't you?"

"I aim to do just that,' Preacher said.

"Well, by damn, I wish you luck," Finch said. "Anyone in this world that deserves to die, it's that son of a bitch."

"Thanks again," Preacher said.

Edgar Toomey looked up from behind the counter that separated the post office area from the customer area.

"Yes, sir?" Toomey said. "What can I do for you?"

"Sometime ago you delivered two letters to Ben Caviness. Both were from Philadelphia. Do you recall that?"

Toomey shook his head. "I'm not at liberty to discuss the U.S. mail. That's confidential information."

"Hell, what's so confidential about it?" Preacher asked. "Everyone in LaBarge's Tavern saw you deliver the letters."

"Well, if you have their word on it, why do you need confirmation from me?"

"I don't need confirmation. I know you delivered the letters. All I want to know is who sent them."

Again Toomey shook his head. "Now, you are really asking me to violate postal regulations," he said.

"You know that Caviness killed Jennie, don't you?" Preacher asked.

Toomey nodded. "I've heard that possibility discussed," he said.

"You know that, but you won't help me find him?"

"I told you, I can't answer your questions. Perhaps you should inquire over at River Bank."

Preacher looked confused. "The bank? What does that have to do with it?"

"They might be able to answer your question," Toomey said pointedly. "That's all I can do for you, do you understand? All I can do is refer you to the bank."

* * *

"I'm not sure it is appropriate for me to be discussing bank business with you," Abernathy said in response to Preacher's question.

"I don't know that we are discussing bank business," Preacher replied. "All I'm trying to do is find Ben Caviness and when I asked Mr. Toomey about it, he referred me to the bank."

"Yes, well, I . . ."

"Tell him what he wants to know, Duane," a woman's voice said.

Preacher turned to look toward the door of Abernathy's office, and saw a rather stout, stern-faced woman standing there.

"Sybil, are you . . ."

"Tell the man what he wants to know," Sybil Abernathy repeated. Her voice softened. "Please, Duane," she said. "I feel responsible for this whole awful mess. If I had not been so insistent that that beautiful young woman be run out of her house, none of this would have happened."

"What do you have to tell me?" Preacher asked Mr. Abernathy.

"Sybil, discussing the business of our depositors is highly unethical."

"So is paying someone to murder," Sybil said. "Tell him."

Mr. Abernathy sighed, then looked up at Preacher. "Caviness cashed two bank drafts, drawn against the account of Theodore Epson, on the Trust Bank of Philadelphia," he said. "The first was for fifteen dollars, and the second was for one hundred dollars."

"One hundred dollars? That's a lot of money, isn't it?"

"Yes," Abernathy agreed. "For someone like Ben Caviness, it is quite a substantial sum."

"Yes, well, I guess murder isn't cheap," Preacher said.

* * *

Once more, Constable Billings was peeling an apple. Two previously peeled and browning apples sat on the windowsill, evidence of earlier efforts.

"I think I know where Caviness is," Preacher said.

"Oh?" Billings was toward the end now, and what was clearly the longest unbroken peel he had yet made lay in a coil below the apple. He was being very careful as he continued to peel. "Where?"

"Philadelphia."

Billings looked up in surprise. "What makes you think he is in Philadelphia?"

"Because Theodore Epson is in Philadelphia."

"Epson? The man who used to be the head teller at the bank?"

"Yes. Did you know that Epson sent Caviness two bank drafts, one for fifteen dollars and one for one hundred dollars?"

"No, I didn't. What the Sam Hill would he be sending Caviness money for?"

"I think he paid Caviness to kill Jennie," Preacher replied. "If the killing had gone smooth, Caviness would've taken the money and been on his way. But it didn't go smooth. Slater got himself killed and Caviness lost an ear. And knowing Caviness, he's going to figure that he's got more money coming."

Billings nodded. "You may have an idea there," he said.

12

Carla and Dog came down to LaClede's Landing to see Preacher off on his quest. The boat he would be taking was a side-wheeler called the *Cincinnati Queen*. Because it was designed for use on the Mississippi and Ohio, both rivers deeper and more stable than the Missouri, the *Cincinnati Queen* was larger and more ornate than the *Missouri Belle*.

There was a great deal of activity around the landing as both people and cargo were being taken aboard the three-decker, red-and-gold painted boat. William Ashley and Constable Billings had come down to the riverfront as well, and all were gathered in a little cluster as Preacher prepared to board.

"I've written a letter appointing you as my deputy," Constable Billings said, handing the letter to Preacher. "To be truthful with you, I don't know how much authority it will have, but if you find a sympathetic peace officer or judge, he might recognize it and grant some reciprocity. Sometimes law officers do that for one another, since our jurisdiction is so limited."

"Thanks," Preacher said, taking the proffered letter.

"And I've prepared several bank drafts for you, which should be recognized wherever you go," Ashley said. "You have fifteen hundred dollars in fifty-dollar drafts."

"I appreciate that," Preacher said. He looked at Carla, who so far had been very quiet. Dog was sitting by Carla's side.

"Preacher, you will be careful, won't you?" Carla said. "I'm not over losin' Jennie yet. It would be awful hard on me to lose another friend just now."

"I'll be careful," Preacher promised. He looked at Dog. "Dog, you did a really good job of looking after Jennie. Now, I want you to look after Carla for me. Will you do that?"

Dog looked up at Carla, then back at Preacher. Preacher smiled, and rubbed him behind the ears. "I knew I could count on you," he said. "And I promise you this. When I return, I'll take you back to the mountains with me."

The dog opened its mouth and let its tongue hang out. Laughing, Preacher rubbed him behind his ears again.

"Yeah," he said. "I thought you would like that."

The boat's whistle blew and, looking toward the boat, they saw the purser coming up to the bow, which was pegged against the bank. The purser raised a megaphone.

"All aboard that's comin' aboard!" he shouted.

There were several last-minute good-byes as those who had remained ashore, including Preacher, started up the gangplank.

"Stand clear!" one of the deckhands shouted as he closed the gate.

"Stand by to cast off!" the captain shouted down from the wheelhouse.

"Standing by!" the deckhand answered.

"Cast off."

The deckhand lifted the heavy rope from its stanchion and threw it toward the bank. The boat's whistle blew two deep-throated blasts that echoed from the opposite side of the river. The engine was put in reverse and the steam boomed out of the steam-relief pipe like the firing of a cannon. Like the boat whistle, the booming came back in echo from the Illinois side of the river.

The wheel began spinning backward, and the boat pulled away from the dock, then turned with the wheel going upriver and the bow pointed downstream. The engine lever was slipped to full forward, and the wheel began spinning in the other direction until it caught hold to begin propelling the boat downstream.

Walking back to the stern of the boat, Preacher looked toward the landing they had just departed and saw that though many had left, Carla and Dog were still standing there, watching as the boat moved quickly downriver. Preacher stood there looking back at them until the boat moved around a bend in the river, taking them out of sight.

The Mississippi River was placid, though with a current powerful enough to push the steamboat south at a fairly good clip. It was nearly dusk and the sun, low in the west, caused the river to shimmer in a pale blue, with highlights of reflected gold.

As Preacher stood on the deck, he recalled his first experience on the river. As a twelve-year-old boy looking for adventure, he had met a man named Pete Harding at a trading post on the Ohio River. Harding was taking a flatboat down the Ohio. The boat was loaded with goods to be traded at the Mississippi River port town of New Madrid, and Harding hired Art as his deckhand and assistant. It was a position young Art accepted readily, for not only was it a job, it provided him with food and transportation for his trek westward.

Fifteen years earlier

"Run away from home, did you, boy?" Harding asked.

"No, I . . ." the boy started to reply, but deciding it would be better to be honest with Harding, he sighed and spoke the truth. "Yes, sir, I ran away from home."

"Having trouble there, were you?"

"No, sir, I wasn't havin' any trouble. It's just that I wanted to . . ." He let the sentence trail off.

"You wanted to see the creature."

"See the creature?"

"That's a saying, son, for folks like you and me."

"You and me?"

"It would be my guess, that you and I are just alike," Harding said. "There are some folks who are born, live, and die and never get more'n ten miles away from home in any direction. Then there's those folks, like the two of us, that's always wondering what's on the other side of the next hill. And when they get over that hill, why, damn me if they don't feel like they got to go on to the next one, and the next one, and the next one after that. They're always hopin' they'll find somethin' out there, some sort of creature they ain't never seen before. I know it's that way with me, and I'm reckonin' that it's the same way with you."

The boy laughed. He had never heard it put that way before, but he knew that Harding had pegged it exactly as it was.

"Yes, sir," he said. "That's the way it is with me. I want to see the creature."

The boy went to New Madrid with Harding, but there, one night, he was hit over the head.

Art felt the sun warming his face, but that was the only thing about him that felt good. He had a tremendous headache, and he was very nauseated. He was lying down. Even though he had not yet opened his eyes, he knew he was lying on sun-dried wood, because he could smell it. He was also in motion. He could feel that, and he heard the creak and groan of turning wagon wheels and the steady clopping sound of hooves.

The last thing he remembered was leaving the tavern to go

to the privy. What was he doing here? For that matter, where exactly *was* here?

Art opened his eyes. It was a mistake. The sun was glaring, and the moment he opened his eyes, two bolts of pain shot through him.

"He's awake," a girl's voice said.

Putting his hand over his eyes, Art opened them again. Now that he was shielding his eyes from the intense sunlight, it wasn't as painful to open them. Peering through the separations between his fingers, he looked at the girl who had spoken. She appeared to be about his age, with long dark curls and vivid amber eyes staring intently at him.

"Who are you?" Art asked.

"My name is Jennie," she replied.

That was Preacher's introduction to the girl, later to become a woman who would be so important to him.

Preacher soon learned that Jennie was actually a slave girl belonging to Lucas Younger, the man who owned the wagon in which he was riding. To his surprise, he discovered that he was being considered a slave as well. Because he had no proof of his identity, the mere suggestion that he was a slave was enough to make Younger's claim credible.

The boy escaped, spent time with the Indians, then found his way to St. Louis, where he worked in a wagon freight yard. Then, two years later, when General Jackson raised an army of volunteers from the Mississippi and Ohio River valleys to go to New Orleans to fight against the British, the boy was reunited with Pete Harding.

Pete Harding was killed in the Battle of New Orleans. Preacher was mustered out of the Army after the battle, and even though he was but fourteen, he was discharged as a lieutenant. And in keeping with his promise to Pete Harding, Preacher went west to the Rocky Mountains to "see the creature."

* * *

After a full day's run from St. Louis, the *Cincinnati Queen* put in at Cape Girardeau, Missouri. There, merchants from the town came on board the boat to sell their goods. This was the ultimate destination for many of the passengers, who disembarked, while others left the boat merely for a stroll around town. In the meantime, the boat took on a fresh supply of wood for its continuing journey.

From Cape Girardeau, the boat continued south on the river until it reached the confluence of the Mississippi and Ohio Rivers. There, the *Cincinnati Queen* turned up the Ohio. Leaving Missouri behind, it journeyed north and east, bordered on the south by the state of Kentucky, and on the north by the fertile farming fields of Illinois.

After it entered the Ohio River, forward progress became much, much slower because it was now necessary for the boat to beat its way against the current. However, proceeding at a pace that was only slightly faster than a man could walk, the boat continued on its journey.

Without even realizing it, Preacher was growing more and more tense until, five days after they turned up the Ohio, he realized what had been making him so tense. He was about to come face-to-face with his past. Standing at the rail, he watched the shore slide by slowly, monotonously, almost hypnotically. And, as vividly as if he were reliving it, he remembered the past.

Fifteen years earlier

Leaving his brother sleeping in the bed behind him, the boy who would one day be called Preacher stepped out of the bedroom into the upstairs hallway. He moved to the end of the hall to his parents' bedroom, where he stood just outside their door for a moment, listening to his pa's heavy snoring.

His pa's snores were loud because he slept hard. He worked hard too, eking out a living for his family by laboring from dawn to dusk on a farm that was more rock than dirt, and took more than it gave.

His ma was in there too, though her rhythmic breathing could scarcely be heard over her husband's snores. She was always the last to go to bed and the first to get up. It was nearly two hours before dawn now, but Art, the boy who would one day be called Preacher, knew that his mother would be rolling out of bed in less than an hour, starting another of the endless procession of backbreaking days that were the borders of her life.

"Ma, Pa, I want you both to know that I ain't leavin' 'cause of nothin' either of you have done," the boy said quietly. "You have been good to me, and there ain't no way I can ever pay you back for all that you have done for me, or let you know how much I love you. But the truth is, I got me a hankerin' to get on with my life, and I reckon twelve years is long enough to wait."

From there, the boy moved down to his sisters' room. He went into their room and saw them sleeping together in the bed his father had made for them. A silver splash of moonlight fell through the window, illuminating their faces. One was sucking her thumb, a habit she practiced even in her sleep; the other was clutching a corncob doll. The sheet had slipped down, so Preacher pulled it back up, covering their shoulders. The two girls, eight and nine, snuggled down into the sheets, but didn't awaken.

"I reckon I'm going to miss seeing you two girls grow up," the boy said quietly. "But I'll always keep you in my mind, along with Ma, Pa, and my brother."

His good-byes having been said, Preacher picked up the pillowcase in which he had put a second shirt, another pair of pants, three biscuits, and an apple, and started toward the head of the stairs.

Although he had been planning this adventure for a couple of months, he hadn't made the decision to actually leave until three days ago. On that day he'd stood on a bluff and watched a flatboat drift down the Ohio River, which flowed past the family farm. There was a family on the flatboat, holding on tightly to the little pile of canvas-covered goods that represented all their worldly possessions. One of the boat's passengers, a boy about Preacher's age, waved. Other than the wave, there had been nothing unusual about that particular boat. It was one of many similar vessels that passed by the farm every week.

To anyone else, seeing an entire family uprooted and looking for a new place to live, traveling the river with only those possessions they could carry on the boat with them, might have been a pitiful sight. But to a young boy with wanderlust, it was an adventure that stirred his soul, and he wished more than anything that he could be with them.

On the morning Art left, he was nearly to the bottom of the stairs when the sudden chiming of the Eli Terry clock startled him. Gasping, he nearly dropped his sack, but recovered in time. He smiled sheepishly at his reaction. The beautifully decorated clock, which sat on the mantel over the fireplace, was the family's most prized possession. His mother once told him with great pride that someday the clock would be his. He reckoned now that it would go to his brother. His brother always put more store in the clock than he did anyway.

Recovering his poise, he took a piece of paper from his pocket, and put it on the mantel beside the clock. It was addressed to "Ma and Pa."

At first he hadn't planned to tell anyone in his family that he was leaving. He was just going to go, and when his folks woke up for the next day's chores they would find him gone.

But at the last minute, he'd thought his parents might rest a little easier if they knew he had left on his own, and had not been stolen in the middle of the night.

The boy had enough schooling to enable him to read and write a little. He wasn't that good at it, but he was good enough to leave a note.

Ma and Pa
   Don't look for me, for I have went away. I am near a man now and I want to be on my own. Love, your son, Arthur.

With the note in place, Arthur opened the front door quietly and stepped out onto the porch. It was still dark outside, and the farm was a cacophony of sound: frogs on the pond, singing insects clinging to the tall grass, and the whisper of the night wind through a nearby stand of elm trees.

Once he was out of the house and off the porch, the boy moved quickly down the path that led to the river. When he reached the bluff, he turned and looked back. The house loomed large in the moonlight, a huge dark slab against the dull gray of the night. The window to his parents' bedroom was gleaming softly in the moonlight. It looked like a tear-glistened eye, a symbol that wasn't lost on him. A lump came to his throat, his eyes stung, and for a moment, he actually considered abandoning his departure plans. But then he squared his shoulders.

"No," he said aloud. "I ain't goin' to stand here and cry like a baby. I said I'm a-goin', and by damn I'm goin'." He turned away from the house.

"Sorry about sayin' 'damn,' Ma, but I reckon if I'm goin' to be a man, I'm goin' to have to start talkin' like a man."

The boy left the beaten path, then picked his way through the brush down to the side of the river's edge. To the casual observer, there was nothing there, but when he started pulling branches aside, he uncovered a small skiff.

He had found the boat earlier in the year during the spring runoff. No doubt it had broken from its moorings somewhere when the river was at its freshet stage, though it was impossible to ascertain where it had come from. He hadn't actually stolen the boat, but he did hide it, even from his father. And he assured himself that if someone had come looking for the boat, he would have disclosed its location. But as no search materialized, at least none of which he was aware, he got to keep the boat.

The boat provided him with a golden opportunity, and it wasn't until it came into his possession that he seriously began considering running away from home. He left, not because of any abuse, but because of pure wanderlust.

13

Preacher thought about it before he left the *Cincinnati Queen*. Should he or should he not visit his family? If he did visit them, how would they react? Would they welcome him, or would they resent him? If they reacted with resentment, it would certainly be an emotion he could understand. In all the time he had been gone, he had never once contacted them, to let them know whether he was dead or alive.

Dead or alive.

He suddenly realized that he didn't know whether or not his parents, or indeed any of his family, were dead or alive. The thought gave him pause, especially because he realized that, until this very moment, it wasn't anything he had ever considered before.

Was it confidence that they were alive that kept the worry from his mind? Or was it extreme selfishness on his part?

He didn't want to face up to that shortcoming in his own personality, but if truth be told, he would have to say that it was because of his own extreme selfishness.

That consideration made up his mind for him. When the

boat reached the point nearest the old family homestead, he would get off and seek them out. He could only hope that they were all still alive, and were still in the same place. Further, he could only hope that they would accept him.

He did not feel that he was compromising his mission by leaving the boat to search for them. After all, there was no sense of immediacy to what he was doing. Jennie was dead, and would remain dead. There was only a need to bring about justice, and that he would do.

Portsmouth, Ohio, was the nearest town to the old homestead. As it turned out, it was also a scheduled stop for the boat, though primarily because it was a place to replenish the wood supply.

As the boat pulled ashore, Preacher visited the purser's office and informed him that he would like to get off there.

"But you've purchased a ticket all the way to Steubenville," the purser replied. "We are quite a long ways from Steubenville."

"Yes, I know, but I would like to visit Portsmouth."

The purser chuckled. "I've seen Portsmouth, mister. Believe me, it isn't much to look at."

"Maybe so. But I'm getting off here."

"All right. Will you want to be going on to Steubenville at a later time?"

"Yes. Can I buy another ticket from here?"

"Well, if you are going through, that won't be necessary," the purser said. "You've already bought the ticket." The purser handed Preacher a little slip of paper. "Just present this to the purser of the next boat belonging to the Ohio and Mississippi Line that stops here, and he will honor it for passage on to Steubenville."

"Thanks," Preacher said, folding the paper and putting it in his pocket.

Several toots of the boat's whistle indicated that it was

about to dock. That was followed by the slight jolt of the bow as the captain pegged it on the shore.

"Make fast the lines!" the captain called down, and at the bow, the deckhands secured the boat to the shore.

Preacher waited until the gangplank was stretched down from the side. Then he left the boat, climbed up the cobblestone-covered riverbank, and stood there for a moment, looking out over the town of his youth. As he stood there looking at the town, the town was looking back at him, or at least, several of the town's citizens. He was not their typical visitor.

Preacher had not brought his rifle with him, deciding to leave it for safekeeping with his friend William Ashley back in St. Louis. But he had brought his knife and his pistol, and he was wearing both of them on a belt that he had strapped around his waist. His clothes consisted of a buckskin shirt and trousers, as well as a rather wide-brimmed hat.

Preacher wandered through the town, looking it over carefully. Oddly, it was a little like trying to recall a dream that slips away so quickly after waking, for while he recognized some of the buildings, many he did not.

One of the buildings that he did recognize was the River-man's Inn, on the corner of Third and Court Streets. He remembered it, even though he had never been inside the building. That was because the Riverman's Inn was a saloon, and as Preacher had been so young when he left Portsmouth, this saloon wasn't a place he had ever visited. Preacher paused just in front, his hand resting on the door frame for a moment before he went inside.

Although this was the first time he had ever been inside the establishment, there was a degree of familiarity about it. Like most of the saloons and taverns he had been in, this one had a bar that ran down one side of the room. The bar had a foot rail, as well as rings every ten feet or so, from which hung towels for the customers' use. In addition to the bar, there was a handful of tables out on the floor.

All of the tables were empty. In fact, the bar was empty as well. There were only two people in the place, a man behind the bar and an attractive young woman who was standing at the far end of the bar. For a moment Preacher felt there was something different about the young woman. Then he realized what it was. She wasn't dressed in the provocative style that he had come to associate with bar girls. Preacher didn't know if that was unique to this particular woman, or if all bar women back East dressed in a more conservative fashion.

Both the man and the woman looked toward him as he came inside.

"Good afternoon, sir," the man said to Preacher, greeting him with a friendly smile. "Welcome to the Riverman's Inn. You just get off the boat, did you?"

"I did," Preacher said.

"I thought so." He tapped his finger to his temple. "I have the power of divination, you know."

The woman laughed. "Don't let Vaughan fool you, mister. It's your clothes that give you away. Nobody around here wears that kind of clothes. What do you call that?"

"Buckskins," Preacher replied. "They are useful in my line of work."

"And what would that line of work be?" the bartender asked.

"I'm a fur trapper."

"A fur trapper, is it?" the man replied. "Well, now, that sounds fascinating. Have a drink, sir. The first one is on the house," the bartender said as he drew the beer.

"And if I don't order a second?" Preacher replied.

The man laughed. "Well, then, the first one is still on the house and I'm the fool for thinking it would generate more business for me."

Preacher laughed as well. "You're no fool, mister. That seems to me like a friendly way to welcome new customers."

"Doesn't hurt to be friendly, and I can afford to give away a drink now and then," the man said. He put the beer mug in front of Preacher. "There you go, sir."

"Thanks," Preacher said. Picking up the mug, he blew the foam off the mug, then took a long swallow.

"A fur trapper, you say?"

"Yes."

"You know, I think folks used to trap some around here years ago. But most of the trapping now is out West somewhere. And from the looks of you, I'd say that's where you would be doing your trapping—out West somewhere."

"Yes," Preacher said. "I trap in the Rocky Mountains."

"I've never seen the Rocky Mountains, but I would truly like to. I've heard they are something awesome to behold."

"They are indeed," Preacher said. He finished the beer. "Now, I wonder if you would let me buy one for each of you."

"Well, sir, that's kind of you to offer," the bartender said. "But if all I did was stay here all day drinking my own product, I'd be too drunk to work."

"And the lady?"

"The lady is my wife," the bartender said. "And she don't drink at all. Can you imagine, marryin' a tavern keeper and not even drinkin'?"

"Yes, if she's drawn to the man and not what he does," Preacher said. "I'll have another for myself then."

The bartender drew a second drink.

"Well, here's to you both," Preacher said, paying for a second drink, then holding it up to them.

"What brings you from a place as glorious as the Rocky Mountains to a tiny place like Portsmouth?" the bartender asked.

"I'm just traveling through," Preacher said. "Heading for Philadelphia."

"Philadelphia," the bartender said. "Have you ever been there?"

"No, I haven't."

"I think you will find it a fascinating place to visit. I was there a year or so back myself."

The woman laughed. "It was more like ten years," she said. "We wasn't even married yet when you went."

"The name is Vaughan Roberts," the bartender said, sticking his hand out by way of introduction. "And whatever it is that caused you to stop by our fair town, you are truly welcome."

"Thanks," Preacher said. "Folks call me Preacher."

"Preacher? And would you be a man of the cloth, Preacher?"

Preacher chuckled. "Far from it, I'm afraid. It just seems to be a name I've picked up."

"Ever been here before, Preacher?" Vaughan asked.

"Yes," Preacher said. "As a matter of fact, I am from here. I used to live here, or not far from here, when I was a boy."

"You don't say? So that explains why you dropped by. You wanted to visit the place of your youth."

"You might say that," Preacher agreed. "I lived upriver a few miles. My folks had a place there, just where the river makes a big sweep."

"Well, there's a couple of places up there," Vaughan said. "But that's pretty good land. Finest land in the country, some folks say. What is it that made your family up and leave like they done?"

"Oh, you misunderstood me. My family didn't leave at all," Preacher said. "They are still here. Or at least, as far as I know, they are still here."

"As far as you know? Here, that's a mighty strange thing to

say about your own family. You mean you don't even know if they are still here?"

"I'm ashamed to say that I don't know," Preacher said. He took another drink before he continued. "You see, I told you I left here when I was a boy, and that's just what I did. As I look back on it now, I probably did a bad thing, but when I was twelve years old, I just up and left on my own."

Suddenly the woman gasped, and put her hand to her mouth. "Oh, my," she said in a soft voice. "Oh, my, oh, my, oh, my."

"Tess, what in the world has got into you?" Vaughan asked.

"Tess?" Preacher repeated in a quiet voice. He looked at the young woman. "Is that your name? Tess?"

Tears sprang into Tess's eyes, and she nodded. "Yes," she answered.

"Would you have a sister named Betty, and a brother named Morgan?"

"I also have a brother named Arthur," Tess replied, now smiling broadly through her tears. "We thought he was lost, but I know now that he has come back to us."

"My God," Vaughan said, now realizing what was going on. He stared at Preacher. "You are Arthur, aren't you? You are Tess's long-lost brother."

"I reckon I am," Preacher said.

With a little cry, Tess ran into Art's arms. He embraced her for a long moment, feeling her against him, feeling her tears wet his cheeks.

Finally, Tess drew away from him. "Why?" she asked. It was more of a sob than a question. "Oh, Arthur, why in heaven's name did you run away from us like that?"

"I'm sorry, Tess," Preacher said. It was the only way he could think of to respond to this question that had no answer. "I'm sorry."

* * *

Vaughan closed his place for the rest of the day, hitched a team to a wagon, then drove Tess and her long-lost brother out to her parents' farm.

"I've got a thousand questions I want to ask you," Tess said as they drove along the dirt road that ran parallel with the river. "But I'm going to save them because I know that everyone else will want to ask the same questions, and there's no sense in making you say everything twice."

"Thanks," Preacher said. "I'll answer all the questions as best I can, I promise."

Tess's promise not to ask a lot of questions caused the ride out to be a quiet one, and Preacher welcomed the silence because it gave him time to reconnect with his past. As the wagon rolled along the road, Preacher looked out over the landscape, trying to reconcile what he was seeing with memories. As it was mostly trees and plowed fields, there wasn't anything significant enough to make an impression on him. That is, until they came around the final bend and he saw the house, a white, two-story house, sitting on a small hill.

The house was exactly the same. The final moments before he'd left, indelibly burned into his mind and heart, were recreated by what he was seeing now. For a minute, all the intervening years between the time he stood there as a twelve-year-old boy, fighting tears, and this moment rolled away. It was as if the years of his life had formed one, long ribbon, and someone had grabbed the ribbon at each end and folded it together, connecting past with present so that it was impossible to differentiate one from the other.

The wagon pulled into the front yard, and his mother came out onto the porch.

"Well, hello, Tess, Vaughan," she said. She was holding a dish towel. "I didn't expect to see you two until this weekend. Who's your friend?"

"Mom, this is . . . ," Tess started, but she didn't finish. Suddenly, the woman on the porch gasped, and put her hand to her chest. Her eyes grew wide and her mouth began to tremble.

"Don't tell me," she said. "I know who it is." With her arms open wide, she hurried down from the porch. "Arthur," she said. "My dear, sweet, Arthur!"

"How did she recognize me after all these years?" Preacher asked quietly as he stepped down from the wagon to go toward his mother.

"Mothers have a way of knowing these things," Tess said. Even though Tess was not a mother, and was younger than Preacher, she was already in touch with the wisdom that is peculiar only to women.

At supper time, Preacher sat at the dining room table with his mother and father, Tess and Vaughan, Betty and her husband, Jim, and Morgan and his wife, Ann, and their young son, Art.

Preacher's father was holding the Bible.

"A reading from St. Luke," Preacher's father began. He looked up at everyone at the table, then, clearing his voice, began to read.

"A certain man had two sons; and the younger of them said to his father, Father, give me the portion of goods that falleth to me. And he divided unto him his living.

"And not many days after, the younger son gathered all together, and took his journey into a far country, and there wasted his substance with riotous living.

"And when he had spent all, there arose a mighty famine in that land; and he began to be in want.

"And he went and joined himself to a citizen of that country; and he sent him into the field to feed swine.

"And he would fain have filled his belly with the husks that the swine did eat; and no man gave unto him.

"And when he came to himself, he said, How many hired servants of my father's have bread enough and to spare, and I perish with hunger!

"I will arise and go to my father and will say unto him, Father, I have sinned against heaven and before thee, and am no more worthy to be called thy son. Make me as one of thy hired servants.

"And he arose, and came to his father, but when he was yet a great way off, his father saw him, and had compassion, and ran and fell on his neck, and kissed him.

"And the son said unto him, Father, I have sinned against heaven, and in thy sight, and am no more worthy to be called thy son.

"But the father said to his servants, Bring forth the best robe, and put it on him; and put a ring on his hand, and shoes on his feet. And bring hither the fatted calf, and kill it; and let us eat, and be merry."

Preacher's father closed the book and looked across the table at his son.

"And, like the father in the Bible, I welcome my returning son. He was lost, and now he is found."

There was a moment of silence; then Morgan spoke. "Hey, Pop, we didn't kill any fatted calves, though. All Mom did was wring the neck of a couple of chickens. You think that will count the same?"

Everyone at the table laughed.

Later, after dinner, Preacher's father took a couple of chairs out onto the front porch, and invited Preacher to join him. Although everyone wanted to talk to him, to hear his story and to find out where he had been and what he had done, they all acquiesced to Preacher's father, giving him his just due.

"Have you taken up smoking, son?"

"Yes."

"Suppose we light our pipes and have a talk."

"All right."

A cool breeze blew across the porch and, from there, they could hear the whisper of the Ohio River as it moved by in front of them. The sun was low, and the river was a translucent blue, gleaming as if with its own light. The two men lit their pipes, then sat there for a long, quiet moment, enveloped in the smoke of their own making.

Preacher knew that his father must have a thousand questions, so he said nothing. He waited patiently for his father to begin the conversation. He was surprised by the first thing his father said.

"It's been my experience that men who wear a gun and a knife like that generally know how to use them. Are you skilled with those weapons?"

"I get by," Preacher said.

"Ever killed anyone?"

"Only in self-defense, Pa. It's not something I take pleasure in."

"Tess said you introduced yourself in the tavern as Preacher. How'd you come by a name like that?"

Preacher told his father the story of how, as a captive of the Indians, he had preached a sermon continuously for twenty-four hours, convincing the Indians that he was crazy, thus causing them to spare his life.

"Folks heard about that," he concluded, "and I've been called Preacher ever since."

Preacher's father laughed. "That's a wonderful story, son," he said. "And a fitting name. But if you don't mind, while you are here, we'll call you Arthur, the way you were born."

"I don't mind at all," Preacher replied.

"Now, tell me, if you can, why you up and left us in the middle of the night, without so much as a by your leave."

"I wanted to see the creature," Preacher said, remembering the expression used by Pete Harding.

"To see the creature," Pa repeated.

"Yes, sir."

"And did you see the creature?"

Preacher was quiet for a long moment before he answered.

"Yes, sir. I think you could say that I have seen the creature," he replied.

"Tell me about it," his father said.

Preacher began speaking then, starting the story from the morning he sneaked out of the house and onto the boat, telling about his encounter with river pirates, about being declared a slave by Lucas Younger, about his experiences in the war, and about his experiences in the mountains.

He left nothing out, including his relationship with Jennie. He even told his father that Jennie was one-quarter black and, according to the laws of Missouri and other slave-holding states, legally considered a Negro for purposes of slavery. And he told his father that the reason he was going to Philadelphia was to find the man who killed her.

"And what do you aim to do with him when you find him?" his father asked.

"I aim to kill 'im, Pa."

His father was quiet for a moment. "Well, I don't hold with killin', but then, that's my world, not yours. I won't fault you for livin' in your world, seein' as it's the only one you've got now, and we all have to do what we have to do."

"Yes, sir, that's pretty much the way I look at it too," Preacher said.

It was now nearly one o'clock in the morning. Tess and Vaughan had left for town long ago, and the others were sound asleep. Still, Preacher and his father talked. Preacher found that it was as necessary for him to fill his father in on what had happened to him over the past several years as it was for his father to know.

Finally, stories were finished and the two men sat in silence for a long moment, listening to the sound of the night creatures.

"I read the story of the Prodigal Son for a reason," Preacher's father said, finally breaking the silence. "Not because I thought you had been a wastrel, living a life of debauchery and sin. You were a good boy when you were twelve, and I couldn't see anything, any temptation, that would change you.

"No, sir. I read the story because I wanted you to know that, despite all that's happened, I'm happy you came back. My one prayer, for all these years, has been that I could see you at least one more time, to satisfy myself that you are still alive and well."

Preacher didn't answer.

"Are you satisfied with the life you are living, boy?"

"Yes, Pa, I am," Preacher said, realizing at that moment that he was very satisfied. "I can't think of anything I would rather do than what I'm doing now."

"I'm glad. You won't mind, then, if I leave all the farm to Morgan, who has stayed here and worked it for his whole life."

"I think that would be the only right thing to do," Preacher said.

"I'm glad you feel that way, for that's what I intend to do. That is, if I'm able to hold on to it."

"Able to hold on to it? What do you mean?"

"You've told me your story," Preacher's father said. "Now, maybe it's time I told you mine."

Although neither Preacher nor his father realized it, Morgan had heard every word of their conversation. His and Ann's room was just above the front porch, and because it was a warm night, his window was open. The breeze the open window allowed in also brought to him, very clearly, the conversation his brother and father were having.

Until his father said what he did to Art, Morgan had no idea that his father was planning on leaving everything to him.

He was pleased to hear Preacher agree to his father's plan. And now, as his father explained the difficulty they were in, Morgan felt that his older brother would be able to help them. He didn't know how, but he was confident that he would.

14

Klyce Blanton owned the Security Bank of Ohio. He had only recently purchased the bank, and immediately upon acquisition had let it be known that it would no longer be business as usual.

"No more mollycoddling of debtors," he said. "From now on, every penny owed to this bank must be paid on the date it is owed, or I will foreclose."

It was no coincidence that Blanton acquired the bank at the time when a severe drought had brought about crop failure for many of the farmers, Preacher's father included. Blanton bought the bank for the express purpose of forcing all the neighboring farmers into default so he could take their land at a fraction of its actual worth. He had already foreclosed on several farms.

Under the previous banker, the farmers had been able to arrange for additional time by paying the interest only when their note came due. It was a normal procedure, and Preacher's father had not the slightest idea that he would not be allowed to do so until he went to the bank to make his payment. That was when he was informed that Klyce intended to exercise his legal right to call the note the moment it was due.

"That's two weeks from now," Sylvanias said. "The land

that my father cleared, and that I have nurtured all these years, the land that I intended to pass down to my children, is being taken away from me, and there is nothing I can do about it."

Preacher said nothing to his father, but at the earliest opportunity he planned to go into town and set things right. It was the least he could do after causing them so many years of worry and heartache.

Getting up early, Preacher came down the stairs and left a note on the kitchen table.

Dear Ma and Pa
  I have some business to take care of so I must be gone
for a while. But don't worry, I will be back today.
                                        Your son, Art

Preacher walked into Portsmouth, arriving around eight o'clock, just as the town was beginning its daily activity. Though it was much smaller than St. Louis, it had a cosmopolitan air about it with its businesses and enterprises. Merchants were in front of their establishments, industriously sweeping their porches. Freight wagons were already rolling in and out of the town, some of them queuing up at the river's edge in preparation for meeting the next arriving boat.

Preacher walked by Dunnigan's Mercantile Store and saw that Mr. Dunnigan, wearing an apron, was putting together a display of some of his goods. Preacher recognized Dunnigan right away because the merchant hadn't changed that much over the last fifteen years. Preacher smiled as he recalled that he had worked for Dunnigan one summer, sacking potatoes.

"Good morning, Mr. Dunnigan," Preacher said, touching the brim of his hat.

"Good morning, young man," Dunnigan replied cheerily. It was obvious that Dunnigan didn't recognize him, and Preacher didn't say who he was because he didn't want to have to go into a long explanation as to where he had been all these years. "Looks like it's going to be a nice day," Dunnigan added.

"Yes, sir, it does indeed," Preacher replied, continuing on toward the bank.

The bank was on Front Street. It was closed, but on the front door was a sign that said it would open for business at nine o'clock. Looking through the window of the bank, Preacher could see the clock inside. It was now eight twenty-three.

For the next few minutes, passersby saw Preacher standing in front of the bank. From all outward appearances, he seemed totally relaxed, with his arms folded across his chest and one foot raised and pressing against the front wall. In truth, he was keenly alert, both mentally and physically, for whatever challenge he might have to face.

Shortly before nine, a fancy carriage, accompanied by a rider on either side, turned onto Front Street and came toward the bank. The carriage stopped in front and the passenger climbed down.

"Will you be needing the carriage this morning, Mr. Blanton?" the driver asked.

"No," the passenger answered. The man was grossly overweight, with large jowls and several chins. He had virtually no neck, so his bald head seemed to rest, like a cannonball, on his round shoulders.

"Very good, sir. I'll be over at the livery if you do need me." The driver clucked to his team and the carriage pulled away.

The fat man looked at Preacher, curious as to who he was.

"Are you Klyce Blanton?" Preacher asked.

"I am he, sir. Why do you ask? Are you waiting for the bank to open?"

"Yes."

"Well, I'm always glad to do business," Blanton said as he unlocked the bank door. "But the bank doesn't open for another fifteen minutes."

"I'll wait," Preacher said, making no effort to move.

"What sort of business do you have with the bank?" Blanton asked.

"I'm here to give you some money," Preacher said.

Blanton smiled broadly. "Well, now, if you are here to give me money, I think we can make an exception and let you in a little early. Come on inside, Mr. . . ."

"Preacher."

"Preacher? Your name is Preacher?"

"Preacher will do."

"Well, Mr. Preacher, come on inside and we'll do some business."

The two men who had accompanied Blanton, both armed and rough-looking, tied their horses off at the hitching rail, then went inside as well. One of them sat in a chair by the front door, while the other walked toward the back office with Preacher and Blanton. This one settled in a chair just outside the door to Blanton's office.

"These two rather formidable-looking gentlemen are my bodyguards," Blanton explained when he saw Preacher looking at them. "A man of my prominence can't afford to be without protection. Now, I believe you said something about being here to give me money?"

"That's right."

"Well, then, Mr. Preacher, come on into my office and we'll take care of business. Are you opening an account with us?"

"No," Preacher said. "I'm here to pay off a loan and pick up the paper you hold on a farm."

The smile left Blanton's face and his eyes narrowed. He stroked his multiple chins as he stared at Preacher.

"What makes you think you can just come in here and buy up a loan?" he asked. He pointed to Preacher's buckskin clothes. "I can tell you aren't from around here, but that's not the way business is done."

"I'm not buying up a loan," Preacher said. "I'm paying one off. I want it returned to the borrower, free and clear."

"Why would you want to pay off someone else's loan?"

"It's the loan my pa borrowed against his farm," Preacher said. "I want him out from under that debt."

"Who is your father?"

"Sylvanias Coopersmith," Preacher said.

As Preacher said the name Coopersmith, he realized that it was the first time he had so much as spoken the name in over fifteen years. When he left home he had purposely dropped his last name in order not to bring any discredit on his family.

Blanton shook his head. "Are you trying to pull something on me, mister? I know Sylvanias Coopersmith's son, Morgan, and you aren't Morgan."

"I'm his other son, Art."

"I thought you said your name was Preacher."

"That's what folks call me, and I'm comfortable with it," Preacher replied.

"You know I think, mister? I think you are a liar," Blanton snarled.

As quickly as a striking snake, Preacher pulled his knife and stuck the point of it into Blanton's left nostril. He sliced the side of the nostril, not a very large cut, but one that went all the way through. It was not only painful, it produced a lot of blood.

"Ahhh!" Blanton shouted, grabbing his wounded nose. "Colby!"

The bodyguard who was posted just outside Blanton's office came running in through the door, his pistol in his hand. Spinning toward him, Preacher threw his knife, and the point of it punched through Colby's sleeve, pinning his gun hand to the wall just inside the door.

The other bodyguard came running in as well, but as soon as he stepped through the door he was greeted with Preacher's drawn pistol, charged, cocked, and leveled right at him. The second bodyguard stopped dead in his tracks and threw up his hands. "No, wait! Hold it, hold it!" he called out in quick fear.

"Mr. Blanton, you might want to rethink what you just said," Preacher said calmly. "You see, where I'm from, a man's word is his bond. When you call someone a liar, you commit a serious offense against his person."

Blanton held his hand cupped under his nose and the palm was pooling with blood.

"What?" Blanton replied, his voice strained with pain and distraction.

"Whenever someone calls me a liar, I take it real personal," Preacher said.

"I . . . I didn't mean that I actually thought you were a liar. I just didn't realize that Mr. Coopersmith had a son other than Morgan," Blanton whined.

"I thought that might be the case," Preacher said. He looked at the two bodyguards, who were glaring at him with anger. "You," he said to Colby. "Bring my knife to me. And be careful how you do it."

Still glaring, Colby pulled the knife from his sleeve and the wall, then brought it back to Preacher, handing it to him handle-first.

"Thank you. Now, I'd like for both of you to put your pistols on Mr. Blanton's desk," Preacher said, motioning with his own pistol.

Still glaring at him, the men started across the room with their pistols.

"Uh,-uh," Preacher said. "Carry them by their barrels."

Both pistols were cocked, and the men stopped, then started to ease the hammers down.

"No, I want you to leave your guns cocked," Preacher said.

"Are you crazy? You expect me to hold a cocked pistol by the barrel?" Colby asked.

Preacher smiled coldly. "Yes, I do," he said. "That way I know you will be careful."

Slowly, gingerly, the two bodyguards turned the pistols around and held them by the barrel. As Preacher had ordered, the pistols were still cocked. Then, carefully, the men walked the rest of the way across the floor and put the pistols on the desk.

"Thank you. Now, if you would, I want both of you to go over there and sit on the floor facing the wall."

"Mister, just who the hell do you think you are, ordering us around like this?" the other bodyguard asked angrily.

"I think I'm the one with the loaded gun," Preacher said. "Now, do what I told you to do."

Reluctantly, but clearly with no choice, the men complied.

Turning his attention back to Blanton, Preacher saw that the banker was now holding a handkerchief to his nose. The slice on his nose was still bleeding, though not as profusely as before.

"I am Sylvanias Coopersmith's son," Preacher said. "I admit that I haven't been much of a son to him." Preacher was speaking as conversationally as if nothing had happened. "But I am his son nevertheless, and I'm here to pick up the paper you are holding against the farm."

"I'll get the paper for you," Blanton said. "You can have it. Just don't kill me."

Preacher shook his head. "No, you don't understand," he said. "I don't want you to give it to me. That would be the same as bank robbery and as soon as I left, you would just send the sheriff out there and take my father's farm. I'm not here to steal the paper, I'm here to pay off the loan. This is strictly a business operation."

"Is it your business to cut a man's nose off?" Blanton asked.

"Oh, but I didn't cut your nose off, though I could have if I had wanted to. So tell me, Blanton, are we going to talk business or not?"

Blanton pulled the handkerchief away from his nose. The bleeding had stopped, though there was quite a bit of blood on his face and the front of his shirt and vest. Blanton studied the handkerchief for a moment, as if unable to believe this had happened to him in his own bank. Finally, he looked up at Preacher.

"You do understand, don't you, that the entire amount is due? That includes principal, interest, and transfer charges."

"Transfer charges? What are transfer charges?" Preacher asked.

"There were expenses involved with transferring all of the loans from the previous mortgage holder over to me," Blanton explained.

"Seems to me like that would fall under the cost of doing business. By rights those are your costs, not the costs of your borrowers."

"All right. You are the one holding the gun. If you say no transfer charges, then there are no transfer charges."

Again, Preacher shook his head. "No, if these transfer charges are part of it, then I'll pay them as well. I told you, I intend for this to be all legal and proper. How much does my pa owe you?"

Blanton opened a drawer and pulled out a file. "It looks like your father, and I see here that your brother Morgan has signed as well, owes this bank a total of six hundred and twenty-seven dollars. "You have six hundred dollars and twenty-seven dollars on you, do you, Mr. Preacher?"

"I have these bank drafts," Preacher replied. Preacher showed Blanton six documents, drawn for one hundred dollars each. "And I have twenty-seven dollars in cash," he added.

Blanton shook his head. "You don't have six hundred dollars. What you have are bank drafts, and they aren't worth the paper they are printed on unless you can get a bank to honor them."

"These drafts are drawn against the River Bank of St. Louis," Preacher said. "Any bank in the country will honor them."

Closing the file, Blanton returned it to the drawer from which it had come. "I have no intention of honoring them," he said cryptically. "Unless, of course, you force me to honor them. As I said earlier, you are the man with the gun, and I never argue with a man who is holding a gun on me."

Preacher stared at Blanton, so angry with the fat man that his temple began to throb. Blanton was a quick learner. He had already learned how to play Preacher against himself. By saying that the only way he would honor the drafts would be for Preacher to force him to do so, he meant that he was inviting Preacher to take the deed by force. That was something Preacher had already said he would not do, because a deed taken by force, even in exchange for valid bank drafts, would be reported to the sheriff as soon as Preacher left.

"Very well, I will find a bank to honor it, and I'll bring cash."

Despite the wounded nose, Blanton actually allowed a smile to play across his face. He believed that he was in control now. This was business, and nobody was better at business than Klyce Blanton.

"You go find a bank, Mr. Preacher, or Coopersmith . . . whatever you are calling yourself," Blanton said. "But when you do find one, understand this. I want the money in gold coin. I'm not interested in paper."

"Why not? I know that you deal in paper money," Preacher said.

"It is my option to ask for payment to be rendered in gold," Blanton said. "And that is what I intend to do, unless you force me to do otherwise." Blanton continued to play the hand he had been dealt. He knew, now, that Preacher wasn't going to force him into any deal that might later compromise the transaction. "So, if you want your papa's loan back, you are going to have bring me six hundred twenty dollars in gold," Blanton said. He snorted what might have been a chuckle. "You can bring me the seven dollars in paper money."

"I'll be back," Preacher said as he left the office.

Blanton followed Preacher to the door of his office, then stood there and watched as Preacher left the bank.

"You two worthless pieces of shit can get up now," Blanton said dismissively, speaking to his bodyguards, who were still sitting on the floor over in the corner of his office.

The two men stood and retrieved their guns.

"I'm going after the son of a bitch," Colby said, starting toward the door. "I'll teach him to treat me this way."

"No," Blanton said, holding his hand out to stop him. "You and McDougal follow him, but don't do anything until he gets the money."

"Then what?" Colby asked.

"I don't want him to make it back to the bank with it."

"What do you want us to do?"

"I don't want him to make it back to the bank with the money," Blanton said again, this time more pointedly than before.

"All right," Colby said.

15

Preacher had no intention of letting Blanton take the farm away from his father. If the bank demanded cash money in order to retire the debt, then Preacher would come up with the cash. Whatever it took to get control of the farm returned to his father, Preacher intended to do.

The first requirement would be to find a bank that would honor the drafts from the River Bank of St. Louis. That in itself should not be hard, though it might be somewhat more difficult to find a bank that would pay in gold coin, rather than paper money.

This was Preacher's original home place, but he had grown to adulthood somewhere else. Because of that, he really knew very little about this area. In order to find a bank that would meet all the requirements, he would have to have help from someone, and he knew exactly who that someone would be. He walked down the street to visit with his brother-in-law.

Preacher thought his brother-in-law's establishment would be closed at this time of the morning, so he was surprised to see that Vaughan Roberts had already opened the Riverman's Inn for business. When he stepped inside, Vaughan looked up at him from behind the bar. Vaughan smiled, and called a greeting.

"Good morning, brother-in-law."

"Good morning," Preacher replied. He looked around the Inn, and saw that there were several people sitting at the tables.

"I wouldn't have expected you to have this many customers at this time of day," Preacher said. "Seems a little early to be drinking, doesn't it?"

Vaughan chuckled. "Not if you're drinking coffee," he replied.

"Coffee?"

"In the afternoon and at night, we are what some may call a tavern. But you notice we call it an inn, not a tavern, so we open in the morning and have quite a brisk breakfast trade. A lot of men, especially the bachelors, come in here for coffee and strudel. Your sister makes the best strudel in the county, and has proven it by winning prizes at the county fair."

"I didn't know that about her," Preacher said. "Actually, I'm ashamed to say, I know nothing about her, or any of the rest of my family."

"You have a wonderful family, I'm happy to say."

"Tell me about them," Preacher said. "Last night, I'm afraid that all I did was fill everybody in on where I've been and what I've done for the last fifteen years."

"All right, I'll start with your sister Betty. She was a schoolteacher until she got married, and she was a very good one. But as I'm sure you know, the school board has a strict rule against teachers being married so when she and Jim got hitched, she had to give up her job. There were a lot of disappointed families in the area, families whose older sons or daughters had been in Miss Coopersmith's class, and who wanted their younger children to have her as well.

"Betty's husband, Jim, publishes a newspaper, and even the governor has read and commented on some of his editorials. There are some who think Jim should run for office, but he insists that he can do more good as a newspaperman by, in his words, 'being the watchdog of the public.'

"Your brother Morgan, like your father, is a farmer. He

works hard, is honest in his dealings with others, and there is no finer man in the county. His wife, Ann, happens to be my first cousin, so if I tell you what a wonderful person she is, you'll just say I'm being prejudiced."

"No, I would say, who has a clearer idea than you?" Preacher replied. "Thank you for filling me in on all of them, Vaughan. But I must say that, after seeing how well they all turned out, it's clear to me that I am the black sheep of the family," Preacher said. He was only half jesting when he made the comment.

"Oh, I wouldn't say that," Vaughan said.

"I know they were all shocked to see me just drop in out of the blue the way I did."

"They may have been shocked—who wouldn't be to have you suddenly show up after such a long time? But I'll tell you this. I know they were all very happy to see you," Vaughan said. "Oh, where are my manners? Would you like some coffee?"

"Yes, thank you, that would be good. And one of my sister's pastries," he added with a smile. "I left the house before breakfast this morning."

A moment later, Vaughan served him.

Preacher took a bite of his sister's strudel. "Ummm, tell Tess this is very good."

"You can tell me yourself," Tess said, appearing in the door from the kitchen. She was wearing an apron upon which there was a light dusting of flour. An errant strand of hair hung down across her eyes, and when she brushed it back, she left a smudge of flour on her cheek.

"All right, I will tell you," Preacher said. "This is very good."

"Thank you," Tess replied. Then, in a more troubled tone of voice, she asked, "Arthur, what are you doing here? You aren't leaving again so soon, are you?"

"Not just yet," Preacher said.

"I'm glad to hear that. And don't think I'm not happy to see you, but I think you should spend more time with Mama and Papa."

"I will," Preacher said. "It's just that I had some business to take care of with Klyce Blanton."

"Klyce Blanton? You are doing business with that disagreeable man?" Tess asked. "Has Papa told you about the loan on the farm?"

"Yes."

"Everything was going just fine until Blanton bought the bank and began foreclosing on all the farmers. Why did he have to go sticking his nose into everyone else's business?"

"Some people are just that way, I suppose. But I do think that Blanton will be more careful about where he sticks his nose from now on," Preacher said.

"What do you mean?"

"Nothing, I was just making conversation."

"What kind of business did you have with Klyce Blanton?" Tess asked.

"Mortgage business," Preacher said, without being more specific. "Vaughan, if you were going to use a bank other than Blanton's bank . . ."

"I do use a bank other than his," Vaughan replied quickly.

"You do? You mean there is another bank in town? Which one? Where is it?"

Vaughan shook his head. "No, I didn't mean to give you the wrong impression. It's not in Portsmouth. The bank I use now is the Ohio Bank for Savings, over in Alexandria."

"Alexandria? Yes, I remember passing it on the way here. It's about ten miles downriver, isn't it?"

"Yes. Alexandria isn't as large as Portsmouth, but it does have a good bank. In fact, since Klyce Blanton bought out the bank here in Portsmouth and turned a good bank into a bad one, a lot of our local folks are doing their business over in Alexandria."

"Who is the head of the bank over there? Do you know him personally?"

"Yes, I do know him. His name is Burt Rowe. He's a good man."

"Arthur, if you are going to go over there to try and arrange a loan for Papa, I can tell you right now it won't do you any good. Vaughan had a new loan all set up, but Papa wouldn't do it."

"Why not?"

"Because Papa says you can't borrow yourself out of debt."

"Yes, well, he is probably right. But that's not what I had in mind."

"What did you have in mind?"

"I plan to pay off Pa's note so that he has the farm free and clear."

Tess gasped. "Arthur! You have enough money to do that?"

"Yes, and I have it with me. But it's not in cash. It's all in bank drafts."

"Bank drafts are fine," Vaughan said. "Why bother to go over to Alexandria with them? Blanton is the one who is holding the note. Why don't you just do business directly with him?"

"Well, like I said, Blanton and I had a brief discussion about that very thing this morning," Preacher replied. "He says he won't honor the drafts, and it is his right not to do so."

"I guess I'm not all that surprised that he won't do it," Vaughan said. "I have believed all along that Blanton isn't really interested in having the note paid off. What he actually wants is the land. He's got his hands on several thousand acres of prime bottomland right now, and your father's land is as good as any piece of land in the entire county. It may be the best land in the county. I'm sure Blanton is just itching to add your pa's land to his holdings."

"Well, he may want Pa's land, but he's not going to get it," Preacher said.

"Arthur, does Papa know you are doing this?" Tess asked.

"No. And don't you tell him until it's already done. I'm afraid he would try to stop me."

"You are right about that. He absolutely would try to stop you," Tess said. "Papa is a proud man who won't accept a handout from anybody. Not even one of his own children."

"Believe me, Tess, when I tell you that this isn't a handout," Preacher said. "The way I look at it, this is just payment for all the hurt I've caused Ma and Pa . . . that I've caused all of you . . . over the years. I'm hoping that once it's done, Pa will look at it that way too."

Tess smiled. "He will," she said. "I'll talk to Betty and Morgan, and we'll make certain he sees it that way."

"Thanks."

Tess leaned across the counter and put her hand on Preacher's. He could smell the scent of cinnamon and the aroma of flour and brown sugar. For just a moment, it caused him to recall his youth. Many times over the past several years, on those long, lonely nights in the mountains, he would sometimes think of his family, and he couldn't think of his mother without recalling that homey aroma. It seemed right and good now that his sister would be carrying that on.

"You're a good man, Arthur," Tess said. "I was very young when you left, and I'm afraid I don't remember you all that clearly now. I've often wondered where you went and how you turned out. I'm glad you came back, just so we would know what a good man you really are."

Preacher chuckled self-consciously. "Don't get me wrong. I'm not a saint, Tess," he said. "I've done things that I wouldn't want Ma or Pa, or even you or Betty or Morgan, to know about."

"You went out on your own when you were twelve years old, Arthur," Tess said. "I've no doubt that you had to do some things to survive. But survive you have, and here you are today, offering to pay off the farm for Papa. Whatever you may have had to do in the past, you are a good man today, and I love you for it."

"Thank you, Tess. I appreciate that coming from you."

The scene of familial affection was interrupted by the boisterous entry of a customer.

"Woo-hoo," the customer said loudly, coming into the inn laughing and slapping himself on the knees.

"Good morning, Ed," Vaughan said. "What's gotten into you this early in the day?"

"Vaughan, pour me a cup of coffee and bring out one of your wife's strudels, and I'll tell you the funniest thing I've heard in a long time," Ed said, taking a seat at the bar.

Vaughan poured the cup of coffee, then set a pre-cut piece of strudel in front of him. "All right, Ed, just what is this funny story?" he asked.

"You know that fella that bought out the bank? The high-and-mighty Klyce Blanton?"

"Yes, of course I know him," Vaughan said. "He is so disagreeable, he has made himself known all over town."

"Yes, sir, that's the one, all right. But you just wait till you hear what just happened to him."

"Wait a minute. Are you saying something happened to Klyce Blanton?" Vaughan asked, glancing with some apprehension toward Preacher.

"It sure did, and Cleetus Butrum seen it all happen, so, according to him, this is the gospel truth."

"What did happen?"

"Blanton got his comeuppance, that's what happened," Ed said. He took a bite of the strudel. "Ummm, Mrs. Roberts, every strudel I have here is better than the one I had the day before. How do you do that?"

"I just follow the same recipe my mama and grandmother used," Tess said. "Tell us what happened to Klyce Blanton."

By now both Tess and Vaughan were staring at Preacher, who seemed to find something interesting to study in his coffee.

"It seems like some feller come into the bank this mornin' to discuss somethin' with Blanton. Well, I reckon the discussion didn't go to the feller's likin', so he took out his knife, then without so much as a by your leave, took him a slice out of the side of Blanton's nose." Ed laughed. "Just like that," he said.

"What do you mean when you say he took him a slice? Are you saying this man cut part of Blanton's nose off?" Vaughan asked.

"Well, no, not exactly," Ed clarified. He put his finger alongside his nose, then made a cutting motion. "He just sliced right through it. Leastwise, that's what Cleetus is sayin'."

"And Cleetus is saying that all this took place in the bank?" Vaughan asked.

"Yes, in the bank. Right there in Blanton's office, accordin' to Cleetus," Ed said. He took another swallow of coffee, enjoying his moment of being the center of all attention.

"What about Colby and McDougal?" Vaughan asked. "They don't strike me as being the kind of men who would just stand there and watch all that happen without doing something about it. I thought they never left his side. Where were they when this was all going on?"

"Well, sir, accordin' to Cleetus, they was right there in the bank at the time and seen everything that happened."

"They saw it, but they didn't try to stop it?"

"Oh, yeah, they tried," Ed replied with a chuckle. "That's the best part," he said. "They did try, but accordin' to Cleetus, this here fella handled the two of 'em like they was no more'n babies. Had 'em both sittin' on the floor, he did, starin' at the wall, like the way teachers sometimes do with their dunces."

"You don't say," Vaughan said. Now the apprehension in his face was gone, and he looked at Preacher with awe in his eyes and a smile on his lips.

"Chris Dumey seen Blanton a while ago and he said Blanton's nose was all red, with a purple scar where the cut was. The scar wasn't all that big, but you could sure see where it was. No, sir, I don't reckon the high-and-mighty Mr. Blanton is going to be so high-and-mighty anymore."

"So," Tess said to her brother. She chuckled quietly. "Klyce Blanton is going to be more careful about where he sticks his nose, is he?"

"That might be the wisest thing for him to do," Preacher replied.

Ed overheard Tess and Preacher, and though he didn't make the connection that Preacher was the one he was talking about, he did make the connection with the remark about the nose. He laughed out loud. "He's going to be more careful about where he sticks his nose," he said. "Yes, I reckon he is, all right." Ed laughed again. "That's a good one, that is. I'll have to remember that while I'm tellin' this story."

Finishing his coffee and strudel, Preacher stood. "I think I'd better be going. Tell me, Vaughan, can I rent a horse at the livery?"

"No need for you to be renting a horse when I can lend you one of mine," Vaughan said. "And I guarantee you, you'll be better mounted on my horse than you would if you rented."

"Thanks, I appreciate that," Preacher said.

"Also, before you leave, I'll write a letter of introduction to Mr. Rowe. That might be helpful to you in case he has any questions about why you want gold instead of paper for the bank drafts."

"Yes, thank you, Vaughan, that would be a big help," Preacher said.

16

It took Preacher less than an hour to reach Alexandria. Armed with the letter Vaughan had written, as well as the letter Constable Billings had given him back in St. Louis, he presented himself to Burt Rowe, the head of the bank.

Burt read both letters, then returned them. "They are good letters," he said. "They speak well of your honesty and integrity. Now, what can I do for you, sir?"

"I need to cash these bank drafts," Preacher said. "I need six hundred dollars in cash."

"Certainly, I see no problem with that," Rowe said. "Step over to the teller's cage, I'll instruct him to honor the drafts."

"I'll need the money in gold coin," Preacher added.

Rowe scratched his chin for a moment. "Gold coin?"

"Yes."

"Why gold coin? We issue United States Bank promissory notes. They are as good as gold everywhere."

"As good as gold isn't gold," Preacher said. He sighed. "I don't mean to be picky, Mr. Rowe. But I'm paying off the mortgage on my father's farm. Klyce Blanton holds the paper, and he is demanding payment in gold in order to release it."

"I see," Rowe said, nodding his head. He sighed. "Blanton is the kind of man that gives bankers a bad name. Very well,

Mr. Coopersmith, I'll honor the drafts with gold coin. I'll even put them in a bag for you."

"That would be helpful," Preacher said.

As Rowe searched for a cloth bag, Preacher happened to glance toward the wall, where there hung several posters. One poster in particular caught his attention, and he walked over for a closer look. As he examined it, he felt a surge of anger and determination.

WANTED FOR
MURDER
DEAD OR ALIVE
Murderer Is
Missing His
Left Ear

Burt Rowe came over to him then, bringing the cloth bag and the money. "Here is your money," he said, counting out the gold coins in front of him. When he counted out the full amount, he dropped the coins into the bag and handed the bag to Preacher.

"I saw you looking at that," he said, pointing to the poster.

"Yes. What do you know about this?"

"Terrible thing, that," the banker said. He then proceeded to tell the story of Billy and Suzie Potter finding their parents dead on the floor.

"They were murdered, both of 'em. Billy chased him with a pitchfork, but the man was mounted and rode away."

"How were Mr. and Mrs. Potter killed? Did the murderer slit their throats?"

"Yes," Rowe answered. He squinted. "Say, how did you know that?"

"Because that's the way he works."

"That's the way who works?"

"Ben Caviness. Could you tell me where the sheriff's is located?" Preacher asked. "I may have some information for him."

"Sheriff Wallace's office is just across the street, down on the corner," Rowe answered. "You can't miss it, it's the only brick building in that block."

Preacher took the bag of coins from Rowe. "Thank you very much for your help," he said, holding the bag up.

"You're welcome."

Sheriff Wallace, a gray-haired man of about fifty, was sitting at his desk, filling his pipe with tobacco, when Preacher came into his office. He looked up at Preacher with curiosity.

"Yes, sir, mister, something I can do for you?" the sheriff asked.

"Sheriff Wallace, my name is . . ." Preacher started to identify himself as Preacher, but thought of the letter his brother-in-law had written for him, so he used his real name. "Art Coopersmith. I wonder if I could speak to you for a moment."

"Sure thing, Mr. Coopersmith. What do you have on your mind?"

"First, I'd like to show you this," Preacher said, handing Wallace the letter Constable Billings had written for him, appointing him his temporary deputy. The sheriff read it, then handed the letter back. "This letter calls you Preacher."

"It's a name some folks call me," Preacher said. He showed the sheriff his letter from Vaughan.

"All right, Preacher, or Mr. Coopersmith, whichever name you prefer. This first letter says you are a deputy in pursuit of a criminal and it asks for my cooperation. I'll be glad to cooperate with you all I can, but we are a pretty small town and I know everyone here. So I can tell you for a fact that the fella you are looking for, this"—Wallace glanced at the letter again—"Ben Caviness, isn't in Alexandria."

"He probably isn't," Preacher said. "But I believe he was here."

"What makes you think that?"

"I was just in the bank and noticed that you have a dodger posted on the wall. You had a murder take place here recently, committed by a man with only one ear."

"Yes, he killed Hiram and Emma Potter."

"I'm pretty sure that may be the same man I'm looking for. Mr. Rowe said that the Potters' son and daughter saw the man."

"Yes, they did."

"I wonder if I could speak with the boy and his sister."

"Yes, I'm sure they'll talk to you," the sheriff replied. "Are you mounted?"

"I am."

"Let me saddle my horse and I'll ride out to the Potter farm with you."

At the Potter farm, Suzie was working in the garden while Billy was up on the roof of the house, replacing shingles. He had just reached for another shingle when he saw two riders approaching.

"Suzie, someone's coming," Billy called down from the roof.

Suzie looked up and used her hand to shield the sun from her eyes. "Who is it, can you tell?"

"Looks like the sheriff is one of them, but I don't know who the other man is."

"I'll make some lemonade," Suzie said. "No doubt they're hot after their ride."

Billy left his shingles on the roof, then climbed down the ladder. He was standing in front of the house when the two riders arrived.

"Sheriff Wallace," Billy said, greeting him.

"Billy, this is Mr. Coopersmith," Sheriff Wallace said. "But he goes by the name of Preacher."

"You're a pastor?"

"No. It's just a nickname people have hung on me. I'm comfortable with it now."

"I see you're keeping busy," Sheriff Wallace said, nodding toward the ladder.

"Yes, sir." Billy pointed to the roof of the house. "Pa kept tellin' me that we was goin' to have to put shingles on the roof this summer, but I kept puttin' 'im off 'cause I didn't want to do the work," he said. "But I put it off too long. Durin' the rain last week, the roof leaked somethin' awful."

The sheriff chuckled. "When shingles go bad, roofs will do that," he said. "How are you and your sister doing?"

"We're doin' all right. We miss Ma and Pa, but we're doin' just fine. Come on in, Suzie's makin' some lemonade."

"Thanks. Sounds good after a hot ride."

The three men went into the house, where Suzie greeted them with glasses of the confection.

"I just drew the water from the well, so they should be cool," she said, offering each of them a glass.

"Billy, Preacher thinks he knows who the fella is that killed your ma and pa," Sheriff Wallace said.

Billy looked at Preacher. "You know this man?" he asked.

"Yes. If he is who I think he is, he also killed a woman in St. Louis a few months ago," Preacher said. "I've been looking for him ever since."

"I wish you had found him before he got here," Suzie said, a tear sliding down her cheeks.

"I do too, miss," Preacher said. "And I'm very sorry for your loss. But I'll tell you this, if it's any comfort to you. I will find him."

"It won't bring Ma and Pa back."

"No, it won't do that," Preacher admitted.

"What's his name?" Billy asked.

"His name is Caviness. Ben Caviness," Preacher said. "He's a big man with dark hair and a crooked nose. And he's missing his left ear."

"That's him!" Suzie said, gasping.

"How'd he lose that ear?" Billy asked. "What he's got left is about the ugliest thing I've ever seen."

"The woman he killed had a dog with her. The dog chewed the ear off."

"Good for that dog," Billy said. "Too bad he didn't kill him."

"There were two men who attacked the woman," Preacher said. "And the dog did rip the throat out of the other one, killing him."

"Good."

"Billy, Sheriff Wallace said that you ran after Caviness, but he was riding."

"Yes. He was riding a bay," Billy said. "If he hadn't been mounted, he would be dead, because I would've caught up with him."

"He went that way, east," Suzie said, pointing. "Of course, he could have turned a different direction after he was out of sight. I think about that, about him still being out there, and sometimes I'm afraid at night, afraid that he may come back."

"I told her I wish he would come back," Billy said. "He got away from me once. If he comes back, he won't get away again."

"He won't be coming back," Preacher said. "He's heading east."

"You say that like you know it for a fact," Sheriff Wallace said.

"I do know it for a fact."

"Where is he heading, do you know?"

"He is going to Philadelphia."

After they finished their lemonade, Preacher and the sheriff took their leave. As they left, the sheriff saw several rusting, iron washers lying on the ground under a tree, and he chuckled.

"You've got a lot of iron washers there, Billy," the sheriff said. "What are you planning on doing with them? Going into the iron washer business?"

"You remember, don't you, Sheriff, how Dad use to run a float line out in the river for catfish?" Billy asked.

"Indeed I do," Wallace said. "I've had more'n one mess of your pa's fish."

"Well, he used these iron washers as weights for the fishing line. He liked to gather them up, but I don't have any use for them."

"You mean you don't fish?" Sheriff Wallace asked. "I figured, as good a fisherman as your pa was, you'd be out on the river too."

Billy shook his head. "No. Dad enjoyed it, but I don't. I wish I did enjoy it. I think Dad would have appreciated it if I had gone fishing with him, but I never did. I just don't have the patience, I guess."

"What are you going to do with all these washers now?" Preacher asked.

"I don't know. Bury them, I guess."

"I'll give you two dollars for the lot of them," Preacher offered.

Billy smiled broadly. "What? You'll give me two dollars for this?"

"For the whole pile," Preacher said. "What do you say?"

"I say that you've got yourself a deal!"

Preacher gave Billy two dollars, then scooped up all the washers and put them in his hat.

"What are you going to do with all them things?" the sheriff asked.

"I don't know," Preacher replied. He smiled. "Maybe I'll go fishing."

Billy and Suzie watched the two men ride away.

"I wish I was going with him," Billy said.

"Why?"

"I think he is going to catch up with this man Caviness. And when he does, I'd like to be there."

Suzie shivered. "Not I," she said. "I never want to see him again. And I don't know why you would want to."

"There's something about this man that tells me that when he does catch up with Ben Caviness, he is going to kill him," Billy said. "And I would like to be there when that happens."

"You mean you could watch something like that?" Suzie asked.

Billy spat on the ground, then started back toward the ladder to resume his work on the roof.

"Watch it?" he said. "I could do it myself."

17

Colby and McDougal knew that Preacher would have to go to Alexandria in order to find a bank that would honor the bank drafts, so, even as Preacher was in the Riverman's Inn, Blanton's two bodyguards were on their way to Alexandria. They got there ahead of Preacher and waited in the saloon, taking a table near the window so they could keep an eye on the bank, which was located just across the street.

"You think he'll get the gold?" McDougal asked.

"I reckon he will," Colby said. He chuckled. "But he ain't goin' to keep it long, seein' as how we'll just meet him out on the road somewhere between here and Portsmouth and relieve him of that burden."

"Yeah, well, if it was up to me, I'd do more than take the money from him. I'd kill the son of a bitch," McDougal said.

"And you'd get hung for it too," Colby replied. "Hell, you'd get us both hung."

"I just don't like the way he done us back in Portsmouth."

"Me neither. I never seen anyone move as fast as he did."

"Yeah, well, iffen he hadn't already pinned you to the wall with that knife, I would'a had a shot at him," McDougal said. "I could'a kilt him then, and it would'a been self-defense."

"Why didn't you?"

"'Cause I told you, you was in the way."

"So you say. But truth to tell, when you come runnin' into the room, he was already standin' there with his gun draw'd, pointin' right at your innards."

"That's the truth," McDougal admitted. "Wait a minute, ain't that him comin' up the road there?"

Colby looked out the window in the direction McDougal was pointing.

"Yeah," he said. "That's him, all right. Couldn't be nobody else, dressed like he is, with them buckskins and that hat."

They watched Preacher ride the length of the street, then stop in front of the Ohio Bank for Savings. Dismounting, he tied his horse off, then went inside.

"Mr. Blanton was right. He come right here to this bank for his gold, just like he said he would."

They waited for several minutes, drinking beer and watching the bank and the street, until they saw Preacher coming back out of the bank, carrying a sack.

"Look at that there sack he's carryin'. Looks like he got the gold," McDougal said.

"Yeah, but he won't keep it very long," Colby said. "I'm going to enjoy takin' it from him almost as much as I would killin' him."

To their surprise, Preacher didn't remount. Instead, he walked across the street, still carrying the sack of gold. They watched as he went into the small brick building that sat on the corner.

"What the hell?" McDougal said. "He's gone into the sheriff's office."

"Yeah," Colby said. "The question is, what's he gone in there for?"

"Maybe he's going to have the sheriff ride back to Portsmouth with him to guard the money," McDougal suggested.

"No, a sheriff ain't goin' to do somethin' like that. He'd have to hire him a private guard."

"Well, maybe he's going to the sheriff to find out where he can come by someone like that."

"Yeah, that could be, I suppose," Colby said. "But to tell you the truth, the way that fella handled himself, don't seem to me like he would be a-needin' no private guards."

They waited another few minutes, watching the front of the sheriff's office. Then Preacher and Sheriff Wallace came out together.

"Wait a minute, this ain't no guardin'. This is somethin' else," Colby said.

Colby was right. When Preacher and Sheriff Wallace left the sheriff's office, they rode, not toward Portsmouth, but in the opposite direction.

"What do you reckon this is all about?" McDougal asked.

"I don't know," Colby replied. "But I reckon about the only thing we can do is trail 'em and find out what they're up to."

Colby and McDougal trailed Preacher and the sheriff, always remaining some distance away so they could keep up with what was going on without compromising their presence. When they saw Preacher and the sheriff heading toward a small farmhouse, they dismounted and moved their horses into a clump of trees so they could watch without being observed.

"You know who I think that is?" Colby said after a moment of watching Preacher and the sheriff in conversation with the person who had climbed down from the roof of the house to meet them.

"Who?"

"I think that's the Potter boy," Colby said. "You mind, it was in the paper back in Portsmouth. He's the one somebody killed his parents."

"Yeah, I remember that. But what's he's talkin' to Coopersmith for?" McDougal asked.

"I don't know, but as long as the sheriff's there too, there's not much we can do but just wait and watch," Colby said.

"So what do we do now?" McDougal asked.

Colby stroked his jaw for a moment as he tried to determine what their next move should be. Finally, he reached a decision.

"Get mounted," he said. "We're headin' back to Portsmouth."

"What?" McDougal replied in protest. "Didn't you say we was goin' to take that gold offen him?"

"Yes, and we are," Colby said. "But not while the sheriff is around. I don't know what all this is about, but I got me a feelin' that it don't have nothin' to do with us. So, I figure the sheriff will go back to his office in Alexandria, while Coopersmith takes the gold back to Portsmouth. Don't forget, he wants to pay off the loan so he can get his pappy's farm back."

"Yeah, all right," McDougal said, remounting. "Let's go."

Leaving Preacher and the sheriff in conversation with Billy Potter, Colby and McDougal started back toward Portsmouth. Almost exactly halfway between the two towns, the road made a curve around a rather large outcropping of rocks.

"Right here," Colby said, pointing to the rocks. "It's perfect. We can see him comin', and he won't see us."

Dismounting, they ground-hobbled their horses, then took up a position that allowed them to see nearly a mile down the road.

They waited.

Colby slapped at a fly.

McDougal got up.

"Where you goin'?" Colby asked.

"To take a piss," McDougal answered.

Colby had turned his attention back to the road when he heard McDougal.

"Woo-wee, look at this," McDougal said.

"Look at what?"

"I'm tryin' to piss this here grasshopper offen a weed, but the little son of a bitch just grabbed hold and is hangin' on," McDougal said.

"McDougal, you are one strange shit, did you know that?" Colby asked.

McDougal came back to the rock, buttoning up his pants as he did so. "See anything yet?"

"No," Colby replied. "If I had seen something, I would've told you."

They waited for several more minutes. Then McDougal spoke again.

"Here he comes."

"And the sheriff ain't with 'im," Colby said. He pulled a hood from his saddlebag and slipped it on over his head. "Let's get the job done."

Preacher was riding back to Portsmouth when two men suddenly appeared in front of him, jumping out from behind a rock. Both men were wearing hoods over their faces, with nothing but tiny holes for their eyes. Both were armed and they had their pistols, charged and cocked, leveled at him.

Had it not been for the fact that they were armed, Preacher might have laughed at them. The hoods over their heads did absolutely nothing to conceal their identities. Colby and McDougal were still wearing the same clothes they'd had on in Blanton's bank earlier this morning. Preacher put up his hands.

"All right, my hands are up," Preacher said. "What do you want?"

"I want you to untie that there money bag from your saddle pommel and hand it over here," one of the men said, his voice somewhat muffled by the hood.

Slowly, Preacher did as he was told, handing it to the one who had extended his hand. The robber tied the sack to his own saddle pommel.

"Hand over your gun too," that same robber said.

Preacher gave the robber his pistol.

"Now, get down from your horse," the robber added, making a motion with his gun.

"What you goin' to do with him?" the other robber asked.

"This is a tricky son of a bitch," the first robber said. "I aim to make sure we get away." He took the horse's reins. "Let's go!" he said.

Preacher stood in the road and watched as the two robbers left with his horse, money bag, and pistol. Inexplicably, he laughed. Then, with no choice but to walk, he resumed his journey back to Portsmouth.

He had gone about a mile and a half when he saw his brother-in-law's horse standing alongside the road, calmly cropping grass. He didn't know if the horse had bolted, or if the robbers had let it go. Either way, the horse was clearly a welcome sight.

"Whoa, boy," Preacher said, speaking gently to him. He went over to the horse and patted him on the face a couple of times, then remounted and continued his journey as if nothing had happened.

Preacher's first stop when he returned to Portsmouth was the bank. Going inside, he headed straight for Blanton's office.

"Here, sir, you can't just go barging into Mr. Blanton's office," one of the bank employees called out to him as Preacher walked by the teller's cage.

"Sure I can," Preacher replied airily. "Blanton and I are old friends now, and he is expecting me."

Pushing the door open to Blanton's office, Preacher saw the angry banker staring down at the top of his desk. Standing to either side of Blanton, with perplexed and frustrated expressions on their faces, were Colby and McDougal. On the desk in front of Blanton was a cloth bag imprinted with the words "Ohio Bank For Savings." It was the same bag Preacher had gotten from Burt Rowe at the bank in Alexandria, and the same bag he had given up to the highwaymen.

Also on the top of Blanton's desk were several of the rusting iron washers Preacher had bought from Billy Potter.

"Good afternoon, Mr. Blanton," Preacher said cheerfully. He was carrying another sack, and from this sack, he began pulling gold coins and putting them in little piles on the top of Blanton's desk.

"I believe you asked for payment in gold?" Preacher said.

"What the . . ." Colby said with a sputter. He pointed to the gold coins Preacher was stacking up. "Where the hell did you get that gold?"

"Why, you know exactly where I got it, Mr. Colby. You and McDougal were sitting in the saloon across from the bank when I cashed the bank drafts."

"What? How'd you know we was there?" McDougal asked, sputtering in surprise.

"Shut up, McDougal," Blanton said with an angry snarl. "Are you that damn stupid that you haven't figured this out yet?"

"What?" McDougal asked, still clearly confused.

"And now, Mr. Blanton, if you please, I'd like the mortgage to Pa's place," Preacher said.

With an angry look and a snort of disgust, Blanton got up from his desk and walked over to a cabinet, where he jerked open a drawer. After rifling through a few papers, he pulled one out, then came back and slapped it down on the desk in front of Preacher.

"Here it is," he said. "Take the damn thing and be damned."

Preacher looked at the document for a moment, then handed it back to Blanton.

"What now?"

"I would appreciate it if you would write, on the bottom, 'This debt is paid in full,' then sign your name, please."

Blanton did as Preacher asked, signing his name in a large, illegible scrawl, before returning the paper to Preacher.

Preacher folded the paper carefully and put it in his pocket. Then, looking at the top of Blanton's desk, he asked, almost conversationally, "Are you going fishing?"

"Fishing?" Blanton replied.

Preacher pointed to the pile of washers on Blanton's desk.

"Yes," Preacher said. "I'm told those make very good weights. And since you aren't a mechanic, I can't think of any other reason you might have them on your desk."

"Fishing weights?" Blanton growled angrily. He swept several of them from his desk and, as they clattered and clanged to the floor, he looked over at McDougal and Colby. "You brought me fishing weights?"

"How were we supposed to know?" McDougal asked. "They were in a bank bag and . . ."

"McDougal, shut the hell up!" Colby shouted.

"Oh, yeah," McDougal said, growing quiet.

Preacher began stacking the gold coins up on the desk. When he was finished with the coins, he piled up an equally high stack of the washers right alongside. Then he put his finger on each one of them.

"You shouldn't be so hard on them, Blanton," Preacher said. "When you stop and think about it, if you put a bunch of iron washers in a bank sack, almost anyone might think they were gold coins."

"You've got the deed to your father's farm now," Blanton said between clenched teeth. "I want you to take it, get the hell out of my office, and stay out."

"It's been a pleasure doing business with you," Preacher said with a little laugh.

* * *

"I just wish I could've been a fly on the wall whenever ole Klyce Blanton dumped out that sack and what he thought was gold turned out to be nothing but iron washers," Preacher's brother, Morgan, said with a laugh.

The others laughed as well.

It was a gala dinner, with Preacher's mother cooking everything she remembered as her oldest son's favorite. The whole family was laughing and talking, celebrating the fact that, once more, the farm was owned free and clear.

Despite the celebratory atmosphere, though, Preacher's father seemed unusually subdued. After a while, he excused himself from the table, then went outside.

"What's wrong with your pa?" Betty's husband, Jim, asked.

"Nothing, he'll be all right," Betty said.

"Sylvanias is a proud man," Preacher's mother said of her husband. "When the rest of us learned what a wonderful thing Arthur was doing, we went to him and begged him to accept this."

"We finally convinced him," Morgan said. "But it's not sitting well with him."

"He'll get over it," Preacher's mother said to her son, reaching across the table to pat him on the back of his hand. "He just needs a little time, that's all."

"Hey, Vaughan, tell me again about Blanton's nose," Morgan said.

Although he had already told the story Ed was spreading around town, he retold it, adding his own embellishments.

"Whatever he looks like now, it has to be an improvement," Tess said, and once again the dining room echoed with laughter.

With the others were engaged in animated conversation, Preacher left. A moment later, he pushed the front door open, then stepped out onto the porch. He saw his father standing against the porch railing, looking down toward the river.

The air was soft and warm, and filled with the sounds of the night: frogs calling for their mates, insects, and night birds. A mule brayed in the barn. Fireflies winked over the rolling land between the house and the river.

"Peaceful out here," Preacher said.

"Yes," Sylvanias answered.

Preacher walked over to stand beside him. A streak of light raced across the sky.

"There's a falling star," Preacher said.

"They tell me stars are really bright out in the mountains," Sylvanias said. "Is that so?"

"Yes, sir," Preacher said. "Sometimes you get the idea you could just about reach up and pull one down."

Sylvanias was quiet for another moment, and Preacher didn't intrude into the silence. Finally, he spoke again.

"Art, I don't want you to think I'm not grateful for what you did," he said. "Paying off the mortgage and all."

"I don't think that," Preacher said.

"But it's hard for me to accept somethin' I didn't earn."

"Pa, when a man has sons, he expects his sons to be a help to him until they get out on their own. Maybe they start small, picking up a few things here and there, then feeding the stock. But the time comes when the son has to carry a full share of the load.

"That happened with Morgan. He came of age and started carrying his full share of the load. But I never did. I left home, and I deprived you of what you had every right to expect. I know that paying off this mortgage doesn't nearly pay you back for all that I owe you, but I hope it helps."

Again, Sylvanias was silent. "You'll be going on tomorrow?" he asked.

"Yes, sir," Preacher said.

"Chasing the man who killed your woman."

"Turns out he also killed the Potters, over in Alexandria," Preacher said.

Sylvanias nodded. "Yes, I remember reading about that in Jim's newspaper. I reckon stopping someone like him is a noble enough deed. Just be careful. Even if you aren't going to stay here, it's nice knowing you are alive somewhere."

"I'll be careful," Preacher promised.

"Preacher, you'll always have a place to come to. I want you to know that."

"Thanks, Pa. I do know it, and I take comfort in it."

It did not escape Preacher's notice that his father called him Preacher. In so doing, Preacher knew his father was letting him know that he had forgiven his young son Arthur for leaving home so long ago, and now accepted Preacher on his own terms.

For the first time in fifteen years, Preacher was absolutely at peace with himself over that rash decision he had made while still a boy.

18

Philadelphia

Caviness had thought that St. Louis was a big city, but Philadelphia was ten times bigger. He had never seen as much activity as he saw when he arrived in the City of Brotherly Love.

He saw a lot of strange things, such as long wagons with several windows down each side, filled with seats on which people entered and left, seemingly without rhyme or reason. Someone referred to the wagon as an omnibus, and it was pulled by a single horse along rails of iron.

In addition to the omnibuses, there were literally hundreds of wagons and carriages of all sizes and descriptions, their iron-rimmed wheels ringing and the shod hooves clattering on the cobblestone-paved streets. Often, several of the wagons and carriages would congregate at a street intersection and some of the drivers would blow through the trumpets they carried, while others shouted impatiently as they tried to disentangle themselves.

In addition to the wheeled vehicles, there were also men on horseback, though there were not nearly as many riders as there were drivers and passengers of the wheeled vehicles.

Even the walks, alongside the streets, were filled with people, rushing to and fro, pushing, crowding as they hurried to wherever they were going.

Caviness saw a man standing on the corner, waiting to cross the street, and he rode over to him.

"Hey, you," Caviness said. "Where at can I find me a man by the name of Epson?"

"I have no idea," the man replied.

"Epson," Caviness said again, thinking that if he repeated the name, the man might be able to answer.

"No doubt there are scores of Epsons in Philadelphia," the man said. "And even if I knew any of them, which I don't, I would have no idea which one you are talking about."

At that moment there was a break in the traffic, and the man walked quickly across the street.

Caviness inquired of several more people, with an equal lack of success. Then, as he was riding along slowly, taking everything in, he heard a trumpet being blown behind him. The horn was so close and so loud that it made his horse jump. He had to jerk back on the reins to keep the animal under control. Looking around, he saw a carriage in which four well-dressed men were riding.

The men were sitting back in the passenger section of the carriage, engaged in animated conversation, oblivious of the traffic around them. But the driver, a large, liveried black man, was acutely aware of what was going on. He was the one who had blown the horn, and now he was standing up, shaking the trumpet at Caviness.

"Mister, if you don't know what you are doing, get out of the road!" he shouted angrily.

Caviness was shocked. He had never heard a black man talk to a white man in such a fashion, and he looked to the passengers in the carriage to see if they would remind their driver of his station.

To Caviness's surprise, they not only did not correct him,

but one of them shouted out, "We're late, James. Get us through all this."

"Yes, sir," James replied. James picked up a whip and snapped it very close to Caviness's face. "Now, mister, do you get out of the way, or do I whip you out of the way?"

With an angry glare at the black driver, Caviness moved his horse to one side. As the carriage passed him by, Caviness heard one of the men laugh.

"Where did that oaf come from?"

Caviness continued to ride up and down the streets, asking about Epson. Most of the time, he got no response of any kind, and those who did reply said that they couldn't help him.

It was nearly noon, and as he rode by a few of the restaurants, he could smell the aroma of cooking food. The smells reminded him that he was hungry, but they also reminded him that he had no money.

Seeing a hitching rail, Caviness dismounted and tied off his horse.

"Mister, you can't leave your horse here," a fancy-dressed man told him.

"Why not?"

"Only members can tie their horses or park their carriages here."

"Only members of what?"

"Why, members of the Philadelphia Social Club, of course," the man replied haughtily.

"Are you a member?"

"Do I look like a member, dressed as I am?" The man was wearing a tri-corn hat, a red jacket with brass buttons, and yellow pants tucked down into highly polished brown boots.

"I don't know, you look pretty fancy-dressed to me," Caviness replied.

"I am sergeant at arms for the group," the man said. "This is my uniform."

"They got 'em somebody from the Army to look after

things for them, do they? I never heard of such a thing. What do them folks do in that club?"

"The same thing as they do in any club," the sergeant at arms replied. "They drink, eat, socialize, discuss matters of importance."

"You don't say. Well, that sounds good to me. Especially the eatin' part. I think I'll join."

The sergeant at arms laughed out loud. "That's very funny."

"No, I'm serious, I'll join. Where do I go to join up with 'em?"

"You have to apply for membership, and you must have two sponsors who are already members. Then, when they vote on you, you must be unanimously accepted. If but one member blackballs you, you will not be allowed in. And if you are allowed in, then you must pay the entrance fee and the dues."

"How much is that?"

"If you have to ask, it is too much," the sergeant at arms said. "Now, please, take your horse and go somewhere else."

Grumbling, Caviness remounted and rode away. He had never heard of such a thing as a private club, but if they ate and drank, it sounded fine to him. Maybe Epson could tell him how to get in. Or maybe Epson already belonged to such a club. That fancy-dressed sergeant had told him that he would have to know someone who already belonged in order to be a member.

Two more times, Caviness attempted to tie off his horse, but he was run away both times, once because it was in front of someone's house . . . though the house was larger than any hotel Caviness had ever seen. The other time, he was told that the hitching rail was for customers only. He was beginning to wonder if there was any place in Philadelphia for a visitor to tie his horse.

Where the hell was Epson anyway? And how was he going to find him?

More important than finding Epson right now was getting something to eat. This wasn't like it was back in St. Louis, where he knew which households he could go to begging for food. Now, with his ear cut off, he made such a terrifying appearance that women were afraid of him. And it was his experience that women would have nothing to do with men who frightened them.

Caviness continued to ride through the city until he reached an area where there were far fewer people. There, he found a sapling, and at last was able to secure his horse.

Looking around, he saw that, though he was still in the city, this particular area had grass, shrubbery, and trees. It was actually a park, though "park" wasn't a term Caviness would have recognized.

Looking across the open area, he saw a man walking along a path. The path led down into a grove of trees, where it disappeared. Moving quickly, Caviness hurried down to those same trees and followed the man along the path. Within moments, the city seemed far away. So isolated were they that they could have been in the middle of the deep woods somewhere. This was more to Caviness's liking.

Caviness knew he would not get a better opportunity than this. Taking out his knife, he moved quickly up the path until he saw, just ahead of him, the man he had seen earlier. Walking quickly but quietly, Caviness moved up on him so silently that his victim didn't even know Caviness was there until he felt a hand clamp down across his mouth.

Caviness pulled the knife across the man's throat, then dropped him to the ground. The man flopped around a few times, like a fish out of water, and died.

Looking around to make certain nobody had seen him, Caviness then bent down over the body and began searching his pockets. A moment later, he pulled out a wallet, and was gratified to see that it contained fourteen dollars in paper money.

"Well, now," Caviness said aloud. "It 'pears as if my luck is changin'."

Sticking the billfold into his own pocket, Caviness hurried back to his horse, mounted, then rode to one of the restaurants. This time, when he tied off in front of the restaurant, he wasn't challenged.

THIRD MURDER VICTIM FOUND
Like Previous Two, Has Throat Cut

Philadelphia is being besieged with a string of gruesome murders. In but two weeks, three of our finest and most promising gentlemen have been killed by an unknown assailant in a manner so foul as to defy description.

The most recent victim was Mr. B.G. Grant, age 31. Like the other two victims, Mr. Grant was found with his throat cut, in a part of the city that is less traveled. It is believed that the murderer lies in wait in these more remote locations, picking his victims at a time when no one else is around to offer assistance.

The constabulary force of Philadelphia is searching for this heinous killer, and asks all to be on the alert for anything suspicious. Our citizens are cautioned against finding themselves alone in such areas, lest the killer strike again.

Theodore Epson was reading the newspaper when an office boy approached his desk.

"Mr. Epson?"

Epson looked up from his paper. "Yes, Johnny, what is it?" he asked.

"Mr. Fontaine asks that you come to his office."

It had been some time since Fontaine had mentioned anything to Epson about the matter in St. Louis, and Epson thought that the matter was closed. Then he remembered that Miller was going to St. Louis.

"Did he say what it was about?"

"No, sir, he didn't say."

"Tell me, do you know if Mr. Miller has returned from St. Louis?"

"Yes, sir, he has," the office boy replied. "He's in Mr. Fontaine's office now."

Once again, Epson felt a sense of apprehension. Had Miller found something incriminating during his trip to St. Louis?

"Are the other members of the board there as well?"

"No, sir. Just Mr. Fontaine and Mr. Miller," Johnny answered.

Epson breathed a sigh of relief. If none of the other board members were present, then it didn't seem very likely that anything was going to happen. Walking erect, as if he had nothing to worry about, Epson crossed the bank to Fontaine's office. He started to knock on the door, but was interrupted by Joel Fontaine's appointments clerk.

"Mr. Fontaine said for you to just go right in, sir," the appointments clerk said. "He and Mr. Miller are waiting for you."

"Thank you," Epson said.

He pushed the door open and, hesitantly, stepped into Fontaine's office.

"Come in, Mr. Epson, come in," Fontaine called. "You remember Mr. Miller?"

"Yes, of course," Epson said. "How was your trip to St. Louis?"

"Tiring," Miller replied. "And disagreeable. St. Louis may call itself a city, but in fact it is nothing more than a frontier town. They have few of the amenities of a real city."

"Have a seat, Mr. Epson," Fontaine said, pointing to a comfortable chair that was close to his desk. This was a much better sign than the last time he was in here, when he was forced to sit in a hard, straight-back chair that was purposely set apart from the others.

"Thank you," he said. Epson was still carrying the newspaper he had been reading, and he held it now, folded across his lap.

"Mr. Miller has a bit of disturbing news for us," Fontaine said.

"You have some disturbing news?" Epson leaned forward in his chair, once more feeling a sense of apprehension.

"Yes, well, disturbing in its content. Though in one way, I suppose it is good news for you. Though not the way you would like to hear it, I'm sure."

"What is it? I don't understand what you are talking about."

"Mr. Miller, suppose you tell Mr. Epson what you told me."

"Yes. Well, as you know, Mr. Epson, it was my intention, when I reached St. Louis, to question this Miss Jennie, to see what I could find out about all these claims she has been filing against you."

"And did you interview her, sir?"

"No, I'm afraid that was not possible. When I arrived in St. Louis, I inquired about her at the bank, only to learn that she was dead."

"Dead? Jennie is dead?"

"Yes. She was murdered."

"Oh, my," Epson said.

"That means, of course, that the constant barrage of charges she has been lodging against you, whether spurious or valid, will stop."

"Yes, sir," Epson said. "And I assure you, sir, they were spurious."

"I'm sure that they were, though now we will really never know. At any rate, tragic though it might be, her demise is to your advantage," Fontaine said.

"Yes, sir, I suppose it is." Epson laughed weakly. "I suppose it is good that I did not go to St. Louis to answer these charges, for if I had, I would surely be a suspect now."

"That is so," Fontaine replied. "But since you were clearly here in Philadelphia when the poor girl was murdered, you are not under any suspicion."

"No, I wouldn't think that I am," Epson said, relief clearly showing in his voice.

"Do they know who did kill her?" Fontaine asked Miller.

"Seems she was attacked by two men, but one of them, a man by the name of Slater, was killed by her dog. They know there was another one, because they found his ear. Seems the dog chewed it off."

"Do they have any idea who the other one was?"

"They are looking for a man named Caviness," Miller said.

Epson gasped slightly. "Caviness?" he asked.

"Yes. Do you know him?"

"I, uh, know who he is," Epson replied. "He was a ne'er-do-well who hung around town. A one-time fur trapper who wasn't very good at it, as I recall. How do they know he was involved?"

"They don't know for sure, but it seems he and Slater had been seen together earlier that night, and Caviness hasn't been seen since."

"Terrible thing," Fontaine said, clucking and shaking his head.

"It is indeed," Miller agreed. "And one might say that the poor girl was murdered because St. Louis is such a wild frontier town that there is little law and less civil behavior. But I understand now that while I was gone, we had three murders in as many weeks right here in our own city of Philadelphia."

"Yes," Epson said. He held up the newspaper. "As a matter of fact, I've been reading about them."

"Ironically, the poor souls who died here were killed in just as gruesome a fashion as was the lady in St. Louis," Miller continued. "They died by having their throats cut. And that is exactly how the young lady of your acquaintance died."

"I respectfully ask that you not refer to her as a person of my acquaintance, since that suggests that there was a relationship when, clearly, none existed," Epson said.

"I'm sorry. I didn't mean to imply that you had a relationship with the lady," Miller explained.

"Woman," Epson corrected.

"I beg your pardon?"

"As I've explained before, the woman in question is, uh, that is, she was a prostitute. A common whore. It seems to me inappropriate to call a harlot a lady."

"Perhaps that is so," Fontaine replied. "But I would hope you could be a bit more generous in your comments about her now that the poor lady is dead."

Fontaine came down harder on the word "lady."

"After all," he continued, "her untimely death has cleared you of all suspicion."

"Yes, sir, it has indeed," Epson said, unable to prevent the smile from spreading across his face.

So great was Epson's relief over how things had turned out that he didn't even notice the disapproving look Fontaine and Miller exchanged.

"That is all, Mr. Epson. You may return to your work now," Fontaine said with a slight, dismissive wave of his hand.

"Very good, sir," Epson replied.

When Epson returned to his desk, he pulled out the newspaper and attempted to read, but though he tried hard, he was unable to finish the story. He couldn't keep his mind off the meeting he had just had with Fontaine and Miller.

Was he responsible for Jennie's death? He could be, he knew. In his last letter to Caviness he had been very specific about what he wanted. He'd wanted his troubles to go away, and he'd said exactly that in his letter.

But he had not been specific as to how he meant for Caviness to make those troubles go away.

It now appeared as if Caviness had decided that the only way to make that happen was by killing Jennie.

Epson felt a momentary twinge of regret over that. He did not consider himself a criminal, even though he had taken 950 dollars that didn't belong to him.

Some might call him a thief for that, but in his mind, a thief was someone who stole by force or stealth, and he had done neither. Although he had not come by his windfall of 950 dollars in what could be described as an honest way, he had not stolen it in any way that he would describe as theft. After all, the money had been dropped in his lap. He'd merely taken advantage of that, as he was sure any astute businessman would.

He was not a thief.

Nor was he a murderer.

He did not kill Jennie, though it now seemed certain that Caviness did. And if Caviness did kill her, it was surely in response to his specific instructions to make his "problems go away."

He wondered where Caviness was now. If, as Miller said, his ear had been chewed off, there was a good chance Caviness was dead somewhere. It would be hard to stop the bleeding in a wound like that. The wound could also putrefy. Either one could kill him.

19

When Preacher awoke, he got out of bed, walked over to the window of his hotel room, and looked out over the city of Philadelphia. Arriving by stagecoach after dark last night, he had gone to a hotel, deciding to start his search today.

There was a knock on his door and for a moment, he was startled by it. Who would be calling on him? Who even knew he was here?

"Breakfast," a muffled voice announced from the other side of the door, and Preacher relaxed. He remembered now that when he'd arrived last night, he'd been asked if he would like breakfast delivered to his room this morning.

Crossing the room quickly, Preacher opened the door to see a young black boy, no more than twelve years old, holding a tray. From somewhere in the back of his mind he knew that a tip was required, so he handed the boy a coin.

"Thank you, sir," the boy said with a wide grin.

Preacher took the tray into his room, put it on a table, pulled up a chair, and began having his breakfast. He chuckled as he compared this breakfast, in a plush hotel room in a large eastern city, with the breakfasts he had eaten in the wilderness over the last several years.

"I'd better watch myself," he said aloud as he reached for a jar of marmalade. "I could learn to like this awfully easily."

Even as he spoke the words, he knew that he couldn't really live like this. Already he was feeling restricted, and he missed the mountains that had become his home.

He also realized that he had better watch himself as far as speaking to himself was concerned. It was a habit he had developed in the wilderness, but that wasn't needed here. In a city the size of Philadelphia, he had plenty of opportunity to hear other voices and to speak to other people. There was no justification for speaking to himself, and if anyone heard him, they might think him crazy.

A newspaper had been delivered with his meal, and as Preacher put marmalade on his biscuit, he glanced through the paper. He had just raised the biscuit to take a bite when he read the headline over one of the articles.

FOURTH VICTIM FOUND WITH THROAT CUT

Preacher read the story carefully, and by the time he finished both his breakfast and the newspaper, he was totally convinced that Ben Caviness was in Philadelphia. He was convinced of that fact because he was certain that Caviness was the Philadelphia murderer.

Preacher stood in front of a rather substantial-looking brick building looking up at the sign over the front door. The sign read PHILADELPHIA POLICE AGENCY.

Unlike St. Louis, which had a constable and a deputy, Philadelphia had a well-organized police agency, consisting of constables, wardens, and watchmen. The watchmen patrolled the city from "watch boxes," which were scattered throughout the town.

Preacher went inside, where he was met by a man who was wearing a domed hat with a badge.

"Yes, sir, can I help you?"

"I'd like to speak to whoever is in charge," Preacher said.

"That would be Chief Constable Dolan," the man said. "May I tell him what this is about?"

"Yes," Preacher said. "I think I know who is doing all the killings here."

"Do you now?" To Preacher's surprise, the man began filling his pipe.

"What is your name?" Preacher asked.

"I'm Constable Coleman," the man said as he tamped down the tobacco in the bowl of his pipe.

"Well, Constable Coleman, are you going to tell the chief constable that I would like to see him?" Preacher asked.

"And just who do you think is doing the killing?" Coleman asked.

"I'd rather give that information to the chief constable," Preacher replied.

Coleman lit his pipe, then drew several puffs, encircling his head with wreaths of smoke, before he responded.

"Well, now, here's the thing," Coleman said. "You are the tenth person to come in here with an idea as to who is doing the killing."

"I am?" Preacher replied, surprised by Coleman's comment. "Have that many people heard of Ben Caviness?"

Coleman had just started to take another puff of his pipe, but he pulled it away from his lips. Now the expression on his face changed to one of interest.

"Wait a minute," he said. "Do you really know who this is?"

"Well, I know Ben Caviness, I know that he has killed like this before, and I know he is in Philadelphia, because I followed him here."

"You followed him here?"

"From St. Louis," Preacher said.

Coleman studied Preacher for a moment longer. Then he said, "Wait here. I'll tell the chief constable that you would like to speak to him."

"Thank you."

A moment later, Coleman returned and escorted Preacher to a room in the back of the building.

"I'm Chief Constable Dolan," a tall, bewhiskered man said, extending his hand. "And you are?"

"Folks call me Preacher," Preacher said.

"Well, Preacher, Constable Coleman here tells me that you know who our murderer is."

"Yes, I do," Preacher said. "Or at least, I think I know."

"Well, which is it? You do know, or you think you know?" Coleman asked.

Preacher told them the story of his quest, beginning with the fact that he was a mountain man and fur trapper who had come back to St. Louis when he learned that a female friend of his had had her throat cut by a man named Ben Caviness.

"She was killed in the same way as the four people in this city were killed," Preacher said. "That is, if the details in the newspaper article are correct." He thumped the newspaper with his thumb.

"And from that you have concluded that this Ben Caviness is the person we are looking for?" the chief constable asked.

"Yes."

"Other than the fact that the woman in St. Louis was killed by having her throat cut, and the victims here were killed by having their throats cut, what possible connection can you make?" Dolan asked. "One event took place in St. Louis, which is at least a thousand miles from here, and the other events took place here in Philadelphia."

"There was also a similar event in Alexandria, Ohio," Preacher said.

"Where is Alexandria, Ohio?" Coleman asked.

"That is a town on the Ohio River, between here and St.

Louis. There, two people, a husband and his wife, had their throats cut."

"And you think the person who killed the two people in Ohio is the same person you are looking for?"

"Yes, I know it is," Preacher replied.

"How do you know it is the same person?"

"Because there were witnesses to that murder. The two people who were killed were Mr. and Mrs. Potter. And their son and daughter saw the killer."

"Oh," the chief constable said. "Oh, my. Do you mean to tell me that those two children saw their own parents killed?"

"Yes. Well, they weren't children exactly. The boy was seventeen years old, and made a very credible witness. There is no doubt that the person he described as the killer is Ben Caviness."

The chief constable clucked, and shook his head. "What a shame they should have to witness such a thing," he said. "But how can you be certain that the man they described is the one you are looking for? I mean, just in a general description."

"This was more than a general description," Preacher explained. "Turns out that when Caviness attacked the woman in St. Louis, her dog chewed off his ear."

"I'll be damned," the chief said. "So what you are telling me is that you have come to Philadelphia to look for a man with one ear, who also happens to be cutting down our citizens like a scythe through wheat."

"Yes," Preacher replied.

"All right, suppose I believe everything you are saying. And, God help me, I think I do believe you. What makes you think that this Caviness person you are looking for is even in Philadelphia?"

"Because I think he has come here to extort money from Theodore Epson. He used to be a banker at the River Bank of St. Louis. But now he is with some bank here." Preacher went on to explain how Epson had stolen money from Jennie.

"And when Jennie started making trouble for him, I believe he hired Ben Caviness to kill her," he said, finishing the explanation.

"That is about the wildest story I've ever heard," Constable Coleman said. He looked at the chief constable. "Chief, I apologize for bringing him in here to see you. I thought he might have something, but he is really clutching at straws to put all that together and say that that we are looking for the same man."

"I'm not so sure, Coleman," the chief constable said. He drummed his fingers on the desk for a moment. "As crazy as it sounds, I think it might be exactly the way he says."

"So, what are we going to do? Start looking for a man with only one ear?" Coleman asked.

"Why not? At least it gives us something and someone to look for. That's better than chasing after a ghost."

"Yeah," Coleman said. "Yeah, I guess you do have a point there."

"I intend to search for him as well," Preacher said. He showed Dolan the letter that had been given to him by Constable Billings back in St. Louis.

Dolan looked at the letter for a moment. "Well, I'm afraid this letter won't have much authority with any of our judges here."

"I see," Preacher said. He didn't react negatively to it because he had already made up his mind. With or without local permission, he was going to hunt Ben Caviness down, and he was going to make certain that justice was done.

"But," the chief constable continued, pulling out a piece of paper, "I can take care of that." He wrote something on the paper, then signed his name. "I'll make you my special deputy. This will give you authority to act in Philadelphia."

"Thank you," Preacher replied.

* * *

Epson had never seen or even heard of Preacher. But when he saw Preacher come into the Trust Bank of Philadelphia, he had a feeling about him. The man wearing buckskins was tall and muscular, like someone who lived and worked in the wilderness. He had seen several such men when he was in St. Louis. And if this man was from St. Louis, that couldn't be good.

He watched as the man spoke to someone, then, with a sinking feeling, watched the man approach his desk.

"Your name is Theodore Epson?" the man asked when he reached Epson.

"I am," Epson replied. "And you are?"

"Preacher."

"Preacher?"

"That's all you need to know. Epson, Jennie was a friend of mine. In fact, she was a very special friend, if you get my meaning."

"Jennie?"

"Yes, Jennie. You will remember her, I'm sure. She is the young lady you stole nine hundred fifty dollars from."

"I did no such thing!"

"Sure you did," Preacher said easily. "Both Mr. Ashley and Jennie gave you the money to pay off her mortgage and you kept it."

"There are no signed papers anywhere that support that claim," Epson said. "You would never be able to prove that in a court of justice."

Preacher chuckled ominously. "You don't understand, do you, Epson? I don't need to prove it. I only need to believe it. I'm the only justice you will ever see."

"What . . . what are you going to do?" Epson asked, his voice quivering in fear.

"Oh, I don't intend to do anything yet. You are my bait."

"Your bait?"

"I'm a fur trapper, Epson. I know that you don't catch your

quarry without using bait. Right now, my quarry is the man who killed Jennie. Things didn't work out quite the way he thought they would, so it's my bet that he'll be looking you up. Since he's already in Philadelphia, all I have to do is keep an eye on you. Like I said, Epson, you are my bait."

"Ben Caviness is in Philadelphia?"

Preacher laughed dryly. "I didn't say anything about Ben Caviness."

At first, Epson thought he had been caught. Then he smiled as he remembered that Miller said Caviness was the murder suspect in Jennie's case.

"No, you didn't say anything about him, but Mr. Miller did. Mr. Miller just returned from St. Louis, and he told me about the tragic events surrounding Miss Jennie. And he said that Ben Caviness was the prime suspect, so naturally, when you said the murderer was in Philadelphia, I made the connection."

"Did you now?" Preacher asked.

"Yes. How else would I have known that you were talking about Ben Caviness?"

"I wonder," Preacher replied. "How else?"

"What makes you think Caviness is in Philadelphia?"

"As he passed through Ohio, on his way to Philadelphia, he killed a man and his wife by slitting their throats. There have been four killed here by having their throats slit. I believe the killer is Ben Caviness."

Involuntarily, Epson put his hand to his own throat. "What I don't understand is why you think he would want to look me up."

"Like I said, things didn't go well for him back in St. Louis. I think he's coming to see you in order to ask for more money."

"I'm . . . sure that I don't know what you talking about," Epson said, though his protest sounded weak even to his own ears.

* * *

Caviness was sitting at a table with three others in the Bucket of Blood Tavern. He no longer resembled the man who had arrived in Philadelphia nearly six weeks ago. His hair had grown long enough to cover the missing ear. And with the money he took from the men he had killed, he'd bought clothes that were more in the style of the average Philadelphia citizen. Because he was now blending in with the others, he no longer drew curious stares from the casual observer. He was still rough-looking, but no more rough looking than the men who were sitting at the table with him.

To the degree that a person like Caviness could make friends, he had befriended these three. Several times over the last few days, he had encountered them here in the Bucket of Blood Tavern. Like Caviness, none of the three men seemed to have any visible source of income.

Caviness bought a round of beer for them. "I need to find me somebody," he said as he lifted the mug to his lips. "I don't reckon none of you know a feller by the name of Epson, do you?"

"I know a man named Epson," one of the men said. This was Jim Gray. "But he prob'ly ain't the one you're lookin' for."

"How do you know he's not?"

"'Cause he's one of them bigwigs that works in a bank."

"Yes!" Caviness said excitedly. This was his first real lead. "The fella I'm looking for works in a bank. It's got to be the same man. Where is the bank?"

Gray laughed. "Well, they's a lot more'n one bank in Philadelphia," he said. "But the one Epson works in is the Trust Bank. What you need to see him for?"

"He owes me money," Caviness said.

Gray stroked his chin as he stared across the table at Caviness. "Does he now?" he asked.

"Yes."

"What's in it for me if I take you to him?"

"I'll give you a dollar," Caviness replied. He could afford

to be generous. He planned to get a lot more than a dollar from Epson.

"Make it two dollars, and you got yourself a deal," Gray insisted.

"All right, two dollars. But for that, I want you to take me to him."

Gray finished his beer, then wiped the back of his hand across his mouth.

"You got yourself a deal," Gray said. "Let's go." He stood up.

Epson stepped out to the privy behind the bank. When he returned, he saw two men standing by his desk, but as there was nothing unusual about their looks or demeanor, he approached them without any sense of concern.

"Yes, gentlemen, may I help you?" Epson asked, greeting them with his practiced smile.

"Hello, Epson," Caviness said.

"Caviness!" Epson said. "What are you doing here?"

"I took care of that little job you had for me back in St. Louis," Caviness said.

"Shh," Epson said, looking around the bank to see if anyone was close enough to overhear them. "Who is this?" Epson asked, indicating Gray.

"This here is Jim Gray," Caviness said. "He's a pal of mine. Now, about that business in St. Louis."

Epson put his finger across his lips in a signal to be quiet. "Let's step outside to discuss this," he said. "I don't want everyone listening in to our business."

"All right," Caviness agreed.

"Mr. Sinclair, I'm going to step out front for a moment," Epson said to the chief teller.

"Very well, Mr. Epson," Sinclair replied.

The three men walked outside, then stood in front of the bank.

"What are you doing in Philadelphia?" Epson asked.

"I need more money," Caviness replied.

"I paid you a fair price," Epson said.

"Yeah, well, things didn't go the way I thought they would."

"Yes, I know, the dog chewed off your ear, but that's your problem, not mine."

Gray laughed. "That's what happened to you ear?" he said. "A dog chewed it off?"

"It ain't funny," Caviness said. He looked at Epson. "How did you know about my ear?"

"Preacher told me."

"Preacher?" Caviness's eyes grew wide. "Where did you see Preacher?"

"I saw him here in my office yesterday," Epson said.

"What the hell is he doing here?"

"He's after you, Caviness."

Caviness looked around, his face clearly reflecting his fear at the mention of Preacher's name.

"How did the son of a bitch know I was here?"

"He followed you here from St. Louis."

Gray laughed again. "What's got you so spooked?" he asked Caviness. "You that scared of a preacher?"

"He ain't a preacher," Caviness said. Then to Espon, "What did you tell him?"

"How could I tell him anything? I didn't even know you were in Philadelphia."

"This is bad. This is real bad."

Suddenly Epson got an idea. "Maybe not," he said. "Not if we're smart."

"You got an idea?"

"Yes," Epson said. "You want some more money?"

"Hell, yes, I do. I told you, that's why I'm here."

"All right. I'll pay you some more money." He looked at

Gray. "And I'll pay you as well. All you have to do is take care of Preacher."

"What do you mean, 'take care of Preacher'?" Gray asked.

"What do you think I mean?"

"I think it means you want us to kill him," Gray said.

This was Epson's moment of truth. He had danced around being a thief, and he had danced around the responsibility for Jennie's death. But things had gone too far now. It was time to fish or cut bait, and the way he saw it, Preacher had left him no choice.

"Yes," Epson said. "I'll give you one hundred dollars apiece to kill him."

"One hundred dollars? Yeah, I'll do it. How hard can it be to kill a preacher?" Gray replied.

"I told you, he's not a preacher," Caviness said. "And he is going to be a hard man to kill. I've run into him before." Caviness looked at Epson. "A hundred dollars ain't enough. You give me one hundred dollars to take care of your problem in St. Louis. Taking care of your problem here is going to be even harder."

Epson smiled. "He's not just my problem," he said. "He's after you too. Think about it, Caviness. You are going to have to face him one way or the other. This way, at least, you are getting paid for it."

"A hundred dollars sounds good to me," Gray said.

"Make it one hundred and twenty dollars," Caviness said.

"Why one hundred and twenty?" Epson asked.

Caviness looked at Gray. "You think Scott and Kelly would throw in with us for ten dollars apiece?"

Gray laughed. "Yeah, if we don't tell 'em how much we're getting. But you really think we are going to need them?"

"I told you. This Preacher is one tough son of a bitch," Caviness said. "Yeah, we're going to need them." He looked back at Epson. "What about it, Epson? One hundred and twenty dollars apiece?"

"All right," he said. He held up his finger. "But not until the job is done."

"We've got to have some of the money now," Caviness said.

"I'll give you ten dollars apiece now, plus ten dollars for your two friends. Come back to me when the job is done, and I'll give you the rest."

"All right," Caviness agreed. "But try and hold out on me when I come back, and I'll slit your throat from ear to ear."

Epson shuddered. How had he ever let his life get so out of hand that he was in league with men like this?

"I won't cheat you," he promised.

20

The lobby of the Federal Hotel had a red carpet and was dotted here and there with potted plants, chairs, and benches. Coming in off Fourth Street, the stairwell to the upper three floors was to the left of the lobby, while the registration desk was to the right.

When Preacher returned to the hotel from lunch, written in chalk on a slate just inside the door was a sign that read: MR. PREACHER TO THE DESK, PLEASE.

Preacher picked his way through the potted plants. The clerk was making entries in a ledger. He looked up as Preacher approached.

"I'm Preacher."

"Yes, this was delivered for you, sir," the clerk said, handing him an envelope.

"Thank you," Preacher said.

Preacher climbed the stairs to his room, then sat in the light of the window to examine the envelope. There was no name or address on the outside. He withdrew a one-page letter.

Dear Preacher,
   Shortly after you called upon me I was visited by Ben Caviness. I confess that I did ask him to frighten Jennie,

so she would stop making false claims against me. But I did not ask, nor did I expect, him to kill her.

Now, just as you said he would, he has asked me for more money. I told him that I would not give him any more money, and I took him to task for misinterpreting my instructions. He grew very angry and threatened to kill me if I did not comply with his demand for more money. Therefore, it is for my own safety that I tell you where to find him.

You will not find him staying in a hotel. Rather, he has made camp in the park area of Kensington, very near a place known as "Elephant Rock." It was in this same area that the first of our recent murders took place, and I am now convinced that Caviness was responsible for those terrible killings.

Therefore, were you to take care of him, you will not only achieve justice for yourself and your lady-friend, but peace of mind for the citizens of Philadelphia, who are now too frightened to leave their homes at night.

Theodore Epson

Preacher did not believe for one moment that Epson's instructions to Caviness had been misunderstood. He was convinced that Epson had wanted Jennie killed.

He was equally convinced that this wasn't a letter giving up Caviness, but was, instead, a letter designed to set him up. He was certain that once he showed up at the park in Kensington, he would be ambushed by Ben Caviness. But as they say, forewarned is forearmed. Preacher intended to keep that rendezvous.

If Epson went so far as to set Preacher up for an ambush, then he was sure that the banker had even more surprises in store for him. Therefore, before Preacher left the hotel that night, he prepared himself for any eventuality. He had two pistols, loaded and stuck down into his belt. He also had two knives—one on his belt and one stuck down into his boot.

Thus armed, he entered the park.

There was no moon tonight, so it was very dark. Even more so because the park was some distance from the ambient light of the city. The night sky was alive with the sounds of insects and frogs, as well as the silent whisper of the Schuylkill River. Although he was in the middle of a great city, Preacher was more at home right now than he had been at any time since leaving the mountains. He was in the middle of a wilderness, albeit a small one, listening to the ebb and flow of the sounds and moving with—not intruding upon— the natural order of things.

As he approached Elephant Rock, he noticed something that not one other person in Philadelphia would have noticed. There was a slight disruption in the sound patterns made by the night creatures, and that disruption told him that someone was very close and watching him. The hackles stood up on the back of Preacher's neck and he eased one of his pistols from his belt, then cocked it.

Suddenly a shot was fired. The night was lit up by the light from the muzzle flash. In an instinctive reaction, Preacher had anticipated the shot by no more than an instant, and he dove to the right.

Hitting the ground, Preacher rolled quickly to his right, as the ball whizzed by where he had been but a moment before. Had he not moved when he did, he would be dead now.

Preacher returned fire, and was momentarily blinded by his own muzzle flash. In addition, tiny bits of expended gunpowder peppered his face. He heard a grunting sound, then the sound of someone falling.

Remaining on his belly, he crawled forward until he reached the body of the man he had just shot. Rolling him over, he saw that the man was dead.

He also saw that it wasn't Ben Caviness.

A second shot hit the rock just above Preacher, then careened off through the park, its transit marked by a whining sound.

"Scott, did you get him?" someone called. Preacher did not recognize the voice. "Scott, did you get him?" the voice repeated.

"Nah, the son of a bitch got Scott," another voice answered. "Scott is dead." Preacher didn't recognize this voice either. How many were out here?

"Kelly, Gray, quit your jabbering and wait for a shot," a third voice called from the darkness.

This voice, Preacher did recognize. It was Ben Caviness.

"Caviness," Preacher called. "I'm coming after you, Caviness."

"Come ahead, you son of a bitch!" Caviness shouted. His shout was punctuated with a pistol shot, and once again a ball passed dangerously close.

Preacher returned fire, and saw his bullet strike sparks as it hit a rock. He also heard Caviness yelp in pain, though he knew that hadn't done any real damage to the outlaw. The best he could have done was to send shards of his bullet into him. That would be painful, but certainly not fatal.

"Kelly, he's already fired twice," Gray called. "Unless he's carryin' a whole bag of guns, he's got nothin' left."

"Let's get 'im!" Kelly yelled.

Suddenly, two men jumped up from their place of concealment, no more than thirty feet in front of Preacher. With shouts of defiance, they rushed toward him, their pistols leveled.

Preacher filled his hands with his two knives. He waited until they had closed to within ten feet, then suddenly stood up in front of them.

"There he is!" Gray shouted.

Gray and Kelly fired simultaneously while, at the same time, Preacher brought both his arms forward, throwing the two knives. The dual muzzle flashes momentarily illuminated the park. In a picture that was frozen in time, the two knives seemed to hang in the air, the points of the blades toward Kelly and Gray, suspended between Preacher and his two adversaries.

The two assailants saw the knives coming toward them, but they had no time for any reaction other than fear. Both blades struck the men in the chests, burying deep. With groans of pain, they went down. By now, the two bullets they had fired were landing harmlessly in the river beyond.

Now Preacher was effectively unarmed. Both pistols were empty, both knives expended. He dropped behind a rock, then moved quickly and silently to his left in order to reload.

His own pistol empty, Caviness left after his brief exchange with Preacher. He was already on his way out of the park when he heard Kelly and Gray's challenge. He also heard the discharge of their weapons. What he did not hear was their shouts of victory, and had they killed Preacher, he knew they would have let it be known.

The silence could only mean that they missed, or even more likely, that somehow Preacher had killed them. And Caviness believed it was the latter. He knew Preacher, had run across him before, and he knew what the man was capable of.

Caviness had only one thought in mind now, and that was to find Epson, get his money, and get out of Philadelphia.

The only way Caviness knew how to find Epson was to return to the bank and stay there all night long. When Epson showed up for work the next morning, Caviness would be waiting for him.

It was daylight when Epson stepped down from the omnibus in front of the bank. Caviness was waiting behind a flowering shrub as Epson, nattily dressed in a suit, vest, and hat, came walking by. When he drew even with him, Caviness suddenly stepped out into the path in front of him.

Epson gasped, then took a step back. "Caviness!" he said. "What are you doing here?"

Caviness looked awful. His face was cut and swollen where the shards of Preacher's bullet had cut into him. He smiled, showing stained, crooked, and broken teeth.

"Well, now, is that any way to greet an old pal?" he asked.

"We aren't . . . pals," Epson said.

Caviness put his hand over his heart. "Well, now, that pains me deeply, that you don't consider us pards," he said. The smile left. "But that makes no never mind. Just give me my two hundred dollars, and I'll be on my way."

"Did you . . . that is—is Preacher dead?"

"No, Preacher ain't dead," Caviness said. "But all my pards is. You're hard luck to be around, you know that, Epson? First off, Slater gets hisself kilt back in St. Louis and I get my ear chewed off. Then my new pards that I met here got themselves kilt last night. Three of 'em," he added. "They was three of them and one of me, so that we was four to one against Preacher. But that didn't make no never mind. He kilt all three of them."

"Four of you against one man, and he got away?"

"Yeah. So you can see, Epson, the best thing for me to do is just get the hell out of Philadelphia, only I can't do that if I ain't got no money. So, I'll take that two hundred dollars you was goin' to give me."

"That money was to be disbursed only if you killed Preacher," Epson said.

Caviness pulled his pistol. "Yeah, well, I didn't kill him, but you are going to *disburse* it anyway," he said mockingly.

Even before sunrise, Preacher was pretty sure that Caviness had gotten away from him somehow, sneaking out of the park under the cover of darkness. He dragged the bodies of the three men he had killed into a spot that was some distance from the normal path people took when walking through the park. With the bodies out of the way of incidental pedestrians, he went to the headquarters of the Philadelphia Police Agency to report upon the events of the night before.

Chief Constable Dolan, Constable Coleman, and a couple of the watchmen, including one whose "watch box" was very near the entrance of the park, were there to listen as Preacher told his story.

"You think it happened the way this man says it happened?" Constable Coleman asked after Preacher was finished.

"Why? Do you think it didn't?"

"I don't know . . . four men against one, and this morning three of the four is dead. It don't ring right to me."

Dolan nodded. "Well, I believe it," he said. "Let's go down to the park and have a look."

Accepting a ride in Dolan's carriage, Preacher led them into the park and to the place where he had left the bodies this morning. They were still there, undisturbed.

Chief Dolan looked at them for a moment, then pointed out the bodies, identifying them one by one. "That's Jim Gray, Luke Kelly, and Martin Scott," he said. "They are the dregs of society, three of the most disreputable men in the city. If they were out here in the park in the middle of the night, you can bet they were up to no good. Preacher did the whole city a favor by killing these three."

"Thanks," Preacher said. "But the one I wanted got away."

At that moment, a constable on horseback came riding into the park at a gallop.

"Chief!" he started shouting, even before he dismounted. Dismounting, he handed the reins of his horse to one of the other watchmen, then hurried over to Chief Constable Dolan.

"What is it, Smith?"

"Some banker has been taken prisoner," Smith said.

"Taken prisoner? What do you mean 'taken prisoner'?"

"A fella by the name of Epson," Smith said. "Witnesses say

another man jumped out from behind some bushes this morning and took him at gunpoint down to the river."

"Epson?" Preacher said. "Chief Dolan, if Epson has been taken prisoner, then Caviness has to be the one who took him."

The recently arrived watchman looked at the tall man in buckskins, then looked back at Dolan. "Who is this?"

"This is my deputy," Dolan said. "Come on, let's get down to the river."

Down at the river's edge, Caviness had commandeered a small paddle boat. Ordering the boatman to build up the steam, he stood there, pointing his pistol at Epson, while a crowd of curious onlookers began gathering around to watch the unfolding drama.

"My name is Constable Marvin Jensen," one of the men in the crowd shouted to Caviness. This was a watchman, a member of the Philadelphia police whose watch box was close enough to the area to arouse his interest in what was going on by the river. He'd arrived to find Caviness standing there by the edge of the water, holding a pistol pointed at the head of a very frightened Theodore Epson. "Just what is it you are planning on doing?" the constable asked.

"I'm going to kill him if anyone comes any closer," Caviness replied with a menacing jerk of his gun.

"You don't want to do that, mister. That would be cold-blooded murder, and you would hang for it for sure," the watchman replied.

"You want to save this man's life?" Caviness called.

"Yes."

"Then you go to this here feller's bank, and you tell the person in charge there that he had better come up with two hundred—no, make that one thousand dollars. Yeah, one thousand," he repeated, getting bolder. "You tell the bank it's going to cost them one thousand dollars to keep me from killin' this here little pissant."

"What makes you think the bank will pay one thousand dollars to save this man?" the constable asked.

"'Cause he ain't just anybody. This here feller works for that bank. I reckon they'll pay to save him," Caviness said with self-assurance.

"Caviness, Mr. Fontaine is never going to agree to something like that," Epson said in a voice that was laced with panic. "He won't pay one thousand, he won't pay one dollar."

"Then you're going to die," Caviness replied. He looked toward the boatman. "How much longer before we have steam?" he demanded.

"Not much longer," the boatman replied.

"Hurry it up," Caviness said.

"You can't make steam any faster than you can make steam," the boatman complained.

While holding the gun in one hand, Caviness pulled his knife with the other. "You'd better figure out some way to do it," he said. "Or I'll split you open like guttin' a fish."

"No, no, it won't be much longer," the boatman promised.

"It better not be," Caviness said. Then he turned to Epson. "The bank has got until this here feller gets the steam built up to come down here with my one thousand dollars," he said.

"What if . . . what if they don't get here before the steam is up?" Epson asked in a frightened voice.

"Then you'll be leaving with me. Leastwise, till I figure out what to do with you."

The drama continued to play out on the banks of the Schuylkill River, the boatman working hard to build up the steam while an ever-growing crowd gathered to see what was going on. Now and then someone would yell at Caviness, imploring him to release Epson, but Caviness paid no attention to them and, eventually, the crowd became still.

The situation became very eerie as hundreds of people

stared in silence at the three men who were standing on the small paddle boat.

Finally the boatman spoke.

"Steam's up," he said.

"All right. Let's go," Caviness ordered.

"Go where?" the boatman asked.

"Downriver," Caviness replied. "As fast as you can make this thing go."

"Wait!" Epson shouted.

"Wait for what?"

"The bank. You haven't given them enough time to bring the money to you."

Caviness laughed an evil laugh. "They ain't goin' to bring me no money," he said. "You done told me that yourself."

At that moment, a carriage arrived at the river's edge, its team pulling it at a gallop. Three men got out of the carriage. Caviness didn't recognize two of them, but he did recognize the third. It was Preacher. Damn, the son of a bitch did get away last night.

"Hurry up! Let's go!" Caviness shouted to the boatman. Seeing Preacher this close put Caviness on edge. "Come on, let's get out of here!"

The boatman cast off, then opened the throttle. The paddles slapped at the water, and the little boat moved quickly out into the stream.

As the space between the boat and the river's edge widened, Caviness began feeling more and more secure. He was going to get away after all. He felt emboldened.

"Hey, Preacher!" Caviness called out to him in a challenging tone of voice. "What are you going to do now, huh?" He laughed wickedly. "Are you going to keep chasing me?"

"Until I catch you," Preacher answered.

"Yeah, well, you better give it up. You're getting too many people killed," Caviness said. "Your woman in St. Louis, them two back in Ohio, the ones here. I kilt them all, but you're to blame for it, Preacher. You're the blame 'cause you're chasin' me, and as long as you keep comin' after me, the more killin' I'm going to do."

"Did you hear that, Chief?" Coleman asked. "That man just admitted to being the murderer we've been looking for."

"Yes, I heard."

"Well, what are we going to do about it? He's getting away."

"There's nothing we can do, right now," Dolan said.

By now the boat was mid-river and making its way downstream. With the brisk current and full power, the little boat was moving much faster than a horse could gallop.

Suddenly, the three men saw a flash of smoke, then heard a pop. Epson fell into the water.

"Holy shit! He just killed Epson!" Coleman said as the crowd gasped at the horror of what they had just seen.

Glancing back toward the carriage, Preacher saw that there was a rifle in the carriage boot. He walked over to it, picked it up, and examined it for a moment. Then he began loading it. Glancing back toward the carriage, the chief constable saw Preacher with the rifle.

"What are you doing?" he asked.

"I don't intend to just stand by and let him get away from me this time," Preacher said as he reached for the powder horn and pouch of balls.

"Are you joking? He's already out of range. By the time you get that rifle loaded, he'll be well out of range."

"Maybe," Preacher said as he poured powder into the rifle. "But I aim to try."

Out on the boat, which was now some distance from shore, Caviness stood on top of the cabin, looking back toward the landing. The figures were growing smaller as the distance widened, and Caviness laughed.

"I beat you, you son of a bitch!" he shouted. "I beat you!"

That was when he saw Preacher come down to the water's edge, kneel, and aim a rifle at him.

"Ha! What do you think you are doing?" Caviness shouted. "Why, you ignorant bastard! You are so far . . ."

Caviness saw a flash of light and a puff of smoke. He saw Preacher rock back from the recoil.

". . . out of range . . . unnh!"

Caviness felt a hammerlike blow, as if he had been kicked by a mule. It knocked him back a step and he put his hand up to his chest, then watched in horror and disbelief as his cupped palm filled with blood.

"Well, I'll be damned," Caviness said just as the world around him began to fade. He pitched forward into the river and floated, facedown, very still.

The Rocky Mountains

When Preacher reached the top of the summit, he stood there for a moment. Gazing down on the vista, he saw an endless slope of mottled treetops—from various shades of green, to golden aspen, to crimson. Across a rolling basin, there was a wall of red rock, broken along its face into points, ledges, cliffs, and escarpments.

An early fall snow had already crowned Eagle's Beak, and once again, Preacher saw feathery tendrils of snow streaming out from it. The crystals glistened in the sun, forming a prism of color that crowned the beauty of the scene.

How different this was from Philadelphia, St. Louis, or even Kansas City. There, amidst the buildings and the clatter of traffic and the crowd of people, he had been totally out of his element. Even while visiting his family—though he was pleased to see them after so many years, and happy that his brother and sisters were doing well—he had felt a nagging discontent, a need to get back where he belonged.

Overhead, an eagle soared, and just before him, Preacher could hear the sound of a babbling creek. He got a whiff of the sweet smell of pine and caught the musk of distant forest animals.

"What do you think, Dog?" he asked the animal who had been keeping pace with him as they traveled higher and higher into the mountains. "Are you happy to be home?"

Dog looked up at him.

"I almost left you with Carla, you know. She begged me to. But I figure, with that restaurant I bought her, she doesn't need a dog around. Besides, I missed you," he said. "Why, if I didn't have you to talk to, folks would think I'm talking to myself."

The mountain man laughed loudly at his own joke, his laughter echoing back from the woods.

FURY OF THE
MOUNTAIN MAN

1

He rode with accustomed ease on the big, spotted-rump appaloosa horse. The gray and-black animal had an ebon muzzle and ear tips that gave it the appearance of a Siamese cat. Any illusion of cuteness ended there. Sidewinder was a killer horse. He had stomped an abusive former owner into a puddle of crimson mud. He had kicked the slats out of more than one stall and severely bitten all the way through the shoulder of another would-be owner. Sidewinder never made trouble for the man riding him now. A mountain-bred creature, he took to the High Lonesome every bit as much as Smoke Jensen. The two had a natural affinity. Off to Smoke's right a catbird made its mimic cry from the branches of a tall pine.

Trees grew taller this far south, Smoke noted. Lower altitude and more sunlight in the broader valleys. Smoke's ranch, the Sugarloaf, nestled between tall, steep walls of granite that provided a natural bastion against the inroads of civilization. They hadn't kept out the telegraph, which reached Big Rock, Colorado, some eight years earlier. Nor the railroad. That was about all of civilization that Smoke Jensen wanted.

Raised from his early teens by the renowned old mountain man, Preacher, Smoke had cleaned his heels of civilization with a will. He gloried in the crisp, clean, sweet-smelling air of the High Lonesome. Cold water to bathe in bothered him not at all. And a splendid diet of succulent venison, beaver tail, hoe cakes and biscuits helped him grow tall, broad and strong. Life in those days—long after the fur trade had died out because of a trendy change in fashions—had been one long, glorious romp for Smoke Jensen. Not always, he reminded himself as Sidewinder picked his way along the rutted highroad outside of the thriving community of Pueblo.

Inevitably, the dark side of life intruded on the idyllic existence in the Shining Mountains. Smoke learned to shoot, not only to hunt for food, but to defend his life. He killed Indians and white men with equal and growing skill in his teen years. Always, though, the peace and tranquility of the sprawling Rocky Mountains soothed his soul. Now civilization had chosen to intrude once more.

This time it came in the form of a letter from an old friend. Carbone had written Smoke to inform him that he had hung up his guns. The notorious Mexican gunfighter had become a gentleman rancher, a *haciendado* as he put it. Also that Carbone's ace boon running mate, Martine, had done the same. In the years since their last joint venture with Smoke Jensen, they had married and produced a flock of kids, according to the letter. And they had prospered.

Only now something threatened their new-found way of life. Smoke wondered what was going on down in Mexico that they should feel it necessary to send for him. Carbone's missive had been less than fully informative. He'd mentioned bandits and an outlaw army, led by someone who called himself *El Rey del Norte*. Smoke's Spanish was limited at best, and rusty from lack of recent use, but he knew that meant "The King of the North." North of what? For all of Carbone's vagueness and the oddity of that name, Smoke was on his way, and that spoke volumes.

Smoke Jensen was, in the original meaning, a man of his word. He never lied. Not to anyone, for any reason. Old

Preacher had taught him the value of honesty, courage, determination and all the virtues that, to his consternation and sorrow, Smoke found dying out far too fast in his own country. Those lessons in basic morality had served him well over the years. Got him in and out of fights far better than sheer brute strength or viciousness alone. Fighting had been a large part of Smoke's life. He recalled that barely a year ago he had been in a fight-to-the-finish against Major Cosgrove and Jack Biggers, with Pasco, the nephew of Carbone, siding him.

That had been up in Red Light, Montana, where Smoke and his wife, Sally, had fought for the rights of Smoke's niece, Jenny. Before that brouhaha ended, nearly half of the trash class of gunfighters west of St. Louis had been hustled off to meet their Maker, a town lay in ruins, and those behind the scheme to defraud Jenny had paid the ultimate price. Pasco had remained behind as a working hand on Jenny's ranch, as had a number of others.

Once more taking in the splendor of his beloved mountains, Smoke Jensen wished them well. Jenny was a good girl and deserved the huge, valley-wide ranch she had acquired. There would be time, too, on his journey south, Smoke speculated, to figure out more of what plagued his old friends.

On the south slope of a long ridge, the three men sat their horses. With the animals shoulder-to-shoulder, they completely blocked the road. Hard-bitten men, their grim expressions reflected the purpose of their presence at this particular spot. Len Banks, on the right, and Lonny Ranks, on the left, were brothers, and shirt-tail relatives of the man in the middle, Myron Forbes.

Neither of the Banks brothers particularly liked what Forbes had in mind. Yet, they felt compelled to see it through. It would take all three of them, they knew that much. One hell of a tall order to face down the man they sought.

"He has to come this way," Myron Forbes said, desperate urgency crackling in his words. "From what we learned, he *has* to."

"Could be he stayed over in Pueblo," Len Banks suggested.

"Then we wait," Forbes bit off.

They saw the hat first. A slowly growing silhouette against the cobalt blue of the Colorado sky. As it progressed over the top of the ridge, it increased in definition: a black, XXXX Stetson Cattleman. Then the face resolved itself: square, rock-hard jaw; long, darkly tanned cheeks, with shadowed holes where the eyes would be; longish blond hair riding the slight breeze behind.

"Gawdamn, I think it's him," Lonny Banks blurted.

"If it is, today's the day he dies," Myron Forbes gritted.

Black-tipped appaloosa ears showed next, then the well-shaped head. The rider crested the ridge in a few strides and started down toward the trio of murderous intent. When he drew within twenty-five feet, he reined in.

"Howdy, boys," Smoke Jensen offered politely.

"You Smoke Jensen?" Myron Forbes growled.

Smoke Jensen recognized the challenging tone and sighed sadly. He released his reins and used his bent left thumb to ease up the brim of his hat. "I might be. Why?"

"If you are, we came to kill you," Forbes snarled.

"Do you mind telling me why, exactly, you intend to kill me?" Smoke asked in the reasonable tone he forced himself to use.

"You oughtta know. I'm Myron Forbes," the big man snarled.

"I'm supposed to know you?"

"Know the name, for sure. You killed my baby brother. Shot him in the back."

Smoke Jensen slowly shook his head, the sadness a heavy mantle around his shoulders. "I've never shot a man named Forbes so far as I know."

"Gawdamn, Jensen, you killed enough you don't know all their names?" Lonny Banks blurted.

Again Smoke sighed, his large, callused right hand resting on his saddle-hardened thigh, close to the smooth butt of his long-used .44 Colt. "I regret to say that is true. Some Blackfeet, Arapaho, a punk or highwayman here and there. But I've never back-shot a man unless he turned at the last second, after my hammer fell. And I've never shot a man who wasn't trying to kill me."

"You seem mighty sure of that," Len Banks challenged.

"I am," Smoke told him, his level, gray gaze never leaving Myron.

"You're lying, goddamnit!" Myron Forbes shouted, working himself up for what he'd come to do.

"I never lie," Smoke said softly.

"Yes, you do," Myron rushed to contradict. "With his dying breath, Bubba told me it was Smoke Jensen who shot him."

"Someone claiming to be, maybe, but not me," Smoke persisted.

Fury suffused the face of Myron Forbes. "You're a coward as well as a liar!" he shouted. "Tryin' to save yer miserable life by hiding behind still more lies. Fill your hand, you son of a bitch!"

With that, Myron Forbes went for his gun. Lonny Banks, beside him and not too bright, did the same. Smoke Jensen moved with a blur. Before the astonished Len Banks could blink, the big .44 came clear of age-worn, well-oiled leather and barked a final denial at Myron Forbes. Myron's thick body absorbed the lead pellet and reacted with only a slight backward jolt. A soft grunt left his lips. Then he completed his draw and fired off a round that went wild, snapping over Smoke's head. Lonny had his .45 Peacemaker in action now and developed a sudden surprised expression when his arm shrieked in pain and went as quickly numb.

His revolver flew from unclinched fingers, and Lonny half-turned toward Myron when the older man centered his muzzle on Smoke and screamed defiance. Smoke Jensen shot him again, this time between the eyes. Myron fell soundlessly from the saddle.

Len Banks already had his hands in the air. Lonny found it impossible to move his right shoulder and merely raised his left paw high over the crown of his hat.

"I'm sorry. I really am," Smoke Jensen told the survivors. "You'll have to get that wound tended soon," he advised Lonny. "Are you related to Mr. Forbes?"

"Shirt-tail relatives is all," Len Banks allowed. "Lord, I never saw nothin' so fast, Mr. Jensen. Y'all know I never touched iron. Never even tried to draw." Smoke nodded acknowledgment and Len went on, his tongue in high gear. "We didn't have much truck with this crazy idea. I mean, who ever heard of Smoke Jensen in south Texas? The real Smoke Jensen, that is."

"I'm headed south now," Smoke observed, still a bit on the prod.

"Uh—yeah, but . . ."

Smoke nodded in the direction of the cooling corpse. "Bundle him up and see he gets a proper burial."

"Yessir," Len gulped. "A right proper Christian burial. 'Twern't your fault, Mr. Jensen. Myron, he sorta pushed it. An' he got my brother shot up in the bargain."

"Not much of a bargain for Mr. Forbes, I'd say," Smoke quipped dryly. "You fellows clean up the mess, then, and I'd say a quick trip back to south Texas would be in order after that."

"Yessir, yessir, that's exactly what I was thinkin'," Len hastily agreed.

Smoke poked out the three expended cartridges and replaced them, then reholstered his .44. He lowered his hat a notch on his forehead and lifted Sidewinder's reins. Without another word, he steered his way around the obstructing horses and continued on south toward Trinidad, Colorado.

* * *

A soft breeze whispered through the tall, stately ranks of pines that scaled the steep slopes forming the valley which housed the Sugarloaf Ranch. It set to trembling the serrated-edged leaves of the aspens. Already some had exchanged their usual silver-green for pale yellow and rich gold. It would be an early winter. The heady aroma of fresh-baked apple pie wafted out the open kitchen window of the tidy house that was home to Smoke and Sally Jensen.

Sally appeared in the doorway, a smudge of flour on her nose, hands on aproned hips. Crocker and the hands should be back soon and Smoke should be with them. She pushed the irritating thought away. They so frequently saw things alike that it was as though they thought with one mind. Friends were in trouble, and it was like Smoke to go at once to their aid. Hadn't they come to help him often enough? Somehow the name, *Mexico,* seemed dark and mysterious. A distant, foreign land.

Yet, Smoke had said that he would be in the mountains there. And mountains were mountains, he always maintained. All a man had to do was get to know them a little and be right at home. At least a man raised by that old rapscallion, Preacher, would be, she amended. Oh, how she loved that big slab of a man, Smoke Jensen. And how she missed him already, with him gone only a week. He'd not taken the train, said Sidewinder might take exception to being in a rattling, swaying stock car, and it would be impossible for any stranger to take care of the Appaloosa stallion. Smoke had not even taken supplies and a packhorse. Said Carbone would provide everything. The rumble of many hoofs sent her gaze to the broad basin at the upper end, of the valley.

Five hands, led by Crocker, the foreman, came on at a fast run. The clear, sweet air of the High Lonesome fogged with dust from the pounding hoofs of nearly two dozen sleek, handsome horses they drove before them. Although Eastern born and bred, educated in the best schools and trained to the duties of a society lady, Sally Reynolds Jensen thrilled at the sight. She loved to ride, and astride, not on one of those silly sidesaddles.

She also loved her husband's decision to reduce their prize herd of cattle to a few for personal meat and milk use and go into the horse business. The nation was growing rapidly, and expanding westward at an alarming pace. Yet that meant more demand for horses, lots of them, and prices had started to soar nearly two years ago. Not that they needed much in the way of money.

She was wealthy in her own right, and Smoke had put aside enough to live in comfort without turning a hand for the rest of his life. Sally waved to the foreman and her husband's employees with the towel she intended to put over the pies while they cooled.

Burt Crocker halooed back with a vigorous wave of his stained and battered old Stetson. One hand sprinted forward and opened a corral gate. The running tide of horseflesh swerved at the prompting of the remaining handlers and surged into the circular enclosure of lodgepole pine rails. Burt trotted up to the house.

"Twenty-three prime two-year-olds, Miz Jensen. Smoke'll be right proud. Suppose it's none of my business, but when you expectin' him back?"

"Not for some time, I'm afraid. He promised to telegraph me from El Paso. Might know more then."

Burt Crocker flashed a white smile. "I'll tell the boys. Say, is that apple pie I smell?"

"That it is. I baked four of them. There's venison stew, the last of the garden greens and fresh bread as well. All of you get washed up and come to dinner. I imagine you'll have an afternoon of it with those rough-run horses."

"That we will. Sure wish Smoke was here to oversee the shoeing. It's gonna be pure he—uh—Hades, ma'am."

"Pure hell, indeed," Sally responded with a chuckle. "My

ears aren't made of velvet, nor rose petals for that matter. If you want, I'll give you a hand."

"Pardon, ma'am, but they ain't saddle-broke as yet," Crocker protested, hat in hand.

"You get the forge fired up, and I'll show you I can fashion a mean shoe," Sally responded. "In fact, I'm looking forward to it. Something to do besides cook and clean house."

Exquisite taste and a sensitive understanding of the arts reflected in the large *sala* of the *Hacienda La Fortuna,* in the state of Durango, Mexico. The vaulted ceiling soared some fifteen feet above the meticulously fitted and immaculately scrubbed flagstones of the flooring. Although a warm day outside, a fire crackled in the walk-in fireplace, where a spit awaited a whole lamb or a haunch of beef to roast. The good taste, however, did not belong to the man sprawled in a throne-like chair at one end of the main hall.

Gustavo Angel Carvajal wore the uniform of a general in the Mexican Army. That he held no such rank, and never had, constituted no bar to his wearing it. The knee-high black boots were smeared with dust, mud and splatters of blood. The ease with which his men had taken the hacienda seemed to heighten his displeasure, rather than elate him. He had a brooding countenance as he listened to the reports of his three most trusted subordinates.

Small of stature, with bowed legs and a growing middle, Carvajal's five-and-a-half-foot frame seemed constructed of spare parts. Close-set, ebon eyes were slightly crossed. The left one had a speck of nebulous gray-white that gave it an odd cast. His ill humor increased as he heard out the last man. When the recitation concluded, Carvajal sprang to his feet and began to pace, hands behind his back.

"Why is it we can take this place with only two losses, yet when I send my best soldiers, my Eagle Warriors, and my

Jaguar Warriors, to exact tribute from two stubborn hacendados, you return empty-handed?"

Embarrassed, and instantly alerted to the edge of madness in Carvajal's tone, the trio of lieutenants pondered how
to reply. His reference to the army of the Aztec emperor,
Montezuma, revealed the possible onset of another of his
flights of fancy, in which Carvajal insisted that he was the
reincarnation of that selfsame emperor. At least, they thanked
the God they weren't entirely certain existed, he did not go so
far in his other persona as to undertake the gruesome ritual of
human sacrifice and cannibalism known to the Aztecs. Finally, the tallest, Humberto Regales, cleared his throat and
hazarded an answer.

"Your pardon, Your Excellency," he began in the fawning
tone so appreciated by Gustavo Carvajal, who called himself
El Rey del Norte in his saner moments. "Both of the gentlemen in question are notorious as *pistoleros*. And apparently
they have done the unthinkable. They have trained some of
their *peones* in how to use firearms. A dangerous precedent
if it were to become widespread. Armed men can determine
their own destinies, and even who it is who rules them."

"Yes—yes, I understand all of that," Carvajal snapped.
"So, what you are telling me is that they resisted, and did so
successfully?"

"It is in our reports," Regales said quietly.

"What I still can't understand is why this unnatural quirk
remains in my fate. In all of three states of Central Mexico,
not a soul refuses to bow down or pay tribute to me, except
for these two stubborn, stupid *hacendados,* Esteban Carbone y Ruis and Miguel Antonio Martine y Garcia. How can
this be?"

All three dissembled. "We do not know, Jef—er—Excellency.
We have already given Carbone what should have been a death
blow. His villages are in ruins, the priest run off, what *peones*
remain on the *estancia* are frightened and cowed. Yet he con-

tinues to resist," Humberto Regales defended the 230 men of Carvajal's bandit army.

"Only through the assistance and connivance of that *cabrón*, Martine," Carvajal snapped. He reached unthinkingly to one side of the thin wisp of mustache that drooped down below his jawline. He tugged on it while he contemplated what his next order would be. With the wide empty space on his upper lip between the two sides of his mustache, and the equally spindly goatee that sprang from his lower lip, his face had a saturnine appearance.

Abruptly he stopped pacing and turned on his subordinates. "Well, then, we will move on Martine now and see if that doesn't break the spirits of those two old comrades in arms. And end their willingness to resist."

2

Pinpoints of starlight showed faintly, low in the eastern half of the sky's dome. Thin slices of pink and blue, shot through with soft orange, still limned the western horizon, though not brightly enough to wash out the evening star. Venus, Smoke Jensen mused as he turned thick slices of bacon in the cast iron skillet. The goddess of love. He cut his eyes to the opposite direction. The moon wouldn't rise until near midnight.

In his reflections, he pictured how the moonlight silvered the tall black pines that rose above his home. He could visualize yellow shafts of light spilling from the windows, a thread of smoke curling from the chimney. Sally would be finishing the details of a substantial and delicious supper. Six hands and Crocker to feed. It made for a lot of work. Sally was up to it, though.

A lot of time had passed since Smoke brought Sally to the Sugarloaf and they realized his dream of a large, comfortable house, its inside walls ringing with the shouts and laughter of happy, healthy children. It had all come with time. Those years had been kind to Sally. To Smoke she still looked the sweet young bride.

In the soft lamp glow of their bedroom, she showed none of the physical traces of bearing three children, two of them twins. They had all dearly loved the High Lonesome, with the same dedication as their father, those kids. And Billy, too, whom they had adopted before Sally's first pregnancy. Their lovely daughter always cried when she had to leave the Sugarloaf for the outside world. All were gone now.

Billy was in the next to last year at the University of Paris. The twins had gone on to Europe, too. Although far from full-grown, the youngest, Kurt, attended school back East. Sally had insisted. They needed to know more than how to ride, rope, brand and shoot. Only spottily did the schoolhouse in Big Rock offer classes, and never beyond the eighth grade. The children of Smoke Jensen, Sally contended, would have need for more than doing their ciphers, reading and writing on an elementary level. And so, beguiled as always by Sally's beauty, Smoke had given in on the point.

Smoke's youngest son attended a preparatory school for "young gentlemen." Smoke snorted at the thought of the term. Kurt Jensen, with his father's broad shoulders, big hands, and, at 13, awkward feet, could hardly be confused with those wet-nosed, simpering, pale-faced sissies with whom he now associated.

From the ranch hands, Kurt had learned to cuss like a trooper from the age of eight. He sat a horse like he'd been born on it. All of the kids did. Lean, hard, deeply tanned, Kurt was a product of the High Lonesome and took to "gentling" with all the resistance of an unbroke mustang to a saddle.

Many had been the letters in the early days. Words of protest and outrage poured from the spirited nature of young Master Kurt Jensen. But never a word of his being vicious, brutal or malicious. After the outrage-venting first paragraphs, the letters always indicated that the boys, whose noses Kurt had bloodied, eyes he'd blackened, and lips he'd split, had all had it coming. No, Smoke conceded, it wasn't the physical punishment meted out by his spirited son. To those docile and controlled Easterners, it was the very idea of anyone standing up for his rights that so outraged them.

To the north, in the gathering darkness, a wolf howled. That surprised Smoke Jensen. He wondered that any wolves remained in so populous an area. Man had always held hatred for the wolf. Perhaps it went back to when man and the wolf vied for possession of a particularly warm and comfortable cave on the edge of a world of ice. Whatever, the emnity, at least on man's part, had remained to this day. For the wolf's part, he simply didn't care. The old timber prowler howled again.

To the south, the high, yapping cries of his lesser cousins, the coyotes, answered. "Hello, Brother Wolf," Smoke Jensen greeted in a low voice. "Go in peace, if other men will let you."

Suddenly, Smoke knew why it was he had turned his thoughts to the children. He did not disagree in the least with Sally's insistence that they receive a quality, university education. Only that he had a deep, serious concern that exposure to Eastern culture might turn his brood into marshmallows.

"Wild and free, like Brother Wolf there, that's what I want you to be," Smoke breathed softly. And it was almost a prayer.

He saw the flurry of activity from a distance that prevented recognizing what was happening. Dust boiled up around the legs of a man who stood in a corral. He raised and flung down one arm as though driving stakes with a sledgehammer. Pitiful squawls and the shrill voice of a child reached Smoke Jensen's ears.

South of Trinidad, Colorado, now, it had been two days since the evening he contemplated his children's future in the socially correct East. The sounds of this almost human agony drew Smoke Jensen closer. What he saw brought a coldness to his heart that reflected in his icy gray eyes.

A man was beating a small pony with a piece of firewood

as long and thick as an arm. To his side, a barefoot boy of about ten looked on in horror and begged the man to stop.

"Please, Paw. Don't—don't hurt Dollar no more. She's bleedin'," the little lad shrieked hysterically. Tears ran down his face.

"You stop that bawlin', hear? Or I'll take this stick to you."

"Oh, please—please, Paw. Take your mad out on me. Don't beat poor Dollar no more."

Swiftly the man rounded on the boy. "Gawdamn you, Bobby, I got a mind to do jist that." He backhanded the child with enough force to split the youngster's upper lip and send him staggering.

Hard, frigid anger burst inside Smoke Jensen. He could never abide anyone who beat women, children or helpless animals. He reined in Sidewinder and dismounted. In three fast strides he reached the corral. Both hands on the top rail, he vaulted over and approached the man.

"I think that's about enough," Smoke growled ominously.

The man rounded on him. "Keep yer nose out of this, butt-face," the red-visaged brute snarled. "Or I'll kick yer tail up twixt yer shoulder blades."

"Start kicking, you worthless son." Smoke's words came heavy with menace as he pulled on a supple pair of thin leather gloves.

Advancing two steps, the man raised his cudgel as he spat words from froth-flecked lips. "No stranger's comin' betwixt a man an' his kid, or his animals."

"He ain't my paw," the boy shouted. "He's my step-dad. An'—an' I hate him."

"Yer gettin' yers next, Bobby, soon's I finish with this no-account," snarled the man, his big beer belly jiggling. Before the last word had sounded, he took a hefty swing at Smoke Jensen.

Smoke calmly made a back-step to avoid the club. "It's

been my experience that bullies are all cowards at heart," he observed in a bantering tone.

Rage caused the slack muscles in arms that could have far greater power to quiver. "I'll show you 'coward,' you bastid!"

Before the billet of stove wood could whistle a quarter of the way toward Smoke Jensen's head, Smoke stepped inside its arc and popped the fat-lipped man solidly in the mouth. It rocked him, stunned him. He tottered backward a little, spat blood, and roared like a bull. Smoke took the charge, slipped a blow with the stick off one shoulder, and went to work on the soft middle.

Grunts and gasps, sickly with the odor of stale beer, came from blubbery lips. Smoke's opponent wobbled on his feet, sucked in a huge draught of air and measured another swing. Smoke Jensen stepped back and let him come. As the club descended, Smoke took his adversary by a thick right wrist and aided in the downstroke. The cudgel left the man's grasp as Smoke flipped him heels over head. A long *whoof* escaped the brute when he landed on his back.

"I could end this right now, since you are a bully and a coward, by simply telling you my name," Smoke advised him factually.

Slower than usual, the man rose to his boots. He cut a wicked gaze at the boy, then sought his bludgeon. "I don't give a damn about your name, saddle-trash."

"I'm curious about names," Smoke taunted. "What's yours?"

"Rupe Connors. An' if you was from around here, you'd be pissin' your jeans ta hear that."

"As it is, I'm terribly unimpressed." Smoke Jensen sighed heavily. "Well, then, playtime is over."

He closed in on the blubber-waisted lout. Hard rights and lefts popped off a head that began to wobble uncontrollably. Connors pawed the air in a feeble attempt to fend off the punishing blows. It had no effect. Smoke rocked back and cocked a hefty right fist. He threw it straight forward with a force that came up from his toes.

Cartilage smashed and bone splintered. A fountain of red gushed from the ravaged nose. Howling now, Rupe Connors stumbled blindly after Smoke Jensen. Pain caused Connors' eyes to squint shut. A sudden hot explosion on the side of his head set his ear to ringing. He turned that way in fury and caught a solid left that mashed his lips.

Smoke Jensen set his boots and went to work on the midsection. Connors grunted and gagged and bent double, sucking in desperation for air. He sagged and slowly went to his knees. Blue-white light flashed off the wicked blade of the knife Connors came up with from the back of his belt. The only effect this danger had on Smoke Jensen was to have him change his tactics.

"There's no such thing as a fair or unfair fight," old Preacher had instructed the boy, Smoke Jensen. "There's only a winner an' a loser. Your mind should be set on al'ays bein' the winner."

Smoke had taken that advice to heart. So now, instead of backing off, giving up in the face of possible death or mutilation, he shifted his weight and kicked Rupe Connors full in the face. Connors went over backward, and his head made a solid *klonk* on the hard-packed ground of the corral.

He moaned and rolled onto one side. Ever so slowly, Rupe Connors forced himself to rise to his knees. Panting, blood spraying from his mangled lips, he got his boots under him and staggered toward Smoke Jensen. He had not lost hold of his knife, Smoke discovered.

Smoke could have drawn his own large, heavy bowie and carved out Connors' liver. But he hadn't taken a hand in this to kill anyone. Maybe he could still avoid it. When Connors made a half-hearted slash, Smoke jumped to one side and stepped past the thick-bellied enemy. Then he drove rock-like knuckles into Connors' kidneys.

Rupe Connors squealed like a pig. Gagging, a pink string of saliva hanging from his chin, he fell heavily on his knees. New pain lanced as a chunk of gravel dug into the vulnerable space below his right kneecap. Screaming his outrage, Connors tried to make his body obey the commands of his fogged brain. It resulted in an agonizing, lethargic turn to his left. Pushing up with his left hand, he came to his boots. Black hate blazing in his bloodshot eyes, Connors duck-walked toward Smoke Jensen.

Again Smoke let him come, always mindful of the nasty tip and keen edge of the big Greenriver knife Connors had fisted. When the distance between them narrowed to arm's length, Connors lunged at Smoke. Jensen parried the attack with a backhand slap, then pivoted around the left side of Connors. He kept turning until he could grasp the knife arm with both hands. Then he yanked down at the same moment he drove his knee upward.

Smoke heard the bone break, a grisly, dry stick sound, a moment before Connors screamed like a woman. The knife fell from numb fingers. Smoke had realized earlier that he would have to go all out. Anything short of killing the man if possible. So he didn't let go. Instead, he yanked on the broken arm with all his force, set his boots and hurled Connors into a corral rail.

Bleating cries of sheer agony fought past the crimson mush of Connors' lips. He could not force his eyes open even when the cascade of powerful, hurting punches pounded his chest and head. He sagged, slumped, wavered, and fell face-first into a large mud puddle.

There had been no rain in a long time. One of the horses that shuffled nervously at the far side of the corral had provided the moisture. Panting slightly himself, Smoke Jensen stood over the fallen man.

"You through showing me manners?" Smoke asked.

Rupe Connors raised his head, smeared with the red-brown

mud of southern Colorado. "Gawdamn you, gawdamn you to hell." Blackness welled up then and Connors slumped back, head resting on his uninjured forearm.

"Gol—lee, mister!" young Bobby gasped. "That was sure some bodacious fight. But, jeez, he'll kill me now for certain sure. Wi—will you take me with you, mister? Please? Take me along."

"Son, I can't do that," Smoke Jensen answered honestly. What would he do with a kid? Especially where he was headed.

"Please, you gotta. He'll do for me like he did my maw."

Coldness touched at Smoke Jensen. "What do you mean, boy?"

"He—he beat on us, like he done my pony. Maw an' me. Ol' Rupe would get all drunked up and come home late. Yank Maw outta bed and whomp on her something awful. If I even let out a squeak, he'd go after me next. Sometimes I didn't even have to remind him I was there. He *liked* it, don't you see? Then—then one time he hurt Maw somethin' awful. That was two weeks ago. She had to lay in bed a whole week, just gettin' worser an' worser. An' then she—she just . . . went away."

Grim outrage fired that special sense of honor and justice deep within Smoke Jensen. "She left? Took off and left you alone with him?"

"No, sir." Tears found their way down Bobby's cheeks. "She died. We buried her over there by the root cellar." The boy gulped down air to renew his plea. "An' that's why you gotta take me along. He'll kill me for sure now, what with Maw bein' dead, an' seein' as how I watched him get so bad whupped."

"I don't think so, son." Smoke gauged the amount of punishment Connors had absorbed. "At least not right away. I'll stop off in the next town, tell the sheriff to come take a look in and ask some questions. You answer him truthfully, and it'll all go right for you."

"B-B-But, Rupe'll beat the tar outta me before that. I know it."

"Listen, boy, where I'm going I can't have a kid along. If you want, ride out of here for a while, keep the place in sight, and come back when the sheriff arrives."

Bobby wiped at his wet cheeks. "If you say it'll be all right," he offered tentatively.

"I'm sure of it," Smoke encouraged, wishing he felt as confident as he sounded.

Early that morning, in the large town of Zacatecas, on the eastern slopes of the Sierra Madre Occidental, Esteban Carbone and Miguel Martine met at a cantina. The mountains around the city, layered in yellow, tan, red, and brown, produced a spectacular effect. Someday this mining town could attract people from all over the world. Now, with the railroad only partly completed, in the easy places further south, it retained some of the sleepy nature of an isolated village. When the saucy young lady brought a bottle of tequila, two shooters, salt and lime, the old friends watched with appreciation as her firm, mobile young bottom retreated to the bar.

"You are a married man, *amigo,*" they said in unison and laughed.

Carbone poured and they went through the age-old ritual of licking the web of one hand, sprinkling salt there from the small dish, picking a wedge of lime. They licked salt, swallowed the clear liquor, bit the lime. The stringent juice cooled their throats as it trickled down. Carbone dispensed more.

"Salud, dinero y amor . . ." He raised his glass in toast.

"Y tiempo de gustarlos," Martine concluded.

"Health, money, and love," Carbone said with an edge of bitterness. "We have plenty of those. But the time to enjoy them . . ." He gave an elaborate shrug. "I fear that is growing short."

"So, then, Carbone, how long do you think it will be?"

"Until the end? Another month or two," Carbone opined.

"No, I mean until he gets here."

"Another week, perhaps. I am to be in El Paso to meet him then. Have you had any further incidents?"

Martine frowned. "I have lost a few head of sheep, some goats. But that could be for some other reason. No fires. My last shipment to the plaza in Ciudad Mexico was not stolen."

Carbone massaged his forehead to rub away the frown lines. "He's not going to like too much what you do for a living, my friend. You know how he feels about animals."

A sigh gusted from Martine. The white cicatrix that extended from the outer edge of his right eye to the corner of his mouth flushed pink. "Oh, yes. I've listened to his lecture on the shabby way men have treated the wolves more than once. Or on how horses have feelings and need to be broken with gentleness. A man of many facets, our Smoke Jensen. Do you think it will be enough? You and I and him? Can we really stop this *loco,* Carvajal?"

"*¡Hijo chingado!*—son of a bitch!" Carbone repeated. "What kind of *rabia* calls himself 'the King of the North'? Five years ago he was a third-rate *bandido,* stealing *centavos* from the poor boxes in mountain village churches."

Martine sighed heavily. "Yes. And now all of Central Mexico lives in fear of his name. We can call him crazy, call him madman and rabid dog, but that fact remains. He is one powerful *loco,* if nothing else. I only hope Smoke Jensen has some ideas on how to rid ourselves of him."

At a table in deep shadows, a short distance away, a man peered from under the brim of his big sombrero and studied the two former *pistoleros.* It bothered him that they spoke in English; he caught only a word or two. Esteban Carbone y Ruiz sat straight in his chair, vibrant with an undiminished vigor, in spite of his being at least in his early forties. His straight, black hair, that pencil-line of mustache and shoe-button eyes never wavered or seemed out of place. No pot-belly on this one, the observer noted.

Nor on his companion, Miguel Antonio Martine y Garcia. Younger than Carbone by at least ten years, he was a big, ef-fervescent man with broad shoulders and a trim body. Even though it was reputed that he and Carbone had hung up their guns some seven years ago, one could almost see them there, poised in their well-oiled holsters, ready to leap to life and spit flame and death. An involuntary shudder passed through the onlooker.

He had recovered his composure when the pair had fin-ished their third shots of tequila and dropped a five-peso gold piece in the girl's tray. They rose and departed, rich cigar smoke trailing behind them. Quickly the man came to his boots and went out the back way. In five minutes he stood in the presence of his *patrón, Don* Gustavo Angel Carvajal, *El Rey del Norte.*

Hat clasped in both hands in front of his pigeon chest, he spoke with fervor and awe. "It is as I say, Your Excellency, Don Gustavo. They talked in English and few words made sense, but it was of en—ending your career. Of that I am sure, And of something called a Smoke Jensen."

Carvajal's crossed, obsidian eyes narrowed, which pro-duced a snake-like glitter. He seized upon the last words of the informant. "Yes. Who or what is a Smoke Jensen? He or it is coming from El Paso in *los Estados Unidos,* eh? That's what I want you to find out," he added in an aside to Ignacio Quintero, one of his subordinate commanders.

"Sí, Excellencia," Quintero responded briskly. "I—uh—I have heard of this Smoke Jensen. He is a famous gunfighter from *los Estados Unidos.* He has killed many men. Hundreds, they say."

"So what? Can he defeat an army? Learn what he looks

like. Then take enough men along to the border, Ignacio. Find this Jensen and watch him. If—" The strange, hot light came into his eyes again. "If he then comes into the empire of the great Montezuma, he is to be destroyed. Go now. I have spoken."

3

Rupert Connors groaned softly and made feeble movements with his arms and legs. A soft buzz in the near distance resolved into human speech. Funny, he couldn't quite make out the sense of what was being said. With enormous effort, he located the bottom rail of the corral and dragged himself to his knees. Rupe's eyes had swollen nearly shut, he found when he tried to open them. He brushed at the burning lids with his big hands and wiped mud from his face. He could see now, through tears that sought to wash away the blood and clotted dirt.

They were there, together, talking. The stranger and that damned brat. What was the kid saying? Something, something about his mother. And—and going with the stranger. Can't let 'im do that. He'd twist everything, make it look like Wilma had been done in deliberate. Rupe knew he had to stop them. He needed something to help him get on his feet. He groped blindly and came upon a long, hard shaft. The pitchfork! Fingers of both hands wrapped around the oak handle, he forced his way to his boots and stood swaying for a moment. Then the inspiration came to him.

Holding the wicked iron tines horizontally before him, he

started toward the man and boy in a shambling walk. "I'll get ya. I'll get ya both," he mush-mouthed.

Those deadly fingers of metal had nearly reached the man's broad back when the stranger turned with a cat-quick speed like nothing Rupe Connors had ever seen. The well-used Colt .44 left the holster in a blur, and surprise widened Rupe's eyes when he saw smoke bloom at the muzzle. By then the pain had already exploded in his gut. The sledgehammer blow doubled him over, and he abruptly plopped on his butt in the dirt. He had already let go of the pitchfork. It was only then that his mind registered the shouted warning of the boy. Could it have been *that* fast? Gasping out his life in a stunned numbness that now washed over him, Rupe Connors struggled to form words.

"You—said—you c-could stop this by te-telling me your—name. Wh-Wha-What is it?"

"Smoke Jensen."

It echoed hollowly in Rupe's head. The words brought with them a glimmer of wisdom. Eternal cold clutched at him as he admitted error for the first time in his life. "Oh, God, I—I done a right stupid thing, didn't I?"

"You chose the path you walked, Connors," Smoke told him, but he was talking to a corpse.

Bobby tugged at his trouser leg. "Now you gotta take me along, mister. I ain't got nothing to stay here for."

Smoke considered that for a moment. After due deliberation he admitted to himself that he couldn't fault the kid's logic. "I suppose I must for a while," he allowed. "D'you have any kin around these parts?"

"No, sir."

A frown came and went on Smoke's broad brow. "Well, I can take you into the next town. Someone there will look out for you. What's your name, son? I heard Connors call you Bobby."

"Robert Edward Lee Harris, Mr. Smoke. An' I've heard all

about you. Gee, that was so fast I didn't even have a warning clean out before you had your gun movin'."

"Fast isn't always best," Smoke found himself explaining. "It's accuracy that counts. Now, Robert Edward Lee Harris, ah, that's for the man who commanded the Army of Northern Virginia, I take it?" At Bobby's nod, Smoke went on. "We'd best care for your pony and saddle her if she can take it."

"What about him?" Bobby asked, pointing to the dead Connors.

"Umm. I suppose we should bury him. Though he could lay there and rot for all I care. Never could abide someone who'd abuse women, children or animals."

"How 'bout we toss him over the plow horse and take him into town? Let *them* bury him."

"The town folks? Not right to saddle them with that expense," Smoke noted.

"No. I mean that bunch he drank with and played cards all the time. They're the closest thing he had to friends."

Amused at so astute an observation from a small boy, Smoke decided to enlarge the lad's knowledge of the world. "You'll find that sort of friend tends to distance himself from a dead man. But it's worth a try."

Half an hour later, they started out for Starkville.

What does one do with a 10-year-old boy? Smoke considered that question as they rode through the splendors at the top of Raton Pass. They had reached Starkville in early afternoon. Smoke Jensen had turned the body of Rupe Connors over to the sheriff and explained what had happened. The lawman made a stern face and questioned Bobby closely. He substantiated what Smoke had said and pointed to his split lip. Then he yanked up his shirt and revealed a multitude of fresh and fading bruises on his skinny chest and back. Smoke also advised the sheriff of the probable cause of the death of Mrs. Connors.

Still gruff, the law dog had grunted and given an "I thought so" nod. When asked about someone to take in the boy, he had raised both hands, palms up, in a resigned gesture. "Ain't no one in this burg," he said tersely.

To Smoke's surprise, two of Connors' cronies agreed to stand the cost of a funeral. Not a fancy one, mind you, they had hastily asserted. Which left Smoke Jensen stuck with Bobby Harris. Man and boy, they rode on south the next morning.

Civilization and progress had invaded this southernmost edge of Colorado, Smoke noted. The Denver and Rio Grande Railroad had track crews busily grading, placing ties, laying rails, and dumping ballast for a new mainline that would connect Santa Fe with the distant East via the shiny ribbons of steel. Hard, numbing work, Smoke mused. Unbearably dull for these workmen, he also considered.

A strict moralist and a teetotaler, the president of the D & RG had hired railroad police to keep away from end-of-track the usual clutter of tents that housed saloons and bawdy houses. The men should be using their hard-earned money to provide for their families, not spending it on whores and cheap whiskey, the head man had pontificated. It didn't surprise Smoke, then, when one of a trio of gandy dancers hailed him as he and Bobby rode by.

"Howdy there," called a big, beefy, red-haired track layer.

Smoke howdied back. The other two stopped work also, in hopes of some novelty, and looked piercingly at the strangers. One of them spat a stream of tobacco juice. Their nominal spokesman pushed more conversation on Smoke.

"M'name's McGuiness."

"Jensen," Smoke gave sparely.

"Looks like you plucked a rat out of a flood."

"What are you getting at, McGuiness?" Smoke demanded.

"That boy there. Skinny little thing, with too long hair. Like a half-drowned rat, you ask me. He kin of yours, or is he along to warm your soogans?"

Well, hell! What sort of imbecile would make such an offensive suggestion? Smoke Jensen's temper flared, then burst into ripe flame as he saw by the blush on Bobby's cheeks that he understood the slur given by the big Irish gandy dancer.

"You've got a pretty nasty tongue on you, McGuiness," Smoke growled warningly. "I think it's dug a hole that's going to be hard for you to get out of."

"Not so long as I get a little help from my friends," McGuiness bantered, all carefree and light, eager for the diversion a fight would bring.

"Make it easy on yourself," Smoke urged. "I'll accept your apology, and so will the boy, then we can ride on our way."

"Sure an' what if I choose not to?" McGuiness taunted.

"Then I'll have to step down from this saddle and kick the living hell out of you."

"Try it," one of McGuiness's companions challenged, "an' ye'll have three to fight. Kid looks like a sissy-boy to me."

What happened next caught Smoke Jensen completely off guard. "You better take that back, mister," Bobby's high, thin voice rang with emotion. "Do it, or Smoke Jensen'll shoot you down like a dog."

"Him? That's Smoke Jensen?" the third gandy dancer chortled. "Not likely."

"Shut up, O'Dwyer," McGuiness snapped, suddenly sobered.

"What the hell for, Mick? Sure, he's a big one, but ev'ryone knows Smoke Jensen is eight foot tall. He wears two guns, too. Left one high up and butt pointed out. Reg'lar top gun." O'Dwyer turned to Bobby. "You're a gawdamn liar, kid. When we get done with this backside of a mule, I'm gonna wash out yer mouth with soap."

Smoke Jensen sighed heavily and handed the reins to Bobby. "Hold Sidewinder for me."

He dismounted and shucked his cartridge belt and holster, looped the free end through the buckle, and hung it on his saddle horn. From his hip pocket he took the pair of thin leather gloves and slowly put them on. McGuiness had a less eager expression by that time. He hung back slightly and took stock of the man facing them.

"Go get 'em, boys," he muttered softly.

The word "easy" didn't touch this one, Smoke knew. He would do well to polish off all three. And that wouldn't happen without taking some damage himself. Smoke stepped away from the horses and set himself, knees slightly bent, arms relaxed and at his sides. He watched the two muscular trackmen advance, their faces darkening as they summoned up the lust to do battle.

"Take him from the left, Sloane, I'll go in from this side. This is gonna be easy as eatin' apple pie."

O'Dwyer began to shuffle his feet then and lifted fists large enough to completely cover the face of Bobby Harris. A lopsided grin split his face widely as he closed in on Smoke Jensen. Smoke wiped the grin from those lips with a hard right he uncorked from the balls of his feet.

He continued in the direction of the punch, pleased at the meaty smack his knuckles made when they connected with O'Dwyer's mouth. His momentum brought him on around, and he swung the leg his weight had left. It swept Sloane's boots out from under him. Smoke stepped to Sloane and drove him flat onto the ground with a shoulder-rolling right. Bobby's yelp of surprise came an instant before O'Dwyer jumped on Smoke's back.

"I got him! I got him!" the burly gandy dancer shouted.

With a roar, McGuiness joined the fray. The powerful, experienced brawler waded in, fists pumping. Smoke absorbed a lot of what most men would consider terrible punishment to his middle and chest before he managed to set his boots and spin so suddenly that McGuiness's next blows pummeled O'Dwyer's back. The smaller—though far from average—sized O'Dwyer dropped his grasp around Smoke's shoulders and fell away. He got an elbow in the sternum from Smoke for good measure.

Gagging, O'Dwyer turned away from the fight. McGuiness tried a kick at one of Smoke's kneecaps. Smoke dropped low and caught the flying boot. With a savage twist, he wrenched McGuiness off his feet. The huge railroader fell heavily to the ground.

"Get 'em, Smoke, get 'em," Bobby shouted encouragement.

When Smoke tried to rise, he caught a set of knuckles in the center of his forehead. Blackness swam behind Smoke's eyes for a moment, and he felt the warm trickle of blood. Outside of hard-rock miners, Smoke knew, they didn't come any tougher than railroaders. He wiped at the rivulet of blood and then swung his forearm horizontally. It connected with O'Dwyer an inch below his navel.

With a whoop and a whoosh, O'Dwyer lost what remained of his lunch. While he was still bent over, Smoke came to his boots and delivered a knee to the middle of O'Dwyer's face. The gandy dancer dropped like he'd been shot. Smoke whirled in time to face McGuiness and Sloane together.

Smoke slipped several blows on his broad shoulders and batted others aside. But he couldn't avoid all of them. McGuiness unleashed a pile driver punch that bruised flesh, and Smoke recognized the sharp twinge of a broken rib. He sucked air and then stepped in close. Smoke snapped fast, hard fists to their faces. McGuiness rocked back, panting heavily as he gulped out words.

"Y'know, might be the kid's right. This is one tough sumbitch."

By then a crowd had gathered, shouting encouragement to their fellow railers. Smoke knew for certain that he had to carry the fight to them in so painful a way that it ended soon. It was that or he'd lose. He would be in real trouble, too, if all three hung on long enough to sap his strength even a slight bit. Accordingly, he sidestepped toward O'Dwyer, who was stirring feebly on the ground. With a swift move, Smoke lifted the man by his shirt-front and popped him solidly on the jaw. A soft grunt and O'Dwyer went off to sleepy land. That left only two. Smoke turned back to see that McGuiness had picked up a spike mallet.

Laughing, Sloane circled Smoke, making light jabs that stung but did no real harm. Meanwhile, McGuiness closed in with the deadly hammer. Smoke Jensen grabbed for the nearest object with which he could defend himself. His fingers closed around a rail alignment spade. The long steel shaft had a shoe-tongue lever and spiked hook on one end. Smoke had time to grasp it two-handed near the middle before McGuiness swung his first blow.

Smoke blocked the descending mallet as though he wielded a quarterstaff. Muscles strained and bulged in both arms of the burly McGuiness, while the crowd shouted approval. Smoke resisted with equal energy. Gradually he gained the advantage of leverage and hurled McGuiness away from him. Windmilling the narrow-faced hammer in a figure eight, McGuiness started back in.

Lightning quick, Smoke Jensen flicked the bare end of the rail spade into the bulging middle of his opponent. McGuiness grunted and went to one knee. His hammer thudded ominously into the ground. Smoke followed up, realizing he could kill the man easier than he could knock him out of the fight.

McGuiness raised his hammer in time to block Smoke's next blow. Smoke reversed ends and smacked the slightly rounded spade end into the side of McGuiness's head. His eyes crossed, and he made a gurgling noise deep in his throat.

Slowly, the huge figure went slack and McGuiness sagged to the ground.

"B'God, I-think-the-kid-was-right," Sloane blurted out in a babble of words. "You are Smoke Jensen."

Smoke ached in more places than he knew he had. Yet, his heart sang with that sweet, keen joy of victory. "I am. You could have saved us all a lot of hurt if you'd listened in the first place. Now, I'm waiting for that apology."

"Uh—right you are, Mr. Jensen. Right sorry about the mouthy ways of m'friends here. They got outta line. Sure did." Sloane waited with caught breath, blood running from one nostril and an ear. Smoke nodded toward Bobby. Sloane took the cue. "You, too, kid. Plain to see you're no sissy-boy. None of us shoulda mouthed off like that. I'm plum ashamed."

"Thank you," Smoke said simply.

He stripped off the light gloves and replaced them in his pocket. At Sidewinder's flank he rehung his gun belt and swung into the saddle. He clicked his tongue, and the Appaloosa started off at a lazy walk. Bobby, eyes as big as they could get, swallowed hard and followed. He quickly caught up.

"I never, never seen anything like that," he gulped.

"Let's hope you don't have occasion to see it again. Any more of that, and I'll never get where I'm going," Smoke told him sincerely, conscious of his cracked rib.

In camp that night, halfway through the steep Raton Pass, Bobby Harris sat hunched and quiet on the opposite side of the fire from Smoke Jensen. The boy hugged his knees up under his chin and took on a "hundred-mile stare." Wise in the ways of youngsters, at least his own, Smoke kept a congenial silence. At last, Bobby sighed heavily and spoke.

"What *are* you going to do with me? I mean, I know you can't be tied down with a kid taggin' along to—to wherever it is you're going."

This kid had a good intelligence, Smoke realized. His

grammar and speech habits had steadily improved the further away they got from the dead Rupe Connors. Now he had seized upon the key question to Smoke's present dilemma.

"That's a good question, boy," Smoke allowed. "Trouble is, I don't have an answer as yet."

"Do you have a home? A real place with a family, I mean," Bobby probed, his smooth brow wrinkled.

"Yes, I do. A horse breeding ranch up in the High Lonesome."

"Huh?"

"That's what the mountain men used to call the high Rockies, northwest of Denver. It means a big, empty place, with tall mountains all around, where even a whisper sounds loud to your ears."

"Gosh. That's po-poetic. You're married, then?"

Smoke chuckled, the image of his beautiful Sally instantly displayed behind his eyes. He cut a shrewd look at Bobby. "Yes. Her name is Sally. She's the most beautiful woman I have ever seen. We have four youngsters, too. They're a bit older than you, living back East and going to school in Europe."

"Ugh! What an awful thing to have to do. I remember being back there before my folks, my real dad, that is, came out to Colorado. Couldn't breathe the air for all the coal smoke. Noisy, dirty, all kinds of mean kids who'd steal your shoes if they had nothing else to take. Cops beatin' on everyone. I think they must have had a rule that someone had to hate kids to be a policeman."

Quite a chatterbox he had turned out to be. "The big cities are like that, true," Smoke admitted. "Fortunately, one of my sons is in New England; green fields and rolling mountains, lazy rivers and sailboats. It's right peaceful . . . if a little dull."

Turned full-face to Smoke, eyes round in wonder, Bobby blurted, "Gosh, you been there, Mr. Smoke?"

"Yes, I have," he replied, recalling that hectic race eastward to save his wife and unborn child from the mad designs of Rex Davidson and the man called Dagget. "But it wasn't a pleasure trip."

Bobby got a sly expression. "Some gun business, huh?"

Damn, maybe he was too astute, Smoke considered. "Sort of."

"Folks say you've killed fifty men in shoot-outs," Bobby hazarded.

For some reason, Smoke found himself uncomfortable under this youthful scrutiny. "At least."

"Others say it's more'n two hundred."

"Bobby, there's something you should learn young. Nobody who's worth his salt keeps count. Killing's not a contest, with prizes for the winner. A man does what he has to do. Deliberately or because he's pushed into it and no place to go to avoid it. Only loudmouthed punks keep score, cut notches in the grips of their six guns. Most often, those are for show and blow, not for real."

"Please, Mr. Smoke, tell me an exciting story about your life," Bobby urged.

Smoke sipped the last of his coffee and poured the dregs into the coals. He chuckled softly before he spoke. "I'll make you a deal. I'll tell you a story about the greatest man I ever knew, and you stop chattering and go to sleep."

Bobby took on a pained expression. "Must I?"

"We've got a long ride tomorrow."

"All right."

"Settled, then." Smoke's voice took on a faraway, dreaming tone. "A long time ago, there was this mountain of a man, name of Preacher. He was in the fur trade. Some said his daddy was a puma and his momma a rattlesnake." A muffled giggle came from Bobby. "To near everyone, he was the biggest and best of all the old mountain men. Now, one day, Preacher came on this scrawny kid, dirty face and somewhat confused, because he'd lost his way in the mountains. Ol' Preacher took mercy on the tenderfoot right then and there.

He . . ." When Smoke Jensen finished the last line of his pean of praise to his mentor, Bobby Harris had snuggled down in his blanket and was breathing softly in deep slumber.

Smoke doused the fire and rolled up in his own blankets. His last thoughts, before sound sleep muffled him, returned to the early afternoon. What the hell was he going to do with a ten-year-old boy?

4

Raton, New Mexico Territory, was wild and wooly. Track crews labored to extend the rails northward to meet in the pass with those inching south. The promise of prosperity that the railroad represented had attracted merchants, entrepreneurs, and of course, bartenders, gamblers and whores. Raw wood buildings went up faster than the track extended. The sawmill aroma and steady rap of hammers filled the air. Smoke Jensen and Bobby Harris rode into this industrious bustle near noon the next day.

"Gosh," Bobby enthused, "this is a regular boom town."

Smoke flashed a small grin. "If I was a betting man, I'd wager that fame and fortune will bypass the good folk of Raton. Popularity is destined to settle on some other place. No doubt Santa Fe. The Atchison, Topeka and Santa Fe already have tracks into there. Any place two railroads meet, that's where the big growth happens. Besides, Raton is Spanish for *rat*. Who ever heard of a great metropolis named Rat?"

That sent Bobby into a wild cackle of laughter. The big Appaloosa horse and small paint pony ambled down the busy main street. A gust of giggles came from Bobby again when they reached the next intersection. Two young men looked their way.

Both had the air of blooming hardcases. Gaunt cheeks, hard, cold eyes, and the ready six-guns, extras stuck into the top of their trousers. They had the practiced sneers, too. Every two-bit punk in every low-class dive on the frontier had its share of these would-be predators. One of the pair reached up to tug at the wisps of a straggly mustache that tried to grow on an adolescent lip.

"You rescue that from a rag bag, mister?" he asked of Smoke Jensen. "Or don't you give enough of a rip to outfit yer kids decent and proper?"

Damn, Smoke thought irritably in his first reaction, the kid drew trouble like horse droppings attract flies. Then Smoke cut his eyes sideways to Bobby. It might seem funny to some, but he'd never given any thought to the boy's clothes.

Bobby wore a handmade shirt, and so did he, to accommodate shoulders too broad to fit off-the-shelf merchandise, Smoke weighed. On closer examination now, he saw that the boy's was made from a flour sack, while his own shirt had been cut and hand-sewn from the finest quality cloth by Sally. Faded, much-patched jeans were belted tightly at Bobby's slender waist by a length of frayed lariat. Bare feet were stuffed into worn stirrups. Not too unusual for a kid from a hardscrabble farm, Smoke evaluated. That summation released a hot glow aimed at the rudeness of these punks. He turned his attention back to them.

"It appears your folks might have dressed you well enough, but they sure neglected teaching you manners," Smoke said levelly.

"Don't!" one rowdie barked, his left hand lifted in a stopping gesture, the right hovered over the butt-grip of his six-shooter. "Don't get lippy with us, mister. You'd be bitin' off a whole passel more trouble than you could handle."

"Gabe's right, mister. You're strangers to these parts, so you don't know who you're mouthin' off to."

Smoke snorted derisively. "And I don't have any burning

desire to find out. Why don't we just ease off and go our separate ways?"

"Are you kidding?" Gabe shouted, warming to the vibrant aliveness of battle lust. "You insult us like that and think you can just turn yer back and walk off? I got a mind to knock you into the middle of next week."

"No," Smoke responded with low intensity. "Not the both of you could do that. On the other hand, if I took a mind to it, I could kick your butts so hard and so high you'd look like you were wearing fur collars."

Bobby's eyes had grown wide and wild, and he squirmed in the saddle in anticipation of another Smoke Jensen solution. Smoke took note of that while the faces of the two punks turned crimson. A sudden jerk of Gabe's head brought his attention back to them.

They couldn't be more than seventeen, eighteen, Smoke decided. Too young to die. Someone else could teach them the hard lessons they needed. He especially didn't want one of them to open the dance when Bobby was in the line of fire. Smoke bit back his own rising call to combat and shook his head.

"I agree." Smoke broke the silence. "The boy could use some dressing up. I'll tend to it today. Now, let's just all back off, and we'll be on our way."

Without waiting for a reply, though a part of Smoke's mind burned with an unaccustomed feeling of humiliation, he lifted Sidewinder's reins and set the big Appaloosa in motion. It took all his willpower to turn away from the confrontation and not give these impudent vermin what they deserved.

"Yer yellah!" Gabe shouted. "That's what. A yellah cur dog."

Smoke cut his eyes to Bobby. What he read on the boy's face profoundly shocked him. Rather than relief, or pride, the lad's expression revealed a deep sense of being shamed by Smoke backing down from the punks. Bobby's lower lip protruded like a pink bulb, and he would not meet Smoke's gaze.

That reaction confused Smoke. Bobby actually looked forward to the violence and blood, perhaps even to a death. Could the boy have already been irredeemably bent and twisted by his drunken lout of a stepfather?

"Over there," Smoke announced a couple of minutes later.

Smoke directed Bobby to a haberdasher's establishment. So far it stood alone, not crowded into a block of other, similar clapboard buildings. Sparkling clean windows, despite the dust haze in the air, displayed a wide variety of clothing items for men and boys. Inside, Smoke oversaw outfitting Bobby with two pairs of new trousers, four shirts, a light jacket, and boots.

"Do I gotta wear these?" Bobby protested, reverting to his illiterate speech pattern. "They're hot, an' tight, make my feet hurt. I done gone barefoot most my life, don't see why I should change now."

Nearing the end of his patience, Smoke Jensen glowered down at him. "Because winter is coming, and it gets damn cold around here. You need to break them in good before you have to wear them all the time."

Hope flashed brightly in Bobby's eyes. "Then I can go without 'em some of the time?"

"When we're not in town," Smoke qualified.

"Shoot!" It came out sounding much like another, nastier word.

All but simpering, a prissy clerk observed, "Your boy has quite a mouth on him, I see."

"Don't you start," Smoke growled and silenced the salesclerk. "Now we need a hat."

Swallowing the knot of fear in his throat, the delicate vender started to a tier of shelves. "I have just the thing. The latest fashion from New York."

He produced a dark blue item with a low, domed crown and narrow, rolled brim. Long azure satin ribbons hung to the rear. Both Smoke and Bobby made expressions of distaste that renewed their mutual bond.

"I think something more suited to this country," Smoke suggested.

Long pale fingers fidgeting, the clerk found another boy's style in brown that matched the vest Bobby had fancied for himself. At least it didn't have ribbons. The youngster gave it one slight glance and turned his button nose to Smoke in appeal.

"I want one like yours."

Smoke grunted. "When you're a man, you can have a man's hat. That'll do fine," he added for the clerk. For some reason Smoke felt eager to get himself and Bobby out of this place.

Out on the street, looking store-fresh in his new clothes, Bobby glanced to the left and right. "Now what?"

"First we find a place to eat. Then we look for someone who can help us locate a place for you to stay."

"Bu-but I don't want to stay here. I want to go with you."

"Look, kid, you said it yourself the other night. You can't go along where I'm headed. So we have to find someone willing and suitable to take you in."

Tears welled, but didn't escape Bobby's big cobalt eyes. "Yes, you're right. I know that. But I hoped . . . for a minute there . . ." He stopped short.

"It's rough, kid. Sure. I got left alone when I was not much older than you. Preacher came along, took me under his wing. Things worked out."

Bobby's face brightened. "Like in that story you told me in camp?"

"True story, Bobby. Let's eat. It's been so long since breakfast my tongue's forgot what coffee tastes like."

During the meal, Smoke decided that finding a minister, if there was one in this raw town, would be the best place to start. On the street once again, they walked three blocks, and Smoke asked several people about the presence of a reverend.

"Oh, there's a church over in the Mexican section. The padre there can probably help you. Ol' Colonel Larson is out ridin' the circuit. He preaches here twice a month. Should be back any day now," one helpful local informed him.

Smoke thanked him and they turned away. That brought Smoke and Bobby face-to-face with the two budding thugs who had earlier taunted them. They blocked the boardwalk in a hunch-shouldered, menacing manner.

"We meet again, you yellow dog," Gabe snarled. "This here is Pete McGiver, and I'm Gabe Winkler. That should have you wettin' yer britches. Now we want you to get down on your belly and crawl for us."

No one who knew him, and most who didn't, ever suggested Smoke Jensen had the least bit of back-down in him, let alone the willingness to crawl for scum like this. "No," Smoke said in the voice of Death. "Bobby, get out of the way. Cross the street *right now.*"

His reluctance to bring grief to these neophyte, callow bullies had been genuine. This latest challenge had simply drained Smoke's supply of compassion. If he worked it just right, they might yet live to profit from the experience. "Do it, Bobby," he demanded again.

"Do it, Bobby," Gabe mimicked.

Frowning, unwilling to go, Bobby took hesitant steps into the street. Smoke kept his eyes locked on the would-be bad men. Pete McGiver seemed nervous; beads of oily sweat popped out on his forehead. Gabe sneered and preened. His right hand hovered over the cheap pearl grips of his .44 Merwin and Hulbert.

"Either you crawl or go for that iron, yellow dog," Gabe challenged.

"No. I don't crawl before any man. Leave it alone," Smoke urged.

"DRAW, GAWDAMN YOU!" Gabe bellowed.

Smoke shook his head. "Sorry. I won't do it. You want this so badly, you draw. Both of you. I'll let you get your irons clear of leather."

"Then what?" Gabe taunted. "You gonna pee your britches and run home to Mommy?"

"No. If I choose, I'll then kill the both of you."

"Haw-haw!" Gabe brayed. Then, with a preparatory nod to Pete, they both went for their six-guns.

He knew it! Gabe Winkler knew he was fast, one of the best around these parts. The old fool hadn't even touched the worn grips of that old hog-leg, and here he had his six-inch barrel clear of leather and coming up on line. Pete had his shooter in action, too.

Then it happened.

And to his dying day, Gabe Winkler could never account for the blur of motion and sudden hot pain in the bulging biceps of his right arm. Only belatedly did he hear the report of the stranger's six-gun.

Gabe's .44 Merwin and Hulbert went flying. The pain had hardly begun to register when the stranger took a quick two steps forward and laid the barrel of his .44 Colt alongside Pete McGiver's head. Pete went to the boardwalk like a poleaxed steer. Then Gabe found himself looking into the coldest set of gray eyes he had ever seen. Like two fancy gun muzzles.

"Don't play with grownup's toys, sonny," the stranger told him.

From across the way, a high, thin voice chirped, "That's showin' 'em, Smoke."

"Smoke?" the aching Gabe worked over his lips.

"That's what folks call me. Smoke Jensen," the deadly stranger told Gabe.

Gabe wanted to puke up his last meal and beg for mercy. Then he realized he had already received the most merciful treatment one could ever get from Smoke Jensen. "You—you let us live."

Jensen's lips quirked at the corners. "You're too stupid to be worth killing. Go back to the farm or your dad's ranch and learn how to be a good farmer or stockman. This life's not for you or your friend." Smoke bent and removed their firearms, tucked them into his waistband and strolled calmly across the street.

"Hold on a minute there, mister." Part of what passed for the local law in Raton had arrived on the scene.

He was young, bull-whang tough, and so thoroughly high-altitude tanned it made his big, boldly blue eyes seem to leap from his face. The little, rectangular half-glasses perched on the tip of his twice-broken nose had to be someone's idea of a bad joke. Smoke touched Bobby's shoulder and stopped walking. The man and boy turned to the lawman.

"You just shot a man, pistol-whipped another, and now you walk off as though you were headed for a cool beer and some fried pork skins."

"Thank you, but we just ate," Smoke quipped with a straight face. "Truth is, since we are strangers here, I was going to have to locate someone to tell me where I could find the law."

"The law's right here," the deputy marshal said nastily. He flipped over the wide lapel of his black broadcloth coat to reveal the badge. "We have a little talking to do about this shooting."

"It's simple, really," Smoke assured him. "When we were riding in, these two punks braced us. I managed to talk our way out of anything nasty. Then, a few minutes ago, they called me out, demanded gun play."

"So you shot one and beat hell out of the other one. That was a mistake. Their fathers are important men in this community."

Smoke eyed the deputy askance. He wondered if the young

law dog was for real. "That's unfortunate. They should have spent more time in the upbringing of their children. Both of them drew first. The one I shot had his hammer back."

"Was that before or after you took it away from him?" the badge asked nastily.

Cold, gray eyes fixed him in place. "I'd back water, were I you."

Weighing the menace, he swallowed hard. "Look, those boys' paws are wealthy, influential men."

In other words they had the local law in their hip pockets, Smoke reasoned. "I don't care if they are the King and Queen of Sweden. I gave you the facts; the least you can do is try to verify them."

"So I managed to ascertain," the deputy said tightly.

Ascertain? What sort did they hire around here for deputies? Smoke put it away. "Then you know I acted in self-defense. So, if you will excuse me—"

"I'm not through yet. What's your name?"

"Smoke Jensen," Smoke provided tiredly.

The lawman blanched. He swallowed hard to remove the lump that had formed in his throat. "I don't need this. Not today, not any day. Smoke Jensen? Well, Mr. Jensen, I have to draw up a report on this. I'd appreciate it if you dropped by before you left town and signed it."

"Fine. Say in about three hours?"

"Excellent. The office is two blocks down, a small stone building on the left."

"No doubt," Smoke offered dryly. "C'mon, Bobby."

"I appreciate your willingness to make the effort on Bobby's behalf," Smoke Jensen stated an hour and a half later in a small, neat house five blocks off the main drag.

He had learned of a childless couple from the padre at the church in the Mexican section of town. "Although they are not of my faith," the priest had added, as though in caution. Smoke found the Goodmans, Marvin and Ella, to be warm, hospitable people who made over Bobby and provided fresh-baked cake and good, strong coffee. Ella even produced a large glass of milk for the boy.

"We—we've been without the happiness of a child in the house for long enough," Marvin stressed.

"Yes, dear. I know how you have longed for a son to take fishing, show off your office to, and make into a friend," Ella cooed. Smoke read her guilt at failing to conceive on her face.

"Yes, well," Smoke injected, not wanting to prolong the farewells. "I have to be on my way. Bobby, the Goodmans very much want you to live with them. You behave and study hard in school. What's happened is in the past. Leave it there."

Smoke started for the door. "Lemme come to your horse with you," Bobby pleaded, rising from the overstuffed chair where he had been sitting.

Out in the street, Smoke self-consciously patted the boy on the head and started to climb aboard Sidewinder. "You take care of your pony, hear?"

Suddenly he was being clutched around the legs by thin, strong arms, and Bobby buried his face into Smoke's shirt, above his belt buckle. "I don't want you to go, Mr. Smoke. You—you saved my life," he choked. "Ol' Rupe woulda killed me if you hadn't come along." Long withheld, tears coursed down the boy's tan cheeks. "I'll be good, I promise. I'll stay with those folks and do what they ask, even—even go to school. But when you come back, take me with you to your ranch, please. I don't want to live in this town."

"I—er—I don't know how long I'll be gone. And the longer it is, the more heartbreak you'll bring to the Goodmans by leaving," Smoke offered.

Bobby hadn't considered that. It gave him pause; then he tilted his head back and gazed up at Smoke with some-thing close to adoration. Close enough to make Smoke uncomfortable. "You will stop and see me, won't you? Just for a while, a visit?"

Smoke cleared his throat. "I can manage that, I suppose."

With a visible effort of will, Bobby conquered his emotions, relinquished his hold on Smoke, and took a step back. He extended his hand to be shaken in a manly fashion. "Then, good-bye, Smoke Jensen. You take care of yourself, too. I—I'll miss you."

Smoke's big hand engulfed that of the boy. They shook solemnly and Smoke swung astride Sidewinder. A light touch of rein turned the spotted-rump steed's head, and Smoke gigged him with blunt spurs. Typical of the breed, Sidewinder fought mastery by a human and looked back at the forlorn figure of the boy sadly waving to Smoke. The big blue eyes of the horse seemed to contain the same sadness the lad's prolonged sigh revealed.

5

With purple-blue shadows touching the eastern horizon, and the mountains on the western vista crowned by a slice of intense orange light, Smoke Jensen made camp for the night. He estimated his location to be about halfway between Raton and Springer, New Mexico. He slipped the cinch and relieved Sidewinder of the burden of his saddle. Trail-wise for many years, Smoke forestalled his own comforts to cool out the big Appaloosa stallion. While he walked the animal and then gave it water, he munched on a cold biscuit. He had some fresh fatback, obtained in Raton, and a can of peaches. It would do.

His ground cloth and blanket went into place next, once he put Sidewinder's nose down in some grass that had survived the worst of the summer's heat. When his Spartan meal had been consumed, Smoke sat hunched over the tiny fire that boiled his coffee. Its orange-yellow light reflected off the rock overhang that Smoke had selected as much for concealment as partial shelter. He'd put plenty of Arbuckle's *Fino* into the small granite pot, and the aroma told him it was ready shortly after the moon rose and a chorus of coyotes serenaded the night.

Smoke had taken only three sips when he heard the

muffled thud of hoofbeats. He tensed momentarily, set his cup aside, and eased back out of the direct light of the fire. His right hand dropped naturally into position by the big, well-worn .44 Colt tied down at his hip. The sound grew louder, and he slipped the hammer thong.

Those spoiled brats back in Raton could take prizes for stupid, Smoke considered. Surely they weren't so dumb as to come after him, in light of their last meeting. The hoofbeats neared the rounded breast of the hillside where Smoke made his camp. Only one horse, which stopped abruptly.

"Hel—hello the camp?" a thin, soprano voice offered tentatively.

Smoke came to his boots in time with the recognition of that voice. "Bobby? What are you doing out here? How did you find me?"

"Can I come on in?"

"I've a mind to paddle your bottom all the way back to Raton," Smoke growled. "Yeah, come on in."

Bobby Harris and his paint pony appeared in the firelight. The boy sighed heavily and dismounted. "Stand, Dollar," he commanded.

Smoke studied him in silence, curiosity growing. "You didn't answer my questions, boy."

Bobby shrugged. "I learned to make out Sidewinder's sign a long ways back. All I needed to do was find it on the road south and follow. Uh—at least until dark. Then I figgered all I had to do was keep on until I saw a campfire."

"You could have gotten the wrong camp, found a heap of trouble," Smoke growled.

"Naw," Bobby said and blushed. "Dollar knew Sidewinder's smell. She whuffled when she caught a whiff."

Puzzled, Smoke frowned. "Where'd you learn all this trail savvy?"

"Before ol' Rupe took to drink so much, he taught me a lot about readin' sign, huntin' an' trackin' men."

"Humm. He wasn't completely worthless," Smoke judged.

"Only the last couple of years. But what he did kilt Maw, so I ain't got a tear."

"Me neither, son," Smoke admitted in sympathy. Abruptly, he grew brusk. "You still haven't told me why you're here."

Bobby studied the toes of his boots. "You ain't gonna believe me."

"Try me."

Bobby's eyes rolled up, and he sucked in air enough to get through his ordeal. "They weren't the nice people you thought, Mr. Smoke. They locked me in a room and didn't give me any supper. They—they were gonna sell me."

"What?"

"It's God's own truth, Mr. Smoke. I heard them talkin' after they ate their supper. They thought I was out in the wash house, takin' a bath." Bobby's expression clearly revealed his opinion of bathing. "I was in the kitchen, instead. They talked about selling me to the highest bidder. Someone who had lots of hard work to get done and didn't want to pay out wages. Or keep me and rent me out. That woman, Ella, said that. I was so scared, I just took all my new stuff and skedaddled."

Smoke mulled that over. The boy's voice held the ring of truth. Eyes big with fear at recounting this outlandish tale, he had a nervous quaver to his small chin. At last Smoke nodded, his plan firm.

"No sense in taking you back there. Time's too short and the law wouldn't be too happy to have me back in town again. He made that clear when I signed that report." The beaming smile Bobby gave him almost changed Smoke's mind. "Though I'd like to bring this little story up to the Goodmans and see how they react. People like that . . . they don't have a jail cell miserable enough or a pit deep enough to keep them in." Smoke sat down on his blanket. "We'll be moving on to Santa Fe."

"Can I—"

"*May* I," Smoke fired back, the father reflex surfacing.

"May I have something to eat? I'm hungry."

Smoke grinned. "There's some cold biscuit, fatback if you fry it, coffee."

"Coffee," Bobby repeated. "For me? Really?"

Oh hell, Smoke thought. *There goes a perfectly simple trip to take a hand in some sort of Mexican range war. What* can *I do with the kid?*

More of the aspen on the Sugarloaf had turned gold. A hint of frost hung in the early morning air. Sally Jensen pushed a stray strand of thick, dark hair away from her forehead. It would be a wonderful day.

Sally knew that from the first taste of autumn, like spices on her tongue. She loved the fall like Smoke savored spring. A smile curved her lips as she visualized Smoke, his massive barrel chest and bulging muscles of his huge upper arms bared to the first warming rays that promised renewed life. He would work like that for hours, alongside the hands, bare to the waist, chopping wood or chucking postholes with an auger.

She knew he had learned that lesson from Preacher, the redoubtable old mountain man who had raised him. Sally could almost hear the words. "No man worth his salt asks another man to do something he wouldn't do hisself."

That was Preacher all right. And that was her Smoke. He'd used another name when they were married. They had met shortly before Smoke nearly wiped out the small town of Bury, Idaho, in vengeance against those who had murdered his first wife and small son, Baby Arthur. Sally, she freely admitted to herself, had been a spirited young schoolteacher who had come West to find a more adventurous life than that offered in staid New Hampshire. They had fallen in love and married.

For several years, she and Smoke lived in peace. Then Smoke's reputation caught up with them. He assumed his real name again and did, as always, what a man had to do. The man responsible for this emergence of Smoke Jensen, gunfighter, was Tilden Franklin. He wanted to be king of the entire valley that countained the Sugarloaf. Worse, Sally recalled with a frown, he had long coveted her and had made the news public.

In the end, all Tilden Franklin got was half a dozen .44 slugs in the belly, from the guns of Smoke Jensen, and an eternal leasehold on a plot of valley ground, six-by-six-by-three feet in size. That had bought the young couple two years of blissful peace. Then Davidson, an old and implacable enemy of Preacher and anyone friendly to the old mountain man, and Davidson's twisted partner, Dagget, showed up to wreak havoc upon the Sugarloaf and avenge their unnatural hate on Smoke Jensen.

They lost in the end, and Smoke became a new father of twins.

Sally loved children. She had to or she would never have become a teacher. The family increased over the years, Sally mused, and grew older, and now resided far from the Sugarloaf. And, oh, how she missed them.

Sally's frown deepened as she looked toward the long, narrow lane that led from the big front gate of Sugarloaf to the ranch yard around the headquarters. Few people would brave Smoke's rather terse greeting posted on one of the tall, lodgepole pine uprights. "If you have no business at Sugarloaf, ride on by," it read. Now a young, slender figure, riding loose and at ease in the saddle, cantered up the final slope toward the house. When he drew closer, Sally noted he had a beguiling grin and wheat-straw hair that stuck out at odd angles.

He reined in and called out from a distance, "Hello, the house. I'm friendly."

"Howdy," Sally answered back. "Ride on in."

The stranger urged his mount forward and stopped at the tie-rail outside the low picket fence. He tipped his hat politely to Sally. "Mornin'. Sure is a fine day, ain't it?" His voice held a whine that detracted from his otherwise good looks.

"Yes, it is that. Do you have some business at Sugarloaf?" Sally asked in a neutral tone.

The young drifter removed his hat and worked plastic features into an expression of wry contrition. "Well, not 'zactly, ma'am. I was wonderin', is the boss hirin'?"

A drifter, Sally recognized at once and pursed her lips. "Not that I know of. You'll have to ask our foreman."

"Where'll I find him?"

Sally handled that one in the manner she and Smoke had frequently discussed. "He'll be in town later this afternoon," she said sweetly.

The drifter's mouth puckered. He spoke in a manner intended to dissemble. "Truth is, ma'am, I'm a bit down on my luck. It's a long ride back to Big Rock, an' I ain't et for some time. If you had any chores to do, I'd be obliged if I could he'p out a bit in exchange for a good breakfast. Sorta pad my innards for the ride back."

"There is some firewood needs chopping," Sally relented, her natural compassion for the hardships of others surfacing.

An eager expression replaced the soulful one. "I'll make the chips fly, ma'am, you can be sure of that. I'm grateful, really I am."

"Might I have your name?" Sally inquired.

"Yancy, ma'am. Named after my uncle, Yancy Yarnell," he went on, inventing a last name, "who served with Colonel Merril during the late unpleasantness. If you'll just direct me, I'll get a start on that firewood."

* * *

Somehow it didn't seem right. The more he worked on it in his mind, the more Yancy Riggs reckoned that life had dealt him a bad hand. He'd worked hard, bone-wearing hard, since he was big enough to take up a hoe and hack at the hard ground of his momma's kitchen garden. Other men did the same and wound up havin' something like this-here Sugarloaf. It stood to reason, then, that anyone who worked hard deserved the same, didn't it?

Another thing. Since he'd been growed enough to knock his paw on his butt and ride off, a saw handle sure didn't seem to fit Yancy's hand. The bow saw he used now quickly produced a rick of stove-length billets and a fresh crop of blisters on his hands. Enough, Yancy figured, for a breakfast. With axe in hand, he set to splitting the thigh-thick chunks into more manageable pieces.

Was this all he had to look forward to? His thoughts along this line brought him to that good-looker who provided this means of earning a meal. Bet she had nice legs under that long, frilly-edged dress. She had the face of an angel. Yancy could hear her rattling pots and pans in the kitchen at his back. A man had a right to have someone like her waitin' for him. That took Yancy to another realization.

He'd not seen or heard from the boss man of this spread. Nor any hands, for that matter. Was that purty young thing all alone? Despite himself, Yancy felt that familiar stirring in his loins. He hit the next stick of firewood with particular force. No, he wouldn't, couldn't let that happen again.

Hot-tempered, and with a quick fuse where women were concerned, Yancy had been forced to drift out of too much of the West to allow himself to indulge in such dreams. She sure had a nice smile and lovely dark hair. Yancy groaned and split another billet. Man would be a fool to leave the side of a woman like that.

Maybe she's a widda woman and in need of the kind of comfort only a man could give? Stop it! his mind demanded.

Too late, though. Yancy was getting in a powerful sweat with such images in his mind. He glanced over his shoulder at the kitchen window. Then cut his eyes to the doorway, where the woman suddenly appeared.

"My, you've certainly done a good job," she declared as she wiped her hands on her apron. "I've some smoked ham, eggs, home fries and biscuits ready. Red-eye gravy, too, if you've a mind."

Yancy's mouth watered. The food sounded marvelous; she looked even better. His pounding heart told him the battle would be a stout one. Yancy forced a smile.

"I'm obliged. I can do more after I eat, if you want."

"Oh, that'll be fine," the vision of loveliness allowed. "Then you can get on your way to Big Rock." Her final statement held a no-nonsense firmness.

Yancy washed up, replaced his shirt over a shallow chest, and entered the kitchen. His driving hunger prevented any conversation until he'd sopped up the last of the red-eye with a half-biscuit. Sighing, he leaned back in the chair.

"That was bodacious grub, ma'am."

Surprisingly, she smiled at him. "My name's Sally."

It had the usual effect on Yancy Riggs, and he cast aside all effort at caution. "Well, then, Sally," he began, grinning. "Maybe you have something else to offer a lonely man?"

"I don't know what that might be." She knew only too well.

"Er—I mean, a woman here, alone like this," Yancy prodded. "Must get somewhat vexin' at times, eh?"

"I am not alone." A lie and Yancy caught it.

He rose, cat-quick, and closed in on Sally. One hand went to her waist, the other tilted up her chin. Lush, full lips waited for him, and he bent toward them. Sally jerked her face away. She felt the hot brush of his lips on her cheek and revulsion rose in her. She spun to the opposite side from his clutch and darted to the corner behind the door. She came up with the Marlin lever-action that always resided there.

Instantly, Yancy went cold. Nothing scared him more than a gun in the hands of a woman. She'd close her eyes and yank the trigger, like any other woman. More than likely she'd ventilate the roof and blow out a few windows before ever getting on target. But that made noise, and Yancy didn't want that. Besides, he had something far more pleasant in mind.

"Put that down. I only want to give you what you want."

"I want you out of this house," Sally snapped.

"Yer hankerin' for it, I can tell. I see it in yer eyes," Yancy cooed.

"You have half a minute to clear that door and get in your saddle," Sally's cold words informed him.

Yancy advanced, his body under command of a surging stew of vital juices. "You won't shoot me, honey. C'mon, admit it, you've got the hots for me," Yancy purred as he closed in.

Sally adjusted the muzzle of the rifle. "I've got hot lead for you, if you want it."

"That's plumb foolish. Wimmin can't use a gun proper," Yancy insisted from five feet away.

Sally Jensen shot him in the left shoulder. Yancy yelped and stumbled backward, the report of the weapon ringing loudly in his ears. A cloud of smoke formed, hovered between them. Dimly he heard her recycle the action.

"The next one will be in your heart," Sally informed him. The next round, she knew, was loaded with stacked shot. Three .33 caliber 00-Buckshot.

This unique load had been introduced to Smoke and Sally by Louis Longmont, the notorious gambler-gunfighter-bonvivant. "The celluloid cap lets it feed like a regular cartridge," he had explained. "It's ideal for house defense and well-suited for ladies to employ." Although too polite to say it, and with Sally an obvious exception, Louis Longmont held much the same opinion of women and firearms as Yancy Riggs.

Riggs moaned now, suppressing a scream of agony, and found his inner demons rapidly cooling. He made a shambling run for the doorway, right hand clasped over the bleeding hole in his shoulder.

"You'll be sorry." He tried to save face. "You'da liked what I could do for you."

"I guess I'll never know," Sally fired back.

"Crazy woman, that's what you are."

All the same, Yancy Riggs spared no time putting boots to stirrups and making speed out of the ranch yard. Gradually a certain peace descended on him. His composure regained in part, he abandoned any thoughts about revisiting that crazy woman. He wanted a quick getaway before she made him a more lasting peace.

6

Santa Fe, New Mexico Territory, sprawled in its mountain valley. Thin wisps of smoke climbed from backyard beehive ovens, placed outside the detached adobe kitchens of most houses. Chickens pecked in the yards and strayed into the street as Smoke Jensen and Bobby Harris rode down the long road from Raton. Half-naked children, with brown skin and big, black eyes, stared shyly at them from the corners of the houses. Bobby drew a deep breath and produced an expectant grin.

"I smell bread baking," he chirped.

"And just naturally, you're hungry," Smoke suggested good-naturedly.

Smoke had made a decision on the way to Santa Fe. He had questioned Bobby closely about his education. Although spotty, he could do his sums, read and write, and tell time. Smoke mulled this over as they made their way to the central business square, the *Plaza de Armas.* A large adobe church dominated the west side. Along the north, the Governor's Palace. The other two faces were given over to commerce. Saloons—called *cantinas* due to the Spanish influence of its Mexican residents—stores selling fresh meat, vegetables, bread and pastry, a plethora of tailors, boot makers, saddle shops and three gunsmiths lined the narrow, cobbled streets that defined the plaza. Smoke reined up in front of a restaurant.

"Comidas Corridas," an easel-like slats board declared in white chalk. Below it, the price in dollars and pesos. Smoke nodded at it. "I wonder what their full course dinner consists of?"

"That what that means?" Bobby asked.

"Yep. Too bad your education hasn't included learning Spanish. It can be useful in this part of the country."

Wide-eyed, Bobby queried Smoke. "Do you mean, you can read and write in Spanish?"

"Not exactly. Enough to get along, though. And speak it, of course."

"Gee, Mr. Smoke, that makes you a right smart man."

"Learning another language isn't all that much, Bobby," Smoke deprecated. "All you need is to have someone who grew up with it to teach you, or go live among people who only speak that tongue. That's how babies learn."

"They do? I always thought they were born to folks who spoke that language, and they naturally did, also."

"That's true, in part. Because the language babies hear spoken around them is the language they'll learn. But if you take a baby, say a Chinese baby, and raise him in a Sioux camp, or in a white man's town, he'll grow up speaking the language of the people around him and never know a word of his native tongue."

Bobby rolled his eyes and cut them to Smoke. "You mean if I'd growed up in some Indian camp, I'd talk like they do?"

"Yep. There's even been cases of captives who were raised on their own language, then spent ten, fifteen years, since maybe your age, among the Indians, and they couldn't remember anything but Sioux or Cheyenne, Comanche or Arapaho, whatever. Now, let's fill that hollow belly of yours." Smoke ended the lesson in languages.

Inside, the menu listed such exotic delights as *Bistek Ranchero, Chuletas de Puerco,* and *Carrie Asada.* It also had roasted pork and meat loaf. Bobby chose the meat loaf and Smoke, after inquiring as to the ingredients, settled for the rancher-style steak. It came, cut in strips and stewed with tomatoes, onions, garlic, and chili peppers.

Hot enough to blister the lips of a brass monkey. Smoke managed it with alternate bites of beans and rice, washed down with cool tamarind water. He would soon learn that in New Mexico they cooked a much hotter style than in Old Mexico. It was the Indian influence, he was told.

"Lucky you picked the meat loaf," Smoke observed as they pushed away their plates.

"Might not be so lucky in the morning," Bobby assured him with a shy, knowing wink. "Who ever heard of *hot* meatloaf?"

Smoke fished a folded brochure from a shirt pocket. "Know what this is?" he asked, handing it to Bobby.

The boy studied it a moment, then said brightly, "Sure. It's a stagecoach schedule."

"Good. I picked it up next door before we came in. You can read it and know what it says?"

"Yes, sir."

"Think you could make out a train schedule?"

"Mostly like this, isn't it?"

"That it is."

"Why you checkin' on my reading?" Bobby asked, suspicious.

"Suppose you tell me what those numbers in the column mean?" Smoke evaded.

Bobby read again and produced a shallow frown on his high, smooth forehead. "That's the times when the stage, or the train in the case of the other, gets to each stop. Also tells the day it runs."

"Good boy. Now, I've decided what we can do to make sure you have a right proper place to live."

Wet and pink, Bobby's pout revealed how he felt about that. Smoke ignored it and ordered pie for the both of them. Bobby only toyed at his. Smoke sighed and consumed the confection before adding to his mysterious explanation.

"I'm sure that if I leave you anywhere along the trail, you'll find some reason to take off and catch up to me again. So, you have to have a good home, one where you'll want to stay. To have that, what I'm going to do is buy you a ticket on the next stage north to the end of track. From there you'll take the train."

"Where to?" Bobby asked, fearing the answer.

"Let's pay up and go get the ticket," Smoke suggested.

Outside, the plaza thronged with shoppers and travelers. Smoke and Bobby entered the stage office. A man with sleeve garters, long, black cuff protectors and a green eye-shade held sway over the grill-fronted ticket window. A buxom woman and two small children turned away as Smoke approached.

"What'll it be?"

"One way to, ah, end-of-tracks for the D & RG."

"That'd be to Trinidad, Colorado. Twenty-three dollars," the clerk snapped.

"For a child?"

"Nope. He goin' alone?"

"Yes."

"Hummm. Says half price if accompanied by a parent."

Smoke's eyes narrowed. "It don't cost any more to haul him if he goes by himself," he said with a hidden menace.

"Someone's got to be responsible for him," came the prissy answer.

"What say he's responsible for himself?" Smoke suggested tightly.

Stretching, the clerk peered over his half-glasses and the lip of the ticket window at Bobby. "Him? That little carpet rat?"

"I ain't so little," Bobby challenged.

"Mind your mouth, boy," the clerk admonished righteously.

Smoke had had enough of this dumpling in men's clothing. "Mind yours. Half price for kids his age, then half price it will be."

"You cheap or somethin', mister?" the clerk sneered.

"Nope. Not near as cheap as you are impudent. Would you care to discuss this outside?"

"That's tellin' him, Smoke," Bobby enthused.

"Smoke? Smoke *Jensen?*" the clerk bleated. Instantly he paled, and a tremor came to his long, white fingers. "No reason to get riled, Mr. Jensen. None at all. Why, we'd be proud to have the son of Smoke Jensen ridin' one of our coaches. Be an honor, yessir, quite an honor."

"He's not my son," Smoke denied to the clerk. Then added, "At least, not yet." He felt embarrassed at the adoration that shone in Bobby's eyes at this.

"Half price? Yessir, that'll be just fine. Eleven dollars, fifty cents. Cash money."

Smoke paid. "When does the next coach depart?"

Consulting the octagonal Regulator clock on the wall, the clerk provided the answer. "Two hours, twenty minutes. Right on time, mind you."

"We'll be there."

On the street again, Smoke turned toward the far corner, closest to the church. A sign there proclaimed a bank. "Let's go get some gold changed into smaller coin. You'll need money for eating, then the train ticket."

"Where—where am I going?" Bobby asked for the first time.

"For now, back to Trinidad. There you'll take the Denver and Rio Grande express train to Denver, then the local to Big Rock, Colorado. There you'll be met by Sheriff Monte Carson . . ." Bobby scowled at this. ". . . and Sally Jensen, my wife. You're going to have a home in the High Lonesome, Bobby. A home at Sugarloaf."

Bobby Harris's chest swelled, and his cobalt eyes grew misty. He slipped the restraints he had kept on himself so far and hugged Smoke Jensen around the waist. "Oh, Mr. Smoke, that's wonderful. I'm plumb bowled over. You mean it? At your ranch?"

"You sure will. For so long as you need a home. You'll also be going to school there."

Bobby's bubble burst at this intelligence. "Why? I can read an' write an' do my sums, tell time, and I know the names of all the presidents."

"That's easy, there's only been twenty-one of them," Smoke teased.

Bobby threw back his head and glanced up at Smoke. "Twenty-two, Grover Cleveland being our president now. So, what more do I need?"

Smoke squatted beside the lad, oblivious of the looks of passersby on the tiled walkway. Wrinkling his brow, he tried to put his experiences and convictions into words Bobby would understand. "Knowledge gives a man strength. It is the way to power. It allows one man to succeed where another falls to the wayside. You can gain knowledge from experience, true. The surest wellspring, though, is a good, thorough education." He was shamelessly quoting Sally, and he knew it. "The more you know, the better able you are to face anything."

"Even a gunfighter?" Bobby challenged, still unconvinced.

"Yes. Even a gunfighter. Being able to read a man's mood shifts helps predict what way he will act under pressure. There are doctors who have written about those things. That's something you can only get from school. Why, back East, they are starting to teach modern languages in the schools, as well as Latin and Greek. A while ago, you seemed so proud that I could speak a little Spanish. I can also hold my own in

Lakota, Cheyenne, Blackfoot and Arapaho. I didn't acquire them by refusing to learn. Think what it would mean if you learned a language well enough to write poetry in it."

"Poetry?" Bobby made a face. "That's for girls and sissies."

"No, it's not," Smoke snapped. "Listen to this: 'Age cannot wither, nor custom stale her infinite variety. Others cloy the appetites they feed, while she makes hungry where most she satisfies.' That's Shakespeare, one of the world's greatest poets."

"What's it mean?" Bobby asked, face innocent of all guile.

Smoke plucked Bobby's hat from his head and ruffled his red-blond hair. "In a few years, I'll explain the relationship between Anthony and Cleopatra to you. For now, let's concentrate on getting you some money and sending you on your way to the Sugarloaf."

Enthused, Bobby set off at a brisk pace, then stopped abruptly. "What about Dollar?"

Smoke had not considered the pony. "We could sell her and her tack, and you'd have more money," he suggested.

Bobby looked stricken. "Bu-but she's been mine since I was big enough to ride. I can't do that."

"The alternative is to take her along on a lead rope to Trinidad, then a stock car to Big Rock. That'll cost extra."

"I don't care. I can get along with one meal a day."

Warmed by the boy's loyalty to his animal companion, Smoke smiled. "Then that's what we'll do."

Bobby's farewell to Smoke turned out to be a tearful one, although the boy tried his best to be manly. Once the stage rattled away from the depot, the paint pony trailing behind on a lead, Smoke turned aside. He had to find the telegraph station and send a wire to Monte Carson and Sally. For a moment, Smoke's thoughts staggered him.

What, he wondered, if Sally wouldn't go along with it?

* * *

Seated alone at a shadowed corner table, Yancy Riggs nursed his wound. He had seen the local doctor, paid him all but the last two dollars of his dwindling reserve of cash, and been patched up. Now he dawdled over a schooner of beer in the Silver Saddle, a new saloon in Big Rock. He couldn't shake the uncomfortable feeling that everyone here knew what he had done and how he had been shot. Even the barkeep kept cutting his eyes to the corner.

Damn that woman, Riggs thought resentfully. The more he drank, the lower his stack of coins grew, the more he returned to the lovely figure in that kitchen. The long, graceful neck, the promise of shapely legs. A warm, pliable body. Yeah, he had to go back and sample that forbidden fruit. Besides, she had to have some cash money around the house. It would get him back on his feet.

"Howie," a newcomer shouted greeting to the apron as the batwings creaked at his entrance. "Set 'em up. I just heard the latest."

"What's that, Mike?" Howie asked in a bored tone. Damn near nothing ever happened in Big Rock, Colorado, not since Monte Carson and that gunfighter, Smoke Jensen, had cleaned out a nest of snakes and brought peace to the valley.

"Burt Crocker and some of the boys just rode in from the Sugarloaf," Mike Hoxsey announced. "Seems she done it again."

Icy fear clutched at Yancy Riggs' spine, cupped his heart.

"Don't try to be mysterious. Did what? I'm all ears," Howie offered, busy with a stack of beer mugs.

Mike walked to the bar. "Beer first, then I'll tell you."

Howie drew a quart-sized schooner and set it before the cowhand. Mike plunked down a nickel and took a long, satisfying swig. "Miz Jensen got put upon somewhat by another drifter. She popped a hole in his shoulder with a rifle, shot him clean through, and he lit out."

Miz Jensen? Where had he heard that name? Why did it

seem significant? Yancy mulled it over while he dulled his pain with more beer.

"Good thing Smoke wasn't around. There'd been a buryin'," Howie opined.

Smoke? "Oh, Jesus, Smoke Jensen!" At first, Yancy had no idea he had said it aloud. Then he took in every eye cut his direction. Recognition highly motivated him. He gulped back his abject terror and came to his boots. "I'm gone from here. I ain't ever been here, an' I ain't comin' back," he babbled as he scuttled toward the tall front door.

Rich laughter followed him out onto the street. Yancy Riggs made record time to the livery. He had his horse saddled, and fogged out of town at a full gallop, within five minutes of leaving the Silver Saddle Saloon.

"Stop it! Do you hear me? Leave me alone."

Smoke Jensen heard the feminine appeal from the intersection of a narrow side street in Santa Fe. In the larger communities such appeals were quite frequently made. Smoke had encountered it before. It usually came from a lady who had crossed her fate with one of the rougher elements. He had about decided not to take a hand in this business when a genuine cry of pain sat him back on his heels.

"Please, *please,* don't touch me like that. Help! Someone help me."

Smoke Jensen reversed his direction and rounded the corner. Immediately he came upon a pair of bucktoothed, cross-eyed young oafs who pawed lasciviously at an expensively dressed young woman. From the style of her lavish outfit, Smoke immediately pegged her for a high-priced soiled dove.

What difference did that make? Smoke decided as he came closer. Even if she sold her favors for a living, that didn't take away her right to say no when she chose to. Some of the finest women he had ever known on the frontier had been ladies of the night. Even his own sister had owned, and left to her daughter, Jenny, the largest sporting house in Red Light, Montana.

Ten feet from Smoke Jensen, one of the louts planted a big, hairy paw on a bosom supported by whalebone stays. "Ouch! Oh, you're hurting me. Please, please someone help me."

Only a scant second later, her appeal for help was answered by Smoke Jensen. He clapped a hand on the shoulder of the offending punk and yanked him around from the shady lady. Smoke's huge, powerful fist hummed forward and knocked the lout's eyes straight with a blow to the forehead. The resultant knot rose between thick sprouts of carroty hair that lined the dense ridge over his pale, watery blue orbs. The offender staggered backward to bump into his intended victim.

"Hey, what are you doin' to my brutha?"

Smoke cut his eyes to the second attacker to see a face identical to the one he had just punished. Twins. Ugly, stupid, and lustful in equal proportion, Smoke judged.

Well, to hell with that. A fast left and right from Smoke Jensen made a raspberry jam of the mouth of the second bucktoothed trash. He stopped asking about his brother and backpedaled rapidly. By then his twin groaned and rolled over on the ground. Smoke ignored him and went after the one still standing. His arms pistoned as he drove one-two combinations into the over-grown lout's mid-section.

All at once, fingers like steel bands clamped onto Smoke Jensen's elbows, and he was lifted clear of the red-brown street by the burly lug he pounded. The huge twin shook Smoke like a terrier will a rat. All the while he called mush-mouthed to his brother.

"Delbert, Delbert, get up, Delbert."

"I'm a-tryin', Albert, I'm a-tryin'."

Held at half an arm's length, Smoke Jensen dangled there for a moment, then worked free his forearms. He spread them, hands open, palms facing, and on the next inward yank, he clapped them painfully over Albert's ears.

"Nunnnnnggg!" The odd sound sprayed blood from rubbery lips. Sharp, ringing agony in his ears caused Albert to release Smoke Jensen.

Although disoriented and hurting, before Smoke stabilized on his boots, the huge twin fisted his .44 Remington revolver. He had it level with Smoke's gut before Smoke could make a move. What should have been a wicked grin spread across the damaged mouth, and Albert gestured with the barrel.

"Pick my brother up," he demanded. When the groggy Delbert had been restored to his boots, his brother went on. "You okay, Delbert? You shoulduna let him hit you like that."

"Wha-wha' hoppen?" Delbert gobbled.

"He done hitten you, Delbert Banner. You stood like a ox an' let him hitten you."

"What now, Albert?" Delbert asked his brother.

"I'm gonna shoot him dead." Albert Banner turned to Smoke Jensen. "You hear me, mister? I'm gonna shoot you dead."

"I think not," Smoke told him quietly, his hand resting on the butt of his .44 Colt.

"Look at me!" Albert shouted. "I done got my iron out, an' I gonna kill you dead for hurtin' us. Dead, dead, dead!"

7

While Albert swung his hog-leg .45 into line, he paused to ask with a sneer, "'Fore I do, I wanna know who it is I'm gonna kill. Whut's yer name, stranger?"

"Jensen," Smoke told him. "Folks call me Smoke."

Albert Banner's ugly, crimson face went stark white. "Aw, sweet sufferin' Jesus. *You're* Smoke Jensen?" The muzzle of his Colt wavered as Smoke nodded. "I—ah—well, I—ah—got outta line, Mr. Smoke Jensen. It's true. It surely is. I—ah—ain't gonna shoot you dead."

"I know that," Smoke offered calmly. "Now, why don't you scoop up your half-wit brother and get him out of here?"

Yellowed buckteeth flashed in a grimace that didn't quite make it to a smile of relief. "Yessir, I'll do that little thing. Right now."

"An apology to the lady would be in order, also," Smoke demanded.

"Her? Why, she's jist a whoore."

"Would you like to be lying there beside your brother?"

"Gosh, no, Mr. Jensen. I reckon we done did act out of line. I—I'm—ah—sorry, miss. We meant no harm."

"I understand," the young soiled dove replied in a throaty voice. After the departure of the Banner brothers, she turned in relief toward Smoke Jensen. "I'm grateful. I'd be happy to show you how grateful, if you've a mind to."

Her sensuality crackled in the air between them. Smoke swallowed in uneasiness. "I'll pass, thanks all the same," he told her.

"Then, I could do with a cup of coffee, Mr. Jensen. What about you?"

"Suits," Smoke agreed curtly.

Thin moonlight filtered down on the *Hacienda El Rayo*. Carbone had named his sprawling ranch estate after the handle tagged onto him by his fellow countrymen, "The Thunderbolt." His speed and deadly accuracy with a six-gun, rifle or blade had become legend.

Esteban Carbone and his wife, Maria Elena, stood before the ample fireplace in the book-lined study. Carbone, in a velvet smoking jacket, held a glass of Pedro Domeq *Don Pedro* brandy. Maria sipped delicately at a new concoction of a famous chef in Mexico City, named a margarita. It consisted of a green-orange liqueur, the national aperitif—tequila—and lime juice. Maria wasn't sure she liked it, but had to admit that it certainly grew on one. Tension deepened the lines around her mouth.

"Are you certain, husband, that this plan of action is necessary?"

"Yes, *amada,* I am sure," the former gunfighter guaranteed her. "We are, after all, considered upstarts. The 'good' families have as little to do with us as possible. The government ignores our pleas for help against this madman. Already he has reduced two of my villages to ruins. Men have been killed, women carried off into who knows what new life." Carbone knew exactly what sort of fate awaited the young women of his villages, but as a gentleman would not mention it before a lady.

"The Rurales?" she asked, and he gave a shrug.

"Everyone knows they are *corrómpido.* If we take our own people into the mountains after this *loco,* El Rey del Norte, they threaten to arrest *us.* No, there is only one answer for this problem."

Maria sighed. "I know. Your mysterious gringo friend, Smoke Jensen. But what can he do in a foreign land, in strange mountains?"

"I am certain that Smoke will be right at home in our Sierra Madre Occidental. He is a mountain man. The last mountain man. If anyone can exact justice out of this dilemma, it is he. Now, drink up. *La cena* will be ready soon."

Maria raised the margarita to her lips. A split second later, the musical sound of shattered glass preceded the meaty smack of a slug as it struck Maria Elena in the chest. The margarita glass fell from her suddenly numbed fingers, and she sagged against the mantel of the fireplace.

In the next instant, Carbone heard the faint, distant crack of the rifle. Seconds later, he ducked low as another hole appeared in the window. The slug spanged noisily off the granite slab that formed the mantel. Crouched, he hurried to his wife's side, as he made note of the report of the second shot.

Her breath came in shallow, rapid gasps, and air whistled out of the entry wound. With it came a pink froth. The shots had come from far off, Carbone's mind told him while he struggled futilely to preserve the life of his beloved. A hidden assassin.

"Santa Maria, madre de Dios," Carbone began to pray.

Maria Elena Carbone shuddered, and her death rattle sounded in her throat. Tears coursed down Esteban Carbone's face, unashamedly. The children. What would he tell them? How could he tell them? Wretchedness assailed him.

"Damn that murdering swine. Call the padre." He began to think rationally again.

"Arrange for the funeral," he said aloud, then lapsed into

thought. See his wife off to eternity, then start north to the American village of El Paso to meet Smoke Jensen. *Then this arrogant* pendejó, *Gustavo Carvajal, will taste the full measure of our retribution.*

From the large front porch, Sally Jensen waved a welcome to the thick-shouldered rider approaching the house. Sheriff Monte Carson howdied back with a ham-fisted swing of his right arm. When he stepped down, Sally put on one of her most radiant smiles.

"You're just in time for coffee and sweet cake, Monte. Fried chicken, mashed potatoes, gravy and jarred beans for dinner later on if you've a mind. I've got pie, too," she added teasingly.

"Sounds dear to a man's heart, Sally. I'm obliged." He dug into a coat pocket and produced a yellowish sheet of paper. "I've come on an errand. Telegraph message from Smoke."

Fleetingly a frown of worry crossed Sally's brow. He couldn't have reached El Paso so soon. "No trouble, is there?"

Carson produced a rueful grin. "Depends on how you define trouble. I got one, too. You'd best read it and make up your own mind."

Truly concerned now, Sally took the missive and spread it wide. Her eyes tracked the page and took in each word with growing trepidation. Whatever did Smoke have in mind?

Seated at the kitchen table, Monte Carson worked on a thick slab of Sally's peach pie and sipped his coffee while she reread the brief message.

"Dearest," it began. "Please be in Big Rock to meet the train on Wednesday. On board will be a boy named Bobby Harris. He is ten years old and needs a home. I reckon the Sugarloaf would fit right nice. Give him the love and protection he needs. Monte will be there with you to meet him. Love, Smoke."

"He is serious, isn't he?" Sally said to Carson.

"Oh, I'm sure of that. The telegram he sent me asked that I meet you at the depot on Wednesday and help corral a youngster name of Bobby Harris."

Sally made a face and produced a mock groan. "What am I going to do with a child that young around this place?"

"You mean, once again?" Monte Carson kidded her.

"Yes, 'once again.' I swear, Monte, sometimes that man exasperates me." She waggled an admonitory finger at the lawman. "But if this is what Smoke wants, this is what Smoke will get."

Trailing through the dry, barren desert south of Santa Fe, along the course of the Rio Grande, Smoke Jensen rode his Appaloosa in a relaxed mood. For better or worse, he had managed the problem of Bobby Harris. Of course, that depended upon whether, when he returned, Sally met him at the door with a skillet in hand to feed him or rap him over the skull.

That gal did have a temper. She was also a fine shot, a cool head and a fantastic lover. No man in his experience had been so richly blessed, Smoke allowed. Sally was a treasure. Wealthy in her own right, she had no need to be dependent upon Smoke Jensen. Yet his Sally let him assume that role. She valued her independence in other ways and often. Like the matter of schooling back East and in Europe for their children. If she took to Bobby, would his future be the same?

Smoke reckoned it would. Unbidden, a smile creased Smoke's leathery tan cheeks. It would be nice having a boy around the ranch. Perhaps too many years had gone by without the shrill laughter of a happy child at the Sugarloaf. He'd soon find out. Once he got this thing with Carbone and Martine out of the way, it would be straight back to the High Lonesome. Another two days and he would be in El Paso.

Funny thing about names, he considered. For all the friction between Texicans and the people of Mexico, when the Mexicans chose to rename El Paso del Norte, the Texicans grabbed it up quickly enough. The little settlement that had been called Bliss, after nearby Fort Bliss, became El Paso, and the thriving community south of the Rio Grande became Ciudad Juarez.

The oddity of names brought Smoke Jensen to that of the man whom Carbone called El Rey del Norte. Did this King of the North have designs on land beyond the Rio Grande? No doubt his plans included the desert state of Chihuahua. Idle speculation produced nothing, Smoke reminded himself. He'd find out more when he got to El Paso.

By mid-morning, the sun bore down with a vengeance. Hard to believe that fall was on the way, Smoke mused. Already the aspens would be turning on the Sugarloaf. Frost in the shadowed folds of the mountains. Maybe even an early snowstorm. Smoke visualized his lush spread, all blanketed with white, big flakes lazily falling through the yellow light from a lamp. Inside, a fire burning on the hearth, and his family gathered around a Christmas tree. And Sally, his beloved, presiding over the distribution of presents. Next he saw Bobby Harris there, eyes alight, eager to tear through tissue paper and expose the delights beneath. A slight twinge of worry touched his mind, quickly banished. Sally would take to the tyke, surely as he had.

That last thought surprised Smoke Jensen nearly as much as the distance-muffled sound of a gunshot that came immediately after. Several more quickly followed. Smoke reined in and oriented himself in relation to the rattle of gunfire. Directly ahead, he decided, over that rise in the road.

Caution directing him, Smoke rode to the crest of the ridge. He dismounted and flattened himself to the ground. A long gaze over the edge showed him a stagecoach, stopped in the middle of the road. Five men, guns drawn, surrounded it.

The shotgun guard lay slumped against the backrest of the roofline seat. The driver held the nervous horses in check. Already passengers began to climb from the coach.

"Stand and deliver," bellowed a burly man, his face hidden by a bandana mask.

"What is it? What's going on? Who is doing that shooting?" demanded a stout matron inside the stagecoach.

"I think it's a robbery," the small, nervous man next to her said.

"That's utter nonsense, Mr. Perkins," she responded. "This is civilized country."

"Not so's you could tell it right off, ma'am," a lean, tanned Texan across from her remarked.

"Everybody outside," growled a short, bow-legged highwayman. "Come on, hurry it up."

"We'll do no such thing, young man," the dowager snapped.

"Shut up, fatso, and get outta that coach."

"Wha—why, the nerve." She turned to the small man beside her. "Philip, are you going to let him talk to me like that?"

"Do it, Mother," her husband urged.

Mrs. Perkins descended ungainfully from the stage and stood dithering. Her husband followed, then the Texan, who turned back to give a hand to an attractive young woman. At her appearance, the eyes of the road agents glowed with lust. Licking full, unseen lips, the short outlaw advanced with a flour sack.

"Now, folks, we're gonna take up a little collection. I want all your money, watches, jewlery, anything of value."

"How dare you," Mrs. Perkins spluttered. "You'll get nothing from me."

Hoisting his six-gun to her eye level, the bow-legged highwayman snarled, "Then I'll take it off your dead body."

Mrs. Perkins let out a whoop of fright and fainted. Her huge body sagged and swayed. Her husband staggered under her weight in an attempt to keep her from striking the ground. Three of the outlaws sniggered.

"Tie off them horses, driver, an' get down here," the burly leader commanded.

"What do you want?"

"You're gonna unhitch them critters, an' we'll run 'em off a ways."

"Y-You're goin' to leave us stranded out here? Man, that's cold. There's Comanches around," the driver protested.

An unseen grin creased the leader's face. "So I've heard. Say, before you climb down, throw off the strongbox."

"We ain't got an express box this run," the driver lied.

"You think we're stupid? We wouldn't have stopped this coach if we didn't know you carried the Y-Bar-R Ranch payroll, along with bank money for El Paso. Get to tossin'."

Eying the highwayman only a moment, the driver relented. The steel-strapped box hit the ground heavily. A moment later a shot blasted the stillness. The lock rattled and slapped and remained intact.

"Darn good lock," one of the bandits remarked, then fired again.

Coming right on his blast, another report went unnoticed. At least until one of the mounted outlaws gave a low moan and fell from the saddle.

"What the hell!" the leader shouted.

Another bullet cracked close by him and knocked the hat from his head. It revealed a bald dome that shone waxily in the sunlight. All heads turned then to a solitary figure who had ridden close in on the robbery. A second holdup man went down before they could react to the sudden attack.

Smoke Jensen rode with his .44 ready. Sidewinder pounded over the ground on the down-slope toward the stalled stage. Shooting accurately from horseback is an iffy thing, and Smoke knew well how to compensate for the motion of his steed. He held off until he came into medium pistol range, then picked the largest target in his line of sight.

His slug smacked into meat a bit high and left of the outlaw's heart, but with sufficient force to clear him from the saddle. His second round took the hat off a barrel-chested masked man. The third put another road agent on the trail to the grave before Smoke reined in and swung out of the saddle.

"Stand," he tersely commanded Sidewinder.

Smoke used the broad side of the coach for cover while he punched out expended cartridges and reloaded. Three of the enemy still remained. The leader, hatless, took it upon himself to terminate this intrusion. He kneed his mount to the left and circled the team. He came into view as Smoke Jensen snapped shut the loading gate of his .44.

Smugly triumphant, the boss robber raised his six-gun. The smirk got wiped from his face by a hot slug from Smoke Jensen's .44 Colt. Disbelieving he could be hit, let alone hurt, the burly outlaw swayed in the saddle and tried to focus on the man who shot him.

Smoke didn't give him time to recover. His next round dead-centered the ruthless road agent and flung him from the saddle. Smoke Jensen reversed himself then and came around the boot of the coach. A lean, rangy redhead got caught off guard, eyes turned to the direction of the leader.

"Over here," Smoke said softly.

Startled, the man turned. Smoke put a bullet in his brisket. He went loose-jointed and began to sag, but not before he got off a shot that punched through the cloth of Smoke Jensen's coat. Smoke put a safety shot into the man's head. With two cartridges left, and no time to reload, Smoke turned toward the last robber.

With a courage-building shout, the bow-legged, squatty highwayman rushed at Smoke Jensen. Flame speared from his revolver and lead smacked into the coach over Smoke's right shoulder. Smoke returned fire, but the man kept coming. At a distance of barely three feet, both men fired again.

In a fleeting instant, Smoke saw the man's head snap backward while his boots kept coming forward. Then a swift, hot blackness swept over Smoke Jensen, and he fell into oblivion.

Rancho Pasaje spread over thousands of hectares of cactus-strewn land. There majestic Iberian bulls grew from infancy into powerful, thick-shouldered fighting machines of raw ferocity rarely matched in the animal world. Urrubio Pinal had spent all his life with the huge creatures. He had worked for the former owner and now remained to serve Don Miguel Martine y Garcia. The *patrón* had been a famous *pistolero*, Urrubio knew that.

Yet his lovely wife and splendid children had mellowed him. Urrubio respected Don Miguel. He would give his life for him. Too old now to wrestle with the stupendous strength of the *torros*, Urrubio worked as cook for the field hands. Early each morning, his wife of forty years would make the tortillas and pack them in wet cloths. He loaded his small carreta with beans, flour, meat and condiments and headed out into the fields.

He was set up on a low knoll, shaded by a big oak, and heated the tortillas now, on a sheet of iron, laid over one of three cooking fires. Another held a gigantic pot of coffee. The vaqueros liked their coffee, a lot of it, fiery hot and strong. Beans bubbled in a cast iron kettle, hung on a trestle, over the same fire. At the third, half a *cabrito*—a young goat—rolled on a spit, turned by his youngest son, Ramon. All was peaceful and full of bounty.

Odd that none of the *vaqueros* had ridden in for coffee before their noon meal. They should be here by now. Urrubio bent to retrieve an iron skillet and came abruptly upright at the stricken expression on Ramon's face.

"Pappa, ¡tien cuidado!" Ramon shouted in fright.

From the corner of one eye, Urrubio saw the wicked glint of a blade and an arm that looped wide to encircle his throat. He reflexively jerked the skillet upward.

Tomas Diaz, one of Gustavo Carvajal's lieutenants, smiled in satisfaction. The large, black mustache under his hawk nose writhed as he worked his lips and spat a blade of grass from them.

"This is going to be easy. Take out the herd guards first. Do it silently, so as not to frighten the bulls. Use your knives," he instructed. "Then we round up the herd and drive them away. Make certain every one is dead. That way we can buy at least half a day to remove the bulls to a place of hiding. Our friend from San Luis Potosi will be delighted with these new animals."

"Sí, Jefe," his second-in-command agreed. "We are fortunate to have discovered them so convenient to us."

They laughed together. Then Diaz made a sweeping gesture. *"Adalante, compañeros*—go get them."

Carvajal's men moved swiftly around the herd on the high plateau of Aguascalientes. With caution and patience, they made their moves on the *vaqueros* watching the fighting bulls. Swiftly the men died. The last man in position had the task of dealing with the cook.

Paco Guzman was as lazy as he was fat. He waddled when he walked, feet wide-spread, toes pointed out like a duck. Hours in the saddle had galled his thighs and made his groin ache. Consequently, he rushed his assignment.

For so big a man, Guzman moved quietly, with an unexpected speed. He managed to close on his victim before he saw the small boy at the spit. When the youngster shouted warning, he hurried his work.

Blood squirted and the man fell. Guzman didn't bother to

check that his knife had gone true and the man's throat had been cut. He advanced on the terrified boy.

Sudden, immense pain exploded in the back of Paco Guzman's head and blackness washed over him as he fell at the feet of the trembling child. His skull split by the heavy edge of a cast iron skillet, Guzman never knew of his mistake as he shuddered his way into eternity. In his dying moment he thought he heard a voice, only a whisper.

"Stay low, *mijo*. Let them think we are dead. We must live to take word of this to the *patrón*."

8

Sensation returned to Smoke Jensen in the form of brightness against his closed eyelids and a special, scented softness surrounding his throbbing head. He also felt a restriction on his legs, as though they had been clamped in a padded vise. None of it made much sense. Cautiously he opened one eye. Harsh sunlight brought a new wave of pain. Through its pulsations he heard a soft, decidedly feminine squeak of surprise.

"Oh, he's alive! Mrs. Perkins, please bring some water."

"Are you certain?" came the other woman's tone of disapproval. "A falling out among thieves, if you ask me."

"No! Oh, no. He saved our lives, don't you see?" The sweet trill of a younger voice tugged on Smoke.

He opened both eyes and groaned. "What happened?" he asked weakly.

"You were shot. Alongside of your head. It must have made you unconscious."

"The other one? The last road agent?" Smoke pressed, recalling some of his precipitous attack on the stage robbers.

"He's—he's lying dead across your legs."

"I'd be obliged if you would have him moved," Smoke

responded, rousing enough to understand the absurdities of the situation.

"Oh! Yes—yes, I'm sorry. Would some of you gentlemen remove that—er—dead man please?"

Smoke Jensen maneuvered so that he could see his angel of mercy. Despite the pain, his breath caught in his throat. She was lovely, beautiful. A face that matched the sweet innocence of Sally Reynolds when he had first met her. He forced a rueful smile through his discomfort.

"Thank you for caring for me. But I'm afraid your dress is ruined. All that blood," Smoke offered.

For the first time, the lovely appeared to take notice of the mess in her lap. "Dear me, heavens, I—I never realized."

A snort of disapproval came from an older woman standing behind her. "Appears some folks have money to throw away on expensive clothes, then soil them beyond repair."

"I had to," the young woman defended herself. "He was hurt, needed help, don't you see?"

Filled with matronly self-righteousness, the elder woman came forward, waggled an accusing finger in Smoke Jensen's face. "You're one of them, aren't you? Had a falling out over the—ah—loot, isn't that it?"

An overpowering urge to bite off that finger swept through Smoke. He suppressed it. "Sorry. You have it all wrong. I heard the shots, discovered the robbery in progress, and decided to take a hand. It seemed you were in considerable need of it."

The dowager huffed her disbelief. "A likely story. What is your name?"

"Jensen. Smoke Jensen." He said it quietly.

"Heaven protect us," the old woman cawed loudly, throwing her gloved hands into the air. "The outlaw and murderer. We're all doomed."

She had gotten to Smoke Jensen with that performance. He levered himself upright and came to his boots, gave her his most icy visage. "I've been a lot of things, madam, but never an outlaw or a murderer. I've never killed a man who didn't deserve it and wasn't trying to do the same to me."

"You're a scourge, an abomination," she spluttered.

"Enough, Mrs. Perkins." The younger woman got into the exchange. "All you know is from that trash in the penny dreadfuls." She turned back to Smoke. "Mr. Jensen, we're grateful for what you have done to protect us from these terrible men."

Mrs. Perkins wasn't through yet. "At least he could have left them alive for the law to deal with, Penelope."

"Excuse me? Did I just imagine the gunshot that knocked me out and left me to stand here in front of you, bleeding from the head?" Smoke made a gesture to encompass the dead outlaws. "They opened the dance, I simply invited myself to attend."

"He's right, ma'am," the driver remarked from where he stood beside the last highwayman to fall. "You've all got your valuables back, we've saved the express box, and it's Smoke Jensen who made that possible."

"But, it's—it's so *uncivilized*," Mrs. Perkins muttered, subsiding.

Penelope recovered her composure and made a gesture toward Smoke's head. "Let me bandage that for you. Are you sure you are all right?"

"Yes, of course. A little patching up and I'll be on my way."

"You should see a doctor," Penelope suggested.

"I will. As soon as I get to El Paso," Smoke assured her.

Her touch proved feather-light as she wound a strip of silk, from a petticoat in her luggage, around Smoke's head. With the bleeding stopped and the throbbing subsided somewhat, Smoke surveyed the scene once more, mounted Sidewinder, and rode off.

Large pools of darkness covered the high pasture on Pasaje Ganaderia. Martine and his *segundo,* Pablo Alvarez, stood looking down on the bodies of his herdsmen. They had all been knifed. Only one had survived long enough to ride to the *hacienda* and bring word of the stolen bulls. The loss, although high in terms of money, meant nothing to Martine like the deaths of these innocent men. *Vaqueros* who trusted him to provide for them and their families. They deserved better than this. He said so to Alvarez.

"That is true, *Patrón*. This Carvajal is an animal. Our men were not armed. They could have easily been run off, frightened into keeping silent for long enough to get the herd safely away."

Martine looked at the pitiful remains of Pepe Lopez. "Carvajal did it because of me. My good *amigo*, Carbone, and I, alone, refuse to pay him tribute. Are we doing wrong, Pablo?"

"No, *Patrón*. You are not the sort of man who could stand by and accept the excesses of one like Carvajal. Nor is *Señor* Carbone y Ruis. We, the men and I, are all behind you. It is said that what *vaqueros* and flock tenders he has left, Don Esteban is arming and training how to fight."

Martine nodded. "That is right. As of this minute, I will do the same. If the men are willing to stay, they should be able to defend themselves. Even *Padre* Lorenzo agrees."

"And this friend, the *gringo pistolero?* What will happen when he gets here?"

Martine smiled at his *segundo*. "Gustavo Carvajal will find Smoke Jensen unlike any man he has ever known before. Much to his regret."

Only three hours off his original estimate, Smoke Jensen arrived in El Paso in late afternoon, two days later. He located the hotel Carbone had named in his letter, registered and took his few belongings to the room. Then he went to the livery and made arrangements for Sidewinder.

"Mind that you never take your eye off of him," Smoke cautioned. "He don't like strangers. The best way to feed him is at arm's length. That way all you might lose is a finger or two."

Stooped and gray-haired, the stable keeper swallowed hard at that and peered with watery eyes into Smoke's face. "Don't I know you, mister?"

"I can't imagine so. I've never been here before," Smoke answered honestly.

"Big feller like you, not many made that size. Seems— somethin' I saw, read somewhere."

"First time in Texas," Smoke assured him.

"Yes. Well, then, enjoy your stay, y'hear?"

"I shall. Two, three days at the most."

"That'll be six bits up front. Ten cents a day extra for double grain."

Smoke doled out a silver dollar and a nickel. He still felt a twinge of discomfort from the bullet gouge along his head, although it didn't intrude on a light-hearted mood that rested on his shoulders as he strolled through town. He decided he might as well wash the trail dust from his outside and innards as well.

He fetched a change of clothing from his room and adjourned to the bathhouse provided for guests behind the two-story clapboard hotel. There he found duckboards set over the hardpacked clay floor. A trough led from there under one sidewall and out into the yard. A piece of pipe extended through the rear wall, up high, under bare rafters. It had been fitted with an elbow, a spring-loaded valve and a spray nozzle from a garden watering can. A string hung down to control the valve.

Smoke disrobed and stepped under the nozzle. Tepid water, from a pair of wooden barrels outside on a platform, cascaded over him. After a long, satisfying minute, he released the string and soaped luxuriously. Thick, corded muscles rippled under his sun-browned skin as he worked up rich suds. He rinsed his hair, face and upper torso, soaped his hard, flat belly, groin and legs, and repeated the process. Again, Smoke let the water run over him in a final cleansing.

He kind of liked this. It sure beat sitting in a tub with the same dirt just washed off. Somehow he felt cleaner. Maybe he should consider something like this for the Sugarloaf. A complaining voice interrupted his contemplations.

"You sure don't mind taking your time, feller."

"Didn't know anyone was there. Be out in a minute," Smoke responded in a pleasant tone.

"Make it fast."

Dressed in clean clothes, Smoke exited the washroom. The man who had complained turned out to be of short stature, with a hard scowl and lippy attitude. Smoke and he sized up one another. The surly one swallowed hard and worked up a few less harsh words.

"No problem, mister. I made a long, hot ride here an' was in sort of a hurry. No offense?"

"Nope. That sure makes a fellow feel good," Smoke commented on the shower, then passed on his way out of the small building.

Behind him, the short, mouthy one thanked all he held sacred that he'd not run his mouth a little longer. A big one like that could chew him up and spit him out and not even raise a sweat.

Smoke Jensen located a suitable saloon, Cactus Jack's, on the corner of one intersection near the final two blocks to the bridge across the Rio Grande to the Mexican city that had once been called El Paso del Norte, and was now calling itself Ciudad Juarez, in honor of the hero, soldier-scholar, Benito Juarez, who defeated the French forces of Napoleon III and ran them out of Mexico. Carbone had not as yet checked into the hotel, so Smoke had time to burn.

Inside the large, well-lighted establishment, Smoke almost changed his mind. Five young men, local rowdies it appeared, lounged along the bar, holding court. Smoke instantly knew the leader, having studied the type for a long time. He leaned back, the long heel of one riding boot hooked over the brass rail. Both elbows supported him on the bar top.

Smoke saw him as a vicious young punk, with close-set, pig eyes of a lifeless blue, a small, mean mouth and a quick, hot temper. It literally smoldered in him. One of the syco-phants called him Herbie. To Herbie's left, another of the same ilk slouched, his body turned a quarter toward the bar. The other three Smoke sized up as working cowboys, perhaps not too bright, but loyal to those they respected.

They wore rugged work shirts, jeans, well-worn boots, and had scarred leather gloves tucked behind their cartridge belts. All talk stopped when Smoke Jensen entered, and the quintet cut their eyes to him, following the big mountain man to the bar.

"Beer," Smoke announced.

"Comin' right up," the apron sang out. He drew a large schooner and plunked it down in front of the newcomer. "Five cents."

Smoke dropped a nickel on the polished mahogany. From the corner of one eye, he took in the way the young hardcase named Herbie stared at him with narrowed eyes. One of the trio of working hands broke the silence.

"What was that you were sayin' about a year ago, Herbie?"

"Huh? Oh, yeah. It was up Colorado way. Little town of Deacon. I'd stopped into this saloon, had a couple of shots and started foolin' around with this fancy gal. She was about to give me her price when *he* came in.

"Are you sure it was him?" another of the hands asked.

"Sure as I'm standin' here. Of course, ev'rybody's scared pissless of him. Except for me, of course. Then he turns those

hard, gray eyes on me. 'That's my woman you're foolin'
with,' he growls."

"What'd you do, Herbie?"

Herbie pulled a grimace that he had practiced for a sneering smile and tossed off the shot of whiskey in his fish-eye
glass. "Give us another round, Myron."

Myron Hardesty moved slowly, awkwardly. He had been
studying the stranger and come to a conclusion of his own.
He knew the tall tale Herbie Cantrell was spinning. The
knowledge made his hand shake when he poured liquor into
their glasses.

"What's the matter with you, Myron? You got a hangover?"
Herbie prodded.

"Naw, Herbie, naw. Only, I think you ought to hold off on
that story of yours."

"Really? Why, Myron ol' pal?" Herbie taunted.

Myron cut a nervous glance toward Smoke Jensen. "I—
well—I just think . . ."

"No. Go on," Smoke Jensen interrupted. "I think it's getting interesting."

"Who asked you, mister? Butt out," Herbie snarled.

Smoke made a deprecating gesture. "Whatever you say."

Herbie went back to his braggard's tale. "Well, what did I
do? I set the pretty dove to one side and turned to face him.
'Who the hell do you think you are to tell me that?' I asked.
'I'm Smoke Jensen,' he says, all cold and hollow-like."

"Glory, didn't that scare you some, Herbie?"

"Nope, Walsh, you see, I already knew who he was. An' he
saw me, saw the way my guns was fixed and figgered out I
was fast and good with them right in a wink. He says once
more for me to let the girl alone, only not so tough this time.
So, I says, 'You make me,' an' went for my iron. I had it out
and on him before he could twitch. He went all white and
his lip trembled. His hand wasn't halfway to his six-gun. He

opened and closed his fist a couple of times, swallowed real hard and jist turned away an' walked out of there."

"Lordy, Herbie, you was lucky he didn't pinwheel you."

"No chance, Evans," Herbie told the middle of the three cowboys. "I had it figgered out long before. Smoke Jensen is an inven—invention of them dime novelists and penny dreadful writers. He's a bag of wind. He saw a real gunman and he turned tail."

Admiration and hero worship glowing on their faces, the three youthful cowhands clapped Herbie on the shoulders and offered to buy him a drink. Herbie nodded as though it were his due and pointed to Myron. "Set up three more for me an' Deake. These boys are payin'."

Myron's hand shook again as he dispensed the whiskey. He slopped some on the bar top when Smoke Jensen spoke up. "That's quite a story, youngster. Considering there's no such place as Deacon in Colorado."

Herbie's face seemed to borrow color from Myron's, as the former turned crimson and Myron went a pasty pale. "You callin' me a liar?"

"Only suggesting you may have made a mistake in the location."

"I think you called me a liar. Now you tryin' to back down. What you got to say to that?"

"I think you wouldn't last five seconds if you challenged Smoke Jensen," Smoke said, realizing that he was enjoying himself.

Herbie and his sidekick paced away from the bar, with Smoke pivoting to keep them in sight. The three cowboys gulped their drinks and departed for a green-covered table well clear of the open space between this hard-eyed stranger and Herbie Cantrell. Behind Smoke, Myron began to swiftly remove bottles from the back bar and set them on a shelf below the mahogany.

Unseen by Smoke, another of Herbie's followers rose from

his captain's chair and cat-footed it on silent boots to the stairway that led to a balcony that wrapped two walls of the saloon. At the same moment, Herbie yelled a fury-heated challenge at Smoke.

"You're a liar and yellah. You don't talk to Herbie Cantrell like that. Nobody does. I got six notches on my guns."

Smoke Jensen's expression of scorn turned Myron Hardesty's innards to ice. "Any fool can take a Barlow and cut notches in a pistol grip."

Herbie began to froth at the mouth. His voice came out, rising in volume and pitch a full octave. "First you call me a liar and now a fool. D'you want to die?"

"No. Do you?" Smoke asked him levelly. He cut his eyes to the three cowboys. "How about you?"

One raised both hands above the tabletop, fingers spread, palms toward Smoke. "We're out of this. We ain't no gun handlers like Herbie an' Deake."

"You don't need this fight, neither of you," Smoke urged on Herbie and Deake. "Step down from it."

"Go to hell," Deake snarled, infected by Herbie's blood lust and confidence.

"Two men at once is a stiff proposition, mister," Wade advised.

"You offering help?" Smoke asked.

"No, sir. Just caution. Herbie is good."

"But not good enough," Smoke confided.

"That does it! That damn well does it," Herbie screamed. "I ain't even gonna wait for you to go outside. You're gonna die right here."

Still unseen by Smoke Jensen, the third hardcase had slipped into position behind him, leaning on the balcony rail, his six-gun in hand and the hammer back. Herbie Cantrell darted a quick glance at him. Good. No problem with this loudmouth. He and his two tough followers had robbed a few mom and pop trading posts, stuck up a stage or two. Herbie had killed two half-growed kids with guns in Tascosa and was proud of it. Still, this hard-faced stranger had not shown a bit of fear. Yet, there was no way to back down.

"Now, Deake!" Herbie shouted as his hand dipped to the butt-grip of his .45.

Half the cylinder had barely cleared leather when the man facing him drew with such blinding speed that Herbie only managed to blink before a powerful blow hit him in the left shoulder. Reflexively, he tottered backward a few steps, saw smoke billow, then another lance of flame and heard Deake cry out.

Struck squarely in his elbow joint, Deake dropped his .45 back into the holster and slammed into a chair. The seat took him at the knees and he plopped into it, one hand clutched to his aching arm. His eyes filled with unbidden tears, but not before he saw Herbie try to complete his draw.

"No! Don't, Herbie," he cried out.

Herbie paid him no mind. There, he had it now, the front sight cleared leather and began to rise. How could any man shoot so fast? Hell, Sam up there hadn't even been able to get off a shot as yet. Herbie found his arm weighed a ton. It moved so slowly. What was wrong with Sam? He lined up the front sight on the man's chest.

A loud, ringing crash blotted out everything else, and blackness washed over Herbie Cantrell as Smoke's third bullet took him between the eyes. Herbie's head snapped backward, and he stared sightlessly at the man who had killed him. A soft sigh gusted out of his dead throat.

"You kilt Herbie!" Deake shouted, clawing for his second revolver. He had it clear and then could not find his target.

Smoke Jensen had ducked down to one knee, as instinct yelled a warning about his exposed back. He wasn't positive someone lurked there, but the lessons learned from Preacher had been deeply ingrained. He saw Deake rise from the chair and swing a hold-out gun in his direction. Smoke fired first.

His slug popped through the upper edge of one rib and plowed into Deake's heart. The young punk's knees sagged, and he fell face first in the sawdust of the barroom floor.

Recovered from his initial numbing surprise, Sam rose slightly to get a shot at the stranger's back. With care, in a world slowed down by the exhilaration of the fight, Sam brought the barrel down into line with the wide space between the man's shoulder blades. His finger tightened on the trigger. Sam took a final, quick breath, held it. Then the stranger moved out of his sights and blasted the life from Herbie and Deake. A split second later, a shot exploded from beyond the batwing doors.

Oh, shit, not another one, Smoke Jensen thought desperately as he saw the flame bloom over the batwings, and smoke billowed to obscure the figure of a man standing there. Caught in the act of punching out expended cartridges, Smoke looked on helplessly as the silhouette advanced.

9

Smoke Jensen quickly poked two fresh cartridges into chambers and positioned the cylinder. Before he raised the big .44 to fire at the new threat, he heard a loud, soulful groan from behind him and the splintering of wood. A quick over-shoulder glance showed a portion of the balcony rail hurtling though the air, followed by the body of a young hardcase. The corpse hit the floor with a muffled thud just as the batwings swung inward.

Through the slowly dissipating powder smoke, Smoke Jensen made out a huge Charro hat, bolero jacket and tight pants of a Mexican *vaquero*. "Ah, *Señor* Smoke, you must mind always to watch your back, *¿commo no?*" Esteban Carbone said through a chuckle as he walked into the saloon.

"Carbone," Smoke exclaimed in relief as he came to his boots. "You old hound, how'd you find me here?"

"And just in time, I suspect," the Mexican gunfighter gibed. "I heard gunshots as I rode by and knew you had to be involved, *amigo.*" He nodded toward the three wide-eyed cowboys, still seated at the table, their hands in clear sight on the green baise. "What about these *gatitos*—these kittens?" he added in English.

"They're out of it, Carbone," Smoke informed him as he finished reloading. "I'm going to have to take to wearing two guns again; that's twice I've been caught short in the past week."

"Excuse me, *Señor*," one of the cowboys said politely to Carbone. "When you came in, you called him Smoke. Smoke who?"

Carbone gave him one of his coldest, deadliest smiles. "Smoke Jensen."

All at once, the trio developed a sickly pallor. Walsh worked his throat with evident difficulty and made an effort to form words. "Th-then Herbie must never backed you down nowhere, Mr. Jensen?"

"No. I tried to tell him that."

"He—he was on the prod. Only this mornin', he got fired for the third time this month. Don't reckon you could have talked him out of nothin'."

Adams nodded enthusiastic agreement. "We—ah—best be ridin' out. Best get back to the ranch before we get sacked, too."

"If it's all right with you, Mr. Jensen?" the third youth spoke up.

"Might need you to tell the law what happened here," Smoke suggested.

"Yessir," Walsh agreed quickly. They all nodded accord. "We'll sure stay long enough to do that."

After the law had come, asked the usual questions, and departed, Smoke and Carbone moved on to an eatery next door to the saloon. Over roasted pork and parsnips, Carbone began the explanation of the troubles that had prompted Martine and himself to ask for help.

"A number of years ago, not long after we assisted you in

that small affair up north, Martine and I decided to hang up our guns. We had both accumulated considerable wealth. So we bought land, and with it came all the villages, people, livestock and the large haciendas. We also took wives of good families. We are gentlemen now, *caballeros,* instead of *pistoleros.* We have lived the good life. At least, until this former hill bandit, Gustavo Carvajal, raised a small army of *bandidos* and began a program of conquest.

"Up until three years ago, this Gustavo Carvajal was a third-rate *bandido.* He commanded, perhaps, ten or a dozen men. Scavengers mostly," Carbone elaborated on the content of his letter. "Half-starved much of the time, taking the leavings from larger bandit gangs. Then . . . something happened to change all of that. He may have gotten some bad tequila, or had a long bout with fever. Afterward, Carvajal claimed to be the reincarnation of the last Aztec emperor, Montezuma. He even dressed up in a feather cape and headdress when the spirit was on him and began calling his followers Jaguar Warriors or Eagle Warriors, after the divisions of the Aztec army."

"Sounds like he's not too tightly wrapped. I'd think what followers he had would desert wholesale from something that crazy," Smoke injected.

"Ah, perhaps. I'm sure many did. It attracted a different type of men, though. Before long his gang grew to over two hundred. They became a small army. At present, he holds sway over three states in Central Mexico: Durango, Zacatecas, and Aguascalientes. Collects tribute from all of the *hacendados,* the villages, even some merchants in the larger cities."

"Except for you and Martine," Smoke provided.

"Exactly."

"What about this King of the North you mentioned?"

Carbone patted at the corner of his mouth with a napkin.

"That is what Carvajal calls himself when he is not being emperor of the Aztecs. When he is, shall we say, sane."

"Can't the army do anything?"

Carbone shrugged at Smoke's question. "The Rurales are mostly untried amateurs. They are policemen basically. The army is busy with an Indian uprising in the south, and bandits in Sonora. Besides, they only defend the property of friends of El Presidente. We are not so big, and with our pasts, we are hardly counted among the close friends of Diaz."

"So that leaves Carvajal to run free over as much territory as he can control with his two hundred plus," Smoke summed up.

"There are only about a hundred and fifty left."

"Left? How's that?"

A sardonic smile creased full lips in the brown face. "These scum hit one of my villages, burned it down, then hit another. Oh, they took it and looted it. But sixty-seven of them were buried there. Now, I strongly suspect, and Miguel agrees, they will attack a village on the Martine y Garcia *estancia*. This is why we decided to ask you to come take a hand in the game."

"Does Martine have a partner?"

"No. That is the way it is here. When one takes a wife, he also takes her family name. So we are Miguel Antonio Martine y Garcia and Esteban Carbone y Ruiz."

"That's what I call being really married," Smoke quipped. Then he grew thoughtful. "Don't laugh, but I never knew you two had first names, let alone this double last name thing."

Another of those eloquent Latin shrugs. "It did not suit us to use our full names, *amigo*. And speaking of the double name, I suppose I am through with that," he added with a deep sigh.

"Oh? Why is that?"

"I had meant to mention it earlier, but we got off on this *cabrón,* Carvajal. Not long before I left to come here, an assassin fired from long range at our *hacienda*. It was no doubt intended for me. My wife walked into the path of the bullet. She is dead, and our children are half orphans."

Raw anger flushed through Smoke Jensen. He recalled the murder of his first wife and their son, Arthur. He thought also of the many close calls Sally had managed to survive. Silently, Smoke vowed to do everything in his power, and more if need be, to bring a world of hurt down on Gustavo Carvajal.

"That was Carvajal's doing," Smoke suggested.

"No doubt. I appealed to the local Rurale company. The captain in charge said too bad, but without seeing who did the shooting there was little he could do. I later learned that he was in the pay of Carvajal."

"And it's like that all around where we're going?"

Carbone produced a somber expression, although his eyes twinkled. "When has the law being bought by your enemy ever bothered you, Smoke?"

Smoke's voice took on a speculative tone. "A hundred fifty of these bandits and their suck-egg law dogs, you say?"

"Yes." The beginnings of a smile added a white line to the twinkle in Carbone's eyes.

"Against you, Martine and me? The odds seem about right, I reckon. Will the workers on your ranches fight?"

Carbone's shrug could have toppled mountains. "Who knows? They are peons. Some will, a few will run and hide, others may even carry information to El Rey."

"Then," Smoke prompted, "we had better get started. First, though, I have some telegrams to send."

* * *

Her dress, a creation in purple velvet, edged with delicate, lighter lavender lace, had come from Bancroft's in New York. The matching hat, huge, feather bedecked, with flowing veil, from Robert's of Paris. Fortunately the hem dropped modestly to an inch off the ground, which hid the utterly practical and utilitarian cowhide boots Sally Jensen wore under her fashionable ensemble. She stood in the shade of the overhanging cupola of the Big Rock Railroad Station of the D & RG.

Beside her, looking grumpy in white shirt, black trousers, cloth vest and tall Montana peak hat, stood Sheriff Monte Carson. Every few moments, he reached up to smooth one side or the other of his full walrus mustache. From far down the valley came the faint, shrill scream of a steam whistle.

Sally's usual reserve faltered, and she asked concernedly, "Are you sure he will be on this train?" With a start, she realized she had asked the same question at least twice before. She was surprised at her nervousness and the unusual desire to please that she was experiencing.

Monte Carson suppressed a grin and spoke dryly. "Either Smoke told him to do it, or the little tyke's got sense enough to have sent me a telegraph message from Denver verifying he'll be on today's train."

"I'm relieved, Monte. I wonder what he'll be like. I've wondered ever since Smoke's first message."

Monte's tone became fatherly. "He'll be just fine. If Smoke Jensen took a likin' to the boy, he'll be first class, you can be sure."

Gradually the shrill blasts of the locomotive's whistle, three longs, a short, and a long, grew closer and more frequent as it encountered more grade crossings. A white-skirted column of black smoke boiled up from the mushroom stack of the American Locomotive Works 4-6-0 Mountain. The ground began to tremble, and the air rumbled with the power of the huge steam loco. Heavier smoke belched from the stack when the engineer backed her down and slowed for the stop in Big Rock. Steam gushed from the fat pistons that worked the driver arms.

Majestically the engine and tender rolled past the platform, followed by a stock car, two baggage-freight cars, and a single passenger coach. The conductor swung down to the platform before the train came to a complete halt and set in place his small boarding step. A moment later, three persons got off the rear of the passenger car. All were adults.

"Monte, is there something wrong?" Sally asked uneasily.

"Why, I don't know, Miz Sally." He frowned, looked around. "Appears he's still inside."

"I'll go see. He must be shy," Sally suggested.

"No, you wait here, I'll go."

Sally laughed, a musical, pleasant sound. "With that outrageous hat, the badge, and your gun, if he's shy, you'll scare the pants off him."

Monte hurrumphed and allowed as how she might be right. Sally stepped to the conductor. "Is there a small boy on board."

"Oh, yes. He's a live wire, I'll say, ma'am. He has a pony in that stock car, too."

"Oh, my. I hope it's gelded," Sally said, devoid of any sensitivity about such direct language.

"It's a mare," the conductor informed her.

"Dear me, Smoke won't like that. Our stallions are all prize stock. Be such a waste. But where's the boy? He didn't get off with the others."

She and the conductor looked around. Unexpectedly the steam whistle shrieked wildly, and a small hand waved from the cab of the locomotive. When the blast of sound stopped, a head topped by a mop of reddish-blond hair and a ridiculous little round hat popped out of the window. A piping voice called with all the stridence of the whistle.

"Are you Miz Smoke Jensen?"

Sally muttered a brief apology to the conductor and started forward. Monte Carson cut diagonally to reach the side of the locomotive first. The boy's head disappeared inside, and a moment later, a beefy, beet-faced engineer handed him down to the sheriff.

"He's a fine lad, he is. Regular chatterbox. Kept us entertained all the way from the water stop at Arapaho." Behind him the fireman nodded grinning agreement.

"How did you get in the cab?" Sally and Monte asked at the same time.

"Well, it was a water stop," Bobby Harris chirped. "So I got off the train to . . ."

"That's enough, boy," Monte warned, pink filling his cheeks. "You're in the presence of a lady."

"Sorry, ma'am," Bobby offered softly and doffed his hat.

"Funniest thing. Here was this little pup wettin' down the tra—ah—er." The engineer's words ground down at the black look Monte Carson cut his way. "Afterward, he asked if he could ride up front, and we saw no harm in it. Made the time go by quicker, if you know what I mean."

"Thank you very much," Sally Jensen frosted at him in her best Eastern hauteur. For once she was glad Smoke wasn't with her. Like most frontier men, Smoke could not abide crude talk around a woman. There would be a fight for certain, and she was sure the railroad needed the engineer to take the train back to Denver.

To Bobby she said, "We'll get your pony and her tack and start for the Sugarloaf."

"Yes, ma'am," a subdued Bobby responded. Then he brightened as they walked toward the stock car. "I learned some keen new words when the fireman banged his thumb on the boiler door."

"I'll bet you did," Sally answered tightly, but she could not suppress the bubble of laughter that rose in her throat. Oh, Smoke, do you have any idea what you've gotten us in for?

10

Handcarts and two-wheel *carretas,* drawn by burro, horse or ox, streamed slowly through the cobbled streets of Juarez. Mounds of beans, onions, chili peppers, lettuce and cabbages filled them. The big horses of Smoke Jensen and Esteban Carbone created eddies among the market-bound merchants in the early dawn light. A gaggle of small, barefoot boys hawked fresh editions of *El Thario,* the local newspaper.

"So this is the town named for the Hero of Cammeron," Smoke remarked as they turned into *Ave. Ferrocarril*—Railroad Avenue.

"You know our history?" Carbone exclaimed with a raised eyebrow.

"Some of it. Preacher helped organize the 'University of the Rockies' for the mountain men. He had even more books than he had reloading gear. This place is growing fast."

"That it is. For all the many Mexicans who distrust or even hate the *nortenos,* they seem fascinated by being close to the border. We'll have time for coffee and *pan dulce,*" Carbone changed the subject, "after we load the horses."

"I'm still uneasy about Sidewinder in a stock car with some stranger," Smoke advised, his thoughts on the animal's penchant for doing damage.

Carbone gave him an easy smile. "The railroad employs older vaqueros, who can no longer keep to the saddle all day, to care for the livestock they ship. They know how to handle spirited horses."

"Sidewinder's more than 'spirited,' he's a killer. I've got another horse like him. Even they don't get along," Smoke added in jest. "I'll have to trust you; if you say it's okay, it is." He pulled a long face. "Hell, I don't have any choice."

True to the temperament of the times, laborers toiled on a huge edifice in homage to the iron rails. A regular cathedral of cut native stone, wide expanses of glass and domed rotundas that inspired a sense of awe. Typically Mexican, though, was the fact Smoke discovered that the new railroad station was being constructed around the old, one-story clapboard one. Carbone led the way to a refreshment counter and called for *cafe cón leche* for himself and a plate of *espirales.* Smoke had his coffee black, with plenty of sugar. He found he liked the coarse, grainy, slightly yellowish sugar of Mexico on first try.

"This is good," Smoke commented as he munched one of the spiral sweet rolls. "Beats a cold biscuit any time. If I eat many of these, though, Sally will complain I'm getting fat."

Carbone laughed. "You get fat? No, amigo, it will never happen. We board in twenty minutes, so you will have to hurry if you want to do justice to these rolls. We're in the last car, *Primera Classa;* only the best for the friends of Esteban Carbone and Miguel Martine."

Smoke found that the Mexican railway had obtained an earlier model of Pullman's sleeping car. They had added partitions between the sets of seats that made up into upper and lower berths. It afforded some privacy. The train started with a snort of steam, a screech of steel wheels on iron rails and the plaintive wail of the steam whistle.

After they settled in, Carbone suggested they take a stroll to the smoking car. There, the dedicated drinkers had already started in on snifters of brandy, shooters of tequila or bottles of beer. Two men at the tiny bar rattled dice in a leather cup and played a game incomprehensible to Smoke Jensen. A card game was in progress at one round table, and two empty chairs indicated a lack of players.

A silver-haired, older gentleman, with the features of a patrician, acknowledged their presence with an invitation to join the game. Carbone turned on Smoke an expression that in a man of a less violent reputation could be called wistful appeal. Smoke gave him a smile and a nod, then summoned his best Spanish to decline.

"I am not familiar with the game, *Señores,* or that deck of cards."

Carbone took one of the vacant chairs eagerly and extracted from a pocket a soft leather pouch of gold coins. Introductions were made around the green felt table. Smoke drifted to the end of the bar, nearest the table, where he could observe. Play began briskly. One player, a small, intense man with narrow face and long nose, soon drew Smoke's attention. He had been introduced to Carbone as Xavier Iturbe, Smoke recalled. He had phenomenal luck, or skill, the mountain man reckoned. He won clearly a third of all hands and every one he dealt.

A warning tripped in Smoke Jensen's mind. Iturbe had too much good damn luck. He started watching closely. Although they played a game he did not recognize, it took little card sense to spot a holdout rig and the deft substitution of cards from an identical deck. The fifth time the man substituted a card from up his sleeve for one in his hand, Smoke eased away from the bar. He bent and whispered to Carbone.

Years of experience at maintaining a cool disposition kept any sign of shock or anger off the Mexican gunfighter's face. Instead, he nodded soberly and spoke with a light air. "Yes, bring me a tequila. Our breakfast seems to be sticking with me rather too firmly."

Smoke returned to the bar. He ordered a shot of tequila for Carbone and a beer for himself. He didn't want it. It only served as a cover to their inspection of the cheat. He carried the salt dish, lime slice and squat, slender glass of clear liquid back to the table.

When Smoke bent to place the liquor beside Carbone, the smoothed back, black hair tilted and Carbone spoke softly. "Next time you see him do it, let me know."

Two others called for drinks from the bartender, and Iturbe asked for coffee. When their orders had been filled, play resumed. Two hands went by with nothing from the cheat. On the first, he failed to take a single trick. On the next, he lost to another player by one trick. The third round went to Iturbe when he took three fast tricks with what appeared to be the highest ranking card in each suit.

Smoke recalled that in the hand Iturbe folded, he had at least one of the cards with a single pip. No doubt an ace, Smoke now considered. It hadn't shown up in the next hand, but Iturbe had just played it to take his third trick. Smoke had to admire the man's talent. He had sense enough to vary his technique. No wonder no one else had spotted Iturbe cheating. Already Iturbe was gathering the pasteboards. Smoke gave a nod to Carbone.

"One moment, *Señor* Iturbe," Carbone snapped. "My friend has a question to ask about the game." Carbone cut his eyes to Smoke, clearly offering him the chance to open the dance.

"I am interested in the number of like cards in the deck, *Señor,*" Smoke worked out in Spanish. "How many are the same?"

"Why, four, as in any deck. One for each suit," Xavier Iturbe answered.

"Odd. I'm willing to bet that there are at least two of each suit at the table right now."

Iturbe's ferret eyes narrowed and glittered like obsidian. "Are you suggesting something, *Señor?*" he asked with menace.

Not exposed to the language long enough to go on, Smoke resorted to English. "I'm saying that the card with the single red diamond pip, and the one with the king and black circle, with which you took the fifth and final tricks, have duplicates somewhere on your person. Also that the black circle, single pip card was withheld from two hands ago and only now reinserted into your hand."

"*¡Gringo cabrón!*" Iturbe shouted, and his hand darted for the front of his frilly shirt.

It never got there. Panther quick, Smoke Jensen made his move well before the cheat had a chance. The wicked tip of the big bowie knife in Smoke's hand bit into flesh, and Iturbe's hand jerked spasmodically. That triggered his hold-out rig and dispensed a shower of cards, which were pinned to the table accusingly by Smoke's blade as it penetrated Iturbe's hand and fixed it, too, to the green felt. Iturbe squealed like a pig.

None of the other players moved. The distinguished gentleman quickly lost his expression of horror for one of chagrin. "My apologies, Don Esteban. I had no idea this *lathróne* was a cheat. We will, of course, make good on your losses. There is no need for—ah—more forceful satisfaction, do you agree?"

"*Sí. Bastante bien,* Don Pablo," Carbone said tightly.

Yes, it was good enough, Smoke considered. Not a carload of these soft-handed gentlemen would stand a chance against Carbone if he called them out. Squirming, the cheat begged to be freed. Smoke's hard, cold gray eyes pinned Iturbe as firmly as his knife. He held him there while Don Pablo plucked Iturbe's ill-gained winnings from in front of him and distributed them among the others, the largest share to Carbone. Only after that did Smoke put one big hand on the wrist above the bowie and pull his knife free.

Blood ran in profusion, and for a moment it appeared that Iturbe would faint. He got shakily to his boots, then started to frame a retort, but was interrupted by one of the other players who had regained his composure.

"We owe you a service, *Señor*. But perhaps it would be better were you to finish the object lesson and dispose of the corpse somewhere along the track?"

Cold, these gentlemen of Mexico, Smoke thought. "I see nothing to be gained by that, *Señores*," Smoke answered mildly.

Burning with hatred of the despised *gringo*, Xavier Iturbe let his impotent rage and frustration boil over. "You let a stinking *gringo* do your dirty work for you. I have been insulted and robbed by such fine gentlemen and their tame dog of a *gringo*. *¡Mierdo en la lache de ellos madres!* I will get even for this insult!" Iturbe shrieked as he wisely made a hasty exit from the smoking car.

Don Pablo, looking droll, sized up Smoke Jensen. "Something tells me that it would not be wise for him to follow up on his threats. We were not introduced, *Señor*. I am Don Pablo Gutierrez y Soto," the elderly patron began and went around the table.

"Smoke Jensen," Smoke responded simply.

Don Pablo cocked an eyebrow. "Ah. I understand the speed with which you acted now, *Señor* Jensen." He cut his eyes to Carbone. "And Carbone y Ruiz would be Esteban Carbone, *pistolero famoso* of Jalisco? Well, gentlemen, we are in momentous company. Shall we resume play?"

Xavier Iturbe fumed as he thrashed through his large steamer trunk in the baggage car. He'd show them. A *gringo!* His mind boiled with the stories his grandfather had told of when he was a small boy, and the gringo soldiers had come, stealing all of the chickens, lambs and young goats, doing evil things to the young women and girls. He had grown up hearing those tales, never once doubting. After all, it was his *abuelo* telling him and the other children. At last, his face a sheen of perspiration, he found what he was looking for. Quickly he located the accessories.

He returned to the smoking car, his face set in granite determination. First the gringo, then his smirking friend, Carbone. Woodenly, Iturbe thrust open the door from the vestibule and entered. He raised his uninjured left arm and thrust it forward. A gentle squeeze and one hammer on the antique double-barrel .60 caliber pistol fell.

The muzzle-loading weapon discharged loudly in the confined space of the railroad car. A huge plume of smoke expended into the space before Iturbe's eyes. A hot three-quarter-ounce lead ball popped a hole through the back and side panels of Smoke Jensen's coat. It did him no harm, but killed a man across from him at another table. All at once, Xavier Iturbe realized the terrible mistake he had made.

Before the assassin's finger could change triggers, Smoke drew his .44, turned and fired. His slug pinwheeled Iturbe, staggered him and sent him reeling toward the closed door. Frantically Iturbe yanked the second trigger. The hammer fell on a percussion cap, and the ancient weapon belched flame and smoke as it sent a ball into the roof of the coach.

Already his vision had begun to dim. His second shot brought another from Smoke Jensen. The bullet burst Iturbe's heart. He hardly felt it as life slipped from him. His knees sagged, and he tumbled into darkness even before his face hit the threadbare carpet on the floor of the car. Smoke had already reholstered his six-gun.

"A masterful piece of shooting," Don Pablo bellowed his congratulations. "We are indebted to you, *Señor* Jensen. *Cantinero,* bring a round for everyone in the car. We must celebrate the remarkable feat of shooting skill by *Señor* Smoke Jensen. Let's make a fiesta of it," he suggested eagerly.

"Won't be much of a party for that feller," Smoke observed, as he nodded toward the dead bystander.

Myron Hardesty didn't like it a bit. Three hard-bitten outlaw types had entered Cactus Jack's shortly after opening, at eleven that morning. Seated around a table in one corner, near the painted glass window, they had been drinking heavily into the late afternoon. Trent, Vickers, and Yates, they called themselves.

Trent had wheat-straw hair that stuck out in all directions, close-set, nearly colorless blue eyes, a gap between his upper front teeth that gave his aspirates a marked whistle, and a decidedly truculent attitude. Vickers was a weasel-faced individual with a penchant for back-shooting unless Myron had missed his guess. He had small, round ears that stuck out like handles on a cream pitcher. Yates filled every bit of the captain's chair in which he sprawled. A dough ball, but Hardesty suspected his fat hid iron-hard muscles.

"Saddle bums," Myron muttered to himself.

One thing Myron Hardesty had learned from the grumbled conversation between one another was that they hated Smoke Jensen. Hated him more than Yankees, politicians or even Mexicans.

"I hate Smoke Jensen," Yates growled as he poured another shot from the bottle in his big, hairy left hand.

"You said that before," Vickers reminded him.

"Yeah. About a dozen times," Trent added. Then, "I hate Smoke Jensen."

"You said that before," Yates reminded him.

"Yeah. About a dozen times," Vickers added. Then, with mounting disgust, he hurled his empty shot glass across the room, to shatter against the plastered adobe wall. "Barkeep, bring me another." Then, "I hate Smoke Jensen."

"Shit," Trent spat.

"Dang it all, we gotta do something about it," Yates said.

"Yeah, only we got here too late. Smoke Jensen's up an' gone. Ain't that right, bartender?" Trent complained.

"Yes, sir, that's quite right, he and the Mexican," Hardesty responded as he brought a fresh shot glass to Vickers.

"Tell me again, where did they go?" Trent commanded.

"To—to Mexico, I think."

"But before he left, he kilt a good friend of ours. Two good friends, right?"

Myron swallowed hard. "Only one. The—ah—Mexican gentleman who met him here killed the other."

"Ain't no such thing as a Mezkin 'gentleman,'" Trent growled, his sneer marred by the whistling of his "s" sounds.

"Who was this Mezkin?" Vickers demanded.

"We've been through this before," Myron protested, sweating. "I've already told you I don't know. Only that Mr. Jensen called him Carbone."

Yates' moon face writhed with agitation, and his pudgy lips worked out the words from his throat. "Jeez, I've been thinkin', fellers. If that's the Carbone I've heard of, maybe we done bit off more'n we can chew."

"Horse plop!" Trent thundered.

Vickers' weasel face squinched and small, deep-set eyes glittered with enmity. "What's this Beaner look like?"

"Big," Hardesty informed them. "A lot bigger than most Mexicans. Hands near the size of Smoke Jensen's. He was dressed up expensive-like." Bryan thought of the dapper, five-foot-nine Esteban Carbone, his slim, wiry frame and lightning-quick draw, the pencil line of mustache. If these saddle trash ever found out he was lying to them, they could be trouble. "He had a big, flowing mustache, drooped clear to his chin."

"What's Jensen doin' in Mexico?" Yates asked.

"I—I don't know. What I heard folks say, he and some

high-and-mighty grandees were going to take on an army of bandits."

Once more the trio cursed their bad fortune in not being in El Paso in time. Hardesty edged away to the security of his bar. At last, Trent, the nominal leader, downed another shot and came to his boots.

"Fellers, there's one thing we can do."

"Whazzat?" Vickers asked, his voice slightly slurred from all the liquor he had consumed.

"We can head south and join up with this El Rey del Norte. My guess is he's the one Jensen's after."

"What do we do when we get there? I can't speak Mezkin," Yates protested.

"All we need do is bide our time. Jensen will show sooner or later," Trent speculated.

"Yeah. An' with my Express rifle an' that telescope, I can pop him and the Beaner easy at a half mile," Vickers gloated. "They'll never know what hit 'em."

11

"¡Torreón! ¡Torreón, Coahuila!" the conductor bellowed as he entered the Pullman early the next morning.

"That's our stop, Torreón," Carbone advised Smoke. "From here we ride. There's a good outfitter in town. Friend of mine. We'll get pack animals, gear. Then some groceries. You can still cook?"

"Oh, yes," Smoke answered dryly.

Preacher had taught him well as a youth to make corn bread, biscuits, fry bacon, to broil beaver tail, grill elk steak and bison hump. Beans became a specialty. Old-timers among the dwindling number of mountain men, proud of their vocabularies, called beans "the orchestral fruit." When young Smoke had asked Preacher why, he had replied with the rest of the old saw, a twinkle in his eye, "the more you eat, the more you toot."

Smoke and Carbone slung their scant belongings onto the platform and recovered their horses. *"Gracias a Dios,"* the harried-looking attendant in the stock car had muttered fervently as Sidewinder clomped down the loading chute.

"Now I wonder why he's thanking God?" Smoke asked, pleased with his rapid recollection of Spanish.

Carbone laughed heartily. "In gratitude for getting rid of your horse, no doubt, *amigo*. Perhaps I misjudged their ability to handle an animal of such magnitude. Come, let me show you this beautiful town."

Immediately outside the small, pink stone depot, on the street side, Smoke Jensen received his first lesson in how pervasive an influence Gustavo Carvajal had over the territory he claimed for his own. Tied by dirty string to a lamppost was a crudely hand-lettered poster.

"¡VIVA EL REY DEL NORTE!"

In smaller print, it announced that the collectors of "contributions" would be in Torreón each Thursday to gather the "gifts" of a "grateful people" for El Rey del Norte. Carbone read it with interest and translated for Smoke. His face twisted, memories of the sweetness of his dear wife a fiery goad in his mind.

"This is a bad one, *amigo*. Now he openly defies the authorities. What law there is in this town, if there is any, cannot be trusted."

Smoke had changed his carrying habits back in El Paso. He now wore two revolvers, one on the left, high up, butt pointed forward, the other low and tied down on his right hip. He reached to slip the safety thong from the hammer of the right hand .44, then did the same to the left.

"Then our welcome might not be entirely warm?" he asked knowingly.

"Just so."

They continued down the long street at the heart of Torreón. On every block they found three or four of the posters. When they reached the main street, which led to the cathedral, professionally printed ones were in abundance. Carbone nodded and pointed with an upraised arm to a storefront on the Plaza de Armas and a slant-roof livery-type building next door.

"There is the establishment of my friend," he announced. "It is best we obtain supplies and leave this place quickly."

"Never had much jackrabbit in me," Smoke observed. "Unless some of Carvajal's hardcases muddy up the waters, I kind of favor taking our time."

Carbone twitched the corners of his mouth. "I know you, *amigo.* You want to try them on, see of what they are made, eh?"

"Might as well know from the git-go, Carbone."

They proceeded toward the outfitter's where four unsavory individuals lounged outside, two leaning on a tie-rail. When they drew nearer, Carbone raised a cautioning hand to halt their progress.

"Uh-oh, I recognize two of those *ladrónes.* They ride for Carvajal," he said quietly.

Smoke Jensen knew the type well. Their mouths and eyelids drooped like their overfull mustaches with an excess of insolence. Always used to being backed by enough guns to avoid risk, they puffed themselves up into an importance they could not support. They would, he decided, be quite easy.

"Shall we go ask them for the next dance?" Smoke prompted.

"It would be my pleasure," Carbone answered tightly.

They separated, Carbone remaining on the elevated boardwalk, while Smoke edged out onto the cobbled street. The four hardcases had seen them and, no doubt, recognition had been mutual.

They knew that their *jefe* had put a price of five thousand pesos in gold on Carbone. Perhaps *la Donna Fortuna* had put them in the way of earning that bonus this day. The long, lanky one gave a sharp whistle and made a summoning gesture with his left hand when the pair neared pistol range.

Three more joined the quartet of Carvajal's *bandidos,* exiting the outfitter's store and blinking at the bright light. Their momentary vulnerability signaled a prime opportunity.

"I think right now," Smoke Jensen said softly.

"¡Los manos arriba!" Carbone shouted at them, then repeated, "Hands up! By authority of the governor of Aguascalientes, you are under arrest for banditry."

All seven drew their weapons as one. The three from inside the store, still befuddled by sunlight, could only fire toward the sound of Carbone's voice. Their shots went high. One of the lead slugs set off a brassy bass note from the huge bell in the cathedral tower across the square. The four without impairment opened up with more haste than the task required. Dust and splinters sprayed upward from the boardwalk around Carbone's feet. A bullet smacked into the thick adobe wall near his head and sent a spray of chips through a cloud of red-brown.

Carbone, cool as ever, put a round in the gut of one bandit. Smoke Jensen had not been lagging. He had triggered two rounds, wounding another of the seven and putting two others into a dive for the protection of a water trough. With more courage than good sense, one of those still standing started toward Smoke, thumb-slipping the hammer of his Mendoza copy of a Colt .45 Peacemaker as he advanced.

"This is going to be work from here on," Smoke advised his companion.

"Too true," Carbone replied as he raised the sights of his six-gun to blast the life from a bandit crouched in the doorway to the outfitter's.

Smoke Jensen had had enough of being a target. He shot the advancing bandit between the eyes. The huge black Charro hat the man wore flew from his head, its silver braid shimmering in the morning sun. He did a brief, grim dance of death and crashed to the cobbles of the street. That made only two down and dead for certain.

A bullet's crack close by his ear turned Smoke Jensen toward the new threat. Fat and flushed of face, a bandit lumbered into the middle of the street, extending the area to be covered by Smoke and Carbone. He fired again, only to receive a powerful blow under his rib cage. It stopped him, and he gave Smoke a curious expression as he fell over his own boots.

One of the wounded had gotten back in action. He put a hole in Carbone's jacket that came close enough for the Mexican gunfighter to dive for cover. A rain barrel under the overhang provided that for the moment. He paused to punch expended casings from his revolver and reloaded. The surviving *bandidos* used the lull in firing to make a run for the screen of trees and shrubs in the center of the Plaza de Armas.

Smoke sent rock chips and lead smears after them, then also reloaded. "We're going to have to hunt them down or be back-shot," he opined.

"We had better split up, go at them from two directions," Carbone suggested.

"Good idea. Ready?"

"As much as I'll ever be," Carborie responded, his easy life of late telling on him.

"Let's do it," Smoke urged.

Smoke Jensen ran diagonally across the bedding of smooth, rounded rocks that formed the roadway. His destination: a cairn of native stones with a polished granite slab that appeared to be some sort of monument. He crossed the halfway point before any reaction came from Carvajal's bandits.

Bullets trailed him, always a scant few feet behind. He reached his objective. It was indeed a monument, to someone he didn't recognize, for something he hadn't time to translate.

Only the date—16 September 1824—had vague meaning. Something about the Mexican revolt against Spain. An angry slug chipped a hunk from the corner of the monument and howled off to bury itself in a tree trunk.

Coldly energized, Smoke Jensen crouched and turned in the direction of the gunshot. He raised his .44 Colt and put a round into a large bush that waggled in agitation and seemed alive with a ball of powder smoke. A scream answered his efforts, followed by two more blasts from a revolver.

Smoke had learned how to fire at a blind target years before. Preacher's instructions had not been wasted. Smoke put two fast rounds to left and right of the point where he saw the muzzle flash, and used the bulk of the cairn to mask his change of position.

From the far side of the plaza he heard a rapid exchange of gunfire and the tinkle of glass as a stray slug took out a window. "One less, *amigo,*" Carbone's voice called out gleefully.

Smoke Jensen nodded in satisfaction. By his count that made three dead, one wounded, only three more to track down. Rusty hinges creaked on a balcony door behind Smoke, and he jerked around in time to see the grinning face of a bandit looming over him. In his hands, Carvajal's follower held a short-barreled shotgun.

"You are the *gringo* el Rey sent us after," he mouthed a moment before he unleashed a slash of 00 buckshot from both barrels.

The double charge obliterated the testimonial to Torreón's hero of Mexican Independence. Through its hellish blast, Smoke Jensen sent a single messenger of death. His .44 slug found a home in the chest of the bandido. Already off balance, he staggered, then lurched forward, crashed through the balcony rail, and pitched headfirst onto the street below.

His head made a wet melon sound a moment before his

shoulders smacked into the cobbles. Obviously in a vulnerable spot, Smoke Jensen made a rapid move toward the large, musically splashing fountain in the center of the plaza. Geysers erupted from the surface of the catch basin as the surviving bandits tried to end the life of Smoke Jensen.

Smoke's second .44 came to life as he neared the base of the stone adornment. He ducked low and returned fire on those so determined to kill him. Small birds, which had been startled by the sudden eruption of gunfire, cowered in the safety of the stone folds of the robe of the Virgin Mother. The force of the muzzle blast from Smoke's .44 set them off again, in a whir of many wings, racing for yet another hiding place.

They burst forth and swung once around the statue in the fountain, then hurtled toward the cathedral. Smoke saw faint movement of a pair of legs through the screen of carefully manicured shrubs. Slowly he edged to a more covered position beside the fountain.

"He's over by the fountain," Diego Bernal informed his companions. "We'll get him now."

"I'm not so sure," a scruffy bandit of slight stature countered. "These two are like madmen. They kill and kill and only joke about it."

Still smarting from the wound he took early in the fight, Bernal glowered at the detractor. "Are you a coward? He is only a man. And a *gringo* at that. He will die begging us for mercy."

He moved to one side and kicked the reluctant outlaw in his side. "Get up, *cobarde*. Move, you dog."

Sudden pain exploded in Diego Bernal's offending right leg, and he looked down in shock and surprise to see fragments of his kneecap fly into the bushes, along with scraps of his trouser leg. He went down like a cutoff stalk of corn. His screams could be clearly heard by Smoke Jensen, who had shot him.

"Jesus, Maria y Jose," the uncommitted hardcase babbled. All at once, he wanted no part of this. Let someone else collect the bounty on the head of Carbone and this gringo. *"¡Oje! Gringo,* listen to me," he called urgently. "I'm out of it. I am through."

"Throw out your six-gun," Smoke Jensen responded in Spanish.

Machismo, the ridicule of his *companeros,* and the sure and certain punishment meted out by el Rey when he returned to the headquarters *estancia* warred with his newfound respect of the deadly guns of Smoke Jensen. He gulped back his fear.

"No, *Señor.* I cannot do that."

"Then you'll die with it in your hand."

"Better that, than a machete across my neck for failing el Rey," he yelled his shaky defiance.

With that, he levered himself to his boots, a Mendoza .45 in each hand. Still more interested in escaping retribution than collecting a reward, he ran toward the sanctuary of the tall, wide double front doors of the cathedral. With every other stride, he turned sideways at the waist and fired blindly back at Smoke Jensen.

Smoke came from behind the fountain and drew a deep breath, his first full one for several long, tense minutes. Taking his time, he raised the .44 in his right hand and aligned the sights. His big, thick thumb eared back the hammer. Ahead of the big front post, the bandido had reached the midpoint of the fifteen stone stair risers at the entrance to the church.

He lurched to a stop there, startled at seeing his enemy so exposed and available. Relieved laughter bubbled up inside him. It was true. All gringos were crazy and would sooner or later lapse into some stupid act. He brought up his .45 Mendozas and slip-thumbed both. He howled with mirth now, his mouth formed into a fat, round "O." He felt the solid shock of recoil as both weapons fired at once.

Totally without aim, the bullets went wide of their mark, albeit close enough for Smoke to hear their crack and thump into a tree to his right. He had fired simultaneously with the bandit. His round went true, straight into the black "O" of that howling mouth. It silenced forever the last laugh of the nameless outlaw.

"That's the last of them, *amigo,*" Carbone opined as he appeared soundlessly beside Smoke.

Smoke Jensen surveyed the scene of carnage. "Seven down, a hundred-fifty to go. Not a bad day's work. Right now, though, I'm hungry. And I could sure use some coffee."

Carbone grinned. "My mouth, she is a little dry, also. If we could have some brandy in that coffee it would help."

Nodding, Smoke reholstered his six-gun. "Suits. Then we get outfitted and leave here. I've got a feeling we're not about to receive the key to the city."

Genuine joy glowed in the eyes of Bobby Harris. His button nose wrinkled and set the freckles over the bridge into a dance of delight. "You mean I really get to have a full-size horse all for my own?"

"Yes, you do. Only you have to pick it out, gentle it, break it to saddle and to ride." Bobby scowled at this, and Sally Jensen added, "This is a working ranch, Bobby. Everyone carries his own load. If you are going to ride for the brand, you'll have to do everything any other cowboy would do."

Bobby toed a dirt clod with his left boot and studied its movement intently a moment. "Yes, ma'am," he managed to get out through the pink pout of his lower lip.

So far, Sally Jensen reflected, all had gone well. Bobby was cute as a button, she acknowledged, although streaks of willfulness often put a brittle edge on their relationship. He was testing her, she realized.

In contrast, Bobby had taken well enough to Burt Crocker, the foreman at Sugarloaf. In fact, Bobby looked up to Burt with almost as much shining adoration as he reserved for her still absent and beloved Smoke. She made an effort to banish her loneliness and put on a smile.

"Look at it this way, Bobby. Once you learn to gentle and break a horse Smoke's way, you will be doing it with the hands. *And* you get a bonus paid on each one of your broken horses when it is sold."

That caught the lad's attention. "I do? Gosh, Miz Sally, that's awful nice. But it takes so long doin' it Smoke's way. Why can't we jist do it the reg'lar way with tie-downs, sharp spurs an' a whip? We could break 'em three times as fast."

Hands on hips, she stood exasperated that the boy had so far failed to assimilate the message of Smoke Jensen. Animals had a right to be treated gently, to live lives as relatively free of pain as any human might expect, given the times and the rugged nature of the frontier. To Smoke, it wasn't a matter of quantity and quotas met, but one of caring and delivering top quality.

"Because, young man, if Smoke Jensen ever caught a hand or anyone else treating any of his horses like that, that man would be fired on the spot. Usually after a good thrashing by Smoke."

Bobby went big-eyed, recalling what had happened to Rupe Connors , and gulped back his belligerence. "I—ah—I guess if that's the way Smoke wants it, that's the way he'll get it," he stammered.

Sally gave him a smile now and reached out to tossle his strawberry mop of unruly hair. "And don't you ever forget it."

"Oh, no, ma'am. Is there—is there any biscuits left, an' some of that blackberry jam? I'm sorta hungry."

Sally made a face of mock resignation. "And here the dinner dishes are not dry an hour. Mind, Bobby, only one, you'll spoil your supper."

Bobby put up two small fingers and peered coyly at her from under long, white lashes. "Two? I'm awful hungry."

Those cobalt eyes melted something in Sally Jensen. "Two, then. But mind what I said about spoiling your supper." Spoiling the kid is more like it, Sally Jensen, her mind chided her. What would Smoke say?

12

It felt good to be in the mountains. Smoke Jensen breathed deeply of resinous pines and relaxed. He let his mind digest the situation they had encountered in Torreón. It seemed to him to be more than coincidence that the seven had been present at the outfitter's shop. It was almost as though they had been waiting for them. He shared his conclusion with Carbone.

"It is possible. If Carvajal knew of my intention to meet with you and bring you south, men might have been waiting in Juarez. There is a telegraph line as far as Aguascalientes. Even in the state of Chihuahua it would only take a little of Carvajal's money to buy information as to our destination."

Smoke gave a snort. "Funny, I had been thinking the same thing. What about their being in that particular place?"

Carbone produced a rueful smile. "Valesquez is not only the best outfitter in Torreón, he is the only one. So, if Carvajal's men knew we were traveling light, they would expect us to show up there."

Smoke began to wonder if retirement to the life of a gentleman rancher had affected Carbone's survival instinct. Too much had been left to chance. These might not be his Shining Mountains, but they were familiar territory. From here on, the big mountain man decided, they would rely on Preacher's tried and proven methods.

"Old friend, I think that we should stay in these mountains awhile, avoid places where Carvajal might have support. If we manage to confuse them, if they lose the trail, we will regain the initiative and strike where they least expect."

Carbone nodded thoughtfully "Of course, *amigo.* You have the right of it. I fear I am out of practice at thinking deviously."

He's still man enough to admit it, Smoke thought with satisfaction. "Where had you intended for us to go?" he asked.

"Directly to my *estancia,*" Carbone responded.

"Um. What say we take the next small trail leading off the main road?"

Carbone considered it a moment. "We would end up in the small town of Pueblo de la Paz. It is a mining town, like many around here."

"Under Carvajal's control?" Smoke asked.

"Not openly, at least. There are some stories I've heard. For some reason, Carvajal has so far left the town alone."

"Then that's where we shall go, friend," Smoke decided.

Luminoso Soto sat in the chair in front of a roll-top desk. He laced pudgy fingers over a swell of belly that would have done justice to a hot air balloon. His small, close-set pig eyes glittered with avarice as he listened to the man in front of him.

Making that report was his partner in the small silver mine above the town of Pueblo de la Paz, Gaston Moro, the *Jefe de Policia*—Chief of Police—who concluded, "You realize what this means, Luminoso. We must have more men at once. This new vein is rich and thick." He spread his hands some two feet apart. "It is nearly pure silver. One can almost gouge it out with a spoon."

"I have no desire to eat the stuff, *compadre.* I don't even like it for itself." Thick lips pursed in sympathy to thoughts

of mounds of rich food, barrels of prize-winning port wine,
bushels of salted sardines. "It's what you can exchange it for
that excites pleasure in my heart."

In contrast to his partner, Gaston Moro had remained
whippet-thin, with the lean lines of a swift hunter. He contin-
ually despaired of Soto's preoccupation with food and drink.
Where Luminoso lived to eat, he, Gaton, ate, and sparingly at
that, only to keep alive. "Listen, *primo,*" he urged his cousin
and godfather of his children, "this is serious. If we cannot
obtain men from outside, we will have to begin using the villagers."

"No!" Luminoso exploded. His fat hand slapped down on
the desk top. "We would be hanged from the belfry of the
church if we tried that. So far the people have tolerated our—
ah—unusual methods and prospered along with us. We must
not turn on them now."

Moro shrugged expansively. "So be it, then. I leave it up to
you to recruit new workers for the mine."

"Never fear, Gaston, there will be an adequate work force
when it becomes necessary to tap this new vein. Meanwhile,
what have you done about Alfonso Lares?"

Moro worked up an expression of distaste. "The *cantinero* with ambitions of joining our partnership? Well, in
light of your opposition to dealing harshly with the locals,
I'm not sure what can be done. If you want my opinion, I
suggest that we need to arrange for him a little accident. A
fatal one."

After closing time at the *Cantina La Merced,* bartender
Alfonso Lares washed glasses and stacked them, while his
young son, Carlos, swept the floor and sluiced out the urinal
trough in front of the bar. Then they helped themselves to fiery
bowls of leftover *caldo de camerón,* a mixture of tiny shrimp,
onions, garlic, tomatoes, and chili peppers. This night, some-

thing must have happened to put off the shrimp broth made by old *Señora* Hurtado.

Alfonso's belly cramped as he and the boy made their way home. Could the shrimp have been bad? Some said the Hurtado woman was a witch. *Bruja* or not, something had certainly put a curse on that batch. New waves of pain, like thin glass spears piercing his stomach, washed over Alfonso. He jerked out of his own misery at a cry from his son.

The boy lay on the dirt of the street, curled into a ball, his small hands clutching his stomach. "Popi, Popi, my stomach hurts. I—I—" His eyes squeezed shut and tears ran down 10-year-old cheeks. He gave a convulsive heave and vomited explosively. Alfonso went to one knee and wretched also. Then a velvet club of blackness bashed his senses from his head, and he fell in his own spew.

He awakened in jail. His head throbbed, his mouth dry as sand. *"Por dios,* what am I doing here?" he demanded in a croaky voice.

"You ought to know," a smirking jailer responded as he rounded the corner of the box-like cell in Pueblo de la Paz's municipal hall. "We found you standing over the body of the son you had just murdered."

"I? Murder? No, it is not possible," Alfonso Lares protested in numb disbelief. "I—I did nothing to Carlos."

"Come, Lares, you're guilty as sin, and you know it. Poison. That's a woman's weapon," the jailer added scornfully.

"The City of Peace." Smoke Jensen spoke as he and Carbone rode past a small sign at the outskirts of Pueblo de la Paz. "I hope it is as good as its name."

"For our sake, yes, let that be so," Carbone agreed.

After arranging for the care of their two packhorses and gear, Smoke and Carbone rode to the smallest of the three saloons in town and entered to wash away the dust. Four men, who looked hard and dangerous, sat at a table near a beehive-shaped fireplace. They eyed the strangers with suspicion and hostility.

"Maybe not so peaceful after all, *amigo,*" Carbone observed of their watchers.

"Time will tell," Smoke replied philosophically. He could taste the hightened tension in the room.

They ordered beer and it came in tall, slender glasses called *tubos.* Smoke tried his and found it a bit rushed on the finish, not so green as to be skunky, but short of the standards of American brewers such as Pabst and Anheuser. Like the United States, every town of any consequence in Mexico had its own brewery. Local brands had a fierce partisanship on the part of residents. Carbone used the back of his hand to wipe foam from his pencil-line mustache.

"Aye, such a dandy," observed one of the card players. "Why didn't he just lick it off like a real man?"

Carbone made to ignore him. Smoke Jensen eased away an arm's length and unobtrusively slipped the hammer thong free on his .44.

"Speak up!" the heckler persisted. "I can't hear you."

"So much for the city of peace," Carbone said with a sigh.

"He's all yours," Smoke offered. "I'll keep the other three off your back."

Carbone pasted a laconic smile on his face and pushed away from the bar. On cat feet, he padded across the floor to the obnoxious local hardcase. With only the table between them, the taunting *pistolero* shoved back his chair and came to his boots, big, cruelly sharp spurs ringing. His hand hovered over the pearl grips of his Mendoza .45 Colt copy while his mouth worked up a new insult.

"You walk like a man with a cob up his . . ." His words ended when Carbone drove a hard, straight right into his mouth. The knuckles of Carbone's fist pulped the man's lips and ground his scraggly mustache into the raw flesh.

Instantly his companions sprang from their chairs, ready to take on this impudent stranger who had offended the town's premier bully. From the bar, Smoke Jensen's voice cracked like a teamster's whip.

"Don't!"

They looked at him, disbelieving. A *gringo* and he dared to interfere? They ignored the source of their agitation and charged Smoke as one. Their mistake, as they quickly found out. Smoke's big, broad shoulders rolled as he kept his fists low, balled and ready. The nearest Mexican overextended in his eagerness to land the first punch. Smoke's right rocketed up from his waist and planted itself firmly under the ardent combatant's chin.

His head snapped backward, and his boots kept coming forward. Smoke Jensen sidestepped him and let his forehead smack into the marble-trimmed bar. He went down soundlessly. A sizzling left blew past Smoke's ear, and he ducked to reposition himself. The remaining two came at him like a pair of wrestlers.

The smaller grabbed him around the waist and, making a growling sound like an enraged terrier, jerked and flailed uselessly. Smoke ignored him to better deal with his somewhat brighter friend. He slipped a short right jab, popped two quick lefts under the Mexican's rib cage.

Air whizzed out of a surprised mouth a moment before Smoke's looping right cracked off the hinge of his jaw. Staggered, the local tough's eyes crossed slightly, and he took a wise step backward. Smoke now gave his full attention to the one who would wear him to the ground. A balled fist, driven downward from shoulder level, exploded bright colored lights inside the growling Mexican's head. His grip loosened and, confronted by a recovered opponent's charge, Smoke wasted no more time on the small fellow.

A swift raise of one knee sent him flying. Smoke pivoted to check the other's advance. Three blows got through, one stinging off Smoke's cheek, the other two bounced off his heavily muscled chest. He produced a fleeting grin and moved in on his assailant.

"*¡Dios mio!* You are a big one," the local hardcase exclaimed. It didn't matter, he still had his *cuchillo.*

He went for his knife, which proved another mistake. Smoke Jensen had anticipated the move and countered it with the toe of his boot in the tender, vulnerable inner surface of his enemy's right thigh. Howling, the man went to one knee. He swung the large, sharp Toledo blade in a menacing manner, which kept Smoke at a safe distance. Slowly, uncertainly, he tried to stand.

"Fight like a man, you pig," he taunted in a spray of saliva.

"Aren't you confused a little?" Smoke provoked back. "Who's the coward who had to go for a knife?"

Unaccustomed to having his intended victims talk back, let alone insult him, the knife artist gaped, his breath rough, words slurred. "*¿Que dece?*"

"I said, you are a coward," Smoke stated simply in his best Spanish.

"*¡Pendjo! Pinche cabrón,*" the cutter snarled.

His knife whirred through the smoky air of the *cantina,* and Smoke Jensen came right behind its movement. He planted a boot solidly in the man's armpit while his fists did considerable damage to the exposed face. Steel clattered to the tile floor in a musical ring. Relentless, Smoke Jensen continued to work on the face of his opponent like a morning's exercise on the light bag. Swift, twisting, one-two, one-two wasp stings that opened a cut over the left eye, then the right cheek. Smoke waded in on the nose then. He felt cartilage give under the pounding of his big, powerful fists.

Blood gushed in a torrent. Smoke realized his attacker had fallen into unconsciousness a moment before a rain of light blows pounded on his back. Unable to square off for a straight punch, Smoke swung his right arm like the shaft of a flywheel. It made solid contact with the smallest of the three who had jumped him.

Bug-eyed, the Mexican tough went flying into the bar again. This time his head cracked hard against the top. With his stomach exposed he suffered mightily when Smoke Jensen took advantage of it. Hard knuckles made meaty smacks as Smoke went to work on the unguarded midsection. Grunts turned to whimpers while Smoke wore down hard belly muscles into slack, defenseless pudding. He stopped short of any permanent internal injury. Smoke paused long enough to wipe sweat from his brow, then turned in time to see Esteban Carbone yank on the front of his tormentor's shirt and drive his head into the solid wooden top of the table. Smiling with immense satisfaction, Carbone strolled toward Smoke.

"That seems to have settled that," he quipped.

Smoke started to agree when a voice that cracked like a pistol shot came from the doorway. "Put up your hands. You are under arrest."

Ramon, Julio, Gabriel, and Victor worked as herd boys on the estancia of Don Miguel Antonio Martine y Garcia. Victor, the oldest at nearly 12, and Julio, who had only turned 11 the previous month, thought of themselves as the ones in charge. Ramon and Gabriel, ten years of age, were more inclined to take advantage of the warm autumn sun in the high valley of Aguascalientes to throw off their responsibilities, and their clothes, and leap into one of the many cooling irrigation ditches for a long afternoon's swim. Fed by the hot water springs from which the state took its name, the boys could bask in these warm waters far earlier and later than lads living on the slopes of the high sierra surrounding this *alta plana* where grapes, sugarcane and fighting bulls were raised.

They were so doing on this afternoon, and had coaxed Julio into joining them, when the bad men arrived. Hard-faced, with mean eyes and cruel slashes for mouths, the band of out-laws, dressed all in black, reined in and looked at the boys without any show of emotion.

"These are the ones?" asked a bandit to the left of the leader.

"They are as good as any," the leader answered with a shrug of indifference.

Suddenly aware of the presence of these threatening strangers, Ramon, Gabriel, and Julio leaped from the bank where they were sunning themselves dry to cover their naked-ness in the water. Julio, bolder than the other two, addressed the men stammeringly.

"Buenos tardes, Señores. Do you work for Don Miguel? Or are you seeking him?"

Sneering laughter answered him. "We came to see you, boy. Come out of the water," the leader ordered him.

"I—I cannot, *Señor.* I have nothing on," Julio gulped.

"Come out," came the cold demand. "All of you."

Wet and crestfallen, certain they would be punished for ne-glecting their duties, the trio of boys splashed up the bank of the ditch. Suddenly, braided *riatas* dropped over their shoul-ders, and they were yanked off their feet. Laughing and shouting gibes, the ugly trio of Carvajal's bandits put spurs to their horses and began to drag the helpless boys across the rough, cactus-studded gound.

Needle spines pierced their flesh, and soon they bled from cuts and gouges. Still the bandit trio yelped with delight. Two others set off after Victor, who had observed their act of terror from a distance. He ran as fast as his sandals would carry him. Growing louder over the frightened pounding of his heart, he heard the approaching hoofbeats.

"He's mine!" the leader shouted with glee as he spun a loop and dropped it expertly over the thin shoulders of the terrified lad. The man had been, before joining Carvajal's army for adventure, a prize-winning *vaquero*.

With a deft snap of the rope, he hauled Victor off his feet and prodded his horse to a gallop. He raced past the fallen boy, the large hoofs of his mount close to Victor's head. When he reached the end of the *riata,* it snapped the boy around violently and sent him to skidding across the ground.

Pain became the whole world for Victor. Faintly he could hear the screams of his companions, whose fate he already knew to be as his own. Their small, bare bodies rolled and dragged over the harsh terrain. His own clothes provided some scant protection for Victor, for which he thanked the kind and protecting God. Only why hadn't God protected them from this? A rock the size of his fist sent a shower of sparks and a flash of blackness through Victor's head and robbed him of questions on theology.

How long could he endure? One by one the voices of his friends quieted. When silence came at last, save for his own cries of agony and pleas for mercy, Victor knew with certainty that they no longer lived. A great sadness burst his heart. He would be next. They would all die here, and no one would know why. Then, miraculously, the torment ended. Victor slid across the ground until his movement stopped at the left side of his torturer's horse. The man bent down, and his long, drooping mustache wriggled as he spoke.

"I have a message for your *patrón*. Tell him to pay the tribute to El Rey del Norte, and to send the *gringo* packing for his own country, or more of his people will be hurt. *¡Bastante! Adalante, compañeros,"* he concluded, loosed the *riata,* and they rode off, leaving a bleeding, aching Victor behind.

It took half an hour before Victor could stand, longer still until he could move around. Sobbing his grief, he went from one to the other still, brown form on the sandy soil. To his surprise, he saw movement in Julio's chest. He still lived. Victor crept on hands and knees, dragging Julio with him, to the edge of the canal and slid into the water with his friend. He stripped off the shredded remains of his clothes and washed thoroughly, bathing Julio's wounds also.

All the while he planned. He would wear Julio's shirt and pants back to the *estancia*. Julio could fit into one of the . . . dead boys' trousers at least. He would have to give the *patrón* the message. If not, those men would return and kill him, Victor reasoned. Then a cold light came to his eyes, and a hard smile touched his lips.

Once the *patrón* knew, the days of those *ladrónes* would surely be numbered. For the *patrón* had been a mighty *pistolero* who would make them pay dearly.

Smoke Jensen looked up as the jailer approached their cell, accompanied by a small, nattily dressed man with a heavy shock of gray hair. He wore a once-white, now age-grayed suit and had a homey face.

"Good afternoon, gentlemen," he greeted cheerily after the turnkey departed. "I am to be your attorney. Do you have any money with which to pay me?"

"First off, what are we charged with?" Smoke Jensen asked, making an effort to throttle his temper.

"Oh, that is simple, *Señor.* You are charged with drunk and disorderly, assault and battery, and resisting arrest."

"*¡Mierda!*" Carbone barked, his own battle with temper lost. "We were insulted, we were attacked."

Fussing with the lapel of his fancy suit, the little lawyer looked Carbone coldly in the eye. "Who threw the first punch?"

"Ah—er—you have me there, *Señor Abogodo.*"

"You know his name?" Smoke asked sotto voce.

"An *abogado* is an attorney," Carbone explained.

"Now then, as to the matter of money?" The attorney made

a circular, scrubbing motion with thumb and two fingers, as though feeling coins.

"We can pay you," Carbone relented.

"Fine then. Your case would be best served if you plead guilty," he said briskly.

"Now, just a minute," Carbone protested.

"Tell us something first. About the man who will be prosecuting us. Are you as good as he?" Smoke prodded.

A thin smile and clever twinkle came to the attorney. "I should say so, since I am also the man who is prosecutor for this court."

Dumbstruck for the moment, Smoke and Carbone cut amazed glances at one another. After a prolonged silence, Smoke Jensen cleared his throat and spoke with quiet control.

"Thank you for your time, *Señor Abogado.* We have decided that we will be quite capable of defending ourselves. Your services will not be needed."

"The man who defends himself, as it is said, ha—"

"Has a fool for a client. We have that saying in our country as well," Smoke told him. "We'll see you in court, counselor."

After his fussy departure, Carbone turned to Smoke. "Do you think we'll have a chance?"

"Do you think we'd have had one with him on our side?" Smoke countered.

"I regret to say that neither way do you *caballeros* have a chance," came the voice of Alfonso Lares. "But still you are lucky. For you it will only mean the mines. I have a more tragic fate awaiting."

"What's that?"

"I am to be executed for murdering my son."

Smoke and Carbone quickly discovered the nature of their neighbor's plight and heard for the first time of the slave labor in the mine. That, Lares assured them, would be where they were going. He was to be silenced for having wanted to invest in the mine.

"My greed cost me my son, and now my life. For we were both surely poisoned. What is there to do?"

"For a start," Smoke Jensen suggested, "we could break out of jail."

13

Several Sugarloaf hands stood around hee-hawing in great amusement. Little Bobby Harris rose from the puddle of mud and cow pies, his face crimson in humiliation. He balled his small fists and advanced on the youngest of his tormentors. Before the lad could defend himself, Bobby launched a wild looping right that smacked the tormentor in his chest.

"Ow! Hey, you hit me, snot-nose," he complained.

Bobby hit him again for good measure. Suddenly he found himself lifted from the ground and turned upside down. When the world stabilized in this topsy-turvy position, he saw the inverted face of Buck Crocker. The foreman shook his head sadly. "When are you ever going to learn to control that temper, Bobby?"

"Leggo me!" Bobby yelled. "I'm gonna kick his butt up twixt his shoulder blades."

"No, you're not. What you are going to do is clean up. Pull off them boots and get yer butt in that horse trough. Wash the mud outta behind your ears, while you're at it."

"You tryin' to kill me?" Bobby complained, lower lip out in a big pink pout. "Nobody around here likes me."

"Why, you little brat, if Miz Jensen heard you whining like that, she'd fix yer behind with a razor strop," Hank Penny scorned him. "You some kind of sissy or what? Can't take a little ribbin' when you get throwed? Haw-haw!"

"Listen to me, Bobby," Burt rumbled good-naturedly. "I generally believe in giving a youngster his head. This time, I'm going to insist you do as you are told. You'll stink to high heaven of cow plop, an' Miz Jensen would come down hard on me for it."

Bobby eyed him suspiciously from his tail-up condition. "That's dif'rent. But I ain't takin' no regular bath. Don't nobody make me do that ev'ry day."

Burt cocked an eyebrow at him. "Oh? Suppose you fall in a cow pattie ev'ry day? You gonna go around stinkin' like the hind end of a cow?" Suddenly Burt heard his voice. Damn, if he didn't sound like an old maid, lecturin' some unruly school kid. He gave Bobby a good shake. "Now, you get in that trough and outta them clothes, or I'll drop your drawers and blister your butt."

Right side up now, Bobby gave Burt a big-eyed stare. "You mean that?"

"Absolutely."

Bobby ducked his head as best he could with Burt's big fist under his chin. "Ooo-kay. Lemme down and I'll slosh off."

"Now that's more like it. Then get yerself back in the saddle and back to work. You're burnin' daylight with all this foolishness."

"Well—ah—well, I reckon it's of yer makin'," Bobby offered the last of his defiance.

"Fine," Burt snapped. "Have it any way you want it. Only get yerself clean."

Snickers came from the crew as they set about cutting out horses and ear-notching those destined for sale. Bobby summoned up as much dignity as he could and entered the cold water of the trough. Thank goodness he'd not have to go through this again this week, he thought to himself.

Darkness had come to Pueblo de la Paz. True to his usual custom, Triunfo Cienfuegos, the fat, easygoing jailer, loosened the belt and chest harness of his uniform and yawned gustily. He seated himself in an oversized chair and tilted it back against the wall. His thick lips had just begun to flutter in the first light layer of sleep when a plaintive voice came from far down the cell block.

"*Socorro. ¡Por amor del dios, ayudamé!*" Alfonso Lares moaned. "*¡Ay, socorro! Estoy moribundo.*"

"Who's dying?" Cienfuegos asked himself as the last appeal from Lares jerked him out of slumber.

"*Ayudamé*—Help me!" Lares repeated plaintively.

"Hey, *carcelero,* this man's sick." To make matters worse, Cienfuegos grumbled, that big damned *gringo* had started yelling at him.

Roused from his usual nap, and pleased by it about as much as a bear disturbed in hibernation, Cienfuegos growled down the barred corridor, "*¡Callerse!* Go to sleep. Stop making noise."

Shrieks of agony added to the pleas. Cienfuegos vaguely remembered something about poisoning being involved with Lares. Frowning, he dropped the chair to the floor and levered his way out of it. He took the ring of keys from a peg in the wall and started for the barred entrance to the cell block.

"I'm coming. Be done with that noise. I'm on my way," he rumbled as he entered the corridor and headed toward the cells.

Alfonso Lares lay on his bunk, doubled up in a ball of pain. His face was wet and shiny in the dim light of a single kerosene lamp that sat on a high shelf, halfway down the corridor. In the adjoining cell, Smoke Jensen and Esteban Carbone stood close to the dividing wall of bars. Their faces wore worried expressions.

"Get back. Get back," Cienfuegos shouted at them. "Now, what's the matter with you?" he impatiently snapped at Lares.

"I've—I've been poisoned. Th-that food we ate," he groaned.

"Nonsense. You're the one who uses poison," Cienfuegos dismissed, his memory reawakened.

"Help me," Lares bleated. He began to shake and slobber.

Maybe he had been poisoned. Cienfuegos shoved the key in the lock case. "Stay where you are. I'm coming in."

Cienfuegos entered the cell and knelt beside the bunk. Lares' teeth chattered and drool ran from the corner of his mouth. Suddenly worried, the jailer reached out and took the prisoner by the shoulders. Gently he lifted Lares to a sitting position.

"Can you stand?" he asked.

Lares nodded. Cienfuegos helped him to his feet. Lares swayed and groaned. He tried to take a step and lurched violently against the turnkey. Cienfuegos slammed back against the open wall of bars with a startled gasp.

Instantly, large, powerful hands grabbed his head, hauled Cienfuegos backward until his shoulders slammed into the steel bars and his head protruded into the other cell. Muscles strained and gave off pain signals as his captor wrenched on his chin and the back of his head. They twisted until his watering eyes focused on the rear wall of the cubicle.

Carbone reached for his bulging waist and plucked the pair of manacles from his belt. Swiftly he drew the arms of Cienfuegos backward and secured the cuffs on his side of the bars. The terrible pressure on Cienfuegos' neck relaxed.

"Get the keys," Smoke Jensen commanded Alfonso Lares.

Lares stood dumbly, mouth agape. "It worked," he muttered in wonder.

"Of course it did. Now move," Smoke demanded.

Carbone tore the tail from the jailer's shirt and stuffed it in his mouth. By then, Lares had their cell unlocked. Smoke directed both doors to be locked in place.

"Bring the keys along, we'll be needing them," Smoke added.

That accomplished, they headed for the office. There they located their belongings and quickly fastened cartridge belts in place. Carbone nodded to a rack of weapons.

"You had better arm yourself, friend *cantinero*."

Lares looked startled. "Me? I am, as you say, only a *cantinero*."

Obsidian glittered in Carbone's dark eyes. "As of now, you are a liberator of your town. Do as I say."

"*Sí, Patrón,*" Alfonso Lares gulped. Then, "What do we do now?"

Smoke Jensen answered him "We're going to round up the rest of the police, the mayor and chief, and lock them in here."

"I never thought I'd live to see the day," Lares stated wonderingly. Then he recalled what had brought about his near death and the murder of his son. "But I am as guilty as the rest. I was greedy and wanted to share in the mine."

"No one need know that, *Señor* Lares," Carbone told him. "If you do your part in freeing this town from Luminoso Soto and Gaston Moro, you will be a hero to your people. Come along now."

They encountered the first of the night police patrol right outside the front door of the jailhouse.

Lorenzo Cruz, Felipe Zargoza, and Diego Santana had been in on the mine scheme from the first. They had been chosen to keep the citizens of Pueblo de la Paz in line after dark. Typical bullies, they swaggered and sneered and generally intimidated the timid folk of the town. All of the violent experiences of their useless lives had not prepared them for Smoke Jensen and Esteban Carbone.

They had been laughing over the hilarious way old Chuchu Bustamonte had wailed and run on his chubby legs when they caught him out after curfew. They stopped chortling when the door to the jail opened at such an unexpected hour. When three men stepped out onto the stoop, they advanced with hands on the butts of their .45 Mendozas.

"Stop right there!" Lorenzo Cruz demanded.

"Or you'll what?" Smoke Jensen asked coldly.

"Por dios, estar el gringo," Diego Santana blurted.

Realization dawned on Lorenzo Cruz. "Escape! Shoot them," he screamed at his companions.

All three drew their weapons. None of them did so fast enough. Smoke Jensen moved with practiced ease; his large, supple fingers closed around the grip of his .44 Colt, and he hauled it free while Cruz, Santana and Zargoza had barely moved their six-guns upward in the holsters. Felipe Zargoza saw death coming his way and uttered a brief, silent prayer a moment before Smoke Jensen's .44 roared to life.

A sledgehammer blow struck the center of Zargoza's chest, and he rocked back on his boot heels. Numbly, he continued his draw. The muzzle of his .45 Mendoza came clear of leather an instant before a second slug burned a hole through his liver and his life ended in a flash of black.

Beside the dying man, Lorenzo Cruz growled an obscenity as he whipped up his weapon and eared back the hammer. His world exploded into a shower of sparks and blanket of darkness as Carbone shot him through the heart. Dead before his body knew it, he continued to stand, finger tightening on the trigger. Esteban Carbone put a safety shot between the corrupt policeman's eyes, and Lorenzo Cruz went off to meet his Maker.

Smoke Jensen had turned his attention on the third of their opponents. Diego Santana had suddenly developed difficulty with his six-gun. He'd quick-fired it into the ground at the feet of Smoke Jensen and now fought against a backed-out primer that hung up the cylinder against the recoil plate. Cursing hotly, he dropped the useless weapon and drew his second revolver.

He brought it into play, only to have it discharge high into the air as Smoke Jensen's next round drilled through his right shoulder. Firing left-handed badly affected Santana's accuracy, the hot pain radiating from his shoulder increasing his disability. His next round split air between Smoke and Carbone and thudded into the door to the jail.

Schooled to calm, controlled shooting under the worst of circumstances, Smoke Jensen was hampered by none of this. He put his fourth bullet in under Diego Santana's diaphragm. Hydrostatic shock drove the air from Diego's lungs, jellied flesh, and reflex lifted him off his feet. Immediately the street became silent.

Only harsh breathing from Alfonso Lares disturbed the graveyard stillness. "I don't believe it. I only blinked my eyes and when they opened, three men are dead," the little *cantinero* babbled. "Wha-what do we do now?"

"Go find the rest and then pay a visit on the mayor and chief of police," Smoke Jensen advised him.

A distant, alarming sound invaded the deep slumber of Mayor Luminoso Soto. Foggily, he pulled himself out of his repose and listened carefully. Had he dreamed it? Gunshots in the dead of night. If not a dream, what could it mean? He turned his head from side to side, seeking further enlightenment.

He heard nothing. He sighed heavily, yawned prodigiously, and broke wind. Those chores accomplished, he lowered his head to the pillow and returned to sleep. Beside him in the bed, his wife lay with open eyes.

Disgust at her slovenly husband kept her awake. She had heard the gunshots also and pondered their meaning. Why, she wondered, had God burdened her with this man for so many years? She sensed, knew, that he was involved in something not entirely legal. It pained her soul. Then a new fear electrified her.

Could the shooting mean that the people had risen in their anger against Luminoso? Could they already be on their way to the *casa* with torches and ropes? What would happen to her? Hesitantly, truly frightened now, she reached out to shake her husband.

Smoke Jensen, Esteban Carbone and Alfonso Lares rounded the corner out of the Plaza de Armas to find themselves confronted by some twenty men. Several bore torches that wavered in the night breeze. The three in front carried old, battered weapons. Two shotguns and a rifle, Smoke noted. The rest had machetes, scythes and other edged weapons. Their faces were taut with determination and anger.

"Who are you and where are you going?" the spokesman demanded.

"That depends on what you have in mind," Smoke responded.

"We are looking for the policemen. We heard shots."

"They are dead," Carbone informed him. "They made the mistake of trying to stop us from leaving the jail."

Some of the tension bled off in an audible mass sigh. The spokesman actually produced an embarrassed smile. "That is why we are here. We are friends of this man, Alfonso Lares.

We know he would never harm his own son. The *jefe* and the *alcalde* are up to some mischief. Of that we are sure."

"That they are," Smoke allowed.

"We know about the prisoners marched off into the mountains," the leader acknowledged. "Are they taken there to be killed?"

"No. Your mayor and chief of police have a silver mine. Strangers are convicted of crimes they did not commit and taken there as slave laborers."

"Slavery is against the law in our country, *Señor.*" The spokesman paused and peered intently at Smoke Jensen. "Your accent, *Señor.* You are not from around here."

"I am an American," Smoke told him simply. To the angry mutters and few curses from the crowd, he went on to explain. "My friend here asked me to come to help fight against El Rey del Norte."

"And who is your friend?" the leader asked suspiciously.

"I am called Esteban Carbone."

Several gasps of surprise accompanied a sudden shift of mood. Men snatched the hats from their heads and clutched them before their chests. All eyes fixed on Carbone. The leader swallowed hard.

"We are at your service, *Don* Esteban. What do you wish us to do?"

"We need to hunt down the remaining policemen," Carbone told him. "Root them out of their homes and take them to the jail. Once they are locked away, we will go visit the mayor."

Broad, white smiles broke out on the upturned brown faces. "At once, *Don* Esteban," the leader vowed. "I am called Ernesto Rubio. These men will do what I tell them."

"Fine. Arm them from the rack in the jail. Round up the police and do with them as I said. Then join us at the mayor's house."

* * *

A sound like a growing, heavy surf brushed at Mayor Soto's consciousness. Groggy, he forced open gummy eyes and blinked. Orange light flickered on the walls of his bedroom. Disoriented, he looked around for his wife. She was nowhere to be seen. Sudden panic touched him when he heard a harsh voice call from the street in front of his high-walled *casa*.

"Come out, Mr. Mayor!"

"Luminoso Soto," Ernesto Rubio demanded loudly, "come out here and surrender to us at once."

"Damn them! Damn peasants. We have been too lenient. They are drunk on tequila and beer. Out of their minds. Where are the police?" Dithering over this strange turn of events, Luminoso Soto hastily donned trousers and a shirt. He slid his feet into Toledo-style boots and clomped to the front door. On the way he saw nothing of his wife.

Soto tried to build a tone of command when he threw open the door and spoke to the gathered people. "Go home at once. You are out after curfew."

Then his sleep-drugged eyes took in the size of the gathering. Torches guttered over the heads of fully twenty-five men. Four more stood in front. Blinking, he identified them.

That greedy *payaso,* Alfonso Lares, the strangers who were jailed, Ernesto Rubio. Lares might be a clown, but he knew all about the mine and knew he had never poisoned himself and his son. Suddenly a skeletal hand of ice clutched at Soto's heart. He was a murderer. Or at least complicit in a murder. Bluster leaving him, he raised his hands, palm outward, and tried to placate the angry crowd.

"My friends. You all know me. I have brought prosperity to Pueblo de la Paz. I have improved the lot of every one of you. What is this talk of surrender? For what crimes am I to stand accused?"

"The murder of Carlos Lares, for one," Ernesto Rubio declared.

"For the false imprisonment of myself and my friend," Carbone told him.

"Who, exactly, are you?" the mayor demanded, some of his courage returning.

"I am called Esteban Carbone. This is my friend from the United States, Smoke Jensen."

Smoke Jensen meant nothing to Luminoso Soto, but the name of Esteban Carbone struck dread into his bosom. He paled visibly. Feebly he waggled his hands. "A mistake, I assure you. You shall be free to go first thing in the morning. There was—ah—some misunderstanding. That is all."

"Stop babbling," Carbone growled. "Come along with us."

Soto half-turned, weakly gestured toward the house behind him. "My—my wife. Who will look after her?"

Ernesto Rubio gave the mayor a nasty smile. "She has already gone to the house of her mother. You have nothing with which to concern yourself, *Señor Alcalde.* Come along peacefully, or we will kick the living hell out of you."

Soto thought fleetingly of darting inside, barring the door against them and escaping out the back. No use, his common sense told him. Head bowed, shoulders sloped, he stepped out into the cobbled street to meet his fate.

Gaston Moro had been awakened by the gunfire that ended the lives of three of his policemen. Unlike pudgy Mayor Soto, he did not cringe in fear and confusion. His first thoughts went to the possibility that Gustavo Carvajal had gone back on his word. It would be just like him. Moro knew Carvajal from the old days.

They had been youthful adventurers together. Robbed and terrorized the peasant villages as part of another man's gang. Carvajal went on to run a bandit horde of his own. Gaston Moro thought of himself as smarter. He lived comfortably, got as much in bribes and salary as Carvajal no doubt did from his raids, and didn't have to take the risk of being shot.

Then along came this King of the North thing. Suddenly his old friend had taken on a grander stature. He now took tribute from every village in three states. All except for those on the estates of Esteban Carbone and Miguel Martine. Fast guns who had retired, married well and lived the good life. Moro had played on this when he and Soto had made their accommodation with Carvajal.

For old times' sake, Carvajal would receive 100 twenty-kilo bars of silver per year. In return, he would leave the village alone, let his old friend have his way within the confines of Pueblo de la Paz. Only now, had greed overcome pleasant memories of past outlaw companionship?

He had armed himself and waited in an upper room of his substantial *casa* on a hillside street of la Paz, ready to meet such an eventuality. A growing mutter of angry voices lent doubt to this possibility. No, Gustavo Carvajal would have come thundering into town on a snorting horse, his men all around him. What could this be?

"*¡Jefe!* Come out with your hands up. The mayor is already in jail," a familiar voice called from the street.

Gaston Moro rose to peer through the firing loop in the shutter that closed off the second-floor window. What he saw chilled him. Torches spluttered and flickered fitfully in a rising breeze. He recognized a dozen citizens standing in the narrow, winding street outside his home. Ernesto Rubio appeared to be leading them. Then he saw the two strangers he had arrested that morning.

They were supposed to be in jail. What had gone wrong?

Gaston Moro heard a faint banging at the rear of the house. He tore himself away from the hypnotic vision of supposedly cowed citizens armed and aroused outside and took the rear stairway to the ground floor. A smaller portal gave access to the alley behind his house. He checked the peephole and opened the door to admit two policemen.

Both appeared frightened. One began talking as he stepped into the kitchen. "We must fight for our lives. The people have gone crazy. They have taken everyone else to jail."

"What's this about?"

"That boy who died," the frightened policeman replied. "And they know about the mine. They are dangerous, I tell you."

"Nothing to worry about. By daylight, they will have run out of energy. We can recover then!"

Glass broke in an upstairs window; Moro regretted his last, overconfident statement. He had not had time to close all the shutters. A loud crash came from the direction of the front door. "Quick," he commanded. "Shoot a few of the fools, and the rest will scatter like chickens."

Swiftly, the terrorized policemen rushed to do their chief's bidding. A thunderous, booming crack came from the direction of the thick front door. Its ominous sound arrested all movement for five long, fateful seconds.

With a loud creaking, the tall, thick panels of the oak door fell inward. Dust billowed from the tile entryway as they struck the floor. Through the cloud, Gaston Soto and his corrupt policemen saw a tall figure sided by two shorter ones. Agitated by fear of the unknown, Soto shouted at his minions.

"Don't just stand there, shoot them!"

The tarnished officers of the law obeyed the orders with alacrity. Not speedy enough, though, as flame split the dust and announced the departure of the lawmen for their final appearance in court.

Smoke Jensen and Esteban Carbone fired almost as one. Smoke popped his cap first by a fraction of a second. His slug plopped loudly into the chest of one policeman, staggering him. The dying cop's reflexes triggered his six-gun in the holster, sending a bullet downward through his thigh and out the front, taking his kneecap with it. With a surprised and indignant expression, he fell backward to strike his head on the lip of a fountain basin.

Carbone did for the second law dog, a shame to his badge, who ended his life in pitiful sobs for mercy. That left Chief Gaston Moro. Frantically the corrupt chief of police waved his small-caliber revolver in the air as Smoke Jensen advanced on him.

One gloved hand slapped the .32 from the chief's hand. The other balled into a fist and landed with astounding force on the mayor's chin. His legs went rubbery. Only conditioning made him recover. He'd been in fights before, knew every dirty trick. His booted foot left the floor, and he aimed a vicious kick at his huge assailant's groin.

Smoke Jensen caught the painful blow on the outside of his left thigh, continued his turn, and brought a roundhouse right to the side of Soto's head. Moro's eyes rolled up, and he went to one knee. He wasn't finished yet; his years as a bandit served him now. Soto pulled a knife from the top of one boot and took a wild slash at Smoke's exposed belly.

Cloth parted in Smoke's shirt and a thin red line, only a graze, showed on the skin over flat plates of muscle. Smoke delivered selective punishment for this offense, lefts and rights to the head and neck of the chief. Stunned, Moro could only swing the blade in directionless arcs.

Blood ran from a cut under one eye; his lip had been split and now grew puffy. Smoke shifted his point of aim and mashed the chief's nose. Then another uppercut to the sensitive point under the side of Moro's jaw, and the venal lawman went slack, out for a long, long count.

Smoke stood over him, panting slightly. "I think we can go to the mine now," he opined to the wide-eyed citizens of Pueblo de la Paz.

14

All of the guards milled around on the fenced-in grounds of the mine. Some, still groggy with sleep, muttered among themselves and sought coffee to stimulate sodden brains. They had heard the rattle of gunfire in the town below and worried over what it might mean. Typical low-grade hired guns, they remained loyal to the man who paid them, so long as he continued to pay. Or until someone else offered more.

Several had gathered at the main gate, and talked in low tones. The topic of conversation was El Rey del Norte, and the possibility he had come to claim Pueblo de la Paz and all it possessed for himself. The prospect did not engender enthusiasm.

"He will shoot us down like dogs," one hardcase guard suggested.

"Why would he do that, Lopez?" another countered. "I have heard that he welcomes men who can use their guns. He is building an army capable of taking on those *corrompidores* in *Ciudad* Mexico."

"What?" a third asked disbelievingly. "Porfirio Diaz is *presidente* and, for once, he has the army behind him He may be corrupt, as are all politicians, but he has the power, *¿no es verdad?*"

"A curse on all politicians," Lopez, the worried one, spat. "But our problem is El Rey. We must decide what we will do when he comes here."

Within a few minutes, they found out their concern had been focused in the wrong direction.

Five men, led by Carbone, approached the front gate to the mine. Fires had been lighted in a scattered pattern. Their fitful light, in a stiffening breeze, allowed a clear view of the compound, and prevented any chance of escape by the slave labor inmates. Carbone halted his followers and they spread out, facing an equal number of guards on the opposite side of the fence.

"Are you from El Rey?" the worried one asked.

"No," Carbone answered. "We've come to tell you you are out of a job."

A couple of the guards snickered at this. "Oh? How is that, *hombre?*" the worried man challenged, grown suddenly bolder now that El Rey del Norte was out of the situation.

"The owners of this mine, who pay your wages, are in jail. They are charged with slavery."

Giggles turned to braying laughter. "These men here have been convicted by a court and sentenced to hard labor. There is no slavery. It is against the law in our country," Lopez sneered in answer.

"Open the gate," Carbone commanded.

Lopez had recovered his usual nasty outlook. "Who are you to give me orders?"

"Esteban Carbone y Ruiz." It came out weighted with menace.

Lopez was stunned by this revelation, though *machismo* would not permit him to show it. "So? An old man who has hung up his guns. A *hacendado,* with soft hands and no stomach for a fight. Go home to your *estancia* and play with the women, *Don* Esteban." Lopez made the honorific sound like an insult.

Was Smoke Jensen in position? He had to be, Carbone told himself. He drew a deep breath. "I had hoped that you would not be so eager to die, *hombre.*"

With that he drew with all the old speed and sureness. His long-barreled .45 made a blur as it left the leather. Its muzzle rose to gut-level in less than an eye's blink. His first slug struck the receiver side-plate of the Winchester in Lopez's hands. Stinging shock and pain ran up the truculent guard's arms, and he let go of the damaged weapon with a sharp yowl of discomfort.

It could be said of Lopez that he was a game fighter. He never hesitated, once in action. His right hand dropped to the pearl grips of his .45 Mendoza, and he hauled it out with alacrity. Unfortunately for him, he remained what he was, a third-rate gun hawk.

Carbone's second bullet slammed into the chest of Lopez with enough force to stagger him. He gulped for air that did him little good, fought to raise his six-gun as the world dimmed around him. To Carbone's left and right, shotguns taken from the jail boomed, and a scythe of buckshot laid low three of the other guards. The fifth turned tail and bolted into the greater safety of numbers. Carbone took note of muzzle flashes from the uphill side of the compound and smiled in satisfaction.

Smoke Jensen hugged the cheek-plate of his Winchester stock to his face and sighted in on a bull of a man who appeared to be in charge at the mine. From this range it would be an easy shot. When Carbone opened the dance, he squeezed off a round.

Almost at once, the boss guard went to the ground, shot through the hips by a fat .45-70-500 Express slug. He bellowed at the other warders, more in rage than pain. At once they scattered out of the vulnerability of firelight. From here on it would be rough. Smoke had identified the guard shack and put three rounds through its flimsy walls. Yelps of alarm and the tinkle of wounded pots and pans coldly amused him. Two slugs turned a watch-fire into a shower of sparks.

Then he returned his attention to the barrack. Men dived through windows and scrambled out the door as hot lead gouged a tabletop, knocked the stovepipe out of alignment in a shower of soot, and wet down the occupants with a spray of tequila from a shattered bottle. Smoke Jensen took time to shove half a dozen large cartridges into the Express rifle before he rose and started downhill.

Well spread out, as Smoke had instructed, eight townsmen accompanied him. At first they met no resistance. All attention focused on the main gate. Smoke saw a guard in a tower take aim at the front of the compound and brought the Winchester to his shoulder. The Express rifle barked, and the man on the elevated platform threw his weapon high in the air as he fell to the side and draped his bleeding body over the side wall.

That got notice from the hardcases nearer to the back of the mine property. Their return fire caused several of the citizens of la Paz to drop to the ground, and one round clipped a young man in the shoulder. His cry of pain could trigger panic among the untrained, Smoke Jensen realized. He had to keep them advancing.

"Everyone down. Crawl forward to the fence," he commanded.

They obeyed at once, grateful for a way not to provide a tempting target. At a crouch, Smoke led the way. He reached the fence and found it to be what farmers in the States had taken to calling "hog wire": big, six-inch open spaces formed by twisted, interlaced wire. It made easy climbing for a human. It would also make easy pickings, like flies on the wall, for the gunmen inside. He summoned one of the volunteers, a thick-shouldered man who had proclaimed himself the town blacksmith.

"Let's take a hold of the bottom of this and see if we can raise it," Smoke suggested.

"Estar facil—that's easy," the grinning smithy responded. He knelt beside Smoke and, together, they prised upward.

Slowly at first, then with a surge, the wire bent to their powerful effort. It rose from the ground, restricted only at the wooden posts where the mesh had been secured with staples. Bullets snapped over their heads and bent backs, and Smoke noticed the stolid blacksmith wince, though he never hesitated.

"You're good at this," Smoke praised when they had opened a swath wide enough for several to cross under at once.

"I have a brother-in-law who is inside there," he answered simply. "He is from out of town, and they . . . took him," he added with a shrug.

"We'll get him back," Smoke assured him.

Once they were inside the compound, the fighting grew close. Knives and six-guns against clubbed rifles and, oddly to Smoke's way of thinking, whips. Advancing with his volunteers, Smoke saw the head guard roll over and prop himself up on one elbow. He had fisted a .45 and sought a good target.

"Some people never learn," Smoke complained to himself as he stepped up close behind the murderous warder.

With an economy of motion, Smoke brought the butt-plate of his Express rifle down on the head of the would-be back-shooter. It made a ripe melon splat, and the .45 slipped from nerveless fingers. Two guards in their union suits burst from the barrack, revolvers blazing. Smoke Jensen stood right in their path.

No time to swing the Winchester Express into line. Smoke let go and, in one smooth motion, whipped out his .44. It bucked and snorted and sent a lethal message to the charging guards. First one, then the other, fell in the dust, but not before a bullet from the second man had put a hot line across the right shoulder of Smoke Jensen. It affected his aim, so that his next .44 round punched a black hole in the forehead of the gunman who had shot him.

Smoke regretted that. These were only hired punks, not soldiers of El Rey del Norte. If they had sense enough to give up, they would be let free. Smoke and Carbone had extracted a promise from the people of la Paz to that effect. They knew better, he reasoned, than to renege. Already he heard Carbone's voice, clear and steady above the tumult, informing the defenders of that fact.

"Stop fighting. Your bosses are locked up. You have nothing to fear from us. Give up and go free."

Gradually a slackening in the melee could be noted. Smoke smiled to himself. Carbone had definitely not lost it. He still commanded while others followed. Smoke added his own imperfect Spanish to the inviting flow of Carbone's urging.

"Throw up your hands. Stop fighting."

A shot cracked past Smoke's head, and he spun to the left, where the enemy lurked in a shadow. Another muzzle bloom gave him a target, and he pumped two fast rounds into the darkness. A muffled cry answered him, and a guard stumbled out into the light of the fires. He tottered, made a futile gesture of surrender, and crashed to the ground, to twitch and die.

Quiet came in an instant. Slowly the groans of wounded and battered men rose. From a locked barrack came the plaintive cry of a prisoner. Quickly the men of Pueblo de la Paz set about freeing the victims of greed. When they lined up outside, Smoke and Carbone addressed them. They told of the depredations of El Rey and asked if the men would show gratitude for their freedom by joining in the fight to rid Mexico of another form of vermin, like those who had made them slaves.

Shouts of approval rose among the former prisoners. In a body they rushed forward to pledge their lives to the effort. When they had been taken into town, fed and armed from the arsenal in the jail, Carbone came to where Smoke Jensen leaned back in a captain's chair, to catch a few badly needed winks.

"What now, *companero?*" the premier gunman of Mexico asked.

"I think it's time we delivered our new recruits to your *rancho,* don't you?"

"*Seguro, sí.* We can ride out within half an hour."

"See to it," Smoke concluded through a tired smile.

They kept with Smoke Jensen's plan. Climbing higher into the Sierra Madre Occidental, the small column of volunteers came to a place where the road split. Carbone called a halt while he studied the map he carried in his mind. At last satisfied, he addressed Smoke.

"This left-hand track leads eventually to my ranch. Ernesto Rubio is a trustworthy sort. I suggest we send the recruits on south to the ranch. My *segundo* can take care of housing and training them."

"And we go where?" Smoke asked.

"This is the long way around," Carbone protested the delay, "but it leads eventually into the state of Aguascalientes near Martine's *estancia.* It is not a well-traveled road, and we should get by without being noticed."

Smoke smiled. "I like that. I've always been a strong believer in surprise. Odds are that if we are out of sight long enough, this Carvajal will start to think I've turned tail and headed back north. By then we should have enough men ready for a fight."

The two friends watched the former slaves depart. Then they gathered up their packhorses and moved out at a brisk trot along the spiny ridge of a lesser sierra. High above, an eagle circled and made its plaintive cry. Somewhere below, furtive prey would be motionless in fearful anticipation of the sharp talons that could close on their small, furry bodies and carry them off to feed a brood of chicks. Smoke Jensen watched the magnificent bird as it soared and dipped in the currents sent up from sun-drenched slopes of pine and balsam.

Cedar trees gave off their pungent odor, which invigorated the big mountain man. With each passing hour Smoke Jensen felt more at home in these rugged escarpments. He made careful, unconscious note of terrain features. Never again would he be a stranger here. Neither man broke the companionable silence until they halted to rest their horses and nibble on cold rations.

"Over beyond this rampart, to the north a hundred leagues, is *Cannon del Cobre.* It is spectacular. Larger even than *Cannon Grande,* in Arizona," Carbone informed Smoke.

"That would be a sight worth seeing."

"It is very rich in copper ore," Carbone added.

"Is it actively mined?"

"No, the terrain is too rugged."

"Well, then, maybe it will last for a while longer," Smoke opined. He strongly disliked and fervently lamented the vast, ugly gashes left in the land of the American West. Hydraulic mining was relatively new, yet it had left its indelible mark on the once-beautiful mountains and valleys.

Sighing, he abandoned such reflections to study the sky. A deep line formed on Smoke's brow as he took note of a growing expanse of black-bellied, towering clouds in the west. In the next ten minutes they seemed to have doubled in number. Smoke called Carbone's attention to them.

"Oh, *sí,*" Carbone responded, relatively unaffected. "A storm is gathering. We'll get wet before we find a place for the night."

Smoke Jensen considered the swift, powerful violence of thunderstorms in the High Lonesome. They could gather out of seeming nothing and dump a cascade of water and hail, and lash the land with tempestuous winds before sailing ponderously away to the southeast. These huge boomers appeared to be kin to those he'd known much of his life. Yet, Carbone seemed indifferent to the menace in the sky.

"We'd better move on, then," Smoke suggested.

Forty minutes later, the entire sky had turned black. It was as though night had fallen on this part of the mountains. Ahead and behind them, bright, golden sunlight sparkled on the snow-capped pinnacles of the Sierra. Muted thunder rumbled to the west. Only a few at first, then wide swaths of tree tops began to sway and twist in a growing wind.

It sang mournfully through the pine boughs. Smoke settled his Stetson more firmly on his head and turned up his collar. Sidewinder twitched nervous ears and rippled his loose hide in agitation. A sudden flash turned the world white around them. The peal of thunder came like a blast of cannon fire to someone sleeping beneath the muzzle.

Their packhorses squealed in alarm. Carbone looked about with newfound uneasiness. Large drops of rain, widely spaced, began to patter down. They bounced high off the ground and rattled the leaves of oak and aspen. Smoke paused to look all around.

"We'd best find some cover. I'm betting on hail," he told Carbone.

"Sí. This is worse than I expected."

"How far are we from somewhere to shelter?"

"¿Quien sabe?" Carbone responded with a shrug. "Who knows?" he repeated. "Maybe half a league. There is, or was, a small ranch in this part of the Sierra. We should almost be there."

"We'll have to be quick about it," Smoke urged, his last

words drowned out in another cataclysmic flash and bang of celestial outrage.

Mixed with the heavy odor of ozone, the wood smoke could not at first be discerned by Smoke Jensen. He caught a whiff of it, though, when the wind shifted and increased in velocity. A billow of gray-smudged white boiled past them.

"That lightning started a fire," Smoke declared. "It's upwind of us. Let's ride."

Carbone took the point, his big spurs raking reckless speed out of his mount. A thoroughly frightened packhorse streamed in his wake. Smoke Jensen followed in the race to get out of this celestial outrage.

Instinctively, Carbone chose a path through the trees that led diagonally across the fire's front, angled southwest. Within minutes, flames licked high into the air behind them. Panicked and riderless, the packhorses tried to bolt ahead of the mounted men. They squealed pitifully and fought their lead ropes. Farther west, it had been raining longer. Smoke and Carbone entered a steady, slow-moving downpour that advanced toward the flames.

It would be a race, Smoke knew, between the deluge and the fire. Their lives quite clearly depended upon which element of nature won. He still fought with his lead animal when a loud, sucking sound came from above them. Wise in the ways of mountains, Smoke glanced upward in time to see a wall of sodden earth pull away from the breast of the mountain and lean far outward toward them. He sucked air and shouted above the tumult of roaring water and thunder.

"Let go the packhorses! Ride out fast," he commanded.

Carbone quickly obeyed. They slipped and slid ahead on the steep path. Once, Sidewinder went to his rear haunches as the great slab of mud and rocks towered over them. Smoke urged the Appaloosa stallion with a smart slap of reins, and Sidewinder surged forward once more. At his side, Carbone had gone pale-faced, and his eyes held a haunted light.

With a tremendous crash, the mudslide slammed to the ground behind them. Tree trunks broke with explosive reports, and branches flew every direction. The mud oozed up to the hoofs of their mounts. Carbone gasped in relief at being spared. Smoke looked hard-eyed at where the hind legs of a packhorse protruded from under the sloppy edge of the cascade. Its companion nuzzled up to the other horses for comfort.

"We've lost that one and the gear," Smoke observed. "At least it was quick. Can you say how far to that old house?"

"If we can find the trail again, perhaps," Carbone answered with a shrug.

Rain still pounded them as Smoke Jensen and Esteban Carbone set off in search of the trail and shelter. A new, ferocious downpour assailed them and drove visibility to a matter of feet. For once, Smoke began to doubt that all mountains were alike. This deadly, powerful tempest, whipped up by a tropical storm, resembled nothing like he had experienced in the Shining Mountains. Reluctantly, he admitted to himself that they could easily die here.

15

Only mental echoes of the violent storm remained when Smoke Jensen and Esteban Carbone rode out of the mountains into the broad, fertile central highland south of Zacatecas three days later. Carbone waved a hand to encompass the upland plateau.

"It is like this from here through Aguascalientes and northern San Luis Potosi. Then the mountains again, and beyond them, Mexico City. We are not far from Limosna. We can stay there for the night."

"Will we be able to resupply?" Smoke asked, concerned over the loss of their supplies, particularly two cases of ammunition.

"It is likely. Limosna is a fairly large town."

"What does the name mean?" Smoke asked out of curiosity.

"Charity. Perhaps that is a good sign, *amigo, ¿como no?*"

"We'll hope so, but reserve judgment."

"Always the cautious one," Carbone observed.

"It's kept me alive a good many years," Smoke remarked, then wished he could recall his words. It was his friend who had left the drapes undrawn in the main hall of his *hacienda,* which cost the life of his wife.

Carbone might have been reading his thoughts. "I will

never forget that lesson, Smoke Jensen. All my life I shall remember my carelessness."

"Carbone—Esteban, I am sorry. I didn't mean to criticize." For once in his life, Smoke felt entirely helpless.

They rode into Limosna in an atmosphere that could accompany a funeral. No children romped and played on the streets. Only a couple of shaggy dogs raised lazy heads to growl softly as they passed by. Here and there a window blind flicked aside to allow the occupant to watch them guardedly.

"Somehow, I do not get the feeling the people are friendly," Carbone observed.

"We'll find out soon enough," Smoke replied. "There's a *posada* up ahead."

Carbone sighed heavily when he read the sign painted on the arched adobe gate to the inn: *PUERTO DEL SOL.* "There must be a thousand *posadas* named Gate of the Sun in Mexico. One would think that a people with the romantic soul of Spain in them could be more original," he lamented.

At least Carbone's spirits had lifted, Smoke thought as he clapped his friend on one shoulder. "We'd better find out if they have room for us."

Inside a man clad in the loose white cotton shirt and trousers of the region looked up from something unseen on his desk and produced a glower. "What is it you want?" he asked inhospitably.

"We're looking for rooms for the night," Carbone told him.

"Do you have cash to pay with?" the clerk snapped.

"Of course." Stung by this rude attitude, Carbone asked facetiously, "Does your employer know how hard you work to fill his establishment with guests?"

"I am the owner," came the surly reply. "I can give you one room together."

"Two rooms, if you please," Smoke Jensen pressed.

"Ah! A foreigner. You are from Europe?" he asked, interest awakened.

"No. The United States."

"Too bad for you. Do you bring a conquering army with you?"

Smoke now burned with temper. "If you're willing to lose the money, we're willing to look elsewhere."

The thought of vanishing pesos improved the *posadero*'s outlook. "Oh, never mind. I do have two rooms, adjoining. On the second floor. Ten pesos a night, each. Another two pesos for stabling your animals."

"Done. Can you recommend a good place to eat?"

"What's wrong with right here?" the innkeeper asked, offended. "And the *cuota* is in advance."

Both men paid for their lodging. They carried their gear to the rooms indicated and stowed it in large armoires. After stabling the packhorse, they set out to locate an outfitter, or suitable shops to replace their missing supplies and another horse.

One square block was formed of wall-to-wall shops, facing outward and inward on a large central courtyard. The sign over the tall, arched wrought iron entrance to the interior declared it to be *EL MERCADO CENTRAL*. Stalls lined the center of the courtyard. The largest store, occupying a corner of the outer rank of merchants, advertised cooking utensils and camp gear. Smoke and Carbone entered.

"Buenas tardes, Señores. How may I help you?" an eager merchant greeted them, briskly scrubbing his palms together in anticipation of a profitable exchange.

"We have a list. Some pots, a skillet, grill, open fire trestle, two big spoons, a tent. Also your advice on who has the least weevils in his flour, where to get the best in smoked meats, dry beans, coffee."

"I—ah—see." The merchant looked closer at Carbone, and on recognizing him, his dream of vast profits vanished. He took on as stern an expression as he could summon. "I am sorry, but you will have to go elsewhere. Your custom is not desired here."

Ruffled, Carbone bristled. "What do you mean?"

"Exactly what I said. You are Carbone y Ruiz, *¿verdad?* The renegade. I will sell you nothing."

"Why is that?" Carbone demanded, though he suspected the answer.

"Limosna has El Rey del Norte as *Patrón.* We are loyal to him. His enemies we spit upon."

Hot anger flared now. "Perhaps you would like to start by spitting on me?" Carbone challenged.

"Get out of my *tienda,* or I will call on others who will remove you," the shop owner ordered coldly.

During their stroll through town to the *mercado,* Smoke Jensen had noticed several men looking suspiciously at them. Since his and Carbone's entering the store, several had gathered in front, peering through the windows. Now some dozen hardcases joined the throng, their cold, black eyes fixed on the entrance to the shop. Before Smoke could advise his friend of their presence, three of them entered.

"You are not welcome here, *gringo,*" one stated flatly.

"Get out of here, while you are still alive," another advised, then added, "and get out of town."

The third walked up close to the Mexican gunfighter and gave him a shove with an extended index finger. "There is a price on your head, old man."

Carbone rocked back on his boot heels, and bleak anger suffused his face. Smoke Jensen pushed up his hat brim and reached for the thin leather gloves in his hip pocket.

"Looks like they're wantin' you to open the dance. You reckon to do that?" Smoke asked his friend in English.

"With the greatest of pleasure, *amigo,*" Carbone responded, recognizing the breed as hired guns in the employ of Carvajal.

Not one of the trio saw his swift move. One moment, Carbone was being pushed a second time. There came a loud crack and a yowl of intense pain as he snatched at the index finger that offended him, bent it until it broke, and shoved its owner back off his feet. He crashed, amid more agony-drawn protests, against a display of buckets. They set off a musical clatter that drowned out a warning shout from the merchant when Carbone unlimbered his six-gun.

He shot the bandit closest to him first. The slug smacked into a leather vest and sent shards flying, along with blood and dust. Stunned, the man jerked backward and attempted to draw his weapon. Carbone sent a second messenger of death his way. His heart blown apart, Carvajal's gunman sprawled on the floor in a grotesque position of splayed limbs and curved torso.

Already, Carbone turned his attention away from the dead man. He tracked the muzzle of his .45 to his left and dead-centered the second *bandido,* who had his six-gun halfway out of the holster. The third had cleared leather and sent a bullet cracking past Carbone's head. It shattered a row of kerosene lamp chimneys on a shelf behind him.

Carbone targeted in on the last of the trio. Wide-eyed, the less courageous outlaw backpedaled toward the door. He waved his revolver aimlessly from a wrist gone limp with fear. Carbone shot him in the leg. The gunhand dropped to his other knee and tried to swing his .45 into line. Carbone didn't give him the chance. His last shot burrowed into the hollow at the base of the hardcase's neck.

He went over backward and twitched violently for several seconds, then stiffened, shuddered, and went slack. In the relative quiet that followed, Carbone heard gunfire from outside and realized that Smoke Jensen was no longer in the store. Ignoring the frightened bleats of the merchant, Carbone took five swift strides to the door and out onto the stone-cobbled street.

Smoke Jensen had a hole in his hat brim, another through a trouser leg. Five men lay huddled in death, pools of blood forming around them. That left four standing. Carbone

reached under his coat for a second gun and laid to rest a nattily dressed *bandido,* garbed all in black with silver conchos
and braid trim.

In the same instant, Smoke dropped two more. Legendary
speed made it seem easy, as though the first report of the gun
felled them by invisible means. The first had his six-gun
aimed at Smoke's chest. Before the hammer could fall, a
hefty .44 slug punched through his sternum, and the revolver
went flying. Its owner staggered backward three steps,
groaned and fell into a puddle in the cobblestone street. Right
on top of Smoke's first round came the second.

Incongruously dressed in bright red, with a huge sombrero
of the same color trimmed in gold thread, the bandit had
launched a large knife at Smoke Jensen. It buried itself in the
frame and plaster false front of the arched arcade in front of
the shops. He had the second behind his head, ready to release, when Smoke shot him in the gut.

Air whooshed out of the wounded man, and he doubled over.
He tottered forward on surprisingly small boots, left hand
groping for the butt of a revolver high on his waist. He cleared
the cylinder and trigger guard before Smoke Jensen downed
him with a bullet in the brain. The remaining member of Carvajal's squad of killers decided to seek safety elsewhere. He
ran blindly for two blocks, to where the horses had been tied
up, mounted, and swiftly galloped out of town.

"I could never tolerate rudeness," Carbone quipped as he
shucked expended rounds and began to reload.

"Nope. Not from the likes of this trash," Smoke agreed.
"We'd best tidy up, eh?"

Working together, after filling cylinders with fresh rounds,
Smoke and Carbone stacked the bodies along the gutter and
then went into the store. Smoke took two dead men by their
collars and dragged them outside to join the others. Carbone
did for the third. Then he returned with his list.

"Now, before we were so rudely interrupted, I had placed an order," he told the thoroughly cowed merchant.

"Y-y-you killed them all," that worthy gulped.

"No. One got away," Carbone corrected.

Meanwhile, Smoke Jensen had drifted toward one corner of the establishment, where he saw a group of shelves that displayed paperbound books. Curious, he perused the titles. It taxed his Spanish, but he made out most of them. *Love for Gloria, Guadalajara Romance,* were two titles. Then he came upon one that caused him to crack a broad, white smile. *Las Adventuras de Smoke Jensen.* He recognized the name of the author. The book was a reprint of one of the penny dreadfuls published some years ago in the States.

Smoke plucked it from its place and carried it to the counter. There he showed it to the proprietor. The man glanced at the cover, started to turn away. "It is not for sale . . . to you."

Smoke bunched up the front of the merchant's collarless shirt and yanked him around close. Then he tapped his chest.

"Yo soy Smoke Jensen," he growled in his most menacing manner, lips curled in a nasty arc.

Images of the quick death of nine men in the street, and knowledge of the identity of Carbone, turned the man's bowels to water. Swiftly the storekeeper crossed himself and bleated, *"Jesus, Maria, y José.* Of course, gentlemen, of course. Your order will be filled with dispatch."

"I AIN'T GONNA!" The words exploded from Bobby Harris as he stood in his underdrawers beside a large galvanized tub.

He and Sally Jensen were in the washhouse behind the comfortable home at Sugarloaf. Steam rose from the water, prepared on the low, two-burner Acme woodstove in a pair of large copper boilers. The chill mountain air caused Bobby to hug his bare chest in an attempt to keep warm.

"Yes, you are," Sally insisted.

"I done took a bath day 'fore yesterday," Bobby protested.

"And you'll take one today."

"An' I washed off down at the corral yesterday," Bobby added, thinking of another unpleasant spill in the muck and consequent bath. "Besides, it's cold," the boy pouted.

"It will get colder," Sally observed. "Besides, there's a fire going, and it'll be warmer after I leave and close the door."

"I ain't dirty. Don't see no reason to risk gettin' the phew-monia by doin' a dumb thing like takin' a bath in this weather."

Sally decided to change tactics. Hands on hips, she produced an expression of disappointment. "I thought you were a brave boy."

"I—I am. Brave enough not to have to take a sissy bath ev'ry day," Bobby countered.

"*I* take a bath every day," Sally pointed out.

"Yeah, an' you're a girl." Bobby's lower lip poked out again. "Takin' too many baths makes a feller weak."

"I'll tell you something else. So does Smoke, when he's at home or in a town where he can."

"He does?" Bobby asked, astounded and very impressed.

"He certainly does," Sally assured him.

A bright light of revelation glowed in the freckle-dotted face. "It sure don't weaken *him* none," he observed.

"I doubt very much that it does," Sally answered, amused now as she realized his defenses had started to crumble.

Without another word, as Sally quietly left the washhouse, Bobby peeled out of his topless long johns and jumped into the steaming water. He splashed loudly and began to soap himself.

They made their explanations to the police, when the gray-clad officers at last arrived, long after the shooting had ended.

The sheer number of bodies argued in favor of the version of events given by Smoke Jensen and Esteban Carbone. Encouraged by the presence of the two famous gunfighters, the store owner found nerve enough to verify their story. He even went so far as to identify four of the dead men as members of El Rey's bandit army. Reluctantly, the police released Smoke and Carbone.

Brief stops in several other shops, and the main marketplace quickly filled their requirements and they returned to the inn. There Smoke and Carbone ate a hot and filling meal, washed down by plenty of the local beer. After cigars on the patio, they retired to their rooms.

Late that night, a small sound awakened Smoke Jensen. He came fully alert out of a sound slumber, as was his nature. Careful not to make any noise that would betray him, he listened in the dark for any indication of the danger that jangled in his head. It came a moment later, a soft-scraping sound outside the door to his room.

Smoke fisted his .44 Colt and made hasty preparations. A long silence followed. Then the door violently slammed open, kicked by two heavy boots. At once, flame lanced into the room from three muzzles.

Hot lead slammed into the huddled figure in the bed. Each of the assassins fired four times, then paused. A thick haze filled the room. Then the apparent leader spoke in a whisper.

"Bueno."

They entered in a rush. The leader made rapid strides to the bed and threw back the bullet-punctured sheet. His gasp of surprise startled the others when he took in the bunched bedding.

"¡Mierda! He is not here," the bandit gasped.

"Buenas noches, gente baja," Smoke Jensen said quietly an instant before his hammer fell on a fresh primer.

And scum they were. The one nearest to Smoke died like it, too, squealing like a pig when Smoke's slug punched him in the belly. He dropped his six-gun and clasped both hands over the hole in a futile attempt to salvage his blasted liver. Already Smoke had ducked and dodged to another part of the darkness.

Reacting swiftly, the leader discharged a round in the direction of where Smoke had been. It did him no good. Already Smoke Jensen had fired again, the bullet making a deep gouge along the rib cage of the leader. It forced him to reflexively jerk his arm and sent the bullet into the ceiling. Plaster dust rained down.

Smoke had moved again. The leader popped another cap, and the clay pitcher exploded, splashed the washstand with water, sent shards whirring through the air. Smoke aimed a little to the right of the muzzle bloom this time.

A noise like a bleating sheep filled the numb silence after the loud report. The leader looked down at the dark stain spreading on his chest, wavered, and fell across the bed. That left only one.

Soft and guarded, a small whimpering sound came from close by the floor. Smoke had moved again and tried to center on the source. His ambush, speedy action and deadly accuracy had driven the macho bravado out of this one, he estimated. If he could only find him. Until he did, danger still lurked for Smoke in the blackness of the room. Ears still ringing, he managed to hear the gathering of courage, born of desperation.

Reaching for the washstand, Smoke closed thick fingers over a bar of soap. With a sharp, hard movement, he hurled it across the room. It smacked noisily off the wall. Instantly, the last assassin fired at the sound.

Smoke's .44 roared into action, aimed a bit to the right of the muzzle flame. Boots beat a mortal tattoo on the plank floor, and a despairing sigh came from the dying outlaw. At last, silence filled the smoke-choked room.

Moving quickly, Smoke located a candle and snapped a

lucifer to life with his thumbnail. He touched the flame to the wick. Quickly, he took stock of the carnage.

None of the trio moved. Vaguely he had a recollection of hearing similar sounds of combat from the room next door. Carbone. He went cautiously to the door, peered around the casing. No more nasty surprises on the balcony. Still barefoot, in long johns and nothing else, Smoke edged along the outer wall to the door that led to Carbone's room.

Silence came from within. "Carbone?"

"Sí, amigo. Come on in."

Candle and Colt leading the way, Smoke entered the room. He found three bodies sprawled in death, a reproduction of what he'd left behind in his room. Carbone sat upright in the middle of his bed, his .45 in his right hand.

"You heard them, too, eh, *amigo?"* the Mexican gunfighter asked with amusement.

"Just in time," Smoke allowed. "They're Carvajal's men, of course. I think we should have a talk with the innkeeper."

"Perhaps we should get dressed first?" Carbone suggested, the brown skin of his bare chest marked with the scars of his former profession.

They found Pedro Rodriguez, the fearful *posadero,* hiding in a big armoire in his bedroom. Smoke yanked him out by a fistful of nightshirt and slammed him against the wall.

"Your loyalty to your guests astonishes me," the big mountain man said sarcastically.

"I—I—I know nothing about what you mean, *Señor,"* Rodriguez protested in a quavering voice.

"Oh, I think you do. Who else knew which rooms we occupied? Or where we were staying, for that matter?" Smoke demanded.

"I—I—It was all a mistake, *Señor. Por amor del dios,"* he appealed to Carbone.

"'For the love of God,'" Carbone repeated. "God spits on

a traitor, *cabrón.* Now you will tell us who these assassins are, or I'll let my friend cut out your liver."

"No—no, please. I—I—I had no choice. They are soldiers of El Rey del Norte. They were left here in the village as 'special policemen' to collect tribute and keep the people in line." Rodriguez gulped hard, his mouth and throat dry. "They came here, demanded to know what rooms you occupied. I had to tell them. They—they were some of Carvajal's best men."

Smoke Jensen and Esteban Carbone exchanged amused glances. The statement elicited a chuckle from both. "If that's his best," Smoke advised Rodriguez, "then I'm looking forward to seeing his worst."

16

Carbone reined in at the edge of a haphazard cluster of small adobe buildings and pointed to a tall cairn of native stone. "There is the marker. We are near the Tropic of Cancer, *amigo*. From here on, the land becomes semi-desert again, and tropical down out of the mountains. There is even jungle."

"I find that not at all comforting, Carbone," Smoke said dryly. "I'll take the mountains any time."

"We head due south from here to Martine's *rancho*. The state of Aguascalientes is within half a day's ride."

"We're going to the headquarters?"

"No. First we stop at the village of Merced. There's nothing else between here and there."

"Mercy, eh?" Smoke observed.

"Yes. The whole name of Martine's village is *Nuestra Señora de la Merced,* Our Lady of Mercy, but that's too much of a mouthful for even those born to Spanish. So it's called Merced."

"I hope Martine has shown more mercy than whoever owns this village," Smoke observed.

He looked around at the scattering of low adobe huts, the narrow, rutted street that divided them. It was a village without a name. Smoke had already noted suspicious eyes watching them from behind drawn shutters. The *cantina,* or what passed for one, had a rank, fetid odor.

When they dismounted and entered, Smoke took note of a man in a white shirt, black trousers, and a big, floppy Charro hat, who bolted from the *tienda* next door and galloped off full-tilt to the northwest. Smoke called Carbone's attention to the messenger.

"One of Carvajal's men," Carbone observed, a fleeting frown dividing his brow.

"So I had it figured. Are we staying here long?"

"Only to rest the horses, refresh ourselves," Carbone advised.

Squalor magnified itself inside the one-room saloon. Smoke made tracks for a small table, while Carbone ordered beer for them both. He brought tepid bottles to the flyspeck-dotted table and produced a sardonic smile.

"The *cucarachas* must run footraces up the walls," he remarked.

"Cockroaches. Not my favorite people," Smoke revealed.

Carbone produced a grim parody of another smile. "You're close. We do have some people here we call *cucarachas.* It's from the song." And Carbone began to sing in a clear, firm tenor voice. *"La cucaracha, la cucaracha, ya no quere cóminar. La cucaracha, la cucaracha, mar-i-juana que fumar."*

Smoke's expression of distaste and contempt shone across the table. "Loco weed. I knew a feller once, got taken by the stuff. All he wanted to do was smoke it, chew it, stopped eating altogether."

"Did it kill him?" Carbone asked.

"No. Some Blackfoot warriors got to him while he was out of his head on the stuff. Served him right."

"Let's talk of more pleasant things," Carbone suggested. "You should know, for instance, that Martine has a bull ranch."

"Bulls, not steers?"

"Fighting bulls," Carbone stated simply. "Oh, we are both

aware of your feelings for animals, amigo. Here it is a way of life, a custom, a tradition. The true *aficianado* looks upon the *Fiesta Brava* as a sort of morality play. Good triumphing over evil, the God-given mind being superior to brute strength. Ah! I see you don't agree."

"I don't," Smoke said tightly. "Nor do I approve. But this is your country and when in Rome . . ."

"Enough said. At least that is out in the open now. Martine has three of the most beautiful children you will ever see. The boy has his father's shoulders already. He's going to be tall, lean, a born *pistolero.* Only Martine won't let him pursue that profession."

They talked on for an hour, ordered plates of beans with cheese—it turned out to be goat cheese—and some stringy roasted meat Smoke hoped he would never be able to identify. Then they made ready to go.

"Dommé la quenta." Carbone asked for the check.

Behind his bar, the *cantinero* spread his hands in a gesture of dismissal. "It is on the house. I know you, *Señor,* and Don Miguel, also. I am proud that there are men with courage enough to stand up to El Rey del Norte."

"Thank you, my friend."

"Your friend here, he is of a like caliber to you and Don Miguel?"

"Only more so. This is Smoke Jensen."

At first the name made no connection for the barkeep. Then his countenance brightened, and he writhed his face in smiles. "Ah, the famous *gringo* gunfighter. Welcome to Mexico, *Señor* Jensen."

"Thank you. I wish I could say I'm happy to be here." On their way out the door, Smoke added for Carbone's benefit, "You know, I think that's only the second welcome we've gotten since we got here."

When they had ridden a mile out of town, his mind on home, Smoke remarked as to how much the nature of life in these parts resembled that in the High Lonesome. Then he queried aloud, "I wonder how Sally's doing with Bobby Harris?"

"We should see the village by now," Carbone announced, a worried tone in his words.

"Might be well for me to scout ahead some," Smoke offered.

"We'll both go. Split up and come toward the village from different directions."

"You think Carvajal might be around?" Smoke asked, not worried, but eager to take the size of the man.

"It could be," Carbone acknowledged.

They swung left and right of the roadway. Smoke headed west for half a mile, before he turned south again. A soft wind spoke in the tall grass around him, and he thought of his infrequent journeys into Kansas. The Cheyenne, who had once lived there proud and free, called it the "talking grass." Now the blades of green spoke in a foreign tongue.

He crested a rise and saw far ahead the spire of a church. It looked somehow odd, the dome skewed to one side. Forewarned, Smoke slid the Winchester from its saddle scabbard and levered a round into the chamber. He advanced at a walk. Clear, sharp eyes took in every detail of the terrain.

Nowhere did he see sign of a man. He negotiated a saddle in the rolling ground, where a lone mimosa stood stark against the skyline. Now streaks of gray and black stood out clearly against the pale blue of the sub-tropical sky. One of them wavered tenuously beside the bell tower of the church. Sidewinder twitched his loose hide, as though conscious of a hidden danger.

Smoke patted the thick neck. "That's right, boy, there's been some trouble up ahead."

He made the outskirts of Merced without taking sight of Carbone. Several buildings had collapsed in on themselves. Smoke from recent fires still spiraled into the air. A deadly silence held over the ruins of the village. Ahead, on the right side of the Plaza de Armas, the fire-scarred walls of the church stood out in stark warning. Black smudges on white plaster gave testiment to the fury of the fire that had burned within. Rafters had been consumed and the roof fallen in. Stained glass windows had burst from the intensity of the heat. Yet the holy place still stood. Smoke sensed movement to his left and swung that way.

Carbone waved to him and advanced down an intersecting street. "We got here too late," he observed of the devastation around them.

"Or just in time. Two more guns wouldn't have done a lot of good," Smoke opined.

Walking their mounts in silence, they proceeded to the center of town. Smoke soon noted that not all of the inhabitants had been killed, captured, or run off. The *cantinero* still conducted business outside his gutted establishment. He stood casually, polishing a glass, behind a wide plank, supported by empty beer barrels. A canvas awning had been rigged to provide shade.

"Buenas tardes, Señores," the barkeep greeted them. "It is not much," he added with a shrug, "but it is mine. For you, the first beer will be only five pesos."

"¡Ladrone! Exploiter of the poor," Carbone roared. "Fifty centavos. Not a cent more."

Blinking in the unaccustomed brightness of his surroundings, the gray-haired bartender formed his mouth into a surprised O. "Don Esteban Carbone? I did not know it was you. Of course, for you, and your friend, there is no charge."

"Gonzolo Ortiz, you are shameless and a thief," Carbone went on, dismounting. "What happened here?"

"Need you ask?" Ortiz responded, palms waggling outward. "Gustavo Carvajal, may his soul roast in Hell, paid us a visit. The *Patrón,* and the armed men, were not close by. Those *hijos de chingada* bandits burned down the town, shot many men, took the young women. Everyone else is too afraid to show themselves. When we heard hoofs, they ran to hide."

"I see." Carbone took charge then, turned his back to the makeshift saloon and bawled loudly, "Come out now. This is Esteban Carbone y Ruiz. It is safe, my children. Come out."

Gradually, the frightened villagers began to poke their heads from hiding places among the rubble. Several younger men came timidly forward. Soon a few women showed themselves, black *rebozos* covering their bowed heads. Finally a handful of children popped from the ruins and ran shyly to their mothers' sides.

"Carvajal will be made to pay for this," Carbone promised.

"This we know," Ortiz agreed. "Only we are so helpless. Unarmed and untrained. And there are so few young enough to carry the fight to that blasphemy of all blasphemies."

"Do you want to learn?" Smoke Jensen asked him.

"Who is your friend, Don Esteban?" Ortiz asked bluntly, a suspicious eye fixed on Smoke Jensen.

"Smoke Jensen. He is a famous gunfighter from los Estados Unidos."

"As famous as you and the *Patrón?*" a young man who came to stand at Ortiz's side asked.

Carbone chuckled. "More so, Pepe. Your illustrious father, our fine *cantinero* here, has surely heard of him."

Gonzalo Ortiz nodded solemnly. *"Sí,* I have heard from the Patrón of his friend with the so-fast gun. Is it true you have killed five hundred men, *Señor* Jensen?"

Smoke pulled a face. "Oh, not by a long sight. Though more than's good for a man's soul, I can assure you."

"It is reassuring to hear you speak of the soul, *Señor* Jensen," the *padre* injected as he appeared in the doorway of the devastated church. He was short and round, moon-faced. His brown Franciscan habit swayed around his bare ankles as he walked toward the *cantina.* Sandals flapped up a cloud of dust and ash.

"Good afternoon, Father," Smoke addressed the cleric respectfully.

"And to you. Don Miguel told of your coming. I am not certain that this event pleases me. There is bound to be more fighting and killing."

"Only if Carvajal refuses to listen to reason," Smoke told him.

Thin eyebrows rose on a wide forehead. "You intend to reason with that jackal? Using what, may I ask, *Señor?*"

Smoke patted the receiver of his Winchester Express rifle. "With this. It's the only argument folks like him understand."

The priest sighed and raised his eyes to heaven. "Like I said, more fighting and killing. Although I will admit in this case it is in a good cause. May God grant you success and soon, *Señor.*"

"Thank you, *Padre.*"

Carbone cleared his throat. "Now then, has anything been done to organize a cleanup? To provide guards for the village?"

"What for, Don Esteban?" another young man asked acidly. "There's nothing worth Carvajal coming back for."

"You're still alive," Carbone reminded him.

"And willing to fight," the youth answered him hotly.

"Good! Good, then. I suggest you make yourself the new owner of one of these weapons we took from some misguided men in Limosna. Six of them."

"Eighteen all together," Smoke reminded him. "They won't be needing them anymore. Take one, and some ammunition, then tell your friends. We'll show you how to fight with them."

Lowering westward, the sun slanted the shade of Ortiz's canvas roof far out into the street. Under Carbone's direction, work teams labored at removing the rubble and clearing side streets. They stopped frequently to wash out the taste of dust and ashes. The women worked lovingly on the interior of the church. Smoke Jensen had taken the young men who had selected six-guns and rifles from the supply obtained in Limosna.

At the edge of the village, he set up a line of damaged clay pots as targets and began instructing them in the use of their new weapons. It proved a more difficult task than he imagined. Not five minutes into his careful lecture on function and nomenclature, an accidental discharge nearly took the big toe off one pupil.

"You were supposed to go through the motions, not actually load that thing," Smoke snapped at him, worried that more accidents could rob him of willing students.

White-faced, the youth responded through chattering teeth, "I thought 'through the motions' meant put in the bullets, *Señor.*"

"Put in the cartridges," Smoke corrected, then hastened to prevent further disaster. "No—no, do not put cartridges in your weapons. Only when I say so. Clear?"

"Claro, sí," came a chorus of answers.

Patiently, Smoke went through the nomenclature again. "Loading gate, half-cock, hammer, cocking lever, cylinder, chamber, front sight, rear sight . . ." On it went.

At last he came to the point when he could not avoid taking the next step. "Load one round," he commanded. "Adjust cylinders to position the cartridge for firing. Full-cock. Take aim. Fire!"

Most of the twenty-seven rounds did mortal damage only to the air. Two clay pot chunks disintegrated. Smoke beamed at his successful students.

"Let's see if you can do that again." To the whole class, he commanded, "Eject your spent round, load one full cartridge."

With that accomplished, Smoke took them through the drill again. To his surprise and pleasure, three pot shards shattered this time. Someone else had gotten lucky.

Encourage, encourage, teach by building confidence, he reminded himself.

"Good. If you can hit that small a target, you'll have no trouble with a man." It wasn't exactly the truth, and for a moment, Smoke's conscience troubled him. During tomorrow's drill, they would come to understand what he meant, he consoled himself. A sudden, growing rumble of hoofbeats interrupted the lesson.

Smoke looked up to see the familiar tall, dignified figure of Martine riding toward him at the head of a sizable number of men. A smile brightened his face for the first time since arriving in Merced. Martine halted his coal-black steed and nodded curtly to Smoke.

The white scar on his long, gaunt cheek writhed when he spoke. "We meet again, old friend. I am sorry it is under such . . ." Martine paused to cut a glance around his ruined village. "Such circumstances."

"I'm glad to be able to help out, Martine," Smoke replied.

"I see you have gotten to the crux of our problem. These men are farmers, *vaqueros,* herdsmen, tenders of flocks, tradesmen. They are not gunfighters. All must learn a new skill."

"They seemed willing enough." Smoke depreciated his commanding role in the target practice session.

"Having one's home burned around one's ears tends to encourage such zeal," Martine observed. "I'm glad you are here," he returned to his welcome. "Now we can concentrate on carrying this fight to Carvajal."

"I'd suggest we meet at the *cantina,* hold a council of war," Smoke put out.

"Yes. A good idea. Diego, go find our friend Carbone and bring him to the *cantina.* It is still standing?" he asked Smoke in surprise.

"Not so's you'd notice. Your man, Ortiz, has set up outside.

Some of the men have rescued tables and chairs. We'll be comfortable enough."

They settled down to a table ten minutes later. After listening to an update on Carvajal's activities since Carbone left for the border, the three gunfighters, along with Pablo Alvarez, Martine's *segundo,* sat in silence digesting the import of this news. At last Smoke broke the quiet.

"I have a few ideas on how to deal with this bandit scum."

"Let's hear them, by all means," Martine urged.

"First off, we send out men who know the country to scout out Carvajal's main camp."

"Consider it done," Martine agreed. To Alvarez he said, "Take five men, good ones, and trail the bandidos to their lair. Send one man back by midnight, another at dawn. We want to know everything we can find out."

"Sí, Patrón." Alvarez rose and departed, shouting as he walked to his horse, "Ricardo, Tomas, Bienvenedes . . ."

"Now," Smoke began again. He spoke for ten minutes, laying out his plans of ambush, fright tactics and confusion, all schemes that had worked well for him in the past. Smiles of renewed confidence and expectation bloomed on the faces of his friends.

17

For all their deprivation, the people of Merced put out a fine feed for the men who had come to avenge their losses. Although inexperienced in fighting with firearms and facing an organized force, the volunteers from Martine's other villages and the ranch put aside their uncertainties to belly up to mounds of *carnitas*—chunks of pork, deep-fried in huge copper caldrons that let the wood smoke of the fire curl and lick over the brown lumps—giant bowls of beans, and ample stacks of late season corn, boiled in blackened tubs.

While the neophyte fighting men filled their stomachs, a guitar took up a sprightly tune. Another joined in. An old man showed up in the plaza with a fiddle. A father and son, a boy of about twelve, appeared in *mariachi* costume with dented but functional cornets.

Their music was raw, wild, and primitive, and appealed to something in Smoke Jensen. He watched the ritual of building a soft taco, in a corn tortilla, with small cubes of the *carnitas,* chopped onion and chilis, sliced radishes, fresh *cilantro,* and seasoned with lemon juice. His mouth watered and he dug right in. While he chomped on one of the savory sandwiches, he spoke earnestly with Carbone and Martine.

"I want to take your men through more detailed shooting

instructions. If they are going to operate on their own, they'll need to handle their guns as second nature."

"It's hard to teach peaceful *peons* to be aggressive," Martine observed.

"True," Carbone agreed. "And those who are mostly *indio* still believe it is the report of the gun that knocks a man down."

Smoke cut his eyes in a sideways glance. "You're kidding me."

"Not at all. Believe it or not, it's a hold-over from the days of the *conquistadores*. The Aztec and Meztec *brujós,* their medicine men and priests, told them that was so, and the belief has lasted until now," Martine explained.

"Only the Yaquis and Apaches in Sonora seem to know better," Carbone added.

"All the more reason for heavy training," Smoke advised.

He carried through on that idea early the next morning. Standing in front of a line of volunteers, Smoke paced back and forth, his voice raised so all could hear. "Aimed shots are what counts," he told them. "There's more air out there than meat. Another thing. I want you to forget all you may have heard about the sound of a weapon's discharge doing the killing. It doesn't knock people down. A man has to hit what he aims at with a bullet to stop an enemy."

"But, *Señor,*" one youthful beginner protested, "I have seen with my own eyes how a *bandido* has fired off his gun, into the air, and a man fell dead."

"Was there more than one bandit around?" Smoke probed.

"Oh, *sí.* Our village was full of them."

"Then someone else shot him," Smoke concluded. "Watch. I'm going to fire five shots into the air. Keep your eyes on those clay targets."

Smoke used his right hand Colt to discharge five rounds into the air. In the silence that followed, the students looked at the undamaged potsherds. Then he holstered his empty weapon and pulled the left hand .44 in a cross draw. This time he fired at the targets.

Five of them disappeared in puffs of dark red dust. "You have to hit what you shoot at to have any effect."

"But, *Señor,* those were only clay pots, and broken ones at that. They do not have the fragile soul of a man."

Smoke Jensen suppressed a groan. Whatever got him into this, he could do well without it. For the remainder of the morning, he continued his instruction. When it ended, some of the men, those with rifles particularly, complained of soreness. Smoke wondered how, with his limited Spanish, he could explain the effects of recoil.

"It seems to me," one of the more talkative volunteers offered, "that a gun punishes at both ends."

"You've sort of got the idea there, Juan," Smoke told him. "It's a natural reaction, called recoil. Those of you who work cattle, or use a hoe and shovel, have strong hands. I doubt you felt much."

Heads nodded in agreement. Smoke favored them with a smile. Most had been able to at least nick their targets by the end of the session.

"We'll do more of this tomorrow. Now it's time to eat."

Halfway through the meal, a rider fogged into town, his horse well lathered, tail streaming behind flying hoofs. He reported to Martine.

"We have found them, Don Miguel."

"Good. Where?"

"There is this wide, deep valley. Up in the mountains to the west. It is not easy to find, for there are no trails."

"Except for the one Carvajal's men made going there," Smoke suggested.

The scout flushed slightly. *"Sí,* that is true. You know the peak called *Cabesa de Borrego?"* This he directed to Martine.

"Yes, the Sheep's Head. Is this camp far from there?"

A shrug. "Perhaps three leagues to the north, then into the Sierra. The trail is harder to follow in the mountains. We are used to looking for stray cattle, not men who can be clever and hide their tracks."

"I understand, Hector," Martine informed him. "You have done well."

"And I think it's time to go get a look at Carvajal," Smoke Jensen suggested.

"You will take some of the men?" Carbone asked.

"No. I can move faster and have less chance of being seen if I go alone."

"This man is dangerous," Martine protested.

"That's something we can agree on," Smoke told him. "I'm only going to watch, learn. They'll not see me. I'll be in the mountains and right at home."

Carbone and Martine sighed and wished their friend well. Smoke wiped up the remainder of his meal with a tortilla and set aside the glazed clay plate. He rose and went to where Sidewinder had been stabled. In ten minutes he had completed his preparations. An old woman came to him with a cotton cloth sack that bulged with its contents and smelled delightful.

"You will need something to eat. *Vaya con Dios, Señor.*"

Moved by her sacrifice in the face of the destruction of her village, Smoke nodded, thanked her and swung into the saddle. He secured the sack by a thong on the skirt and edged Sidewinder out of the half-collapsed barn. At a brisk canter, he soon disappeared from view.

Cook fires flickered randomly among the small army of bandits in the hidden valley, secure in the folds of the Sierra Madre Occidental. At the largest, an elaborate pavilion had been erected. It resembled one of those fancy tents depicted in medieval paintings. Pennons fluttered from the spike-topped center pole and from each corner. It was square, about twenty feet on a side, with a scalloped overhang from the roof.

Inside, a painted hanging divided the tent into private sleeping quarters and a rudimentary office. A trestle table and huge, thronelike chair occupied most of the public area. Gustavo Carvajal sprawled in the seat of honor, his face illuminated by candles in wrought iron sconces, rammed into the ground before the flooring had been laid out. Yellow light reflected from the rings that adorned each of his fingers.

"They are beautiful, no?" Carvajal raised his hands and waggled them to show off some of the booty taken from Merced. "This one was taken from the *padre*. He squealed like a pig when Montez ripped it from his hand. Said it was his ordination ring. Too bad, no?"

"They are nice," Humberto Regales said tactfully. "But don't you think they might get in the way of your gun hand?"

"*¿Que?* Why would I need to use a gun? I have all these fine warriors to protect me. Now, what of the loot taken from the church?"

"The door to the tabernacle," Ignacio Quintero declared proudly. "It is heavy, of pure gold. Also the chalices, gold and silver. There is much gold and jewels from the statue of Our Lady. A bag of coins."

"How much?" Carvajal demanded.

"We have yet to count them, Excellency."

"Do so. Right now."

Quickly his three lieutenants stacked the coins according to their value and totaled them. Quintero raised his eyes to El Rey with a light of greed burning in them. "Five hundred pesos, Excellency. Not a fortune, but plenty for so small a village church."

"Go on."

"There are crosses of gold, and other items, perhaps two thousand pesos' worth."

"What about the rest?" Carvajal snapped, impatient.

"Outside, Excellency," Tomas Diaz informed him. "There are bolts of cloth, boots, saddles, tools, ammunition, liquor, and . . . women. Fifteen young women, Excellency."

"How young?"

"From twelve to twenty-five, none have started to go to fat."

Carvajal smiled. "I will take my pick later. Then the men can have the rest. Tell me, the youngest ones. Do they have pleasant shapes? Nice . . ." His hands described a pair of breasts. ". . . *nalgas?*"

Regales gave a snort of disgust. "They are shaped more like boys, Excellency. There are others, still tender, that will please you, I am sure."

"Well, then, on with it. How much do you value the things taken from the village?"

"I would say at least twenty thousand pesos," Regales estimated. "We can use the food and ammunition; there were no guns that we found. The rest can be sold, the money used to pay the men. With those *torros* we sold, we are able to keep ahead of expenses for at least three months."

"Good. I like to hear that. We will grow stronger, you know. Men are coming to us nearly every day. They know where the power lies."

"What plans do you have for Martine y Garcia's other villages, Excellency?"

Carvajal leaned back in his throne, a small smile playing over his face. "We must wait and see about that," he stated flatly. "After all, the *burro* may see the light now and give in. It is much easier to collect tribute than to wrest it from the hands of the *peons.*"

"Safer, too," Ignacio Quintero observed.

Carvajal and his band of ruthless predators were about to find out how much safer when Smoke Jensen arrived in the area. It had taken him until mid-morning the next day to reach the craggy granite outcropping called Sheep's Head. He halted there, munched on cold tortillas and beans, some dried, powdered beef, called *machaca,* washed down with long draughts of water. He rested Sidewinder, then changed out of boots into soft moccasins and a dark green shirt and tan vest. Then he stowed his hat in a saddlebag.

He wound a green and brown bandana around his head and studied the results in the reflection from a stream that meandered out of the mountains ahead. Satisfied he would better blend with the terrain, he turned Sidewinder northward, to parallel the lofty range of the Sierra Madre.

Nightfall caught him an estimated half league from the turning point. Smoke made a cold camp and soon dropped into a light, trail sleep. Through the night, he marked the chomp of Sidewinder eating grass, the occasional swish of his tail and stomp of a hoof. Nothing else disturbed the mountain man's rest. He awakened refreshed, a vague demand for coffee teasing in his head. He would have to forgo that pleasure, Smoke ruled. With dawn spreading pinkly out of the east, he saddled Sidewinder and rode on.

A broken branch of chaparral provided Smoke the first clue to the outlaws' trail. More disturbed underbrush led him onward. He encountered his first hoofprints after he had selected a likely avenue and turned west. Encouraged by this, he pressed forward.

Two hours later, by the big turnip watch in his vest pocket, his keen sense of smell alerted him to the odors of cooking food. The mighty King of the North had not been entirely clever in selecting this hideaway. Smoke had found it easily. But then, he was accustomed to tracking Blackfeet and Cheyenne warriors who left no trail.

Smoke gauged the steepness of slopes that had become canyon walls and settled on the right side. Within minutes of leaving the one-time trail, he had disappeared into a heavy screen of trees. Feeling more at home with each passing minute, Smoke let his imagination range over what he might accomplish. He kept a tight rein on the more outlandish ideas that presented themselves. Through it all, he kept alert for any sign of the enemy.

He came upon the thin, white plumes from cooking fires before he expected it. Some twenty minutes' meandering through the pine forest had brought him to a broken-off ledge that provided a clear view of a moderate-sized valley. Hunkered down, Smoke Jensen peered over the rim at the barbaric display below.

Carvajal's army had fashioned rude shelters of brush and pine boughs. Here and there, rings of stones contained fires that apparently were kept in perpetual use. The aroma of roasting meat, baking tortillas and chili-rich pots of bubbling beans tantalized his nostrils. His stomach rumbled, and he reached absently for a tortilla, now grown somewhat stale.

His teeth fought with the hard corn cake while he made a mental count of the men below. They walked about freely, totally at ease. Men swigged from bottles of tequila, scooped morsels of food from pots. They laughed and talked among one another. From one lean-to, Smoke heard the shrill cry of a young woman. Her pleas to be left alone went unnoticed by the outlaws. Her cries of pain and terror when she was violated brought forth laughter and amused grins from the hard-bitten men in the camp.

Smoke silently cursed the animal who had had his way with her, conscious of the futility of that. He eased a pair of field glasses to his eyes and made note of the man's face when he was summoned from his pleasure in late afternoon to ride guard on the camp. A smile creased Smoke's weather-seasoned face. Maybe his anger wasn't so futile after all. He kept the offender in sight until certain of the sector he would patrol. Then he slid back from his observation point and rejoined Sidewinder. Now he had to wait until darkness fell.

* * *

Smoke Jensen's premonition proved right. Although the bandit chieftan maintained a loose net of sentries, men riding watch around the valley rim, he apparently had not established a set schedule. Individuals among the army of hardcases rode out to relieve a comrade whenever the mood struck them, or someone with more authority told them to. So far, the bandido that Smoke had targeted had not been replaced.

He rode with his head down, face in a pool of shadow from the huge sombrero he wore. Riding along a well-defined track, he let his horse have its head while he took short nips from a bottle of tequila. Once, he paused to light a small, crooked cigar. The flare of the match utterly destroyed his night vision.

Which aided Smoke Jensen as he ghosted along with only a thin screen of scrub and trees between him and the Mexican gun hawk. Briefly, Smoke wondered what his old friend, General Carpenter, would think of a man who lit a smoke on sentry duty at night. His own intended punishment would be far more severe than that meted out by the general. And he would have to move fast after he accomplished it.

Satisfied he knew the routes taken by all the watchers, Smoke decided the time had come. He urged Sidewinder through the trees to an open spot beside the trail. There he shook loose a large loop of a braided leather lariat. Its soft whir through the air partly alerted the half-drunk sentry.

He glanced up in time to see a darker curve, like a falling branch, descend directly in front of the brim of his sombrero. Then he felt a touch on the points of his shoulders. His mouth opened to shout an alarm. Breath flew from his mouth instead when Smoke Jensen yanked tight on the rope and hauled him from the saddle.

Smoke dropped to the ground and swiftly closed along the taut rope, expertly held rigid by Sidewinder, and stuffed the man's neckerchief in his mouth. Then he took charge of the bandit's mount. From the saddle, he stripped a leather *riata* and rigged the bite end of the rope over a stout live oak limb. He fitted the loop around the struggling outlaw's boots, above the ankles. Satisfied with his preparations, Smoke rocked back on his heels and drew his big bowie.

Instant terror widened the eyes of the captive, the whites starkly bright in the night's gloom. He knew for a fact he was about to die. Instead, this unknown mountain of a man bent over him and used the sharp blade to slit his trousers, legs, seat and front, then pull them away. Next the silent menace rolled him on one side and cut through the back of his jacket. The shirt followed.

Completely naked now, the lax sentry shivered in the mountain chill. The silent giant of a man withdrew from his line of sight, and he tried to quell his panic. Then he felt a tug on the rope around his legs. Painfully, and utterly without dignity, his assailant dragged him across the rough ground. Prickly oak leaves bit his flesh. Small rocks became daggers that gouged him. Slowly, his legs elevated.

Sudden comprehension struck fear in the *bandido*. He was being hanged upside down. Reflexively he tried to scream, gagged on the cloth in his mouth, and wildly flailed his arms. *¡Dios mio!* his liquor-addled mind shrieked. No one would find him. The blood would drain to his head and burst it like a rotten gourd.

Smoke Jensen kept hauling on the *riata* until the bandido hung between heaven and earth; his fingertips, extended beyond his head, missed the ground by a good two feet. Then he tied off the bite end of the man's own rope and walked around to where the swinging captive could see him.

He knew from past experience that the upside-down view of one's captor could be most disconcerting. Smoke watched the play of emotions on the face of his first client. Slowly he bent and spoke softly into an ear.

"I have a message for you to give to Carvajal. Tell him that his days of playing as king are over. Tell him that I'm coming for him."

Silently as he had come, Smoke Jensen faded into the darkness. He retrieved his Appaloosa stallion and headed off for his second encounter of the night. He found his choice with little difficulty, clomping along noisily on a sway-back horse. The bandit gnawed on a rolled tortilla filled with what smelled like roasted goat.

His indolence proved deceptive, however. When Smoke made his move, the man dropped his hand to his six-gun with surprising speed. He had it nearly clear when the tip of Smoke's bowie pierced his chest and sliced through his heart. Uncocked, his Mendoza .45 fell to the ground without discharging. Twitching out his life, its owner followed. Smoke dismounted and retrieved his knife, wiped it clean on the dead outlaw's shirt.

"Oh, well," he muttered to himself. "I'll leave another message with the next one."

Smoke came upon the third one right where he expected him. One surprise greeted him. The bandit sat slumped in his saddle, chin on chest, sleeping away the boring hours. A macabre sense of humor assailed the mountain man spirit in Smoke. He eased up beside the drowsing man and gave him a solid rap on the skull with the barrel of his .44 Colt.

Quickly dismounting, Smoke went to the man, stripped him of clothing. At least this one wore underdrawers, he noted. These he parted with his knife blade and used a small pot of black horse salve to decorate certain parts of the unconscious outlaw's anatomy. Then he swung the helpless gunny in a tree like the first.

Once again, Smoke disappeared into the friendly darkness. The fourth night rider caught a smack to the head also.

Smoke had him ready to tree when he groaned and began to show signs of consciousness. Gag ready, Smoke stuffed cloth in the captive's mouth the instant he opened it to call for help. Too groggy to put up resistance, the bandido swung free of the ground minutes later. Smoke went to him and bent low.

"Tell Carvajal that if he is Montezuma, I am his Cortez."

18

Smoke's next stop brought him to a younger, less seasoned bandit. A boy, actually, hardly seventeen, Smoke judged when he had the lad off his horse and face-to-face with the muzzle of his .44. All thoughts of machismo, of swaggering glory in the ranks of Gustavo Carvajal's outlaw army, fled and the youngster turned a sickly slate-gray. His lips worked with a noticeable tremble.

"Please, *Señor,* please do not harm me. I—I was thinking a-a-a—"

"About what?" Smoke demanded in a rough whisper.

"I swear on the heart of my mother, *Señor.* I was truly thinking that this was not the life for me. Poor food, drunken companions, cold nights riding in these woods. I would give anything to be back home, on the *estancia,* working for my *Patrón."*

Smoke prodded him in the ribs with his six-gun. "You mean that?"

"Oh, yes, yes, I swear it." He was all but sobbing.

"Where is this *estancia?"*

"La—La Gloria, in Durango."

That seemed reasonably far enough away. "Would you

leave right now, not turn back, not even look behind, and go to your home?"

"*Seguro, sí,* and my mother would bless you in her prayers forever."

"Then get up, take your horse and get the hell out of here." Smoke had already taken the revolver from the young man's holster. Now he reached for the saddle. "Here, I'll take that. You won't be needing it anymore," Smoke informed him as his fingers closed around the butt-stock of a Winchester.

Smiling to himself, Smoke Jensen watched the youngster out of sight. He felt good about that one. Now, on to the rest.

Slowly, the night wore on. Not surprisingly, considering the lack of discipline in the camp, none of his victims had as yet been discovered. No one had even come out to relieve them. Smoke nearly bumped into the next guard.

He had dismounted to relieve the strain of hours in the saddle. Keeping him company was the inevitable bottle of tequila. He roused it at the dark shape of a man on horseback.

"*Hola, compañero.* You've come at last," he called out expectantly. "Have a drink before I go."

Smoke Jensen swung down from the saddle and approached. "Thanks, but I prefer bourbon," he quipped softly a moment before he stuffed the muzzle of his .44 Colt into the mouth of this hardcase. "Now, you will do exactly as I say." Smoke's hand worked at the buckle of the man's cartridge belt, freed it.

"Unbutton your trousers and shirt. Do it," Smoke added with menace.

Silently, sweating, the bandit complied. By then Smoke had his captive's neck scarf wadded and replaced his gun barrel with it. "Take off your shirt. Slowly, no funny moves." That accomplished, he added, "Stand up and pull down your trousers."

Muffled bleats of protest came from the gagged mouth. Eyes fixed on the deadly Colt, he did as instructed. Smoke prodded him over to his horse. Then Smoke bent low and used his bowie to cut through the crotch of the man's trousers.

"Step up there with your right foot in the front of the stirrup."

Glittering black eyes seemed to say, But that will put me in the saddle backwards.

Smoke smiled at the silent communication. "Swing your left over and settle in."

A little assistance was required to seat the outlaw backward in his saddle. Quickly, Smoke took a short length of rope from his hip pocket and tied the bandido's ankles to the stirrups and joined them under the belly of the horse. He prodded the man in the ribs with the cold steel of his .44.

"Hands behind you."

That done, Smoke bound them also. He noted with pleasure that these men had shown no difficulty in understanding his Spanish. No doubt the Colt had a lot to do with that. He inspected his handiwork, then stood where the wilted hardcase could clearly see him.

"When you get back to camp, tell Carvajal that he had better abdicate his throne, or I'll be on him like stink on a rotting corpse."

Smoke's captive had little doubt as to the identity of that decomposing body. He nodded vigorously to indicate his agreement. Smoke took up the reins of the outlaw's mount and led it into the trees, far enough off the trail to not be readily noticed until daylight. There he tied it off to a tree.

Satisfied with his night's work, Smoke Jensen returned to Sidewinder. Quietly he mounted and set off toward the exit to the valley. He would return to Merced and a long, peaceful sleep.

Gustavo Carvajal's face turned black with rage. He hurled the glazed clay tequila bottle he held against the wall of the tent. "Who was it? Carbone? Martine? Goddamn them for this insult!"

"The—the men said it was a *gringo*. He spoke Spanish, but

they could see he was a *norteño,*" Humberto Regales informed him.

An unexpected chill ran along the spine of the King of the North. "He's here, then. This Smoke Jensen. He has come because these *hijos de la chingada* have asked him to come. What is he, that he can do this to—to me?"

"He is only a man, Excellency. No, that is not accurate. I have found out more about this *Señor* Jensen. In his country, some call him the 'Last Mountain Man.'"

"¿Que es esto? Un hombre de la cordillera?" Carvajal repeated the accolade given to Smoke Jensen. "What is so important about such a man?"

"The mountain men were fur trappers, and mighty Indian fighters. They lived in the *cordilleras* of the United States all alone, facing impossible odds and triumphing over them. This Smoke Jensen is said to be the last of their breed, a truly awesome man, who has killed nearly three hundred men in stand-up fights."

"¡Mierda! No man can live through so many gunfights.*"* Carvajal's countenance darkened again. "But what he did to our men, this insult to my manhood is an abomination. He cannot get away with it. We must make him suffer for this. Only how? Attack Carbone again? Carbone has lost nearly everything. But Martine y Garcia has much wealth left to him. Yes! We will retaliate against the oh-so arrogant Martine and bring them all to their knees." A wild light came to Carvajal's crossed eyes. "I know exactly how to do it. Pick fifty men. They will accompany me on a bold raid against Martine's *rancho.* It will be the Mother of all Raids."

Bone-sore and muscles aching, Bobby Harris had time to reflect on the fact that riding full-grown horses on the Sugarloaf wasn't exactly like forking his little pony down Trinidad way. His misery even overcame his reluctance to bare his bottom in front of a female woman. All four of his cheeks flushed bright pink at the thought of it.

"Aaah," he sighed when the liniment touched his throbbing thigh. It was so cool and nice. No! It burned like fire. "Ouch! That's awful," he complained.

Sally Jensen suppressed a giggle. "Hush up and take it like a man. I don't understand why Burt Crocker couldn't take care of this."

"Oh, he offered, Miz Jensen. Said he'd do it with a pot scrubber."

"Umm. I can see why you declined."

"Did what?" Bobby asked, the burning sensation forgotten for a moment.

"Declined," Sally, the perpetual teacher, explained. "Said no."

"Uh. Yeah. I declined *that* right enough. Oowie! Owie! That stuff smarts."

"If you would have quit at noon, when I said you should, you wouldn't be so stoved up," Sally lectured.

Bobby had ridden out with the hands for the first time that morning. He had needed help swinging the saddle on a full-grown horse, yet it didn't deter him from "earning his keep," as he put it. He walked with a hitch in his get-along when the hands came in for their dinner, but said nothing. Sally suggested he take the afternoon to rake down the barnyard, or some other non-horse-related job, and Bobby had hotly refused. Now he paid the price.

His lower lip slid forward in a pout, miffed that the application of the fiery liniment didn't come with at least a large spoonful of sympathy. "Aw, I carried my load all right, didn't I?"

"So Burt told me," Sally answered neutrally. She agreed with Smoke that excessive pampering made weak children.

"Then you—you don't need to put that stuff on so much," Bobby complained, wondering if coming here was such a hot idea after all.

* * *

Smoke Jensen rode back into Merced shortly before night-fall. Already the steady efforts of the people had made inroads into the devastation brought on by Gustavo Carvajal. He found Carbone and Martine at the resurrected *cantina*. Starlight gleamed through the burned-out roof by the time they had heard a report of his visit to Carvajal's camp. Carbone chortled at the messages Smoke had left for the bandit king.

"That ought to drive out any sanity left," he remarked. "I especially like that part about being his Cortez. Any lunatic who thinks he is Montezuma will have a fit over that. Seriously, though, can we get at him? Can we hurt him?"

"Oh, yes," Smoke said with satisfaction. "What we must do first is get those women out of camp. No doubt Carvajal intends to sell them to the brothels. They have to be safely away before we do any real damage to El Rey. I think the three of us are best suited to that job."

"Like the old days, eh, *amigo?*" Carbone recalled.

"Right. Only this time we don't go in shooting. More about that later. Now, do either of you have access to any dynamite?"

"No," Martine responded. "It is expensive and not too popular in Mexico. We can get *Gigante.*"

The large-grain black powder was not as powerful as dynamite. Smoke was well familiar with it. Done in grains bigger than No. 3 mortar powder, the explosive had been used for many years by miners and others before Nobel came up with the idea of stabilizing nitroglycerine with sawdust. Smoke nodded his approval.

"Be sure to get plenty of caps and fuse too," he advised. "What our volunteers lack in marksmanship, they can make up throwing blasting powder into that camp."

"You are so . . . inventive, *amigo,*" Martine complimented the mountain man.

"Trying to earn my keep," Smoke deprecated. "We'll set off charges once we get out of Carvajal's camp. Gather the men and tell them what is in store. We'll leave at once and infiltrate the valley tomorrow night."

"None too soon, believe me," Carbone allowed.

While they addressed the small force of volunteers, a hatless rider rushed into the village shouting for Martine. He hurried up to them on a lathered horse.

"Don Miguel, there is terrible news. That *bastardo,* Carvajal, and his army have been seen riding toward your *hacienda.* It is feared they will attack it."

"They're certainly not coming to surrender," Martine observed, his anger rising.

Smoke Jensen thought fast. "I'll take half the men and head that way. With them out in the open, it will be easy pickings. We can cut down the odds, too."

"I'll go along, of course," Martine stated.

"I counted on that," Smoke told him. "Let's get going. The sooner we reach your headquarters, the sooner we can hurt Carvajal."

They came out of the rising sun. Fifty hard-bitten men and Gustavo Carvajal. Rudolfo Malendez saw them first. He scratched his gray hair and rose from his resting place against the tree trunk. One of the bandit army killed him with a knife. The sheep Malendez had watched through the night made tiny, frightened sounds and scattered from under the hoofs of the horses.

"This is going to be easy," Pedro Chacon boasted. "These people are like the sheep they tend. Baaabaaa!"

Father Xavier had just finished reading a passage in his brevery and set about lighting oil lamps in the small chapel when the sound of approaching hoofs drew his attention. Could it be the *Patrón* returning? He swung open the tall, wooden portal and stepped onto the wide landing in time to catch a bullet in the chest.

He staggered and fell, sprawling on the three low steps at the front of the church. Immediately the bandits opened up, firing through windows and open doorways of the ten small two-room adobe houses around the high wall of the *hacienda*. Death and fire had come to Rancho Pasaje.

Women and children screamed in fright. An old man, the former gatekeeper of the main house, snatched up a shotgun and blasted the life from one hardcase. He broke the single-barrel weapon, and aged fingers trembled with the urgency he put behind reloading. Three .45 slugs smacked into him and ended his efforts. Pedro Chacon watched smoke curl from the muzzle of his six-gun and grinned broadly.

"Didn't I tell you? Easier than rabbits."

Twenty men, with Carvajal in the lead, went directly to the *hacienda*. They found the wrought-iron gate closed against them, along with the high, double-panel door. Carvajal did not waste time trying to breach this obstruction.

"Get ladders. We go over the walls," he commanded.

"Why are we taking the risk of going in here?" Tomas Diaz asked. "Just to burn it?"

"No. I have something special in mind. That's why I have the best men with me. I sent Pedro Chacon to round up the girls and young women. I expect he'll amuse himself with a few of them while he's at it. I can trust you and these others to hold your fire when I say so."

"'Hold our fire'?"

"Yes, my loyal Tomas. We are going to take prisoners inside this oh-so-fine *hacienda.*"

Several *bandidos* returned with ladders, and the picked men swarmed up and over the walls. A brief rattle of gunfire followed; then the doors and gate were swung open. Carvajal entered, swaggering. Three white cotton-clad bodies lay on the ground, diminished in death. He waved an arm to illustrate his instructions.

"Secure the patio, dig out the servants. Tomas, you and I will go visit the lady of the house."

They found her door bolted against them. "Go away," a feminine voice demanded from inside. "I have a gun in here, and I'll use it."

"Go get something to use as a ram. Bring four men back with you," Carvajal ordered.

Tomas hurried off on the errand. Meanwhile, Carvajal studied the stout oak door. It would take some effort. Well worth it, though, he considered. Curious, he strode along the hallway. The door next to the master bedroom yielded to a stout kick.

She sat in the middle of the bed, sheet and blanket gathered around her. Big-eyed, the girl of six or so had a hand over her mouth and tears trickled down her cheeks.

"Would you like to take a trip with me, little one?" Carvajal asked pleasantly. Solemnly, she shook her head no. "Oh, come, we'll have a lot of good times."

From the hallway, the sound of the men employing the ram interrupted his game of cat and mouse. Carvajal gave her a cheery wave and returned to her mother's room. The muffled report of a firearm came between the crashes of the ram. The bullet sent a shower of splinters from the face of the door and struck one young bandit in the chest.

He winced and looked down, then plucked the spent slug from his leather vest. "That's a thick door," he observed, then went back to hurling the ram.

El Rey del Norte quickly became bored and impatient at the efforts to breach the portal into *Señora* Martine's room. He prowled the hallway, hands behind his back, the long, split-tail coat of his general's uniform flapping against his calves. He stopped at one door and flung it open.

A brown-faced boy of seven hurtled at him, a tiny dagger

in one hand. Laughing, Carvajal grabbed the lad by his extended wrist and yanked him off his bare feet. "So," he chortled. "You inherited your father's talent with weapons, *niño*. I like to see high spirits in a boy." He took the knife from limp fingers and sat the child on his feet. "You are going on a long trip with us. Go get dressed."

"I won't!" the boy shouted defiance.

Carvajal gave him a sound swat on the rump that sent him staggering into the room. "Do as I say."

From the inner courtyard came the wails of women servants and pleas for mercy. Ruthlessly, the bandits slaughtered the older ones, reserving the younger for a different fate. Highly satisfied, El Rey paced back through the hall, located the third of Martine's children and put them in the charge of Tomas.

"We'll be leaving soon," he advised. He paused, snapped his fingers. "Martine y Ruiz will have heard of this. He will come. We leave a rear guard of twenty men to give him a small surprise, eh?"

"That will be most fitting, Excellency," Tomas agreed.

"Fine. Bring the women and the brats, and we will head for our camp."

19

An hour later, Smoke Jensen and Martine rode in with Martine's retainers. They saw the smoke of burning buildings at a good distance. It prepared them, in part, for what they saw. Every structure outside the *hacienda* itself had been put to the torch. At a distance of a hundred yards the bodies could be seen huddled on the ground. Carvajal's rear guard had opened up on them at that range also.

A bullet cracked overhead, and Smoke Jensen swung the column to the right. More rounds followed them. The lack of accuracy didn't impress Smoke about the ability of Carvajal's men. He led the small troop wide of the settlement until the *hacienda's* walls came between them and the defenders.

"We haven't any choice but to go right at them," Smoke declared.

Martine nodded agreement. "If they don't shoot any better than they have so far, we have a good chance."

Smoke cracked a grim smile. "You may lose a few good men."

"From what I see, I already have. No, my friend, worry over that is time wasted." Martine settled the reins over the huge horn of his saddle and drew both revolvers. "I say we get in close and clean out this scum."

"Suits," Smoke agreed. He fisted both of his Colts.

They came like a whirlwind. Smoke and Martine took five men each and split around the walls of the *hacienda*. Pablo Alvarez waited for the signal, with the other ten, to make a frontal attack. Some among the outlaws congratulated themselves in so easily running off their opposition. Quickly and bloodily, they learned of their mistake.

Smoke Jensen saw a fat bandit giving more attention to a tequila bottle than his area of responsibility. The bottle shattered an instant before Smoke's .44 slug punched through the inebriate's head. Smoke saw movement to his right and turned his torso from the hips to meet the threat.

A grinning soldier of El Rey widened his eyes in surprise at the speed and girth of the *gringo* on the spotted horse. His rifle cracked and disturbed the air over Smoke Jensen's head a moment before blackness claimed him and Smoke sought another target.

Two *bandidos* rushed into the street from what had once been a small *cantina*. They appeared directly in front of Smoke Jensen. One died before he realized his mistake. The other unlimbered his six-gun and burned powder in a useless effort to stop Smoke.

Smoke felt the passage of the bullet an instant before his hammer dropped and the .44 Colt bucked in his hand. His aim proved much truer than his enemy's. The outlaw buckled in the middle and did a little knock-kneed dance while his life leaked out through a hole in his belly.

Martine appeared then, herding two of Carvajals bandits ahead of him. His smile made a white slash in his dark face. "It worked perfectly. They were all concentrating on Alvarez and the men who came at them from the front. I have two wounded. How about you?"

Smoke had not checked the five who came with him. He did so quickly. "Looks like Negocio got a scratch. Nothing more. We've won a cheap victory. Something tells me that these aren't the only men Carvajal sent to visit your *hacienda*."

"Most likely. I am sure these *cerdos* will tell us all we want to know."

An eerie silence settled over the ruins outside the *hacienda*. Weeping, one man brought news of the wanton slaughter inside. Martine's face hardened and he spoke in a near whisper.

"What of my wife and children?"

"*Gracias a Dio,* they are not among the dead," the sad-eyed man reported. "But we can find them nowhere in the *hacienda*."

"Where are they, you pigs?" Martine demanded of the captives, addressing them as he had before. "What has been done with my family?"

They might have been eager enough to surrender, but they showed themselves reluctant to talk. Smoke Jensen dismounted and walked up close to them. He towered over the uncomfortable pair. He produced a nasty grin and drew his bowie from its belt sheath. Slowly he waggled it before them.

"It's remarkable what a heated knife blade can do to loosen a tongue," Smoke remarked lightly.

Eyes fixed on the wicked blade, they listened to Martine's translation. They both paled and one lost control of his bladder. Smoke Jensen nodded to a bed of coals, a blue flame flickering from the ruins of the building.

"Since you have so conveniently provided us with a fire, I see no reason why we should not take advantage of it."

The one who had wet his britches fell to his knees. "I will tell you what you want to know, *Señor*," he blurted.

"*¡Callerse!*" his companion hissed.

Smoke made a nasty face and moved closer to the defiant one. "Have you always been a thief and murderer? Or did you once work on a *rancho?*" The surprise in the man's eyes confirmed Smoke's speculation. "Then you've seen horses gelded, bulls cut?" Without giving the man time to answer, Smoke growled to one of Martine's men. "Take down his trousers."

Uttering a great sob, the man fainted. Smoke Jensen looked down at him indifferently and turned to the other man. "Still willing to talk?"

He swallowed hard and nodded, eyes glazed and fixed on the knife. *"Señor* Martine, your wife and children were taken by El Rey del Norte. They are to ensure your cooperation. His Excellency demands that you give up this attempt to hinder him in rebuilding the empire of the Aztecs. Your wife and children will live so long as you obey him."

Martine wanted to smash this low brute, grind him into the ground. Fury and worry for his family mingled in his mind. He smashed a fist into his open palm. "If only we could have gotten here sooner."

"They didn't come by the way we had been told. Must have spotted your man and changed routes after he rode off," Smoke surmised. He asked the captive, "How long ago did Carvajal leave here?"

"Oh, it has been some time. An hour and a half, perhaps."

"No problem trailing them," Smoke stated. "I'll take most of the men and start at once. You'd best do what you can for your people here."

Half an hour along the clear trail of Carvajal's bandit army, Smoke Jensen reined in. An old man stood at the side of the road, hat removed respectfully and held in front of his chest.

"You are looking for the *ladrónes* who rode this way, *Señores?"* the old-timer asked.

"We are," Smoke told him.

"They are far ahead of you."

"We know that."

"What is it you wish to do when you find them?"

"Kill them," Smoke said simply.

Light twinkled in the ancient's eyes. "I hoped you would say that. I am called El Viejo, the old one. As you can see, I am a woodcutter." He gestured to his burro, heavily laden with bundles of firewood. "Do you know where it is they are going?"

"There is a camp in the mountains to the east of here," Smoke told him. "In a large valley surrounded by high crags."

"I know this country well. Would it please you to find another route that would put you in front of these *hombres malos?*"

For the first time since they had reached the *hacienda,* Smoke Jensen produced a warm smile. "It would indeed."

"I can lead you."

"Then show us the way," Smoke invited.

"I must take care of my burro first," El Viejo diverted.

"Unload him and put him on a long tether to graze. We'll leave some water."

"Gracias, Señor. I am yours to command."

They entered the mountains twenty minutes later, cut across a hogback ridge, and dropped into a deep, lush valley. The vegetation seemed tropical to Smoke Jensen, who missed his pines and aspen. Tall, scaly trees rustled and sighed, bent in the strong breeze that blew above them. Colorful birds, whose names Smoke did not know, flashed through the limbs, chattering to one another. Unexpectedly stout for his great age, the woodcutter maintained a good pace on horseback. By noon the rescue party had crested the spine of the range and begun to descend among lower, rounder mountains.

"We are not far," El Viejo advised Smoke Jensen. "Another hour maybe."

Impatience put hothooks in Smoke Jensen's mind. With two dozen men along, he felt certain they could best the bandits, particularly if they set a good ambush. Could they do it, though, without bringing harm to Martine's wife and youngsters?

That consideration urged caution on his plans. He'd know

more when he found out where they would come out of this part of the range. Gradually, the terrain took on a vaguely familiar appearance. The old man had led them close to Cabesa de Borrego and the valley where Carvajal had his camp.

"You've done a good job. Now if only they are behind us," Smoke told El Viejo when the old man called a halt and indicated the scant trail left by comings and goings from the hidden valley.

"Traveling as they were, they must be an hour or two behind us," El Viejo speculated.

"Then we had better get started," Smoke prompted.

He and Martine's men set about felling several smaller trees. These they topped and trimmed away excess branches. "Leave some of them long," Smoke instructed. "Put a point on them."

Unaccustomed to thinking like Arapaho or Blackfoot warriors, the workmen from Martine's ranch had no idea what Smoke planned to do with the logs. Most accepted that they would be used to block the trail. Not so, they soon learned.

Smoke gathered up half a dozen braided leather *riatas* from the *vaqueros* and rigged the poles into deadfalls. At his urging, two men backed their horses, drawing the heavy, green logs into the air and securing them to the trip line. Smoke approached an agile youngster of sixteen or so.

"Take these branches we've cut and shinny up that tree. Work your way out on the limb and use these to hide the deadfall."

Grinning with suppressed excitement, the youth followed directions earnestly. With swift, sure moves, he wove an overlapping pattern of branches that caused the deadly trap to disappear into the background. Smoke then located some springy young saplings at the edge of the trail and fixed wooden spikes to them. Then he bent them back away from the pathway and secured them to trip lines.

"No time to dig a proper pit," Smoke complained aloud.

Mention of it brought smiles to the faces of several men. They had used such means to trap bears and other large game.

When the last of their preparations had been carefully hidden, Smoke selected positions for the men. "You'll be up in these rocks. Pick a spot that leaves the trail open to you for a long way. Let the head of the column get through to me. I'll drop the first ones in line and get them to run through here without paying much attention to the surroundings. You men who will be farther down the trail, close off their rear when you hear the first shots. Push them hard. Don't give them time to think about *Señora* Martine and the children, or any other captives."

All they could do now was wait, Smoke thought as the men faded into the underbrush. The position he picked for himself was the most dangerous. He would remain on horseback, in the middle of the trail, around a bend from the center of the ambush site. If all went well, he should be able to fight his way to the side of Martine's wife and free her and the kids. Yeah, all he had to do was wait.

Smoke Jensen heard them long before any of the outlaw army came into view. They laughed and talked loudly. Squeals of protest came from the women captives. Lewd suggestions dominated the conversation. A thick, soft layer of leaves muffled hoofbeats so that Smoke caught sight of the first bandit before he heard their horses.

Surprise painted the face under the big brim of a fancy sombrero. Its owner knew the huge man in front of him did not belong to El Rey's army. His hand dropped to the butt of his .45, and he pulled it halfway out of leather before a bullet sped from Smoke's .44 and stopped his heart. Smoke Jensen triggered a second round and spilled a mean-faced bandit out of the saddle.

"Release *Señora* Martine and the children," Smoke demanded in a roar.

Emboldened by what appeared to be a single man challenging them, the confused *bandidos* at the front of the column spurred their mounts forward. Smoke emptied his first six-gun and had the second in action as the bandits flashed past him. Then he heard the snap and whir of the first trip line.

A shriek of agony came from one throat as the bandit took a whiplash of sapling that left, his companion stopped the other with his gut. It cleared him from the saddle, and he dangled there, a grotesque fruit on a red-splattered tree. Smoke saw the frightened face of Consuelo Martine in a swirl of surprised bandit visages.

There, beside her, the two small boys and her daughter. Smoke spurred Sidewinder toward the captive woman. One hardcase saw his determined approach and grabbed the reins from Consuelo's hands. Smoke shot him out of the saddle while more of the bandits and the women captured at the *hacienda* raced past. A loud swish sounded, and men screamed when impaled on sharpened stobs. Gunfire erupted from the rocks.

Yelling in consternation, the bandits fought to escape the ambush. Another deadfall accounted for three more. A second bandit had grabbed the reins of Consuelo Martine's horse and that of her daughter. He ripped his mount's flanks bloody with huge, cruel rowels and spurred away from the milling confusion. Down-trail, the stopper had been applied.

Gunshots echoed off the slopes as the rest of the ambush went into action. Pressed from all directions, most of the bandits sought to flee. Smoke downed one and worked closer to the two boys, seated on one horse. He reached them a moment before one of the desperate *bandidos* decided to take revenge on the youngsters.

His hammer already on the way down when Smoke saw the bandit, it became a close call. Smoke put a .44 round between the snarling outlaw's eyes. Reflexive action put off his aim a bit and the slug intended to kill one of the small boys merely grazed his rib cage. He cried out and clung hysterically to his older brother. More bandits streamed by, with the *vaqueros* of Rancho Pasaje hot after them.

No time to make a try for Consuelo Martine and her daughter, Smoke silently cursed. Close as they were to the valley hideout, reinforcements would already be on the way. He sheltered the small lads with his body and pumped more rounds into the panicked outlaws until they rode out of sight. Even then, the final deadfall triggered, and two throats went raw with screaming.

"Round up our people, and let's get out of here," Smoke said, his voice heavy with regret over being only partly successful. How could he look Martine in the eye and report failure?

20

Another day had gone by with Martine close to losing hold of his reason over the thought of his wife and daughter in the hands of a madman like Carvajal. Back at their main base in Merced, he had been reunited with his sons. His eldest boy had bravely fought off tears while he told of their capture. When he got to the bandit riding off with his mother and sister, the water spilled down his face. His father wept also. Smoke Jensen turned away. No man appreciated witnesses at times like this.

But they had come in the life of Smoke Jensen. When his first wife and infant son had been murdered. And again when he thought he had lost Sally to the bloody hands of demented men. He had never mourned for his parents, forgotten people from an obliterated past. Now he stared at the setting sun until he heard Martine clear his throat and send his son off to be with his brother.

"What about this ultimatum?" Martine asked, recalling what the cooperative bandit had told them.

"It sounded menacing even from the mouth of a man who was about to die," Smoke told him calmly. "Demands on you, your people. Carvajal will not be satisfied until he possesses all of central Mexico. I suspect he believes himself able to take on the federal troops and win."

"His men are good. Look what he did to my *hacienda*. But they are not that good. Give us a month, two months with these men, and we can root him out of anywhere."

"Speaking of which," Smoke changed the subject as he poured a cup of steaming coffee, "there's no doubt that Carvajal took your wife and daughter back to the camp in the mountains. How long they'll stay there is open for guesswork. So I suggest we return to our original plan. Only we have more women to get out of there now."

"Yes, I can see the sense of that," Carbone agreed.

"And I," Martine added. "Of course, I will be coming on the next raid as before."

Smoke cut his eyes to Martine's ravaged visage. He regretted having to say what he planned next. "No. I don't think that is wise."

"Why not?"

"You would be subject to letting emotion cloud your skills when most needed, old friend."

"Nonsense!"

"Look at it carefully. Think it through. Who would you go for first?"

"Why, my wife and child, of course," Martine allowed.

"And they might be the most difficult to get out of there," Smoke revealed to his friend. "It could alert the whole camp. I don't like this any more than you. It is reasonable, and it's the way we're going to do this. You can pick the men you want to go with you and head for your other village. Prepare the people there to defend themselves. Carbone and I will lead the rest to the valley and spoil some of Carvajal's plans."

Smoke Jensen's war party set out after dark. A quick scout of the area had revealed watchers in a ravine a quarter mile from Merced. Rather than eliminate them, Smoke opted for a ruse. The hoofs of their horses padded with gunnysacks, the detail heading for Carvajal's camp walked their mounts out of town to the west.

Smoke had insisted that everything that could rattle, scrape or jingle be secured. No one spoke, and most muffled their horses' nostrils to prevent tell-tale whinnying. The ploy worked quite well. A mile away on the plain, the grim-faced troop removed the coverings from the hoofs, mounted up, and turned to the northeast. Although it was the dark of the moon, they made good time. These young men of the two ranches adapted quickly, Smoke thought with satisfaction. Now if they only remembered what he had taught them about shooting, they might stand a chance of pulling this off.

"It's over the other side of that long ridge," Smoke informed the riders that sat in a semi-circle around him. "Get the men out of sight and settled down. After my last visit, and that set to on the trail, I'm sure our friend El Rey has tightened his security."

"You are the boss, *amigo*," Carbone informed him.

"You know more ways to be nasty in the woods than any of us."

"You're no helpless infant, yourself, friend."

"Me? I have fought in the streets of a hundred villages, maybe two hundred. I have ridden the central valley, but mountains are not my natural surroundings. You grew up in them. I marveled at the traps you set for Carvajal. I only wish you would have squashed that *chingaso* with one of them."

"I might get lucky and land a stick of giant powder in his lap," Smoke suggested. "I'm going to take a little scout around, check on our opposition. It's a long while until nightfall. Cold rations for everyone and no smoking."

Two of the company, who understood English, cut angry

eyes at Smoke Jensen as he and Sidewinder ghosted away toward the camp of Gustavo Carvajal. Who was this *gringo* to deny them the comfort of a little tobacco? Carbone read them with ease.

"He means you, *compeñeros,* and so do I."

Bobby Harris sat in a thicket of wild blackberry and some stray aspens, some five miles from the Sugarloaf. He sipped at a canteen of tepid water and munched on a biscuit. It wasn't fair, his self-pity spilled out.

He worked hard, like any of the hands. They got paid regular wages, but he only made money when he topped off a horse. And—and everyone treated him like a baby. He was lonesome, too.

At least down south, he had friends his age. Sam and Petey, Little Joe Butler. When he could get away from Rupe Connors, they'd gone swimming in the old Dutchman's pond, fished, hunted rabbits in the fall. Here he had no one to pal with. Now, school was going to start.

He hated school. Funny, he loved books and spent more time reading here on the Sugarloaf than he had had time for at home. But *school?* Doin' dumb drills in handwriting and arithmetic because some dried-up old woman said you had to? Awful. Why wouldn't Miz Jensen listen to him? He crinkled up his button nose, and his lower lip slid out in a big pout. The effect was spoiled somewhat by biscuit crumbs clinging to it.

He'd taken Dollar and run off in the night. Show them, he thought. It would drive them wild. Maybe he would head south, hunt for Smoke Jensen. Smoke let him drink coffee and talked to him like a growed man. Only how could he do that? It was a long ways off. He had five dollars, saved up from what Miz Jensen let him keep of his earnings. The rest she banked for his future.

Some future. Forever messing with horses and cleaning up after them. And going to school. That five dollars wouldn't buy many supplies. Nor a train ticket. He'd do it somehow; he'd show them all. Late afternoon sun touched his bowed shoulders and sent the warmth of Indian summer into his thin frame.

Not so thin anymore, he thought with a snatch of pride. He'd been filling out with Sally Jensen doing the cooking, and the work that strained and strengthened muscles in arms, chest and legs. Why, he already wore a bigger shirt than he had only weeks ago, when Smoke had bought some for him. A lump formed in Bobby's throat, and he fought back tears.

"Oh, Smoke, why did you send me away to this lonesome place?" Bobby lamented aloud.

"Because he cares a lot about you and wanted you to have a good place to live." Suddenly Sally Jensen appeared in the small clearing Bobby had cut for himself with a hand axe.

How had she done that? He'd not heard a sound. Not a horse or a person. Bobby looked up, blinked cobalt eyes and flushed with shame and embarrassment. So much for his great plans to run away. He'd only gotten this far and already he'd been caught.

"I gather you needed some time by yourself," Sally offered when Bobby remained silent.

"Yes, ma'am. Som'thin' like that," he responded in a subdued voice.

Sally produced a bright smile. "I'll bet you're hungry."

"No, ma'am." Instantly, Bobby's stomach called him a liar. "Yes. I guess I am."

"You missed breakfast and dinner, no wonder. Everyone has a heavy burden on his mind once in a while. Have you come to grips with yours?"

"No, ma'am."

"Tell me about it," Sally urged.

"I—It's just that I'm so lonely up here. Got no friends, no one to do things with," Bobby began to unload his misery.

Sally pressed her lips together, eyes weighing the boy's discomfort. "Well, if I told you that one reason you need to go to school is to meet other boys in the valley, would you believe me?"

"Huh? I—I never thought of that." Bobby brightened slightly. "Yeah, I guess I would. That might make it worth it, after all."

"There's something else, isn't there, Bobby?" Sally's intuitive sense had brought her to the core of his problem.

Bobby's lower lip began to tremble, and his eyes filled with moisture. "I—I miss my maw. Miss her somethin' awful. I never cried when we buried her. Rupe said he'd whup me if I did. Now . . . now . . . oooh, Miz Jensen, I hurt so bad."

Suddenly the dam burst, and Bobby let go his deep grief over his mother. Sally knelt in front of him and took him in her arms. Bobby hugged her and sobbed wretchedly. His whole body shook, and Sally projected her growing love for the boy through her arms, so tightly holding him. She offered soft words of comfort and rocked him as she had her own brood when internal hurt from childhood tragedy had spilled over. At last, the spell passed.

Bobby rocked back on his boot heels, dried his eyes with a grubby hand and wiped his nose. "I reckon I made a fool of myself," he said tightly.

"Yes, you did. But not here, now. You did that last night when you ran away. It was a spiteful act, wrong and unmanly. The Sugarloaf is your home. I've come to love you very much, Bobby. Smoke thinks the world of you and expects to find you here when he returns.

"But for running away there has to be some punishment," Sally went on, then produced a big wink. "No pie for three days, how's that?"

Bobby hugged her again, this time with genuine affection. "Oh, Miz Jensen, I'd move a mountain for you. I surely would."

* * *

Half a day of observation had given Smoke Jensen the location of all of the captive women, including Martine's wife and daughter. He carefully stored in memory each hut or lean-to where one of the prisoners could be found. He returned to the waiting avengers and changed clothes.

Everyone now wore traditional Mexican clothing, in black or dark brown, with the big sombreros that Smoke had come to identify with the bandit army. Carbone had already picked out the brighter, more aggressive among the ranch hands, flock tenders, and shopkeepers. They gathered with Smoke Jensen at the crest of the ridge.

"Down there, in that big tent. *Señora* Martine and her daughter are in there. It belongs to Carvajal, so we have to be sharp in what we do to get them out. Over there, two women in that lean-to," Smoke instructed in the waning light. When he had completed pointing out the locations of the captives, they withdrew.

"Everyone get something to eat. No fires, and still no smoking. We wait until three hours after dark, give them time to fill their bellies and get drunked up, then we simply walk in," Smoke informed them. "You all know which captive you are going after. Be natural, relaxed. Talk and laugh with them and each other. Make it appear you belong. Be sure to get the women out the back of whatever they are held in and into the dark as quickly as possible.

"Once they are all clear, you men on the ridge will let go with our surprise for El Rey," Smoke went on. "We'll be upstream with the women, so don't throw any sticks that way. Once the fun starts, we should be able to get away without being discovered."

"If we have good fortune," Carbone suggested.

"We make our own luck," Smoke said gruffly, concerned

about the state of mind of their volunteers. "Are there any questions?"

"What if they find out we don't belong there?" one of the group asked.

"Then we have to shoot our way out of there," Smoke told him.

"What if some of the women are hurt, or sick?"

"Carry them out," Smoke told the young shepherd.

"Why can't we smoke? Some of the men I am to lead have complained about it," Juan Murial asked.

"Because tobacco smoke can be smelled for a good distance. And a burning match can be seen for a mile at night. I found one of their sentries that way the other night."

"What happened to him?" Murial inquired.

"I strung him up by his heels in a tree."

"Ummm. I do not think our men would like that to happen to them."

Smoke responded to several more questions and then dismissed their sergeants. They had a long wait ahead.

Several of Carvajal's bandit army lounged around fires, drinking from glazed clay jugs of tequila. They talked in low voices, and some of them had eyelids that drooped toward a drunken stupor. With Carbone and Smoke in the lead, the avengers filtered into the camp. One fast thinker fumbled with the buttons of his fly, as though to give reason for his sudden appearance out of the dark.

No one paid them any attention as they spread through the camp. No more than three came from any one direction, and they angled indirectly toward their objectives. Carbone did the talking, Smoke's accent likely to give him away. Smoke nodded and smiled and said an occasional *"sí."*

He noted the tension among the infiltrators, though he doubted that any of the bandits would recognize it. Many of the huts lay in darkness, and the men assigned to them approached quietly and unobserved. Smoke Jensen's keen hearing picked out several soft grunts as men in the shelters met death by a knife or were knocked unconscious. Smoke, Carbone, and Juan headed for Carvajal's large tent. On the blind side from the dying cook fires, they listened for any sound from inside. A soft whimper could be heard.

"The girl," Smoke mouthed silently. Carbone nodded. "We wait," Smoke added.

While they bided time, Smoke kept track of the women being spirited out of the camp. By his count, all but three, plus Martine's wife and daughter, had been slipped away to safety when a sudden roar of surprised anger broke the silence of the night.

A soft, rasping sound got through the tequila haze spiraling in the head of Montez. Groggy, he cracked one eye and saw the figure of the young woman from Merced standing over him. She was hastily dressing. Then he sensed the presence of someone else.

By damn, no one was taking the woman away from him. He bolted upright, a wicked knife in one hand. "Get out of here, *cabron,* or I'll cut your liver out," he bellowed in anger.

Another blade swished in the dark and cut through the veins and tendons of Montez's knife hand. He howled in pain. Immediately, questions came, shouted from different parts of the camp. Spraying blood on the walls and floor of the hut, Montez dove for his cartridge belt. He came up with his .45 Mendoza and fired point-blank into the chest of the unknown man who had cut him. But not before the soft-spoken saddle maker from Merced buried his knife in Montez's chest, spearing his heart.

Confused and terrified, the woman barged from the shelter and bowled over one of the outlaws who responded to the alarm given by Montez. An arm came out of the darkness, and the hand grabbed her by the wrist. Yanked off her feet, she squealed in fright as the man who held her pulled her out of sight. Muzzle bloom from several six-guns brightened the night.

Befuddled by tequila, the *bandidos* began firing at shadows and each other. More alert, several of their number heaped wood on the fires to provide light enough to find out what had happened. Growling like a baited bear, Gustavo Carvajal burst out the entrance to his tent.

"There goes our perfect plan," Smoke Jensen stated dryly when the first shout aroused the camp. When Carvajal bulled his way out of the tent, he drew his knife. At once he slashed the tent wall with his bowie. "You'd better go in; she knows you," he told Carbone.

Carbone wasted no time. He climbed through the slit and gathered little Alicia in his arms. To Consuelo he said gruffly, "Get your clothes. We've come to get you out of here. Hurry!"

Smoke Jensen assisted Consuelo Martine through the opening in the tent wall and started off at once for the rally point. Consuelo took one startled look at his mountainous size and spoke with conviction.

"You are Smoke Jensen."

"I am, *Señora*. Now please hurry. We go that way." He directed with his free hand.

Bullets flew freely inside the camp. Leaves and small branches showered down, and the startled outlaws made an uproar that only added to the confusion. Two bandits appeared in Smoke's path, and he whipped out his .44 Colt in an eyeblink. Hot lead ripped into flesh and sent one of Carvajal's men staggering into a lean-to. His companion made the mistake of trying to raise his revolver into firing position.

Smoke shot him through the breastbone. A stupid expression came on the face of the hardcase, and he abruptly sat down hard. His Mendoza .45 grew too heavy to hold, and he let it slip from his fingers. Determinedly, Consuelo bent and retrieved it.

"I can shoot," she assured Smoke.

"You may have to," he advised her.

Lances of flame came from the edge of the trees where the rescuers gave covering fire to those still caught inside the camp. Carbone joined up with Smoke, his arms filled with Martine's daughter.

"Juan Murial is wounded, but he's coming behind," Carbone informed the mountain man.

"I'll wait for him," Smoke decided aloud. "You take these two on to safety."

"Going to make some of that luck you talked about, *amigo?*"

"That I am, Carbone. Now get."

21

Smoke Jensen felt a tugging at the hair on the back of his head. A sudden wind had come up, to moan mournfully through the trees and whip up the flames of the fires. Showers of sparks rose, and smoke rolled along at ground level. It gave a nightmare quality to the frenzied scene, as bandits shot at each other and the unidentified targets beyond the lighted area. Indistinctly, Smoke saw Juan stumbling through the swirl of white. A bandit knelt in the doorway to a brush hut and aimed at the young man from Merced.

Swinging his right arm to the side, Smoke took a quick sight and shot the bandit through the meaty part of his left shoulder. The rifle fell from nerveless hands, and the outlaw toppled over. Towering above most of the hardcases, Smoke made a sweeping gesture, directing Juan his way.

"Got me in the side," Juan panted as he drew near. "It is nothing."

A trio of bandits skidded to a halt, realizing the small youth and huge man to be strangers. They fired hastily. One bullet popped a hole through Smoke Jensen's big sombrero brim. Another cut the heel from Juan's boot. The third cracked harmlessly overhead. By then, the three gun slicks were in the process of dying.

Smoke Jensen shot two of them before they realized they had been seen. Juan put away the third with a round through the throat. One of those attended to by Smoke remained on his feet. A wicked grin waggled the drooping mustache that framed his face as he took an unsteady step forward.

"I am going to kill you, *cabrón,*" he told Smoke Jensen, his beady eyes glittering with pain and rage.

"No. You'll be dead before you get the chance," Smoke informed him. Then he tripped the hammer of his .44 and sent a message of termination to the bandit.

Staggered by the impact, eyes already glazing, the *bandido* rubber-ankled it another three steps toward Smoke, his Mendoza .45 belching flame. Rock chips flew from the ground, the disfigured slug moaning away into the trees. Dust plumed between Smoke's legs. When he reached arm's length, the man stopped. A pink froth foamed on his lips. He panted with the exertion of his approach.

Smoke extended his arm, shoved the muzzle of his .44 into the chest of the walking corpse, and pushed him over on his back. Dust rose from the body's impact. "Time to be going," Smoke advised Juan.

"*¡Dios mio!* How did you know he wouldn't hurt you?"

"It's the eyes," Smoke told him. "He had that look that said nobody was home."

"Tha's cold, *hombre,* real cold."

"Only tellin' it like it is."

They reached the edge of the tree line without any further interruptions. There Smoke produced a capped and fused stick of giant powder from inside his shirt. He struck a match and touched it to the frizzed end of the fuse. With an eye on Carvajal's opulent tent, he held it for a three count, then hurled it with everything he had.

It landed short, but touched off pandemonium. At once Smoke watched three more high arcs of sparks tumble into camp. One landed at the edge of a fire ring. The roar of the explosion echoed off canyon walls. The force of the blast sent firebrands into some brush shelters nearby. They burst into flames at once. Smoke lighted another fuse and hurled his second stick.

It landed in the bed of a *carreta* and created instant wooden shrapnel when it went off. Blind hysteria erupted. One bandit staggered a few paces, a chunk of wheel embedded in his forehead, then fell face-first in the dirt. Another gripped the shaft of a forearm-sized sliver driven into his belly. Two more shrieked while blood ran from their blinded eyes. Men began to scream in total loss of reason. Some ran about aimlessly, in circles or zigzag lines as more and more explosives landed among them.

Carbone pitched one that blew a fat bandit high in the air. He landed in a soft, boneless splash. Then, from up on the ridge, more sticks of deadly powder rained down on the camp. Mind-numbing terror seized everyone. They howled in agony, bumped into each other, and sought some means of escape from the merciless bombardment. A few took to their horses. White-eyed with sheer honor, the animals fought their masters. All the while Smoke Jensen, and the wounded Juan Murial, led the rescued women to where horses had been staked out for their escape.

Carbone clapped Smoke on the shoulder. "Well, my friend, Carvajal will not soon forget our visit tonight. I am only sorry that we couldn't finish it."

"There are too many of them." Smoke gave reason. "Another time. And soon, I figure. Carvajal will have to do something drastic, the way he sees things, and we need to be ready for him."

"Ah, yes. He will be coming for us. I can feel it in my bones," Carbone predicted.

Gustavo Carvajal had been shaken to the toes of his size-seven feet. No one could create such destruction. How had it happened? He had guards out. Good men, trustworthy to keep watch. Had they been killed or run off like before? He suspected so. His camp was a shambles. Smoldering ruins reminded him of the villages he had raided. *He* did the burning, the looting, the stealing of women. That last thought struck him suddenly and sent him over the edge.

"Eagle Warriors, to me! Come, my brave Jaguar Warriors, rally around," he shouted into the flame-ripped night.

The final echoes of the blasting powder explosions died in the distance. When only familiar faces could be found, the men stopped shooting at each other. Silence from the woods and the rim above ended their futile shots into the dark. Gustavo Carvajal stood in a growing ring of bandits. He panted like a racehorse, and his face shone with oily perspiration. It dripped from him, staining the front of his nightshirt. Only then did he realize his state of undress. The rocky ground hurt his tender feet.

"Everyone gather here, right on this spot," he demanded. "I will return in a while. We must plan to avenge this insult to the empire of the Aztecs."

He hopped gingerly from foot to foot on his way to his tent. One wall, facing the direction of the blasts, had been blown to shreds. They fluttered fitfully in the wind. Carvajal took in the state of his lodging and groaned aloud.

Inside, he howled in fury and foully cursed Martine and Carbone. The back wall of the tent had been slashed and the woman and child gone. He hastily dressed while his mind ran over various means of exacting revenge. One of them centered on skinning alive and roasting over a low bed of coals.

"They must . . . not . . . get away . . . with this," he bleated in a strangled voice.

Fully dressed in the feathered regalia of what he imagined the emperor Montezuma to have worn, Carvajal ordered his subordinates to line up the men in ranks. He paced before them, hand on the heavy gold pommel of the sword at his side. For nearly an hour he harangued his army. Throughout, he emphasized the need to take vengeance for what he called a cowardly attack. He named several trusted aids to leave at once to seek reinforcements.

"Make deals. Victor Husango is in Zacatecas. Tell him we will pay him and his men well. Tell him we can conquer all of Mexico." And later, "Go to Albedo-Portales in Nayarit. He can be trusted to bring in thirty men. Cutthroats, but good men. Say the time has come to repay old favors."

Carvajal stomped around the clearing, kicked over a burned-out shack. "We are going to make life miserable for Martine y Garcia. First we attack his second largest village. Then we take the last one. Then the *hacienda*. We are going to take everything away from him, even his life. As for this *gringo*, Smoke Jensen, five thousand gold pesos for his head!"

Esteban Carbone stood off to one side while the Martine family lost themselves in the joy of their reunion. At one point, while he bounced his daughter on his knee, Martine cut his eyes to his old friend and sadness darkened his face. He sat the girl aside and rose to cross over to the *cantina*, where Carbone stood.

"Run along, Alicia," he called to the girl. "Go to your mother." Pain shadowed his eyes when he took Carbone by one arm. "I am selfish, old friend. It is not right for me to be so happy at this reunion, when you can be reunited with Maria Elena only beyond the grave."

Carbone sighed. "It is no matter. I am glad for you. And I have almost lost the terrible empty ache Maria Elena's passing has given me. What we must do is concentrate on what Carvajal will do next. We should be meeting with Smoke."

"There is time, *amigo*. The youngbloods want a fiesta to celebrate the victory."

"There's little enough to celebrate," Carbone observed. "We should join him. They can be quite persuasive."

Martine clapped Carbone on one shoulder. "Right as usual. He is at what's left of the *posada*."

They found Smoke Jensen in the inner courtyard of the inn. A dozen young men from the ranches and Merced surrounded him. They clamored for his attention, talking excitedly about dancing, music, feasting, and a lot of drinking. Smoke didn't notice his friends enter. After several seconds more of their enthusiastic chatter, he held up his arms for silence.

"It is true," he said in labored Spanish, "that we won a victory. We won the battle, but the war isn't over yet. Carvajal will be sure to raise some particular hell now. What you need now is some rest. Go to where you are staying, clean your guns and go to sleep. Believe me, you are going to need both."

Disappointed, they departed in silence. Carbone and Martine approached. "What do you think we should be doing?" Carbone asked.

"We agree that Carvajal is most vulnerable when he is exposed. We need to draw him out in the open. I suggest we fortify one of your villages, Martine."

"Pueblo Viejo," Martine came back at once. "It is the smallest, but also the richest. He will want to come after that for sure."

"Good. We'll take the whole company of volunteers over there. Fortify the place and force Carvajal to throw away men trying to get us out of there."

Carbone and Martine looked at Smoke. One after the other, they nodded in agreement. "You have been thinking about this," Martine offered.

"All the way back from the valley camp," Smoke told him. "First, the men did well with the ambush. The traps they set were perfect. Then we hurt him last night in the camp. How badly we don't know. Chances are some of those who joined him recently will be having second thoughts about staying on. Getting caught in the open and being cut to pieces will nudge them along with their decisions. Most important is that we make sure every man will stand behind us. Go among them and make it clear how important this is."

Castigador sat on the brow of a low hill. Its name was the Spanish version of the Meztec Indian god of the underworld: the Punisher. Not since the *conquistadores* had any punishment been visited upon the residents. Not even the cruel French, under the command of Maxmilian of Habsburg, had harshly dealt with the populace. It took one of their own, a fellow Mexican, Gustavo Carvajal, El Rey del Norte, to bring fire, the knife, and the gun to the people of Castigador.

They came out of the rising sun, as the bandit army had done at the *hacienda* of Rancho Pasaje. Few citizens had crawled from their beds at that hour. The outlaw horde descended on the surprised folk with yells and the thunderous crash of gunfire. Quartero Ybarra dropped the lead rope to his burro and ran between two low adobe houses. Laden down with huge jars of oil pressed in the local olive groves, the animal stood stupidly while the bandits raced past the first houses on the eastern edge of town.

Clay vessels shattered on both sides of the small beast of burden, and it went to its knees in a lake of olive oil, shot through the heart and both lungs. Quartero Ybarra impotently cursed the howling swarm and shrank further back in the passageway. Hinges creaked on a door in the side of one house, and an arm thrust a shotgun into Ybarra's face.

"Here," a voice from inside growled. "If you won't fight for yourself, fight for your sainted mother, who still lives in this village."

"Wha—What are you going to do, Bernardo?" Quartero asked of his childhood friend.

"I have an old rifle in here. I will use it to kill any of these *cabrones* who enter my house. The *patrón* warned us of this, you know," Bernardo prompted.

Ybarra felt shame flush his face. "I do know," he admitted as he reluctantly took the shotgun. "Only, I don't know how to shoot a gun."

"With that, all you need is to cock the hammer, point, and pull the trigger. Do it now," Bernardo added as he pointed toward the street.

Galvanized with sudden fear, Ybarra turned to see two of the bandits rushing at him. He fumblingly eared back both hammers and awkwardly pointed the scattergun at his enemies. He closed his eyes at the same moment his finger jerked both triggers.

Recoil knocked Quartero from his feet. The jolt of his butt against the hard ground opened both eyes. He saw one bandit as a headless corpse, still on its feet, the other had an ugly red smear where his chest should have been. The door opened again, and a sisal-fiber mesh bag clunked at his side.

"Reload, idiot," Bernardo growled.

Ybarra stared in awe at the dead men and fiddled nervously with the barrel latch. The shotgun popped open and extracted the spent brass shells. Ybarra crossed himself, and his lips moved in prayer as he inserted fresh casings. He had barely closed the breech when a hardcase on horseback pounded into the open space. The animal reared and threw off the man's aim.

Ybarra fired a single barrel this time. It took the horse in the chest, and it went down squealing. Its rider managed to roll free and came to his boots glaring hatred. Quartero Ybarra put his second load in the gun hawk's chest. From inside he heard Bernardo's rifle discharge. Strangely, he began to feel good about his ability. Then three more *bandidos* showed up and blasted Ybarra into eternity.

* * *

Gustavo Carvajal had flecks of froth at the corners of his mouth. He waved his fisted .45 Mendoza over his head and shouted somewhat incoherently at the bandits gathered around him. "I'll kill the men who broke those jars of olive oil. That's hundreds of pesos wasted!" He whirled on Tomas Diaz. "Find out who it was. Bring them to me." He looked down again at the pool of oil and dead burro, and some of his men would swear he was going to cry.

A woman's terrified screams came from a house two doors down and drew Carvajal's attention. "Amuse yourselves with the older ones. Save the young things for our friend in Mazatlán," he instructed.

Rapid shots crackled farther into town, near the central plaza. Carvajal remounted and started that way. So far the raid had gone well. These *peons* must have been warned. Someone had been keeping watch in the bell tower and given the alarm. Seven men had been killed so far, with thirteen wounded. Twenty of the villagers had died. Humberto Regales had been right. Martine y Garcia had armed his retainers. And they had fought back. Not skillfully but with a will.

No matter, he decided. They would all die anyway. Near the Plaza de Armas, he saw more white-clad bodies sprawled in the dirt. After the ignominious bombing of his camp his men would be ruthless, he felt certain. No man could tolerate such an insult. He reined in as the big glass window of the *cantina* came flying outward, accompanied by the fat bartender.

"Hola, cantinero," he called to the dazed apron. "Don't tell me you are closed for the day? My men have a great thirst."

Dusting off his scraped hands, the barkeep came to his boots. He read pure malevolence in the slightly crossed obsidian eyes that bored into him a moment before Carvajal's bullet. Jerked back on his heels, the barman staggered drunkenly and put a big, soft hand over the hole in his belly. He groaned weakly.

"You have killed me, *Señor.* Why?" He didn't live long enough to hear El Rey del Norte's laughing answer.

Some of Carvajal's men busied themselves stacking some beautiful, well-made furniture in the street outside the shop next door. El Rey ambled his mount over and bent to appraise it.

"This is of good quality. Is it made here?" he asked Pedro Chacon.

"It was, Excellency. The man who carved it is dead."

"Oh, well. See that it is loaded in carts and hauled to Hacienda la Fortuna. Those padded chairs look comfortable."

"It is fine leather, Excellency, with horsehair stuffing," Diaz explained like a furniture salesman.

"They are fit for an emperor, no?" El Rey demanded.

"Most certainly. You will treasure them, I am sure."

"So, then. Let's get on with this. Empty out every building, every last thing. We'll take it all. Then burn this place to the ground. Not one stick, one block of adobe standing on another. I have ordered all the young women to be saved for the *putarias* of Mazatlán. Kill all of the men and boys, the old people and babies. But . . . take your time. Enjoy your work."

With a shots of exuberance, the bandits set to their tasks with a will. The destruction, rapine, and slaughter grew terrible in Castigador. El Rey set up his headquarters in the church. He amused himself tormenting the elderly priest with blasphemous artocities, committed by his men upon the altar. At last, after hours of suffering and horror for the people of Castigador, Carvajal oversaw the murder of the remaining few and rode out, highly contented.

22

Following his new plan, Smoke Jensen and the Mexican volunteers arrived at the small village of Pueblo Viejo—Old Town—third of Martine's villages. At Smoke's direction, they set about at once to fortify it. At first, the *alcalde* offered protest when the newly trained soldiers came to conscript all of the adobe blocks in his workyard. He made a good profit selling them to himself for municipal projects. Now they were to be pressed into use to construct connecting walls between the outermost buildings of the community. In high dudgeon, he went to complain to the man in charge.

At the first sight of Smoke Jensen, the mayor began to regret his hot and hasty decision. The man was huge, looking up on him from *Alcalde* Torrez's five foot five. Those gray eyes were almost colorless. At least until he blurted out his objections to the confiscation.

"You cannot do this. It is my livelihood you are taking away," Torrez whined.

Smoke Jensen turned a bleak visage toward the mayor. Glacial ice formed in those large, fulminating eyes. Torrez cringed inwardly. Smoke's words turned his innards to jelly. "You'd rather we left you to El Rey del Norte? He'd take your life, not just the product of your labor."

"But I must pay my workmen. I must have some form of compensation," Torrez babbled.

Smoke Jensen reached out in a friendly-appearing gesture and clamped one big hand on the narrow shoulder of Mayor Torrez. While he spoke in a low, reasonable tone, he began to squeeze. With each word the pressure grew greater.

"You must understand the point of all of this, Mr. Mayor. We are here at the direction of your *Patrón,* Don Miguel. He has instructed us to fortify this village against attack by the self-proclaimed bandit king, Gustavo Carvajal. We know that this attack is certain. Now, you wouldn't want the deaths of your fellow citizens on your hands, would you?"

By that point, Torrez had gone to his knees. Tears stung his eyes. His mouth flapped like an outhouse door in a stiff wind. Only a pained gasping came out. "You do comprehend what I'm saying, right?" Smoke asked.

Surrender shone in the frightened eyes of Torrez. "Go—go ahead."

Rapidly, the adobe bricks disappeared. Willing hands mixed a slush of the clay soil to serve as mortar. The walls rose swiftly. Smoke turned his attention to other matters.

"We need women who can quickly weave coarse nets of canvas strips and sisal rope. Also," he told Juan Murial, "get men to work with picks and shovels to dig pits outside the town. Stagger them, some far out, some in close. A few right across the only road we'll keep open. Rig some spiked logs to drop over the walls to clear off Carvajal's men if they're smart enough to bring scaling ladders, Also, I want a trench, five foot wide, dug ten foot deep, all the way around town. Set spikes in the bottom and line the sides with tinder-dry wood."

"You are playing very nasty, *amigo,*" Carbone observed.

"I want to bring an end to this thing." Smoke turned back to the men. "When you have the brush in place, soak it with oil, then cover the whole thing with thin branches, canvas or some cloth, and dirt."

He and Carbone went next to where Martine's trained men were teaching new volunteers how to use firearms taken from Carvajal's outlaw army. They watched in silence for a while, Smoke frequently nodding approval of the teaching methods. Then Carbone asked a question that had been troubling him for a while.

"If we are turning Pueblo Viejo into a walled city, why the nets?"

"We'll put them between buildings, cover them with a layer of dirt to hide them from sight. When and if Carvajal's hard-cases get inside town, they'll do like before, ride in between houses and business places and fire through the windows. This time people inside neighboring buildings can pull up the nets and snag the riders off their horses." Smoke winced on the last two words.

A frown of concern creased Carbone's brow. "Is something wrong, *amigo?*"

"Nothing. A little twinge in my stomach," Smoke dismissed. "Let's go by where Blanco is inventorying the ammunition."

Twenty minutes later Smoke and Carbone strolled outside the squat building where Rudolfo Blanco presided over the amassed supply of ammunition. Smoke removed his hat and mopped at oily sweat on his brow. He found it hard to swallow. He replaced the big sombrero and directed their course toward the brickyard of the mayor.

"I've been thinking about those tile waterspouts the mayor has in his yard. If they could be capped at one end, a stick of giant powder and a couple handfuls of bent nails and scrap metal from the blacksmith could turn them into remarkable weapons."

Carbone grimaced, visualizing the terrible effect of the flying bits of iron. His mood lightened as he took in a serious-faced deputation of small boys, around eleven years of age, who approached them, straw hats in hand, over their hearts. Their spokesman addressed himself to Smoke Jensen.

"Señor, we boys want to help, too."

"There's not much youngsters your size can do," Smoke tried tactfully.

"Oh, yes, you will see. We can keep watch. Give signals when we see the *bandidos* coming. We can bring water and food to the men working or fighting on the walls."

After witnessing the remains of wholesale butchery in Merced, Smoke Jensen retained no doubts as to the savagery of Carvajal's bandit army. Nearly a third of the children had been killed. Still, he couldn't expose them to the full fury of so implacable an enemy.

"You could not expose yourself to their fire. And never be seen in the open. They have killed other boys like you."

"Tienenos hondas, Señor," the small spokesman said proudly, displaying his slingshot. "We can protect ourselves."

Such courage and confidence should not be scorned, Smoke thought. "All right, you can fetch and carry for the men. Until the fighting starts. I'll think about using some of you for sentinels."

"Gracias, Señor. Llamado Raul. This is Gaspar, Felipe, Miguel, Armando. We will serve you well."

Smoke bent to pat the lad on his head, and a sharp shaft of pain speared through his stomach. Beads of perspiration broke out on his forehead and upper lip. For a moment, the world whirled around him.

"What is it, *amigo?* " Carbone asked, concern coloring his words. "You are suddenly so pale, white as snow in the Sierra."

"I—ah——I don't know. Something hurting inside. I've got to hit the outhouse," Smoke declared brokenly.

He made a hurried dash and made it to the chicksale barely in time. A terrible stench accompanied the gush of fluid from his body. Wave after wave of knifing pains assailed his intestines and dizziness robbed him of any awareness of his surroundings. Chills came next.

Smoke's teeth chattered and his shoulders quaked. He burned on the inside and froze on his exposed skin. Another wash of watery matter ran from his body. Again the slivers of agony attacked him. He had heard of such ailments. Often the condition came from eating tainted pork or corned beef. Weakness tried his patience. Two more onsets of the fetid discharge occurred before the malady eased off. Intensely weary and shaken, Smoke left the outhouse. His throat and mouth clamored for water. A glance at his reflection in a glass window revealed a ghastly pallor. Carbone came to him, worry painted on his brown face

"You are sick, my friend. Have you eaten something bad?"

"I don't know. I'm having gas pains, then cramps and all I did in there was pass water."

Carbone's grave expression conveyed his grim news to Smoke. "Dysentery. It is common in our country. It comes from bad water, or uncooked foods that are not raised properly or cleaned well. Somehow it has taken a hold of you."

"I haven't time to be sick," Smoke protested.

"All the same, you are," Carbone said simply.

Smoke Jensen never had a cold, let alone major illness. Gunshot wounds or the result of a furious fight were all that ever laid him low. He experienced an unaccustomed helplessness at the thought of his condition.

"What can I do?" He gave in at last.

"Lie down, rest. Take lots of liquids, everything must be boiled first. And something to force the sickness out of you," Carbone advised.

"There's a doctor here?" Smoke asked hopefully.

"There is an old woman who dispenses herbs and medicinal teas. I will bring her to you. Meanwhile, old friend, find a place to rest, go to bed . . . and keep a chamber mug close at hand."

Smoke took a corner room in the *posada*. It contained a large, comfortable bed, an armoire, a dresser and a washstand. The thunder mug sat prominently on a lower shelf of the comode. Smoke eyed it with resentment. He drank three clay cups of water and sat on the bedside. Within a minute the cramps returned, then the rumbling in his bowels.

He made it to the chamber pot only a fraction of a second before he unloaded again. The dizziness nearly knocked him over. When the spell passed, he returned to the bed, pulled off his boots and cartridge belt and lay out on the covers. He had almost managed to drift into sleep when a soft knock sounded at the door.

He rose and admitted Mrs. Martine. "I heard you bad been taken with the dysentery," she announced in a practical manner. "I have come to care for you."

"*Señora,* you have your children to look after, your husband's needs," Smoke protested.

Consuelo Martine raised a hand to silence him. "We owe you much for coming to our aid, Smoke Jensen. I will tend to your needs. There will be someone here at all times. Now, you need to drink more water, and take this herb tea. It will wash out your system."

"It's been fairly well washed out already," Smoke observed wryly.

Smoke Jensen awakened without any memory of having gone to sleep. No, he had lost consciousness, his mind supplied. Sometime during the afternoon, racked by alternating chills and fever, his body dehydrated by diarrhea, he had simply dropped into blackness. He stirred and ran his tongue over dry, cracked lips. Shakily, he reached for a clay cup of water on the bedside table.

"Please, *Señor,* let me help you with that," a strange woman's voice urged him.

Smoke turned his head to the right and concentrated on focusing his eyes. He didn't see Consuelo Martine as expected.

Instead, he gazed owlishly at a slender young woman with an angelic face, dominated by hypnotic eyes. She rose from the straight-back chair and came to him. She took the cup and pressed it to his lips, giving Smoke a close-up of her lush bosom.

His thirst abated, Smoke tried to speak. *"Señora* Martine?" he croaked.

"She is with her family. Resting."

"She was here a while ago," Smoke pressed.

A radiant smile, touched with sadness, lighted the beauty's face. "That was yesterday, *Señor."*

"Who are you?"

"I am called Mirabella. I—I don't deserve to be serving you, *Señor."*

"Say, now, what's this?"

She cast her gaze to the floor. "The people of Pueblo Viejo say that I am a fallen woman."

"Hummm." Smoke considered this a moment. She certainly had all the best qualifications for the position. He held no prejudice against ladies of the evening. She could be whatever she wanted to be, so long as she helped him get over this infuriating sickness.

"What is it you are supposed to do?" Smoke asked.

"To see that you get your herbs, *Señor.* I must mix some now and brew a tea. Also I am to help you to—ah—to—ah . . ." Her embarrassed glance cut to the chamber pot.

"I can take care of that on my own. If I can't, what I need is a diaper," Smoke answered gruffly.

Mirabella looked relieved. "Can you eat, *Señor?"*

"I don't know if I can hold it in place," Smoke answered honestly.

"We can try some soup," Mirabella suggested. "I will help you with it while the herb tea steeps."

Smoke missed part of the Spanish, his head still whirling. He ate the soup, and lost it five minutes later. He also found to his shock that he could barely hold himself upright over the basin on the washstand. He rinsed his mouth and returned to the bed. Mirabella helped him sip the tea, and he lay back with a determined effort not to groan. The room swam and he slept.

A huge grizzly bear chased Smoke Jensen through the tall pines and slender aspens. No matter how he zigged or zagged, the bear kept to his trail. Smoke felt himself growing weaker. A quick glance over his shoulder showed the bear to have gained fifty feet on him. The big clawed paws reached for him, almost a come-here gesture. Smoke tripped over a fallen tree and fell hard on the ground. The bear closed in, saliva dripped from its huge, pointed teeth. Smoke could feel the animal's fetid breath on his cheek . . .

. . . And he snapped awake. For a moment the ceiling of plastered *viegas* swirled in a mad spiral. Then it steadied and Smoke found himself clear-headed for the first time in . . . how long? He looked for Mirabella and found her standing behind the high-back wooden chair, in which sat Consuelo Martine.

"You had a bad dream," *Señora* Martine told him.

Smoke produced a weak smile; the grizzly still danced in his head. "I remember some of it," he rasped.

He propped himself on one elbow and reached for the water cup, got it without assistance. It felt marvelous as it trickled down his parched throat. He drank it all, wanted more.

"The worst is over. You will be weak for a, while, but you will live," *Señora* Martine advised.

"I . . . came close to dying."

"Yes, and in more than your dream, Smoke Jensen. You must eat. Rebuild your strength."

"How long has it been?"

"Three days after the day you became sick."

"I owe you a lot. And you, Mirabella. The old woman who provided the herbs. I must pay her," Smoke added.

"They were given freely, to heal you. There is no need."

"I insist." Smoke sat up, found himself bare to the waist and quickly covered his torso with a damp, rumpled sheet. "Was I much of a burden?"

"No. The crisis came yesterday. You were delirious, could not leave the bed. But the herbs purged you," *Señora* Martine informed him.

"Couldn't leave . . ." Smoke became aware that he had a fresh, scrubbed clean scent about him.

"Mirabella tended to you," *Señora* Martine said to ease his obvious embarrassment.

In half an hour, after the ladies had excused themselves, Smoke was up and dressed. He ravenously ate two bowls of thick soup and demolished a stack of half a dozen tortillas. He could feel the energy pouring back into him.

Shortly before sundown he stepped out into the courtyard of the inn. The cooling air tantalized his nostrils. Carbone rose from a stone bench and came to him.

"We were worried," he stated simply.

"I was too sick to worry," Smoke admitted. "I hope I'm never so helpless again."

To Smoke's surprise, Carbone produced an amused smile. "Foreign visitors to our more attractive seaports have taken to calling it Montezuma's Revenge."

Smoke gave in to the humor of it. "I don't suppose our sawed-off friend, Carvajal, had anything to do with it."

"No. It is as I told you before. Something in the water or the food you consumed. It is important that everything be well cooked, the water boiled."

"The voice of experience?" Smoke asked lightly.

"Yes. No one is immune. It can strike anywhere. Now, let me tell you how the training is going."

"Let me sit down first," Smoke proposed.

For the next twenty minutes, Carbone brought Smoke up to date on progress in the village. He concluded with, "The men are filling bags with dirt to raise the level of the low wall to the east. When that is done, everything will be in readiness."

"You've done well," Smoke praised his friend. "I'm sorry I haven't been able to help more."

"The news that you are well has raised spirits already, *amigo*. Just knowing you are on your feet is a great help. Now, are you up to a real supper? No more of that foul-tasting roots and bark and crushed beetles, or Consuelo's famous chicken soup."

"I think I can handle it. I want to talk with both of you, and the men we've picked to lead. Four days of a complete blank leave me with the uneasy feeling that Carvajal has given us all the time we can expect."

23

"Martine y Garcia is a menace," Gustavo Carvajal announced forcefully to his gathered subordinates. "I am convinced that he will continue to resist until he loses everything. So be it! Tell the men that the fiesta is over. They have gorged themselves and drunk to stuporousness for a week. They are to start preparations immediately to attack the last of the villages on Rancho Pasaje."

"Our informants in Santa Rita have told us that Martine is making a fortress out of Pueblo Viejo." Humberto Regales gave his leader the bad news.

"How is this?" Carvajal asked coldly.

"They have built walls between all of the outer buildings. There are firing parapets behind them. The big *gringo,* Smoke Jensen, is directing everything like a general. He's made the *peons* into an army."

"He has an army? What about my army?" Carvajal snapped.

"We are two hundred ten strong as of this morning, Excellency," Ignacio Quintero informed him.

"Will we be any stronger this time tomorrow, or the day after?"

"Who is to say, Excellency? There are men coming in all the time."

"Humm. So, we wait awhile. To the end of this week. We will attack on Sunday morning, just in time for Mass, eh?"

Although greatly weakened, Smoke Jensen made an inspection of the defensive works the next morning. Warm fall sun on his back did wonders to restore him. By noon he felt nearly his old self. He took the noon meal with his friends.

"You've done a good job," he praised. "There isn't anything I would change. All we have to do is wait. We could use a little scout-around to see Carvajal's degree of readiness."

"I'll send some of the *vaqueros*," Martine offered. "They know how to get around unseen."

"No. I think I need to do this myself."

"Impossible, Smoke," Carbone protested. "You nearly died only days ago. You are in no condition to undertake any long ride around Carvajal's army."

"Esteban is right, Smoke," Martine added his support. "Think what would happen if the dysentery came back."

"It's not," Smoke said decisively. "I'm drinking only boiled water and peeled, cooked vegetables. No more flirting with Montezuma. Besides, I figure to reduce the odds a bit on this trip, spread a little worry among the hardcases."

Sighing, Carbone cut his eyes to Martine, who shared his expression of resignation. Short of tying him down, they could do nothing to stop Smoke Jensen.

After Smoke's departure, four spies, in the employ of Gustavo Carvajal, managed to evade discovery and sneak out of Pueblo Viejo. Once certain they had not been followed, they stopped to decide their course of action. One made a troublesome suggestion.

"It will be easy. He will not be expecting us. We can sneak

up and kill Smoke Jensen and take his head to El Rey del Norte for the five thousand peso reward."

"You are crazy. Have you not seen or heard of the terrible speed of his gun?" one of the quartet objected. "We would not stand a chance."

"Yes, we do. He has to sleep sometime. We can sneak up then and all shoot into him at once."

"I say we go make our report on what has been done to the village. It is important for El Rey to know these things."

"You, too, Chatto?" the bloodthirsty one said sadly. "Listen to me. How much bigger our reward if we kill Smoke Jensen too? Think about that, *hombre.*"

"You have a point, Geraldo. It would be like opening a big old safe and finding something in it," Alberto suggested.

"Exactly. In our case it will be a big stack of ten-peso gold pieces," Geraldo described for them.

"Still, I think, the report . . ."

"Be quiet, Chatto," Alberto griped. "I say we can do it. You are ready to lead us, Geraldo?"

"Of a certainty. We can follow him easily. Then tonight we can do it."

"We must do it quickly," Chatto pointed out.

"Of course," Geraldo responded warmly, satisfied he had won over the other three. "That's the way we do it. Quick like a cat, eh?"

Smoke Jensen heard the soft crunch of gravel under bull-hide sandal soles. Quietly he eased back the hammer of his .44, and waited, unmoving. The fire burned low, nothing more than a bed of embers. An owl hooted. Far off another night bird gave a cry of victory as it seized its small prey off the ground. Four youthful figures appeared around the edge of the lighted area. As one they raised the revolvers in their hands and pumped three rounds each into the figure reclining under a blanket.

It jumped and twitched with the impact. In the shocking silence that followed, a voice sounded eerie as it came from a dark jumble of boulders. "Picked the wrong target. I'm over here."

Horror filled Chatto as all four turned at once, raising the muzzles of their .45 Mendozas. Bright yellow orange lighted a crevice in the nearest boulder as a powerful Winchester .45-70-500 Express fired at them. Alberto screamed and went down, shot through the hips. It had been a lucky shot, Smoke Jensen knew as he released the end of the twine attached to the trigger.

Hot lead howled off rock as the traitors of Pueblo Viejo blasted in response to the wounding shot. By then, Smoke had circled from the jumble of rocks and appeared at the edge of firelight on their right flank.

"Not your night," he told them, then shot Chatto through the chest.

Immediately he dove into the covering darkness and crawled away from the spot. Geraldo and his friend, the surviving pair, reacted instantly. Frantically they emptied their six-guns in the wrong direction. Silence came, broken by the click of their cylinders as they reloaded and soft sobs from the wounded Alberto.

"Can you still shoot?" Geraldo asked him.

"Yes. I think I can. If someone can sit me up, against those rocks."

"Do it, Valdez," Geraldo commanded.

"I think this is crazy," Valdez protested. "We should take Alberto and get away from here."

"Wise words," Smoke said from behind them.

They whirled together. Geraldo fired a split second before Smoke. His bullet came close enough to Smoke that he could feel the wind of its passage. It clipped bark from a tree and howled off into the night. Smoke's slug took Geraldo in the stomach. He went to his knees. In desperation, Valdez discharged his Mendoza wildly. Bullets peppered the air. Two cracked close by Smoke's ear, and he shot the panicked spy between the eyes. Smoke started forward to where Geraldo tottered and tried feebly to raise his six-gun.

A shot blasted from the base of the rocks. It tore skin over the top of Smoke's left shoulder. Careless, he blamed himself. He had not been watching the wounded Alberto. Must still be fog in his brain from his illness. He noticed Alberto now, .44 tracking onto the pelvis-shattered traitor.

Wide-eyed in terror, Alberto threw out his hands in appeal, palms facing Smoke Jensen. "No!" he shrieked.

Smoke's bullet punched a neat hole through Alberto's left palm before it smacked into his chest and burst his heart. He gave a mighty shudder and relaxed against the rocks in death.

"You knew we were after you," Geraldo panted through his agony.

"I saw you go over the wall," Smoke told him. "Kept an eye on you from then on."

"We—we walked into a trap."

"You were stupid. And I suspect greedy," Smoke told him without pity.

Geraldo tried to speak again, but a fountain of blood welled up in his throat and spilled from his lips. He bent at the waist and ended up a human arch, with his forehead on the ground.

"Carvajal needs to pick a better caliber of men," Smoke Jensen observed to the dead.

Midmorning heat made the bullet scrape sting on Smoke's shoulder. He endured it until he identified the type of moss he wanted, removed it from the tree, and soaked it in water. This he applied and the discomfort reduced to a level he could handle. Having hovered so close to death recently,

Smoke thought about the close scrapes he had endured over the years.

There had been too many, he allowed. Far and away he saw the figure of Preacher standing in a clearing and a skinny, if wide-shouldered, kid looking up at him in awe.

"You mean you can make the hurt go out of a cut or some-thin' with that?" the young Smoke Jensen asked.

"Sure's shootin'," Preacher said. "Ol' Injun trick. They use roots and herbs and such for medicine. Now our fancy doc-tors pooh-pooh that sort of thing. But it's worked for the Cheyenne an' Blackfeet an' such for more years than I can think about. Say you got a big head from some pop-skull at Rendezvous. You gather a little red willow bark, scrape the lining off of the inside, and pound it in a mortar. Mix it with some coffee or such-like and swaller her down. Next thing you know, the headache is gone."

"You know most about everything, don't you, Preacher?"

"I wouldn't say that, youngin'. But I know a little some-thin' about most things. Now lemme put this moss on your head there. Sure that fall from the tree didn't make you a little addlepated?"

"Huh? I'm not dizzy or anything, if that's what you mean. Does that sting?"

"Nope."

"Then I'm ready," young Smoke offered.

To this day, a small white scar remained on his forehead from where he'd struck a rock after a fall from a bee tree. The multiple stings he had received, in an attempt to raid the honey in the tree, Preacher treated with a paste of alum and willow bark. Smoke smiled fondly at the recollection. If he hadn't been so light, a condition that mountain man cooking soon rectified, Preacher had sworn he would have been squashed like a bug when he hit the ground. Close call number one.

If one didn't count his childhood. Smoke rarely looked beyond the mental veil he had put between life with and life before Preacher. Now he admitted as he rode along that it had been something out of that buried past that had opened his compassionate nature to Bobby Harris. For the hundredth time, Smoke wondered how Sally was taking to the boy.

Yes, there had been days of danger, violence and death when he had traveled the far fringes of the frontier with Preacher. Some of his greatest memories of beauty and serenity came during those years, too. Smoke mulled over the dangerous time, many years later, when that lunatic German count had set up an expedition to hunt him down like a wild animal. That had been one hell of a cattle-buying trip.

He recalled the troubles that had taken him to Montana to settle the hash for Clint Black. It had started out as a trail drive of 3,500 head to a buyer in Montana. Smoke had taken literal cowboys along, lads hired from local ranches aged from fourteen to sixteen. Some had gotten murdered by riders for the Circle .45 Ranch of Clint Black. Others became men in the fight to avenge their friends and end the rein of terror conducted by Black. His ruminations brought Smoke to a surprising conclusion.

Taken in all, Smoke worked around the burgeoning idea that the essence of growing up, or growing older, is not that one acquires wisdom. Rather that one has memories, a sort of scale in which to balance the experiences of life. If a man could keep that balance level, he could be said to have had a rich life indeed.

Smoke Jensen took a circuitous route to the valley campsite. He arrived to find it deserted. All that remained were the litter, scars, and destruction caused by careless, indifferent men. Smoke searched around and found a few ammunition and food caches. Apparently the outlaw army intended to return. He rigged them with bundles of blasting powder and long fuses. After lighting them, he got well clear and let them blow.

Reasoning rightly that the army was on the move, Smoke chose the direct trail out of the mountains. In the open, he would be more vulnerable, Smoke assumed. He hated to admit it to himself, but his body rebelled against further strain. Less than three days away from delirium and fever, he had already come close to taxing his reserve of energy to the maximum. He pondered the wisdom of heading directly for Pueblo Viejo.

Naah, his fighting spirit urged him. Much better that Carvajal's army arrive to put the village under siege in a demoralized condition. He recalled a story Preacher had told him about the Cheyenne. It had happened in the olden times, before the horse.

Warfare had been carried out then on foot. A Cheyenne war party had set out to revenge some child-stealing by a band of Flatheads, according to Preacher. They made their outward journey without incident. Carefully the leader planned their attack on the village.

While the Flatheads slept, the Cheyennes scaled the lodgepole pine stockade around the enemy camp. Like shadows they flitted through the open spaces between birch bark lodges. "One old man who couldn't sleep got clonked on the noggin," Preacher related. "Other than that, them fellers found all but one of their stolen children and strode out the main gate bold as brass."

They went down a swift river in stolen canoes. The old man survived and described the raiders to his brother Flatheads. A party set out at once. A count of damaged canoes left behind told them the number taken by the Cheyenne. They ran along the bank of the river until they found the place where their enemy had come ashore. Then they took off with the speed of a wolfpack.

"They caught up to the Cheyennes, who were slowed by

the youngins. The fighting was fierce. The Cheyennes broke off and got to a narrow pass that led down out of Flathead country," Preacher told Smoke. "Two of them had been so badly wounded they could not keep on the trail. They stayed behind to hold off the Flatheads while their friends took the kids home.

"Well, sir, their defense was so awesome that the Flatheads lost heart and quit the fight. They never went after the raiding party. The bones of the two heroes were recovered the next summer. Now the point of all that, Smoke, is that even if you are bad hurt, but can still demoralize your enemy, chances are he'll not carry on the fight. Those warriors gave their lives for their brothers, but at such a cost the Flatheads didn't want any part of unwounded Cheyennes."

Smoke Jensen smiled at his reverie. Leave it to old Preacher to have as many parables as the Carpenter from Nazareth. Though Preacher's stories of life and how to live it were a considerable lot more bloody than those told on the shores of Galilee. Which brought Smoke's thoughts around to something that had been nudging him since his bout of dysentery.

He and Sally attended church irregularly at best. Smoke's having been reared and educated for the most part in the High Lonesome, the white man's God seemed not so practical as the beliefs of the Indian tribes he had encountered, or the quiet, often unspoken, reverence of the mountain men. Yet, dredged from his delirium, Smoke held a vague memory of the finger of God reaching out of a cloud to touch him when he lay at his lowest point, teetering on the lip of death. He would have to look into that, ponder it. Perhaps he would even share the imperfectly recalled experience with Sally.

Steeling himself to fatigue and discomfort, Smoke put aside his study of mysticism and directed Sidewinder into a ground-eating lope. He wanted to catch up to Carvajal's army as far from their intended target as possible.

* * *

By his second night out, he knew he could not be far away. The signs had grown fresher, men long in the saddle had grown incautious. Directed by their outlaw natures, lacking the discipline of seasoned soldiers, they began to cast off broken gear, the corn husk wrappings of tamales, papers that had held tortillas. Smoke had a regular trash trail to follow. He made camp early, so as to be able to eat a warm meal and enjoy coffee before darkness fell.

After the meal, his tiny, smokeless fire buried under handfuls of dirt, Smoke settled in to wait. The onset of darkness gave him confirmation of his closeness to the bandit horde. Many fires put an orange glow on the horizon. Once the blazes died down, and the lethargy of midnight settled over the enemy camp, Smoke made his move.

24

True to form, Carvajal had sentries out riding circuit around the camp. Smoke found them as sloppy and inattentive as ever. After careful study of their circuits, and a positive count of numbers, he angled into position to intercept the first of his victims.

Smoke first came upon a pair, who had drifted together to share a smoke, a bottle and some chatter. He worked up a wide lariat loop and dropped it over the both of them when one leaned close to accept a light for his small, crooked cigar.

Sidewinder's jump-start yanked them off their mounts with enough force to drive the air from their lungs. Smoke followed up his advantage by trotting back on them, the line kept taut. The black eye of his .44 muzzle looked down on the pair, who struggled for breath.

"Do you two like what you're doing?" Smoke asked quietly.

"For one, Señor, I have done more pleasant things," a slender, rat-faced individual replied with equal quiet, forcing his lungs to fill again.

"Would you like to go back to doing them? Think hard. Your life depends on it."

The other hardcase worked his mustache-encircled mouth into a sneer of contempt. "You would not use your gun, Señor."

"No. I'd get down and slit your throats," Smoke told him coldly.

Frightened, the rodent-faced one blurted, "He means it, Anuncio."

Anuncio Conti spat at the hoofs of Smoke's horse. "He hasn't the *cojónes* for that."

Still covering them with the .44 Colt, Smoke dismounted and crouched close to Conti. His bowie appeared in his left hand, the keen edge glowed a wicked blue in the pale light of the new moon.

"I've got balls enough," Smoke told him levelly. "Do you want to try me?"

"Jesus, Maria, y José," Conti's small companion squeaked. "Look what your mouth has brought on us, Anuncio."

Still defiant, Conti snarled at him, "And you run your mouth like a frightened woman, Gabriel. Do your worst, *gringo*."

Smoke laid the barrel of his .44 against Conti's temple with enough force to make a deep give in the bone. Gabriel watched wide-eyed. He swallowed with difficulty.

"It is he who said those things, *Señor,* not I. I would be most grateful to leave this madman's army and go back to my home."

"And where is that?"

"Jalisco."

"What did you do there?"

"I—I was a—a bandit."

"Too bad," Smoke informed him, then batted Gabriel alongside the head.

Quickly he stripped them naked and tied them with short lengths of rope. Smoke hefted them belly down over their saddles and secured ankles to wrists. The small one would awaken with a powerful headache. Conti would wake up in Hell. That accomplished, he faded off into the night.

* * *

Three boys, not a one over seventeen, drew comfort from the presence of one another. They had come because their fathers had answered a call to join El Rey del Norte. In the presence of the hard-bitten outlaws they swaggered and made loud noises about what they would do to Miguel Martine and Esteban Carbone. Alone on sentry duty they admitted to themselves that it was all show. They sought each other in the night to inflate their courage. What they found was Smoke Jensen.

"Oje, gatitos," Smoke called softly to them from a thicket of brush. "Over here, little kittens," he repeated the taunt.

Curious, yet not alarmed, certain this was one of the older men who had taken to making life in camp miserable for the trio, they walked toward the brush, leading their horses. When they drew close, Smoke emerged from his shadowy hiding place, a .44 Colt in each hand.

"You are about to become very suddenly dead, unless you do exactly what I tell you. Get on those horses and ride out of here. Don't even look back. Keep going until you get to wherever it is you came from."

One brighter boy made walleyes. "You are the big *gringo*, the one His Excellency always curses, no? Smoke Jensen?"

"Yes. Now that we've met, I think it would be wise for you to leave this place while you still can. A life of crime is one too short for you."

His Spanish fell strangely on their ears, his vocabulary limited, but his message came across loud and clear. "Oh, I agree, absolutely. I am going now, *Señor* Jensen, watch me." He turned away from his friends and the frightening mountain of Smoke Jensen and put a foot in one stirrup.

"He is even bigger than El Rey said," one of the remaining lads whispered to his friend.

From his height of a mere five-four, the last one could only nod dumbly. His feet found purpose, and he moved his boots in the direction of his horse. Smoke racked back the hammer of one .44 and put the reluctant one in motion.

"What about our fathers?" the already mounted boy asked. "They made us come."

"If they don't have as much sense as you three, then they have a good chance of dying with El Rey del Norte," Smoke told them. "Now be on your way."

"Ay, sí, sí, believe me, we're going."

Smoke suppressed a chuckle as they directed their mounts out of sight at a brisk trot. Then his lips formed a grim line as he thought of the other sentries out there in the night.

Gustavo Carvajal awoke in a screaming rage when he learned the disposition of the night guards. Of the twenty-five on duty, five of them had deserted during the night. Ten were dead. The rest had been left in degrading, humiliating conditions. One had been staked out in the grass. Humberto Regales translated the message left in English.

"Next time he'll be left over an anthill."

"Better if he had been, this time," Carvajal ranted. "That way the men would hunger for revenge. I am right, Humberto. We must march on this fortress village of Martine y Garcia and muddy the soil with the people's blood."

One of Regales' men brought in the not-so-arrogant punk at that point. His eyes liquid with fear, he repeated the message given him by Smoke Jensen. Carvajal's face became a ruby of fury.

"Take this puppy out and put a riding crop to him," he screamed. "Teach him respect for his emperor."

"Excellency, it is not the messenger, it's the message," Regales reminded him.

"Oh, yes, so it is. Never mind whipping him," he countermanded his earlier order. "Let him walk through camp naked as an oyster. That should instruct him in how to properly deliver a message." Carvajal paused then, a finger beside his nose. "I must say, this man, Jensen, has a way with his tongue."

El Rey del Norte had cause to awake screaming the next morning also. This time it was in abject terror. Brought out of deep slumber by an oddly familiar, wet-copper odor, Gustavo Carvajal opened his eyes to see Ignacio Quintero staring at him from the foot of the bed. His mouth was twisted in a grimace of horror and pain, and his body was nowhere to be seen. The head sat on the bed, inches from Carvajal's feet.

Quintero had been assigned the duty of supervising the sentries, Carvajal recalled after his initial shock lessened. The man who would be king had believed that this precaution would prevent any repetition of the desertions and deaths of the previous night. Deeply shaken by this evidence of his error, Carvajal gasped and gulped his way from fear into rage.

Quickly he pulled on boots and burst from his sleeping quarters into the front of the tent and on out the flap to confront two startled guards. "Bring Regales and Diaz, have the men called together here. At once," he demanded.

Sullenly, the bandit army assembled in front of their leader's tent. Many suffered from hangovers. Most were groggy from being jerked out of a deep sleep. All had heard of the terrible events of the night. Not a few had second thoughts about the wisdom of following Carvajai. Before the day was over, several of these would find opportunities to turn away from the route of march and speed off to safer climes.

"*¡Compañeras!*" Carvajal shouted above the murmur of uncertain voices. "I have come to a momentous decision. We must continue our advance on Pueblo Viejo. As you know, our numbers have been reduced over the past few days. I call on all of you with friends or family willing to join us to go round them up. Tell them of the brutal murders of our friends. Tell them of the outrages of this *gringo cabrón pistolero,* Smoke Jensen. He is but one man.

"He can be captured and made to pay for what he has done," Carvajal concluded.

"Do you mean only one man has been killing our night riders?" an astonished bandit inquired.

"No." Carvajal quickly reversed himself. "There must be a dozen men crawling through the grass like snakes. But we are men, not the lowliest of creatures. They can be defeated."

"What about the walls at Pueblo Viejo?" another hardcase asked.

Who let that out? Such knowledge, in the hands of these men, could be dangerous. It gave Carvajal pause to consider before he answered.

"They will be of no consequence to us. As I said, we must continue on to Pueblo Viejo. Those walls cannot be well settled as yet, nor very thick. Therefore, we will take a day right here to devise a means of defeating them." Warming to the idea blooming in his head, Carvajal spun out his new aspirations to his followers.

"We will build a large ram, on wheels, to smash the walls. Others of you are to find suitable materials and make scaling ladders." Carvajal congratulated himself for having read those ancient books on siege warfare. "Then, when all is in readiness, we will advance to victory!"

"*¡Viva el Rey! ¡Viva el Rey!*" Humberto Regales led the cheering.

From the distant brow of a ridge, Smoke Jensen watched the confusion in camp through field glasses. He remained long enough to identify what the flury of activity implied. Two large *carretas* had been connected by makeshift running gear before the men stopped for breakfast. Outriders returned with suitable trimmed logs, and the carpenters among Carvajal's army began to construct a framework atop the carts.

Others he saw at work on ladders. Satisfied that Carvajal would remain in camp until the completion of these projects, Smoke withdrew, mounted Sidewinder, and set off for Pueblo Viejo. By pushing hard, he arrived shortly after darkness.

He found the only gate secured, and he was challenged by a sentry with an old Hopkins and Allen break-top rifle. *"¿Quien passa?"*

Smoke identified himself and rode on in after the gate creaked open. He found Carbone and Martine in the courtyard of the inn. He greeted them with an easy smile.

"You have them well organized. Even the gate guard challenged me with a very military 'Who goes there?' Good, because it's going to be needed," Smoke added, growing serious again.

"Sit down, my friend, you look tired," Carbone invited, his face showing his concern.

Smoke settled in a large, carved wooden chair and leaned into the welcome cushion. Smoothly, with pauses at important points, he gave an account of his activities since leaving Pueblo Viejo. Martine cursed the traitors, and informed Smoke that they had been missed the next day. Naturally they had no idea that the four men had made an attempt on Smoke's life.

"Hardly an attempt, I'd say," Smoke assured him dryly. "Amateurs," he dismissed.

He went on to describe what he had observed in the valley camp and the destruction of the cached supplies. Then he got into his thinning of the ranks and they listened raptly. Smoke concluded with a simple statement that summed up the fate of Ignacio Quintero.

"The last thing I did was deprive Carvajal of the services of one of his lieutenants."

Carbone and Martine exchanged surprised glances. "How did you manage that? Did he desert his master?" Martine asked.

"In a manner of speaking. I'm not right proud of what I did, but it's had its effect. Carvajal's gone into camp on the plain east of here to build siege machines."

"Come on, *hombre*," Carbone urged, eager to learn. "What did you do?"

"I left Quintero's head on the foot of Carvajal's bed," Smoke admitted, eyes averted.

"*¡Que bueno,* Smoke!" Mactine rejoiced. "That was a brilliant tactic."

"Oh, yes. Cold, calculating, absolutely guaranteed to terrify. Also totally lacking in any redeeming human quality."

Martine sobered. He cut his eyes to Smoke with a serious demeanor. "We are at war, *amigo*. We may talk of the enemy general as a buffoon, a poseur, but he is not the least bit more harmless by that. He has to be deeply shattered by that, unsure of himself. In a war, my friend, one must do what must be done to win."

"It could backfire on us. What if he calls for no quarter? Not spare even the young women and boys?"

Carbone knitted his brows, weighing his remarks. "We are a different people from you *Anglos*. It is our Indian ancestry, I suppose. If Carvajal declares no quarter, it will only make our people fight the harder. They, too, will give no quarter. No prisoners. It will be a terrible slaughter."

"Yes, damn it, and I thought that's what you sent for me to help prevent. I'm sorry. I may have brought more trouble right to your door."

Martine brightened. He rose and placed an arm around Smoke's shoulder. "We'll ask the people. In the morning, you can tell them what we have discussed and let them make the decision. Any who wish to escape will be free to go. No conditions, no prejudice. They will remain my people, and Carbone's. Now get something to eat, take a few drinks with us, and have a good night's sleep."

He had his mind set. He would do it this morning. Nothin' could stop him. He'd show 'em all that he belonged. Wrestling with the heavy saddle in the chill air and soft gray light of pre-dawn over the Rockies, Bobby Harris left the tack room and rocked on unsteady boots to the corral. He had already picked out the one of his string that he would use.

He had worked with the critter just like Smoke Jensen wanted it. Talked soft, made gooey sounds and always had a supply of rock candy or a carrot from the winter garden. If any horses had been gentled, this one had. Bobby had caught him in a half doze in the darkness and slipped the bridle over his head before the animal knew what happened.

Now he stood tied up close to the snubbing rail, Bobby's lariat double-dallied over the post. He could free it with a flick of the wrist and then let the steamboat go. First he had to put the saddle blanket on and secure the heavy saddle.

For the thousandth time since coming to the Sugarloaf, Bobby cussed his small stature. He wished for a ladder to help heave the heavy leather contrivance onto the back of the quiet horse. Not quiet for long, he thought ruefully.

With a lot of grunts and strain, Bobby got the saddle in place. The pad was only slightly askew. He tightened the cinch straps and put one foot in the stirrup. Instantly Favor— officially No. 57-A— brought up his head. Bobby's small hands could not reach the horn, so he pulled on latigo ties to swing himself aboard.

Once settled in the hurricane deck, he shivered in antici-pation as Favor gave a pre-emptory snort. Bobby leaned for-ward and loosed the lariat. Favor came alive in a burst of energy that left the boy breathless. Grunting and sorting,

Favor crow-hopped across the corral, head low, nostrils flaring. He tried to sunfish, and Bobby held him with his knees.

A pale, pink band sawed up and down, back and forth on the jagged crests of the eastern mountains. Favor came down stiff-legged and jarred the air from Bobby's lungs. Blackness swam around the boy. He gigged with blunted spurs—the only kind Smoke Jensen would allow. Favor sprang, antelope-like, into the air. He whirled and squealed and snorted. Dust rose in a thick haze.

Bobby's head snapped back and forth. His thin chest burned for want of air. Shoulders bowed, he hung with the rampaging horse, sawing the reins, fighting for control. His vision blurred again, this time with involuntary tears, and he reeled in the saddle, a straw dummy tossed about by satanic force. Sharp, hot pain radiated up from his groin. He sensed unpleasant changes there and had his first serious doubts about the wisdom of his decision.

Not even Rupe Connors had given him so fierce a whupping as his sudden descent on a rising saddle produced. Bobby tasted salt on his tongue and realized his nose was bleeding. Favor became a whirlwind.

Dizzied, Bobby clung with stubborn knees. The next time Favor rose off the ground, Bobby arched his back and hauled on the reins with all his slight strength. To his amazement, Favor came down, not stiff-legged, but in a fast run. Around the corral they streaked.

"Woah, boy, woah," Bobby coaxed. The pace lessened. Favor's head came up. "That's a boy, that's my good boy," the battered lad cooed.

He reined in the sweat-lathered horse, gigged him to a walk, then a trot. Grinning like a ninny, Bobby sat atop the stallion and guided it wherever he wanted. After a few minutes, boy and horse had bonded to the point Bobby started didoes across the center of the corral.

"Bobby Harris, what in the world do you think you are

doing?" Sally Jensen's voice crackled over the corral rail. "You'll get yourself killed."

Grinning despite his pain, Bobby walked Favor over to where she stood. "No, ma'am. I just topped him off. A couple of more goes at it, and he'll be ready to sell."

Sally fussed over him a bit longer, then got him off the horse and into the house. There he listened to a lecture on never handling horses without at least two hands present, while he gobbled down fresh, hot biscuits and wild blackberry jam. Later in the day, he confided his satisfaction to Burt Crocker.

"He durn near split me from crotch to craw, but I did it all on my own."

25

Dressed in his splendid general's uniform, his divisions of troops displaying the ornate feather banners and other regalia of their Aztec ancestors, El Rey del Norte rode at the head of his bandit army. Early the next morning they spilled over a low saddle between two substantial hills that blocked the view from Rancho Pasaje eastward.

At shouted commands, they split into two parts and circled the village. Save for the rumble of hoofs and cartwheels, no other sound broke the daybreak quiet. When Pueblo Viejo had been completely surrounded, Gustavo Carvajal sat his handsome palomino with a smug smile on his face.

"Let them observe our splendor and know fear," he declared to those near him.

Confident that he had halted his powerful force well out of rifle range, he firmly believed this display would have the desired effect. A puff of smoke bloomed over the wall before them, and the King of the North laughed disdainfully. Then he heard the hiss and crack of a bullet and the meaty smack as it struck the chest of his personal standard-bearer. The young bandit dropped the banner and folded over his saddlehorn before falling from his mount.

"*¡Imposible!*" the King of the North blurted.

Already another ball of gray-white appeared on the wall. A moment later the slug struck Carvajal's gaudy, plumed, fore-and-aft hat and sent it spinning from his head. He uttered an unheroic yelp and ordered his men to immediately attack.

Alerted to the outlaw army's approach by small boys serving as lookouts, the defenders of Pueblo Viejo went directly to their assigned positions. Grim-faced, they watched the empty ground over the ramparts. First they saw the youngsters scrambling over the rocks and ravines on their way to safety inside the walls. Then the feathered banners rose over the foreshortened horizon.

Drumming hoofbeats and the squeal of ungreased cart axles increased in volume. Huge, floppy sombreros seemed to rise out of the ground, followed by nodding horses' heads. Reinforced to a strength of 245, the outlaw horde advanced over the saddle and spread out to encompass the village. Below Smoke's feet, the recently made gates slammed shut.

Smoke Jensen cut his eyes from left to right, sized up the defenders standing with him. He gave a nod of assurance and returned his gaze to the east. Lifting his field glasses, he studied the center of Carvajal's line. The little lunatic seemed satisfied enough of where he had halted his troops. No doubt he expected to frighten the people inside the walls. Time to shake him up again, Smoke decided.

He put aside the field glasses and raised his Express rifle. He made a careful estimate of range and adjusted the rear sight. Smoke fitted his cheek to the stock and focused on the circular spot of light in the tang sight. He settled it on a splash of white and a bandolier of ammunition slung across a shallow chest. Then he raised the front sight until the blade centered in the rear peep.

Slowly his linger took up slack. The Winchester .45-70-500 bellowed with authority. Dimly, Smoke Jensen felt the recoil. Already he cycled the lever action and chambered a second round. The slight breeze slowly dispelled the gray haze in front of him, so that he was able to see the standard-bearer pitch from his saddle. Now for the finishing touch.

Smoke Jensen's second long-range shot clipped the fancy general's hat from the head of Gustavo Carvajal. Moments later, the entire double rank of bandits charged downslope toward the narrow valley that lay at the base of the knoll on which Pueblo Viejo had been constructed.

"Looks like I might have riled him some," Smoke observed to Esteban Carbone.

Humberto Regales commanded on the west side. His men swooped down on the town in time with the rest. He developed a sinking sensation as he watched the walls loom over them. It indeed gave the aspect of a fortress. Spears of flame came from the top of the wall, and three of his men cried out as two took bullets in their chests and the third had his horse shot out from under him.

Damn, Regales thought, these peasants had been taught well. When they drew close enough to distinguish individual heads above the parapet, he gave the command to halt and open fire. The superior marksmanship of the bandits showed at once.

Here a rifle fell outside the wall, its owner dead with a bullet through his head. There a man jerked upright and fell backward. Regales quickly noted that all access to the town had been closed off. Even the windows had been bricked up. After three rounds, according to the plan, he ordered the bandits to stop firing, and they rode back out of range and rounded the village to the eastern side.

"We can't get in and they can't get out," he reported to Gustavo Carvajal.

"The ram will destroy that gate," El Rey stated decisively. "Concentrate fire on this side while it is moved into place."

"We charge them again?" Regales asked.

"Yes. Keep them busy."

Now in a crescent shape, the lines of horsemen thundered down on Pueblo Viejo. Spirits ran high and they fired wildly at the walls. Then three bandits abruptly disappeared into the ground, covered by a huge cloud of dust.

Terrible shrieks of men and animals came from the pit that had suddenly opened. Without warning, camouflage covers came off of rifle pits in the grassy meadow, and village men fired point-blank into the advancing enemy.

Smoke Jensen watched with a grim expression while more men and horses plunged to death or maiming in the pits so skillfully hidden. He deeply regretted the harm done to the animals. They weren't responsible for what had necessitated building the terrible traps. He gave the signal and the selected men, those with good throwing arms, began to light and toss out at the enemy the tile tubes with sticks of blasting powder.

Powerful explosions, and whistling shards of scrap metal, provided cover for the men in the rifle pits to withdraw to a small portal cut into the main gate. For all their inexperience, Smoke noted, they made it through the bottleneck with remarkable discipline and no sign of panic. More blasts shattered the air. Smoke took a check on the advance of the battering ram.

"They should reach the pits in the road any time now," he informed Carbone. "Have everyone concentrate fire on the men around the ram."

Three bandits died. More rushed forward, dodging the exposed pits, and came at the walls with scaling ladders. At once the men designated to the task dropped spiked logs over the side. Outlaws screamed and dropped from broken ladders. Several died horribly under the falling logs. Still the ram advanced on the main gate.

Certain of its destruction, Smoke turned to the scaling parties. Rocks were hurled down on them, and a number found the buried trench the hard way. Their screams joined those of others. Suddenly the call rang out to fall back.

Shaken by the ferocity of the resistance, the *bandidos* wasted no time in retreating. They sprinted for their horses and rode out of range. The ram continued toward its objective.

Then fate took a vengeful turn against the defenders of Pueblo Viejo. A horseman blundered into the deep pits in the road, revealing them to the driver of the ram carriage. While man and bone disappeared in a billow of dust, the double *carreta* turned ponderously away from danger and maneuvered around the traps.

Smoke Jensen took a quick count. Fifty-five bodies littered the ground outside the walls. Yet he knew Carvajal had enough men left to continue the attack. And they still had the ram to contend with. It began to look to Smoke as though his idea for a fortified village had turned into a prison for them.

Gustavo Carvajal also made a count of his strength. Less than a hundred fifty now. Part of him found it hard to believe that these peasants could show such fury. Another part wondered why those of his men who had survived remained loyal and had not deserted due to the high loss. Tomas Diaz provided answer to the latter.

"They are good and mad now, Excellency. Friends have been killed and maimed. They taste *peon* blood and want to get to it. We should attack again, at once, not give those in the village time to rest or get fresh ammunition."

"Yes, it is best. And the men on the ram need protection to do their work," Carvajal observed.

A minute later, the bandit army hurtled toward the walls of Pueblo Viejo again. Their battle cry came with a low, animal ferocity that chilled many among the neophytes on the walls.

Smoke Jensen turned to face his friends. "We're not going to hold," he told them bluntly.

"Why not?"

"Most of our men are fighting their first battle. Fear is

going to catch up to them when that ram starts pounding on the gate. If Carvajal manages to get anyone over the wall, it will turn to panic." He considered what he had to say for a moment before he went on. "I want you both to take selected men and fall back to the Plaza de Armas. Alert everyone there and put your men in position."

"But our place is on the wall," Carbone protested.

"I know it's a matter of honor for you. I learned this from the Indians. A man who fights and is wise enough to withdraw to a better position lives to fight again. I'll keep the defenders here as long as I can, then join you."

"It is better if I stay with you," Carbone urged. "Martine can prepare at the plaza. They are his people after all."

Smoke pondered this. "All right. Take the south side, that's where the walls are lowest. I'll stay here."

Gunfire began to crackle along the walls. With a mighty roar, the bandit army closed and began to raise ladders. They took care to avoid the trench, the ladders slanted sharply so that men had to bend forward to ascend. Smoke Jensen stepped to the parapet to look down.

Below he saw that planks had been stripped from outbuildings and used to bridge the trench. Slowly the ram rolled into position. Riders at the end of heavy ropes spurred their horses away from the wall. The arm of the ram swung backward. One of the bandits pulling on it took a round in the shoulder. He jerked in reaction and continued to haul on his rope. At a signal, they let it go.

A loud crack and boom sounded when the heavy head smashed into the thick planks of the gate. Smoke felt the impact through his boots. At once more riders took up the ropes and hauled the ram back again. Shots cracked all around them.

"They're excited, not taking time to aim," Smoke Jensen told Juan Murial.

The wounded man from Merced nodded understanding. "What comes next?"

"We shoot our last round," Smoke told him. He leaned over the inside edge of the battlement and shouted below, "Fire the trench!"

Another tremendous crash came from the gate, while men bent to touch torches to the oil-soaked wood in the trench. Slowly the branches caught fire. Another hollow, shuddering boom came from the gate, accompanied by a splintering sound. Black smoke began to coil up from the trench. Tongues of flame licked high here and there The clothing of the men on the ladders began to smolder.

Spurred by this incentive, the bandits scurried up the ladders with alacrity. They smashed aside the resistance and shouted in triumph when they set foot on the battlements. The ram hammered into the gate again. Hinges creaked and the crossbar splintered. Smoke Jensen looked around and made a painful judgment.

"Pull back! Off the walls!" he bellowed his command.

"They've carried the walls, Excellency," Humberto Regales shouted exuberantly.

"Splendid. One more try with the ram, then get it out of the way," Carvajal answered soberly, his mind on the toll this had taken.

A messenger sped up on a lathered horse. "Fifty men are inside. More go over the walls every minute. The people of Pueblo Viejo run like frightened sheep."

"Good. Good. We will join our victorious soldiers at once," Carvajal decided.

Another thunderous smash of the ram was followed by a screech and roar as one panel of the gate gave way and fell inward. A ragged cheer rose from the bandits as they surged through the opening. Behind them, flames licked hungrily at the bridging planks and wheels of the lead cart. Smiling, eyes alight, Gustavo Carvajal gigged his palomino and advanced on the doomed village.

One hundred five men entered Pueblo Viejo. They soon found that the "frightened sheep" had sharp teeth. Every window of the dwellings near the walls had been heavily shuttered, with firing loops cut in them. Doors had been re-inforced also, and from all of these, rifle and revolver barrels protruded. Muzzle flashes spurted into the streets and powder smoke combined with dust to obscure the view. Shouting and cursing, the bandits pressed into the face of unexpected fire.

Screams came from behind them as the ram caught fire and blocked the gate. It spurred the attackers to greater effort. Slowly they fought their way past the defenders, isolating them and ignoring their deadly stings. The cost was counted by those who followed.

Angry, the last of the outlaw army to scale the walls set fire to the houses. Mercilessly they gunned down the occupants as they rushed outside to escape the flames. Salvador Montez felt a sharp pain between his shoulder blades as he blasted the life from an old man in the doorway of one house.

A spent round? he wondered a moment before another hot point of agony exploded along his jaw. He ignored a third hit as he angrily sought the source of the torment. He saw two small boys with slingshots on the roof of an adobe hut and raised his .45 to end their harassment.

Little Raul cheered lustily when his father popped out of an alleyway and used his machete to decapitate Salvador Montez. Then he sobered as his parent shook an angry fist at him.

"Stay out of this, *nino*," his father roared. "Keep out of sight."

"*Sí*, Pappa," a subdued Raul replied.

Eighty-nine of Carvajal's army of hardcases survived to reach the Plaza de Armas. Half of them were mounted.

Swelled with victory, they sensed the end close at hand. With a howl of glee they chased the fleeing *peons* across the park in the center of the square. Suddenly the cry of kill lust ceased in the throats of four horsemen. Seemingly out of nowhere, a narrow net, much like that the pampered elite used to play badminton back in the American East, swung up in front of them.

Unable to halt their horses in time, they went headfirst into its mesh. It broke the neck of one and hanged the other three, suspended off the ground by some five feet. Their mounts charged on, riderless. For a while the net jerked and swayed, then sagged motionless.

Elsewhere, *bandidos* came under fire from second-floor windows. Quickly Gustavo Carvajal took stock of what this meant. To his dismay, he discovered this, too, was a trap; *Smoke Jensen!* The name reverberated in his mind. *He* was behind this. Carvajal shouted commands to rally his remaining troops. He looked about, expecting them to comply.

That's when he saw the carts being wheeled into place to block all of the streets. They had been piled high with shocks of tinder-dry straw and sticks of firewood. Slowly they began to close all avenues of escape. Grinning peasants put fire to the loaded vehicles. Frantically, Carvajal screamed for his men to join together and force their way out.

"This way, this way, you fools. Form up and ride down those *peons.*"

Few listened to him. The volume of gunfire had increased, and the plaza cracked, hummed, and howled with a deadly rain of bullets. Speechless, Carvajal watched dumbly while two men flew from their saddles, shot by snipers strategically placed on rooftops.

"Ruin—ruin!" El Rey del Norte wailed. In that terrible moment, he saw his world crumbling all around him.

Smoke Jensen stood slightly back from the open doors to the largest *cantina* on the plaza. He took time to reload one

.44 Colt, while the fighting intensified all around him. Over at the bar, Carbone conferred with Pablo Alvarez, Martine's *segundo*. Their words came to Smoke as from the bottom of a well.

"Miguel has done well," Carbone observed.

"Men are closing off the six exits now, *Don* Esteban. All but a handful of Carvajal's men are in the plaza."

"Good. Smoke, what do you think, *amigo*? Should the snipers concentrate on those outside our little trap? Smoke?"

Smoke Jensen brought his random thoughts back to the present. "If we have control in the plaza, yes. Are we sure the fires from those carts won't spread?"

"All of the buildings are adobe. There is a bucket brigade standing by," Carbone stated.

"Then set the carts on fire and let's see what Carvajal does," Smoke ordered.

So many men dead, Smoke's thoughts continued to mock him. Farmers, herdsmen, shopkeepers, all dead to achieve what? To keep this land and the right to hold up their heads in freedom, another part of him answered. What was it that Ben Franklin said? *"The tree of liberty must often be watered by the blood of patriots."* These Mexican peasants and trades-men knew that well. Not twenty years ago they expelled the ambitious French from their country.

It's been longer than that since we Americans have had to fight for our beliefs, he acknowledged. Tempered by that, Smoke's rebellious imagination surrendered. Jefferson said it all, he admitted. *"Eternal vigilance is the price of freedom."* If these folks had been prepared, guarded against slime like Carvajal, none of this would have happened.

"The *bandidos* are rallying," came a shout through the doorway.

More trouble, Smoke admitted as he started out the door to direct the fight.

26

Two slugs smacked into the carved and painted wooden representation of a large glass of beer next to Smoke Jensen's head. He ducked the flying splinters and snapped off a round at the bandit who had shot at him. He fired again as he moved to the protection of a stone water trough.

A cry of anguish rewarded his shooting skill. Smoke cut his eyes to the left and saw a weakness. Some better shots among the outlaws had cut down the *peons* who tended to the *carretas* that should have closed off the western exit to the plaza. Already a dozen bandits streamed through the opening. Smoke opened fire and shouted to attract the attention of other defenders.

"Over there. Pick them off. You men, close that gap."

At once Smoke set off to the far side of the plaza, where the heavy rattle of gunfire advised him the bandits had gathered to offer resistance. "Come with me," he ordered half a dozen men crouched behind the fountain in the center of the square.

Smoke's boots pounded the grass into pulp as he closed on the growing firefight. His .44 Colt leading, Smoke Jensen stepped into the clear. He came nose-on against three of Carvajal's gun hawks. Crossed bandoliers of ammunition decorated their chests, brown and brass slashes against white shirts. The wide, upturned brims of their *Charro* sombreros undulated with the movement of their bodies. The first to snap alert to the threat of Smoke Jensen and six hastily trained *vaqueros* raised his Mendoza .45 and fired point-blank.

His slug cut down a young ranch hand next to Smoke, who pumped a round into the precise center where the cartridge belts crossed. The bandit's eyes bulged, and his lips formed a perfect, mustache-rimmed circle as he did a little dance of death. Smoke dropped to one knee and took aim at the outlaw on his right.

Boots thudding to a halt, the advancing gunslinger met death with a curse on his lips. He shot the hat from Smoke Jensen's head and died a moment later when hot lead from Smoke's .44 ripped through his chest and exited alongside his spine. He fell bonelessly to the flagstone paving of the plaza walkway.

Over the head of the last one, Smoke Jensen saw the gaudy uniform of Gustavo Carvajal. He raised his point of aim and fired. A billow of gray obscured his vision for a moment. When the air cleared, he saw that Carvajal had moved in the critical last second. But by then, Smoke had his hands full with the third *bandido*.

Knife in one hand, the outlaw leaped on Smoke Jensen. Smoke deflected the first slash with the barrel of his Colt. The big .44 roared beside the attacker's head and burst his eardrum. Painfully shaken by this, he nevertheless pressed his assault. Smoke's left hand went to his waist and drew his bowie. Off balance, he felt his back slam against the lip of the fountain basin.

Their impact drove the chest of the bandit against Smoke. He used that split moment of advantage to drive the blade of his knife between two ribs and deep into the outlaw's chest cavity. Quivering with outrageous agony, the wiry thug clung to Smoke until the moment of his descent into eternal darkness. Smoke flung him away and turned to his stunned companions.

"Why didn't you stop him?" he demanded.

"You—you were everywhere. All at once," one awed young shepherd blurted. "It happened so fast, and we were afraid of hitting you."

"Remember what I said about using a gun. Don't wait for them to come to you. Act quickly and be accurate." Letting off a little steam calmed Smoke's racing heart. He looked about the plaza, conscious of diminished fire. "We're too late to stop Carvajal from making an escape. Go, spread the word to keep them under fire until they are out of range."

Quiet came at last to Pueblo Viejo. Sadly, Miguel Martine and Esteban Carbone went about counting the toll for their victory. The total seemed appalling.

"Over thirty wounded," Martine reported to Smoke. "Fifty-three dead."

"How about the women and children?" Smoke asked.

"None, thank God," Carbone informed him.

"We'll start the clean-up and restore that gate. Carvajal might be back."

Gustavo Carvajal also took inventory of the army that had made him so proud. Staggered by the terribly reckoning, he looked over the survivors with a pale face and wan expression.

"Only fifty-seven came out of there," Humberto Regahes advised his leader.

Carvajal studied the faces of the survivors. With one accord they bore the stamp of defeat and dejection. How could this have happened to him?

"They can't be that good," Carvajal protested to his remaining handful of subordinate leaders. "Not Carbone, not

Martine, not even Smoke Jensen. Has Quetzelcoath turned his face from me?"

Por Dios, he's going into that again, Regales thought forsakenly.

Fury flushed the face of Gustavo Carvajal. "It must not be! No mere man can drag down the son of the sun! Smoke Jensen is not Cortez. We cannot stop here. We must pull back to Hacienda la Fortuna and regain our strength, our numbers. Then we'll show them. Then we will ride out in the splendor of all Tenochtitlan and devour the enemy. Ride on! Ride on to la Fortuna!"

Willing hands quickly put out the fires in the *carretas.* Men and women went about repairing the walls of Pueblo Viejo. Teams of horses dragged away the charred remains of the battering ram. A new gate was under construction. Smoke Jensen took in all the activity and felt pleased. Yet, it kept nagging him that Gustave Carvajal had managed to escape with at least some of his bandit army. Somehow, sitting behind these walls, waiting for another attack chafed at his spirit.

Carvajal would discover that his supplies and ammunition had been destroyed in the valley camp. He would push on to somewhere. To that end, Smoke sought advice from Carbone and Martine.

"Where will he go? I would say to that grand *hacienda* he took over in Durango," Carbone opined. "La Fortuna. It is as much a fortress as we made of this town."

"I agree," Martine added. "It could be taken, but . . ." he added a huge shrug.

"I feel the need to get into motion. To carry the fight to Carvajal," Smoke stated flatly.

"That's easy to understand. So long as he is alive, he will be trouble," Martine acknowledged. "You have done so much for us, Smoke. Perhaps it is time to leave the end to us, no?"

"I've gotten a lot of good men killed, women, too," Smoke shot back. "And I've never left a fight before its end. No, we have to lay plans, and that takes some knowledge. I'll ride out at dawn."

Carbone put a friendly restraining hand on Smoke's shoulder. "Not this time, *amigo.* You need rest, that wound on your shoulder is festering. Let our *vaqueros* handle this. We know for a fact that Carvajal hasn't enough men to send any chasing after them. They can be our eyes and our ears."

Fatigue and strain had become more than padded clubs for Smoke Jensen. They struck at him like mailed fists. "Maybe you're right."

"Besides," Martine said brightly, "the people want us all here tonight. There's to be a big fiesta to celebrate our victory. Feasting and plenty of drink. You should rest up now for that."

"I don't feel much like partying, and I don't like crowds," Smoke answered curtly. Visions of the hopeful, grateful faces of the people of Pueblo Viejo came to him. He sighed heavily. "I suppose we have to go through the motions."

"That's the spirit. At least it's close. You'll like the music."

"I have a tin ear."

"Come on, Smoke, try to get in the right mood," Carbone urged.

A bright-eyed, attractive teenaged girl approached them. She held a covered basket that proved to contain a woven straw bowl of strawberries and a cut and trimmed pineapple. "It is to say thank you, *Patrónes,*" she shyly advised in a near-whisper.

"See? The people don't see it as a defeat, Smoke," Carbone urged on him.

"All right," Smoke relented as he chose a strawberry. "I'll give it a try. You know, I don't think I'll ever get used to strawberries ripening in the fall." He took a bite of the large, sweet, juicy fruit.

* * *

When initial word came back that Gustavo Carvajal's rag-tag remnants of his once fearsome army had marched through their old camp, found the damage, and hurried onward, the grateful people of Pueblo Viejo and both ranches continued the celebration.

Conditioned by centuries of mandatory religious feast days, the habit of parties and dances, masked and costumed parades, and copious eating was deeply ingrained. After the first two days, Smoke Jensen accepted it philosophically. They had been living under the strain of Carvajal's presence for nearly six months. Work went on, at a slower pace, on the defenses. People of the other villages gave unstintingly of their food and labor, and feasted with the rest. The third day, some of these began to make departures for their own homes.

Promises of help were given by the residents of Pueblo Viejo. They would finish up and journey to aid the others. The holiday atmosphere persisted. Only one incident occurred to encourage Smoke that Carvajal would eventually be dealt with.

Young Raul came running to where the gate was being raised into place after several days of effort to make repairs. His straw sombrero flew from his head in his haste. Eyes wide, he sought out Smoke Jensen.

"Señor, strangers are coming. *Gringos.* They look big and mean."

What, Smoke wondered, could that mean? He thanked the boy and strolled out beyond the partly filled-in trench. Raul padded along at his side. He gazed in the direction the boy pointed and saw the figures of seven mounted men on the near slope of the saddle notch.

They approached the town at a casual walk, though Smoke's keen vision picked out the constant alertness to their surroundings that their posture and head motions betrayed. It suddenly came clear to him who they must be.

"Are they bad men, *Señor?"* Raul asked apprehensively.

"Oh, some might say so. I think they are looking for me."

Boyish bravado filled Raul's face. "We'll not let them take you, *Señor*. You saved our village. We will fight."

"I don't think that will be needed," Smoke said kindly.

"Hello, the town! Or should say fortress?" a familiar voice called out from a hundred yards' distance.

"Howdy yourself," Smoke greeted.

"Smoke! Be damned. From the looks of all this damage, we figgered we might be too late. We're ridin' in."

"Come ahead," Smoke called back, suppressing a chuckle of delight.

At a brisker pace now, the seven men rode up to where Smoke stood. A grinning Jeff York bent forward and extended a hand for Smoke to take. "Good to see you, Smoke," he said softly.

"And you, Jeff. It's been a while."

"Sorry I couldn't bring more men," Jeff apologized. "That's all right," Smoke assured him. "Seven Arizona Rangers look magnificent enough to me."

"I had a hell of a time convincing the captain to let us go," Jeff went on, determined to get out his explanation. "There's all hell to pay in the Territory right now. Rustlers, turncoats sellin' liquor to the Apaches, gunrunners, you name it." York lightly touched the place on his vest where his ranger's star usually hung. "As it is, we had to come all unofficial like."

"I reckoned you would when I sent that telegram. You didn't run into anyone else, did you? Louis Longmont? Big Bull Stebbins?"

"You sure put out a general call. Must be big," York observed.

"It is, or was. You can see the mess around here. This feller, Carvajal, has a regular army of bandits. Uses military tactics in attacking any who won't cow down to him."

"Looks like you have a regular get-together," York suggested, eyes taking in the signs of battle.

"That we did," Smoke acknowledged. "Cut Carvajal down to size. Our best count has his strength at around sixty."

Jeff York's eyes widened. "What size was it to begin with?"

"Close to three hundred."

York whistled through closed teeth. "That's before you took a hand, eh, Smoke?"

"Yep. Me and Carbone and Martine, anyway." Smoke glanced back at the village. "I'm forgetting my manners. Come on in, rest a spell, and wash the dust from your throats."

"Obliged. We'll get the introductions taken care of then. C'mon, boys, there's cold beer waitin'."

Three *gringos* had been waiting for the return of Carvajal to Hacienda la Fortuna. Trent, Vickers, and Yates had not enjoyed the opulent comforts of the *hacienda*. They had been locked in the small stone hovel that served as a sort of jail. Dirty, unshaven, and starved, they were dragged out and thrown roughly to the flagstone floor in front of El Rey del Norte's throne. Trent caught himself on his hands and was first to look up at the man to whom they had come to offer their services.

Oh, Lordy, he thought, *he's plumb jaybird crazy.*

Carvajal wore a fresh, new general's uniform, this time that of the artillery branch. His thick lips curled in disdain at sight of the wretches. He peered at them through a pair of opera glasses, held by a ornate silver handle. With a flip of a scented handkerchief to his nose, he spoke with no less disdain.

"What are these?"

"They say they are notorious yanqui gunfighters. They've come to offer you their services, Excellency," his majordomo replied.

"They are *gringos*," Carvajal dismissed.

Humberto Regales edged close to his master. "So is Smoke Jensen, Excellency."

A flash of fury colored Carvajal's face, then faded. "So he is. Tell me, *gringos,* do any of you know Smoke Jensen?"

"I hate Smoke Jensen," Trent declared acidly.

"So do I," Vickers growled.

"I especial hate Smoke Jensen," Yates added.

"I didn't ask how you felt about him; I asked if any of you knew him," Carvajal rejoindered in a whip-crack tone.

Trent considered how to answer that, deciding upon the truth. "Nope. Never laid eyes on him."

"Nor me. We just know he's bad medicine. We come to kill him," Vickers offered enlightenment.

"I've done had some of them stories about him read to me. They're all bullshit," Yates opined. "'Sides, he done kilt some good friends of ours. We want him dead."

"No more than I, *hombres,*" Carvajal offered them whole-heartedly. "Tell me honestly, would you take orders unquestioningly?"

"Who from?" Trent asked resentfully and ungrammatically.

"From me," Carvajal replied.

"Who'er you?" Vickers rasped.

"I—I am the emperor Montezuma of the Aztecs." Carvajal actually preened himself.

Oh, Jesus, Jesus, Jesus, he's a screamin' loony-tick, Trent thought in utter desperation. His reason suddenly warned him that they'd better play this one right, or they would all wind up dead. He tried desperately to catch the attention of his companions. Not entirely certain he had their thoughts meshed with his own, he winked furiously at them before he spoke.

"We'd be deeply honored to take your orders, ah, Excellency."

"Humph! That's more like it. To use good manners is a mark of respect for your betters. You show some promise, young man."

"Thank you, Excellency. Is there anything more you wish to know?" Trent offered.

"For the time being, that is enough. Humberto, here, will find you a place to stay with the other of my warriors. Do you wish to belong to the Eagle Warriors or the Jaguar Warriors?"

"Uh—ah—wherever you need us the most, Excellency."

"Oh, my, I do like your attitude. How are you called?"

"I am Trent. This is Vickers and Yates."

Carvajal tried to mouth the unfamiliar *Anglo* names. "Unusual. I shall call you Lazarus One, Two, and Three."

"May I inquire as to why we will all have the same name? Why Lazarus?" Treat hazarded.

Carvajal produced a quizzical expression as though to imply that everyone should know the answer to that. "Why, isn't it true that it was Lazarus whom Quetzelcoatl, in his guise as *el Cristo Rey,* raised from the dead? And, most assuredly, since you chose to show the proper humility and respect, you have certainly been raised from the dead. Take them away, Humberto, and settle them in with the men."

Jeff York paced the large *comedor* of the inn like a caged panther. He held a rolled tortilla filled with *carnitas* in one hand and munched while he spoke.

"Now we know that this Carvajal is in Hacienda la Fortuna. When are we going after him?"

"We'll leave tomorrow morning," Smoke Jensen told his old friend and co-godfather to the twins Louis Arthur and Denice Nicole.

"We takin' this whole scratch-together army?" York asked, uncertain of the quality of the Mexican *peons*.

"No. Only you seven Rangers, Carbone, Martine, and me."

"Son of a bi——" York blurted and broke off. "You're kidding, aren't you?"

"Not a bit. Of course, we'll have along twenty of Martine's best *vaqueros*. They can ride and shoot."

"Man, that last *vaquero* who came in said their numbers had grown to near a hundred-twenty."

"Um-hum. We can live with those odds, I'd say," Smoke told him, eyes twinkling.

27

"Hacienda la Fortuna." Martine identified the large, high-walled quadrangle that rested on a rise in the sheltered valley.

"Looks tough to just waltz in an' take," Jeff York observed.

"Carvajal did it with only fifty men," Carbone informed the Arizona Ranger.

York whistled softly. A moment later, his facial muscles tightened at a slight rustle of fallen leaves. Smoke Jensen came into view beyond the low, heavy boughs of a thick-trunked pine. York gave him a wave and relaxed. Smoke reined in and dismounted.

"Carvajal's there, all right," he informed the others.

A thick stand of first- and second-growth timber blanketed the gradual slope of a minor peak that marked the mouth of the valley. The trees were so dark green as to be almost blue-black. They adequately concealed the score of *vaqueros* who had accompanied Smoke, Carbone, Martine, and the Arizona Rangers.

"There's thirty of us," Jeff York remarked. "But we have Smoke Jensen." Friendly laughter danced in his words.

"I've been thinking about putting all this talent to work," Smoke advised the others.

"Your *vaqueros* were right," Smoke told Martine. "Carvajal

is growing stronger every day. I think we should pay him a visit tonight."

"What I can't understand is how he manages to attract men to his army." York put his thoughts to words.

"It has to do with the nature of our people," Carbone explained. "No, don't take me wrong, *Señor* York. Your Spanish is excellent, better than Smoke's, although it's border dialect. I'm sure you've grown up around Mexican people. The thing is, you don't *feel* like a Mexican."

Jeff York cocked a sandy eyebrow. Carbone chuckled and enlightened him. "Not long ago, I told Smoke that his skin was that of a *gringo,* but in his heart he was Mexican." He went on to relate the play on names Smoke had employed, comparing Carvajal's mad obsession of being Montezuma and the dead Aztec emperor's nemesis, Cortez. "You think and feel like an American, my friend," he added for York's benefit. "You see, we are all good Christians, proud of our European heritage, but in the breast of every Mexican beats the heart of an Indian savage. The flair, the romance of wild adventuring with a bandit warlord appeals to many of our men. Especially the young ones."

"Sorta like rutting young *javelinas,"* York suggested, calling to mind the wild boars of Arizona Territory.

Martine laughed heartily. "Just so. Smoke has convinced a number of them to abandon their high life with Carvajal and return to normal pursuits. I have a feeling he's about to try the same thing tonight."

"We are going to do some convincing, my friends," Smoke amended. His expression grew serious. "Any of those who don't see the light will have to be disposed of. That's hard, cold, I know. But we can't afford to have them at our backs when we go over the walls."

"¡Dios! You're serious about paying Carvajal a visit," Martine exclaimed.

"Of course," Smoke answered mildly.

* * *

Sentries started disappearing shortly after darkness fell across the valley. Smoke Jensen had a definite plan in mind. Risky, although entirely necessary from how he saw the on-going problem with Gustavo Carvajal. In truth, the bandit king remained entirely too strong for a heads-on confrontation. Doctors had not yet come up with their ideas about men and the role their subconscious minds played in their lives. Even so, Smoke Jensen had acquired a sound understanding of what moved men who seemed to be on a fixed point.

It wasn't what one could see that frightened most; it was the unseen. To put it simply, Smoke Jensen wanted to scare the living hell out of Gustavo Carvajal. To accomplish that, he decided to combine the attrition of guards with an appearance in the dead of night. Silently, he wished for a *conquistador's* crested helmet, breastplate, and scarlet cloak.

He would have to make do with what he had. And that included a personal talk with the would-be emperor of the Aztecs. Smoke set about his preparations. He used dead coals from a small fire to blacken his face. He removed his boots, in favor of a soft pair of Cheyenne moccasins. He, like all of the small force, would rely on silent weapons. In Smoke's case, that would be his bowie and a tomahawk.

He had not used the deadly hand ax in some while. Its results could be quite unsettling. Smoke counted on that. He had taken it out of his saddlebag earlier and honed its edge to a keeness. Now he slipped it under his cartridge belt and set off silently toward the distant walls of Hacienda la Fortuna. While he covered ground, he wondered how Jeff York and his Rangers were doing.

Seated at ease in his saddle, Jeff York had made a half circle of the valley and came at the *hacienda* from the north.

When a darker mass in the starlit night resolved into the figure of a man, he hissed a soft greeting.

"Hola, hombre."

"¿Quien es?"

"Beltran." Jeff invented a name of convenience. He had to get the man in closer.

"You are new."

"I just came down from Nogales, Sonora," Jeff spun. A little closer now.

"That explains why you talk funny," a rat-faced bandit with a scraggly mustache responded.

Closer still. "*I* talk funny? It's you who talk funny,"

Jeff kept the conversation going. Close enough.

Jeff's knife slid between two ribs and pierced the *bandido's* heart. He sighed gustily and went slack in the saddle. Jeff eased him off onto the ground. "One less," the Ranger muttered to himself.

Five minutes later, Lathrop, one of the Rangers, appeared out of the night. "We've got three of them in a bunch, up ahead," he informed Jeff.

"We'd best not keep them waiting," Jeff suggested.

Together they closed in on the sociable outlaws. Lathrop got right up close to one, whose back was to him. He plunged his wide-bladed bowie into a kidney, then the other in the same instant that York dropped a loop over the other pair and yanked them off their horses. They landed solidly enough to drive the air from their lungs.

York finished one and turned to the other as Lathrop stepped away, his knife dripping blood. "Won't need to bother with this one," he said.

"Damn, you move fast."

"Keeps me alive," Lathrop observed. "Let's go find some more."

* * *

Smoke Jensen hugged a deeper shadow in the midst of the one cast by the wall. Five of the *vaqueros* had managed to penetrate the *hacienda* by simply walking through the small portal built into the main gate. They laughed and talked with the guards, killed them, and took their place. Had the entrance been secured, Smoke would have been required to use his lariat and climb the outside wall.

This way made getting in easy. Getting out would be another matter. He edged along the base of the thick stone and mortar palisade toward the front of the enclosed dwelling. One of Martine's *vaqueros* stepped outside the portal and lit a cigarette. It was the signal Smoke waited for. He rapidly closed the distance on cat feet.

"All is secure, *Señor* Smoke," the *vaquero* assured him.

"Be ready to leave fast," Smoke advised.

Silently, he faded into the inner courtyard darkness. The moon, a fatter slice now, shed light in the center of the garden-like patio. It set off silver sparkles from the water that splashed high arcs in a fountain. Good, Smoke thought, small though it might be, that noise would cover his movements. And he would be making quite a few.

He had no way of knowing which room Carvajal used for sleeping. Logic, directed by the man's mania, dictated that the King of the North would use the grandiose master bedroom. It made sense. Only, could he rely on Carvajal to make any sense at all? He would have to seek the bandit king out, and that meant opening a lot of doors. Smoke's moccasins made no sound at all on the polished flagstones of a corridor formed by the room overhang above and open archways that gave onto the courtyard.

Smoke had glided past two doors, when the latch of one gave a distinctive click. He froze in midstride. "You must be Smoke Jensen," a voice in English accused.

"No entiende Ingles." Smoke pulled a bluff. A Yankee here?

A dry chuckle answered him. "Oh, come now, Smoke Jensen. You're caught fair and square."

Smoke let his shoulders sag, and he sighed in what he hoped sounded like resignation. "Who is it that's caught me?"

"The name's Trent, and I hate you, Smoke Jensen."

He'd heard that before. Smoke tensed and let his right hand drift toward his belt. Trent spoke again, in a whisper as before.

"Turn around. I want you to get it face-to-face."

Smoke turned, and in the same smooth movement, swiftly drew his tomahawk. He threw it underhand, an awkward maneuver, but one that proved effective. Trent gasped when the steel edge bit into his chest. It sank into the hollow at the bottom of his throat.

He tried to cry out, his mouth working spasmodically. Nothing came but a hot, wet flow. His knees loosened, and he slumped to the tile walkway. Smoke went to his side, removed the hawk, and dragged the body to a niche recessed in the wall. He stuffed the corpse of Trent into the depression and hurried on his way.

Passing the first-floor rooms that opened onto the corridor, Smoke went directly to a stairway that gave access to the second level. He had reached the halfway point when his keen hearing brought the crack of boot heels on the stones of the corridor he had just left. Crouched low, and breathing softly through open lips, Smoke waited out the nocturnal wanderer.

Boots grew closer, paused. Smoke heard the scritch of a match and yellow light blossomed around the opening to the stairway. The acrid odor of Mexican blend tobacco reached Smoke's sensitive nostrils. The match light went out. More purposeful and rapidly now, the boot heels clacked on the flagstones, approaching his exposed and vulnerable position.

A man in *vaquero* costume swung around the bottom end of the stairwell and started upward without looking. Smoke tensed, his leg muscles drawn like coil springs. Any second, the bandit would see the toes of his moccasins. In the last possible instant, the bowie fitted Smoke's fist.

He launched himself at the unsuspecting *bandido* and drove the point of the blade in under the ribs, slanted upward. It pierced the diaphragm and severed the hapless outlaw's aorta. Shocked motionless by the incredible pain, he died without a sound.

A few twitches and a violent convulsion signaled the departure of life. Smoke eased the corpse to the stairs and withdrew his blade. He wiped it on the dead man's white shirt and started upward again.

Here the layout was in reverse of downstairs, with the corridor running along the outside wall of the *hacienda*. Smoke turned to his right and started off to his dangerous task of opening doors. The first knob turned easily. He eased the portal inward, hoping for well-oiled hinges. A guttering candle revealed a sleeping form, much too large to be El Rey del Norte. Smoke closed the door and moved on.

At the next one, he found the handle unmoving. He put an ear to the oak panel and heard the rhythmic creak of leather bed supports and the soft sounds of a woman in passion. A smile creased his grim lips, and he advanced on the next. This one opened entirely too easily, and Smoke found himself face-to-face with one of Carvajal's lieutenants.

Before Tomas Diaz could raise a shout, Smoke belted him with a hard right to the forehead. The head of Diaz snapped back, and his eyes rolled upward. Only the whites showed when Smoke put a left to the weak spot under the jaw hinge. He caught Diaz on the fall and dragged him back into the room. A little quick work with pre-cut lengths of rope secured the bandit leader to the bed, one of his soiled socks stuffed between unresisting lips for a gag.

Cautiously, Smoke eased out of the room. At the far end of the corridor a large door denoted the master bedroom. It drew Smoke like a longing for the High Lonesome. To his surprise, he found the door unlocked. Heavy rests the crown on the royal head, he thought jokingly to himself. The portal swung as though on a counterbalance.

A huge canopied bed occupied a low platform in the center of the room. The five-foot-six form of Gustavo Carvajal lay sprawled in the center of turned-back sheets. He breathed stentoriously through his mouth. The passing wind stirred the stringy wisps of his mustache. Smoke Jensen stood over him, studied his sodden slumber. With the suddenness of lightning, a new idea came to him.

Quietly, Smoke exited. He went first to the room of Tomas Diaz. Hefting the big Mexican bandit over one shoulder, he carried him back to Carvajal's room. He sat Diaz upright in a Tudor chair, facing the bed. Then he went for the dead bandit on the stairs. He brought him there, also, and placed the corpse in another chair. Pleased with his efforts, Smoke decided on adding to the collection.

At the opposite end of the hall, another corridor intersected. Smoke went along it to the first unlocked door. Inside he found another ranking bandit stacking snores in a wide bed. A young lady, her lips swollen in a love pout, lay sated beside him. Moving with extreme caution, Smoke Jensen went to Pedro Chacon and rammed a wad of cloth into his open mouth.

With care and near silence, Smoke mouthed the words "Move, make a noise, and you're dead."

Chacon went stiff. His eyes, open wide, swiveled from side to side in an attempt to identify his assailant. Smoke obligingly gave him a look. Pedro Chacon swallowed hard in spite of the gag and tried to cringe away from the iron-band grip with which Smoke Jensen held him.

"Time to go back to sleep," Smoke advised as he tapped Chacon solidly with the barrel of his .44 Colt.

Exercising the greatest care not to awaken the passion-sotted young woman, Smoke gathered Chacon onto his shoulder and hurried to the master bedroom. With Chacon also in a chair, Smoke felt he had set the stage well enough. He made a quick inventory of two large chests and came up with a large white sheet. This he draped over his head and arranged it to cover his body. He located the place for eyeholes and cut them with his knife. Now he was ready to awaken the King of the North.

Someone was calling his name. *All* of his names. Mind numbed beyond ready response, Gustavo Carvajal struggled to push away the thick, cloying tendrils of stupor that contained him. He had become besotted in drink. And, as he suffered from the same affliction as his famous predecessor Miguel Antonio de Santa Ana, the smoking of opium, Carvajal's consciousness returned, although some of the gears didn't mesh, and a few cogs might be said to be definitely missing.

"El Rey del Norte," the sepulchral voice intoned. "The Grand Emperor Montezuma. The most famous *bandido jefe* of them all, Gustavo Carvajal."

Carvajal opened bloodshot eyes. "What? Who? Wh-where am I?" His bleary focus rested on the corpse of the bandit in the nearest chair.

"You are in the hall of the dead. You have been brought here to be judged."

"Why, that can't be. I feel my heartbeat, I can breathe, I can feel my skin."

Smoke Jensen, inside the white sheet, let out a mournful wail. "You were brought here in corporeal form to be weighed in the balance of the Eternal."

Finally, Gustavo Carvajal fixed his gaze on the white wraith that seemed to float at the end of his bed. Painfully his thoughts began to grind together. He winced and looked to his left. Tomas Diaz slumped in a chair at that side. He too could well be dead. Shocked, his superstitious childhood and youth welling up to haunt him, Gustavo Carvajal sought surcease in a fast cut of his eyes to the right. Pedro Chacon lolled in the chair at the edge of a faint candle glow.

"*¡Dios mio!* Are they dead? Are they all dead?"

"Yes," the terrible spirit told him. "It is time to decide your fate."

Carvajal began to regret he had taken that second pipe of the sticky brown happiness. If only he could think clearly. This could not be happening.

The sickening odor of burned opium had given Smoke Jensen his sudden inspiration. Now he wondered how he would break off the charade and get away without Carvajal becoming wise to the whole game. He raised one arm, a finger pointed accusingly at Carvajal.

"Murderer. Thief. Assassin."

Fortunately, Carvajal solved Smoke's problem for him. Hearing the list of indictments against him, he sought escape in oblivion. He uttered a tiny gasp, his eyes rolled up under brushy brows, and he fainted.

Smoke Jensen left the unfortunate outlaws, living and dead, in Gustavo Carvajal's bedroom. The thought crossed his mind that he could have easily killed the mad bandit chief with a quick slash of his knife. But Carvajal was unarmed, helpless and unconscious. To Smoke Jensen, that smacked of cold-blooded murder. The sort of thing that Gustavo Carvajal might do.

Most Easterners, Smoke knew, made light of the so-called Code of the West. Not those who lived by it. Not Smoke Jensen. Killing a man in a gunfight, or at long range in a pitched battle or to escape an ambush, was an ordinary occurrence on the frontier. Back-shooting, back-stabbing and other cowardly ways of dispensing with an enemy were hanging offenses, same as stranding a man without horse or gun in the middle of nowhere.

Smoke had put under a number of men guilty of such crimes. He had no desire to join their ranks at the present, no matter how tempting the proposition appeared. No, Gustavo Carvajal would live to fight another day. Only now Smoke believed he had the measure of the man. For all his swarthy complexion, the King of the North had turned a sickly, pasty green-white when his befuddled mind had bought the play-acting of Smoke Jensen.

Which meant that Smoke could yank his chain any time, anywhere. That's the way Smoke wanted it. There would be enough killing tonight to add to Carvajal's unsteady memories of the midnight encounter. More than likely a few desertions of men newly joined in the ranks of the king's army. That aspect brought a smile to the lips of Smoke Jensen. It had been easy.

All he had to do was get out of the *hacienda* undetected. Yeah, that was all. He paused at the top of the stairwell to listen for any sounds of roaming bandits. Relieved when he heard nothing, Smoke started down the stairs.

He'd put the toe of one moccasin on the tenth tread when a voice spoke from behind him. "That, *Señor,* will be far enough."

Humberto Regales stood at the banister, an oil lamp in one hand, a big, nasty-looking Mendoza .45 in the other.

28

Humberto Regales produced a cynical smile. With studied casualness he reached up with his left hand and stroked one thick wave of his black mustache. Smoke Jensen felt like a fly on a sticky tape.

"It appears you have the advantage," Smoke told him in Spanish.

"Ah, you speak our language. Good. It makes it much easier. You will put your *pistola* down gently. On the step at your feet."

"Could you speak a little slower? I can't quite understand you," Smoke pleaded, playing for time.

"Do as I tell you, or I'll shoot you where you stand," Regales ordered cracklingly. Slowly, Smoke bent at the knees. "Use your left hand, so I can see what you are doing."

Smoke complied. He held the butt of the Colt .44 with forefinger and thumb as he edged lower. His right hand, out of sight of the bandit lieutenant, worked up the cuff of his trouser leg. Carefully, Smoke laid his six-gun on the tread.

"Excellent. Now walk down the stairs. I'll be right behind you," Regales commanded.

Taking the steps one at a time, Smoke Jensen concentrated

on appearing casual as he moved his right hand in front of his body. At the bottom of the flight, Regales had more orders for him.

"Over against that wall. Put your nose on it."

Smoke did as he was told. A moment later he sensed a light touch as Regales relieved him of his second revolver and bowie. Imperceptibly, Smoke tensed. Regales stepped back and chuckled softly.

"You're not so dangerous after all," he congratulated himself. "Turn around. I want a good look at the famous Smoke Jensen."

Smoke spun on one heel, rolled out the small .38-40 Smith, and shot Regales through the heart. "Well, there goes our element of surprise," he sighed.

"Who's shooting? What's happening?" an alarmed, sleepy voice called out.

Thinking fast, Smoke replied, his voice deliberately slurred. "It is nothing. I—I was cleaning my gun and dropped it." He ended with a hiccough and a belch.

"¡Estupido! You are too drunk to clean your gun. Go to sleep."

"Sí, sí, I don' feel so good." When his interrogator did not come to check on the careless drunk, Smoke breathed easier. No one, apparently, was curious enough.

Wrong, he found out a moment later. The sound of hurried footsteps carried across the courtyard. A slightly built bandit ran into the moonlight, one hand clutching at his unbelted trousers to keep them up. He darted between two arches and under the overhang, and ran right into Smoke Jensen's knuckles.

Shock from the impact shot up Smoke's arm. The nosy *bandido* went rigid and fell over backward. Smoke dragged him out of sight against the low courtyard wall. He headed for the staircase once more.

Fat chance he would have getting out the front gate. The

nastiness the *vaqueros* had come to do would have been completed by now. They would be gone and no doubt more than one man responded to the gunshot with attention to duty. Smoke took the stairs two at a time, retrieving both of his Colts on the way. He entered the room from which he had taken Tomas Diaz and crossed to the window.

A quick glance showed him it would be a dangerous jump to the ground. Particularly for someone in moccasins. Smoke took quick stock of the contents of the room. True to his former life as a *vaquero,* Tomas Diaz had a large coil of *riata* hanging on one wall. Smoke recovered it and slipped the loop around a bed leg. He paid out the rope and dropped it through the window. Now, with a little luck, he might yet get away in one piece.

Smoke climbed through the casement and gripped the rope tightly. He swiveled around and braced his moccasins against the wall. Carefully he began his descent. The scrape of his moccasins sounded thunderous in his ears. Nothing for it, though, but to keep going.

Two-thirds of the way down, the first explosion went off. Shouts of alarm followed, with lights glowing to life all over the *hacienda.* Smoke had his moccasins under him on solid ground when the powder magazine blew. It rocked the ground and sent pieces of the roof sailing above the walls. Screams of pain joined the uproar from within.

In all the confusion and damage inside, no one thought to look outside. Smoke had started off at a gentle lope when mounted men came toward him out of the darkness. The one out front led Sidewinder by his reins. Grateful, Smoke swung into the saddle and caught up to Juan Murial.

"I think we just spoiled their day," the mountain man observed with a chuckle.

* * *

Rudolfo Blanco brought the news to Smoke Jensen. "They're pulling out. Every last one of Carvajal's bandit scum are riding away from the *hacienda* as though Satan himself was after them."

Smoke pondered this a moment. "That's something we didn't anticipate. Are they scattering?"

"No. They ride together," Blanco informed him. "What direction?"

"To the northwest, *Señor* Smoke."

"What's that direction?"

Rudolfo Blanco shrugged. "If you go far enough, there's *Cannon del Cobre*."

"That makes sense," Smoke speculated. "Go tell Carbone and Martine. We're going after them."

Eyes dancing with excitement, Rudolfo questioned Smoke. "This time we finish it, no?"

"I think you can count on that," Smoke advised him.

Three days' hard riding, through increasingly more rugged mountains, brought Smoke Jensen, Carbone, Martine, and Jeff York to the high rim of *Cannon del Cobre*. Gustavo Carvajal headed unerringly to the sanctuary of the twists and turns of the great canyon. All the way, York and his Rangers and the *vaqueros* kept up a steady harassing fire that whittled at Carvajal's numbers. When the last of the bandit army disappeared down a steep trail, their pursuers reined in.

"Where do you suppose he is headed?" Smoke asked.

"He has something in mind, *amigo*," Carbone said thoughtfully. "He came to this exact spot; we didn't drive him here."

"You said earlier that Carvajal disappeared for some while," Smoke considered aloud. "Could he have been building a hidey-hole in this canyon?"

Carbone cut his eyes to Martine. "It might be possible.

No one saw or heard of him for six months. Then he came out with this King of the North nonsense," Carbone summed up.

"I think we should let them settle down a little, then go have a look," Smoke suggested.

Jeff York's eyes had widened at the vast expanse of the copper canyon. Huge walls of amber, russet, and jade climbed to the rim where they stood. Fully five miles across, the opposite monuments to nature's power repeated the spectacle. It went on for miles. Far below, a rapid river, redder than the Colorado, twisted sinuously through the confines of the bottom. He spoke now with a hint of the awe he felt. "Me an' the boys will go along, Smoke. We've had some experience chasing bad men in the Grand Canyon."

"But that's nothing like this place, eh?" Smoke said with a chuckle. "Carbone warned me in advance. I assume there's another way in here," he said to Carbone.

"Oh, yes. The mouth of the canyon is ten leagues to the west."

"Maybe some men should be sent to plug that hole," Smoke offered.

"At once," Martine agreed.

"We'll go along and scout out the whole canyon," Smoke decided.

"That could take days," Carbone protested. "We have him trapped. Now's the time to close in and end this."

"Could get costly," Smoke suggested. "Even a cornered squirrel will fight to save its life."

Carbone rethought his brash statement. "You're right, as usual, *amigo*. This trail is so narrow that only one at a time could come up it. Half a dozen men could hold the top against an army."

"Then why don't we do it that way? Leave ten good men and the rest start a sweep of the canyon."

* * *

Gustavo Carvajal paced the ground behind the high, man-made stone wall early the next morning. "Here! They follow us here and come in at night to kill or run men off as though this was their canyon. I can't let that happen, now, can I? They are only men, after all."

A ghost of memories floated in Carvajal's muddled mind. Vague images of a spirit and the dead bodies of his most trusted men added to the opium-induced confusion of thoughts. He had awakened from his comatose state to find that Humberto Regales was indeed dead. That left him with only Tomas Diaz and Pedro Chacon to give purpose and direction to his less than rational life.

Far from relishing his increase in status and power, Tomas Diaz wished fervently for the steadying influence of Humberto Regales. He knew only too well the extremes to which his leader could go when the fantasy of being the emperor of the Aztecs seized him. It helped little, he considered, that Pedro Chacon had been elevated to fill one of the gaps left by the death of Ignacio Quintero and Humberto Regales. Tomas considered that he might have been wise to ride the other direction when the army, now thirty-five stronger, had headed for *Cannon del Cobre*. He suddenly realized that Carvajal expected a response.

"Sí, Excellency. Only men."

"Then we will defeat them. I know exactly how."

Tomas wondered how. Worried, he tried to reason with Carvajal. "They are all around us, Excellency. Even the trail we entered by is blocked."

A glint of madness twinkled in Carvajal's eyes. "We are going to compel them to let us get away unharmed. Gather up every captive in camp. Bring them down to the gate. I have a little exhibition to present to Carbone and Martine."

Twenty minutes later, Tomas Diaz reported to the King of

the North, "It is as you wish, Excellency. The captives are at the gate."

"Excellent. Now help me into my robes."

"Something's goin on," Jeff York murmured softly to Smoke Jensen.

Smoke, his hat tilted down over his eyes, lay against a scrub cedar to catch a little sleep. He heard Jeff clearly, though, and sat up. "Any sign they plan to counterattack?"

"Nope. They have a crowd of plain folks up close to the gate. A second ago, one of the hardcases opened the whole shebang. Uh-oh, what's that feller figure he can do? He gonna try to fly out of here?"

Smoke came forward and peered over the lip of a low ridge in front of the rock fortification. Obviously of recent construction, it answered part of what Carvajal had been doing in the missing six months. The pint-sized outlaw king had come out from behind the walls, wearing his Montezuma regalia. Head swiveling left and right, he paced back and forth on short, stocky legs. He made a colorful spectacle. His feather cape and huge, ponderous headdress swayed and rippled in the breeze. At last he stopped and turned to face outward. Arms raised, he shouted slowly and clearly.

"*Oje,* Carbone, Martine, Smoke Jensen. I have gathered up some of your friends and neighbors. They are all under the guns of my men. I have also given the order that they will be sacrificed to Huitzilopochtli, the war god of our ancestors. Their hearts will be cut out of their living bodies. Unless . . . unless you allow us to depart from this canyon unharmed. And further, that you will submit to my will in all things, pay tribute and provide men for the army of the King of the North. You have one hour to decide."

"I've decided already," Carbone growled.

"So have I," Smoke added.

"Not so fast, *amigos,*" Martine cautioned. "I have been thinking. We have done enormous harm to Carvajal and his bandits. What would it matter if we agreed to his terms? We could always attack him under far better conditions out in the open."

Worried over this apparent change of heart, Smoke eyed his friend. "Do you actually think Carvajal would let any of the three of us live?" he asked rhetorically. "Not after what we've done."

"It is obvious he has completely lost his mind. He means it about the captives. He'll put them over some rock and cut their beating hearts out of their bodies."

"I suggest that you put the threatened executions out of your mind for the time being," Smoke stated patiently. "I want you to listen to a plan I have worked out."

Immediately after Carvajal issued his ultimatum, feverish activity began right in front of the main gate. Squarish stones were manhandled into position, and a large, flat rock placed atop them. The whole structure had a barbaric menace about it. It recalled images from Mexico's dark past. Sharpshooters among York's Rangers sighted in.

Their Winchesters cracked, and three bandits fell dead in the sandy red soil of the canyon. Immediately, rifles fired inside, and the wails of frightened people rose. While the besiegers looked on helplessly, three bodies were handed up and dropped over the wall.

Martine cursed himself and Carvajal with equal fervor. "I never expected that," he protested.

"Carvajal's in a fast canoe with a broken paddle," Smoke Jensen remarked. "Expect anything from now on."

"Such as *gringos* fighting alongside this bandit trash?" Carbone asked, pointing toward two taller figures on the ramparts.

"Um. I killed one *yanqui* inside the *hacienda,*" Smoke recalled. "Appears he had friends."

"What are we going to do about them?" Jeff York asked.

"If they don't give up, kill them." Smoke condemned them.

When the prescribed time had elapsed, a young woman was dragged, shrieking in terror, from the crowd at the gate. Four men held her down across the stone table while a fifth approached with a long, slim-bladed knife. He took his position above her head, which hung over one end of the flat block, and raised the knife in both hands.

Smoke Jensen watched the deadly drama unfold over the sights of his Winchester Express. Before the executioner could start his downswing, Smoke squeezed through on the trigger, and the .45-70-500 slammed against his shoulder.

Instantly, fat sticks of giant powder arced through the blue sky to land inside the fortress. By then all five bandits lay dead, and the frightened girl struggled to free herself from the death grip of her captors. At once, the entire force of volunteers, Rangers and the three gunfighters attacked.

Smoke Jensen led the way. Everyone had been given a specific target, and for once, Smoke noted, they went about doing their jobs in a direct, efficient manner. The canyon walls echoed with a steady pulse of gunshots. Rifle and revolver fire crackled on all sides. Smoke sought out and headed directly for the long, lanky form of Tomas Diaz. Separating them, however, were three of the bandits. Hemmed in on all sides, the trio fired blindly into the rush of a mere twenty-seven men.

Two of Martine's volunteers went down before Smoke popped a round into the head of one outlaw. Dead before he hit the ground, the head-shot bandit flopped reflexively until the Great Leveler claimed him. Startled out of their daze by something so close and personal, the other two concentrated on Smoke Jensen.

"By God, it's him, Yates, it's Smoke Jensen," Vickers bawled as he turned in Smoke's direction.

"I hate you, Smoke Jensen," Yates shouted, spittle flying.

Bullets snapped past Smoke's head, and one tore cloth in his left armpit. Coolly he swung the muzzle of his .44 toward the offenders and let fly. His aim proved far better than theirs. Yates went to his knees, gut-shot and whining in a thin, breathless voice. Vickers ran his six-gun dry and, in stupid desperation, threw it at Smoke. Smoke dodged to one side and pinwheeled the shooter with a .44 slug in the sternum.

Doubting that the attackers numbered less than a fifth of their strength, the bandits ignored their captives, who ran screaming among the combatants. Smoke never lost sight of Diaz. He stepped over the dying Vickers, using his last shot on a fat, ugly bandit with a shotgun and a terrible attitude. Quickly Smoke changed revolvers. At that moment, Diaz cut his eyes in Smoke's direction.

In a flash, Smoke realized the other man had gleaned his intention. He hated to be rushed on a shot, but he had to get off one first to rattle his opponent. The .44 bullet cracked close by through the legs of Diaz, and the latter immediately had visions of an unspeakable wound. He yelled in alarm and jumped behind a *carreta*.

Smoke went after him. Caution took command as Smoke neared the tailgate of the cart. He paused a moment, mentally tracking the rhythm of battle, then rounded the high-sided vehicle with his .44 leading. Diaz fired in too great a haste.

His round careened along the thick sideboard of the cart and showered Smoke Jensen's face with splinters. Smoke's bullet struck Diaz in the upper left chest. Staggered, Diaz's eyes narrowed, and he racked back the hammer of his Mendoza. Smoke fired first. Hot lead sped true to the target and slammed Tomas Diaz into the edge of the huge, tireless wheel. He hung there for what seemed a long time.

Long enough to bring up his .45 and thumb-slip a round that ripped leather from the side of Smoke Jensen's boot. Smoke's ankle gave off a sharp report of pain and promptly went numb. Powder smoke obscured the scene before him. With instinct as a guide, he shot through the haze and heard a soft cry from his enemy.

A running captive and random breeze cleared his view, and he saw Diaz pitch forward into the broken rubble on the ground. Smoke also discovered he had been holding his breath. He let it out in a gust and paused to reload. He had nearly run both weapons dry.

Not the sort of thing he wanted to do in his present circumstances. His mind began to record cries for mercy and the sounds of surrender. Most men, he conceded, could put up with only so many assaults with explosives. The giant powder had shaken the bandits far more than anticipated. Now they gave up to a far inferior force. Both Colts reloaded, Smoke started out, with a pronounced limp, to find Gustavo Carvajal.

He found Pedro Chacon first.

Chacon's eyes widened when he recognized the big *gringo* who had so easily bested him inside the *hacienda*. His boots wanted to run, while his head told him his only chance was to be faster and better. Why, the stupid *gringo* didn't even have a gun in his hand. Quickly, a wild laugh on his lips, he swung his treasured Colt .45 Peacemaker upward in line with the *gringo*'s chest.

A loud flash and a report surprised Pedro Chacon. Pain exploded in his chest, and his precious *yanqui* six-gun felt like it weighed a ton. How could that be? He'd never even seen the *gringo* draw. Yet, his dimming vision showed him fuzzily the image of Smoke Jensen with his .44 Colt in hand, a dribble of white still trickling upward from the muzzle.

Then he saw only blackness and the flickering fires of Hell far down the tunnel.

Smoke Jensen saw the muzzle of Chacon's gun rise toward him, and he drew with legendary swiftness. His hand and the gun were a mated blur. The .44 Colt jolted in his hand, and he sensed the aim had been true. When Chacon dropped to his knees, Smoke knew he had been right. A new sound, or rather the lack of it, reached through to his consciousness.

All around, bandits stood with their hands in the air. Powdersmoke wafted away on the stiffening breeze. Carefully, Smoke Jensen went among the prisoners and their former captives. He peered intently at all those of short stature. Carbone came to him on his second circuit of the captured bandits.

"What are you looking for, *amigo?*"

"Carvajal. He's not among our prisoners."

"Hummm. That would spoil our fun some," Carbone observed.

"I thought so. I'm going to look for him. He can't have gone far in that feather cape get-up," Smoke advised.

This could not be happening. His men deserting him, surrendering to a handful of enemy. It was . . . like the time before. So few, the men who came with Cortez. Yet, in the end they had vanquished a mighty army and put a whole people in bondage. No, it was all wrong. Not again. He was the magnificent Emperor Montezuma. He was El Rey del Norte. He was . . . he was—Gustavo Carvajal, one-time petty bandit, with delusions of greatness.

He saw reality clearly now, with his army collapsing around him, and it dragged down the corners of his mouth in sadness. He also saw what the future held for him. *El Paridón*—the firing wall, and a squad of soldiers. But he would not go alone.

He watched closely as Smoke Jensen searched among the captured bandits. Gustavo Carvajal knew full well whom the *gringo* sought. Well, he'd not disappoint the *yanqui* interloper. He had a secure place in these rocks. From there he could watch everything that happened. It would make a good place from which to avenge himself on Smoke Jensen.

Only a little closer now, he mentally urged the huge *gringo*. Closer. Then the image of the spectre in white imprinted on his mind. And the ignominy of the firing wall. Relentlessly, Carvajal fought those impressions. With deliberate care he cocked the Mendoza .45 in his right hand and began to raise it.

Smoke Jensen came on, as though drawn to the jumble of boulders at the back of the small fortress. As he glided past the hiding place of Gustavo Carvajal, the bandit king raised his revolver the last few inches.

The shot brought Smoke Jensen around in a half crouch, .44 Colt at the ready. What he saw was a wet, red smear on the rocks that had been behind him. Flecks of white and brown tissue spattered it. He stepped to the opening and looked into the hidden pocket.

Gustavo Carvajal lay sprawled in a half-sitting position against the erosion-carved back wall. He had taken the only escape he had to avoid capture, humiliation and eventual execution. The muzzle of his .45 Mendoza still remained inside his thick lips.

A week later, Smoke Jensen rode north in company with Jeff York and his Arizona Rangers, Esteban Carbone and Miguel Martine. Their mood was high and light. A lot of rough jokes flew among the members of the party. Smoke found himself enjoying it.

He knew the Rangers would go back to keeping the peace in Arizona Territory. His Mexican friends, the new-made *hacendados,* would raise their families and restore their ranchos. Carbone would marry again within two years and produce four more progeny. Martine would grow fat and gruffly affable in his declining years. All would be well with the world again. Except for Smoke Jensen, whose reputation kept catching up with him. But that's another story from the life of the last mountain man.

When Smoke Jensen parted company with his friends, his thoughts turned to home and his beautiful wife. Particularly to Sally, and he wondered how she was getting along with young Bobby Harris.

When I was a kid, my parents took me to all sorts of specialists to find out what was wrong with me. I wasn't afraid of anything, not spiders, snakes, heights, wild animals—nothing. That's when they figured out that if there was a fear gene, I was missing it. So I guess you could say I'm fearless. Like if I see some big guy beating up a little guy I just dive in and finish off the big one—and I can, because my dad trained me to. He figured if I was going to keep getting myself into trouble I might as well have the skills to protect myself. And my dad knows trouble—he's in the CIA. At least I think he is. I haven't seen or heard from him since, well, since something happened that changed our lives forever.

Anyway, you'd think that because I'm fearless my life would be pretty great, right? Wrong. In fact, if I had three wishes, one of them would be to know fear. Because without fear, I'll never know if I'm truly brave. That wouldn't be my first wish, though—my first wish would be to have my dad back. For obvious reasons. My last wish . . . well that's kind of embarrassing. I'd like to end my unlucky seventeen-year stint as Gaia-the-Unkissed. Do I have anyone in mind? Yeah. But I'm beginning to think it'll never happen. . . .

Don't miss any books in this thrilling series:

FEARLESS™

Available from SIMON PULSE